Tales of the
Wonder Club

Tales of the Wonder Club

Volume 1

M.Y. Halidom
writing as
Dryasdust

LEONAUR

Tales of the Wonder Club: Volume 1
by M.Y. Halidom writing as Dryasdust

Leonaur is an imprint of Oakpast Ltd

Material original to this edition and presentation of the text in this form copyright © 2012 Oakpast Ltd

ISBN: 978-0-85706-894-1 (hardcover)
ISBN: 978-0-85706-895-8 (softcover)

http://www.leonaur.com

Publisher's Notes

Contents

A Peep at the Wonder Club

Towards the close of the last century there stood in one of the Midland counties of England, in the centre of two cross-roads, a venerable hostelry, built in the reign of Elizabeth, and known by the sign of "Ye Headless Lady." Its ancient gables were shaded by luxuriant elms and beech trees. The woodwork of the building and its weather-stained walls of brick were partially overgrown with thick ivy, while its high, dingy-red roof was tinted with every variety of lichen. The windows were narrow, and the framework heavy, as is usual in houses of that period.

The host of this establishment, one Jack Hearty, was one of the old school of landlords—robust, jovial, and never above his business. His fathers had owned the inn before him, and "he never wished to be a better man than his father, nor a worse either, for the matter of that," as he would say. All day long, when not engaged with his customers indoors, he was to be seen at the door of his inn, with his apron girt around him, and a "yard of clay" at his lips, straining his eyes down the long cross-roads for the first glimpse of a customer.

Often after gazing long and intently into the distance he would turn back with a sigh, knock the ashes from his pipe, refill it, take a deep draught of his own home-brewed ale, then, if none of his customers required anything, and the affairs of his household permitted it, he would sally out again. This time, perhaps, his eyes would be greeted by the sight of a solitary wayfarer, or, better still, the stage-coach. Then it was that the honest landlord's face would brighten up, as it was certain to bring him some of the "big-wigs" from town. He would rub his hands and chuckle, while Dame Hearty would begin to bustle about to welcome the fresh arrivals. It was not often, however, that the "Headless Lady" was entirely deserted.

A small clique or brotherhood, known as "The Wonder Club," had been nightly in the habit of assembling here for years, and this served to bring grist to the mill. Some of the eminent men from the neighbouring village, among whom were the doctor, the lawyer, an antiquary, an analytical chemist, and others, had formed among themselves a club, which was to consist only of very choice spirits, like themselves, and if any guest were introduced among them, it was only to be with a letter of introduction and the full consent of all parties. By these strict rules they hoped to keep the club select. A room at the inn was set apart for them, into which no one not belonging to the club ever presumed to enter, unless it was the landlord, who would be called every now and then to replenish the bowl, and whom sometimes the guests of the club would "draw out," as it was whispered in the village that the landlord of the "Headless Lady" knew a rare lot of stories, he did; also how to tell 'em, too, my word! but these he generally reserved for his more intimate customers. One strict law of the club that we have not yet mentioned was that no guest invited was to be a "business man." Should a commercial traveller ever have the hardihood to enter the sacred precincts of the club, he was assailed with a battery of glances from the members that must have completely cowed him, unless he were a man of more than usual strength of nerve; but as this rarely happened, all such outward manifestations of contempt were kept within due bounds. Business was, of course, tabooed; even politics were only admitted on sufferance and by a special permission of the chairman. There was one evening in the year, however, when the chairman never granted any such permission, and that was on the anniversary of the founding of the club. On this evening such subjects as business and politics would have been cried down, and the daring introducer of the obnoxious themes would have been condemned to drink a cup of cold water on his bended knees by way of expiating his offence. No subjects of public or private interest were tolerated on this evening, or, indeed, on any other. The chief delight of this club was to tell or to listen to stories which were all more or less of the marvellous class, and which each took it by turn to relate to the rest, the strictest silence and order being preserved during the recital. The evening that we are about to describe to the reader was the tenth anniversary of the founding of the club. This was a very grand event. For any one of its members or guests, whether married or single, to have been absent, on this occasion would have been little less than an insult to the rest.

8

Let us try to give our readers a glimpse of the club room and its guests on this memorable evening.

Imagine, then, a large room with low ceiling and walls of dark oak panel, a large old-fashioned fireplace with dogs, and a Yule log blazing on the hearth. The curtains are old and embroidered, and closely drawn. The room is well lighted, and in the middle is a long table, at which, through a cloud of tobacco smoke, a party of nine—all lords of the creation—may be discovered. A bowl of punch is in the centre of the table, at which every now and then each guest replenishes his glass. Mr. Oldstone, the antiquary, has been elected chairman. Watch with what dignity he fills his post of honour. Look! he rises and thumps the table. He is going to make a speech. The strictest silence reigns; you might hear a pin drop.

"Gentlemen," began the worthy chairman, after one or two preliminary "hems," "it is with feelings of mixed pride and pleasure that I feel myself called upon tonight to preside at this most honourable meeting." (Hear, hear!) The chairman resumed, "This is the tenth anniversary of our club of choice spirits (cheers), and so shamefully nicknamed by our enemies 'The Morbid Club.' (Groans.) Irritated at our exclusiveness, and envious at the reports of the superior talent that circulates nightly at our table, and which bursts into a halo of genius on our great saturnalias, what wonder, gentlemen, if the worthy members of our select club should make enemies out of their own circle? Only 'birds of a feather flock together,' and perhaps the contempt of our enemies is the best compliment they can pay us." (Hear, hear! and various shouts and yells of delight, amid clapping of hands, stamping, and rattling of glasses.) Here the chairman paused to take breath, and then, after a preliminary sip at his glass of punch, proceeded.

"Gentlemen, I feel duly sensible of the honour conferred upon me this evening in being selected to preside at our meeting on this very important occasion, an honour which I feel unable to support, and for which I feel my abilities so inadequate. (No, no!) Gentlemen, we are a company of nine this evening, the number of the muses—the omen is auspicious. I see around me faces that were present at the inauguration of our club, ten years ago, though others, alas! have gone to their long rest." Here the speaker was visibly moved, and passed his hand over his eyes to wipe away an incipient tear. Then, recovering himself, "Need I proceed, gentlemen? Need I trespass longer upon the time and patience of guests so illustrious? (Yes, yes!) Then, gentlemen," continued the speaker,

"I would but detain you one moment longer, to propose the following toast, to be drunk with three times three. (Hear, hear!) 'Long live the "Wonder Club," and all its choice members.'" Here the president, at the conclusion of his speech, held a bumper above his head, and repeated the toast with the rest of the company, with a "Hip, hip, hip, hurrah!"

"May their brains be as fertile as the plains of Elysium, and may the fame of the 'Wonder Club' spread to the ends of the earth."

This sentiment was followed by a burst of applause.

In the midst of the stamping, cheering, and rattling of glasses that ensued a knock was heard at the door. Who could it be? The landlord? It was not his wont to disturb the club for a trifle. He only made his appearance when called for. What was it? Was the inn on fire? Who could venture to disturb the solemn meeting of the "Wonder Club" on their tenth anniversary? One of the members rose from his seat and opened the door ajar, still holding the handle in his hand.

"Who is it? What do you want at this hour?" he asked.

"I beg pardon, gentlemen," said the voice of the honest land-lord without, "for disturbing the company; but a gentleman has just brought a letter for the chairman, and I thought it *might* be important. Leastways, I thought it wouldn't be much harm to deliver it at once. The gentleman has sent in his card. Excuse the interruption, sirs; I hope no offence."

The letter was delivered to Mr. Oldstone. He glanced at the card.

"What, a visitor!" he said; "and at this time of night. Let me tell you, landlord—ahem—that this is a most unwarrantable infringement of—er—er—of the rules laid down by—er—eh? Stay, what have we here? Excuse me, gentlemen, while I break the seal. Ha! from my old friend Rustcoin. You remember him, gentlemen—my brother anti-quary, formerly a member of our club. He writes from Rome:

"'*My Dear Friend*,—I dare say you are surprised to hear from me again, after my long silence. The fact is that I had put off writing to you, having some time ago formed a resolution of returning to England, when I hoped to surprise you by suddenly appearing unex-pectedly in time for the tenth anniversary of the inauguration of our club. Certain affairs, however, have prevented me from being present myself in the flesh, but I beg to introduce to your notice my young friend, Mr. Vandyke McGuilp, an artist who has for some time past been prosecuting his studies here in Rome. He is a young man of tal-ent and genius, possessing a great fund of stories of the marvellous and supernatural order, such as your club particularly prides itself on. He is quite one of our sort, and you would be doing me a great favour to introduce him to the rest of the members. If he could arrive in time for your grand saturnalia, I should be doubly pleased.—Your old friend, "'*Charles Rustcoin.*'"

"Well, gentlemen," said the president, "what do you say to that? Shall the neophyte be admitted? You see, he is not a commercial traveller, nor a business man, but an artist; one of those restless strivers after the ideal. A traveller, too—a man full of stories, like one of us. What do you say—shall he be admitted?"

The guests gave an unanimous consent, and the next moment our host ushered the stranger into the club-room. All eyes were directed towards the stranger. He was a young man, bordering on thirty, about the middle height, who, contrary to the custom of the period, wore his own hair, which at that time was considered extremely vulgar. He wore a slouch hat instead of the usual three-cornered shape, and an Italian cloak thrown over the left shoulder.

He doffed his hat with dignity and courtesy as he entered the apartment, and after shaking the snow from his cloak (for it had been snowing hard without that night, being in December), he handed cloak and hat to the landlord and accepted the offer of a chair that Mr. Oldstone had placed for him near the fire.

"Here! mine host," shouted Mr. Oldstone, "bring another log, and see that you make this gentleman comfortable tonight, for I see without asking him any questions that he is one of our set."

"Ay, ay, sir," said the landlord, who was just leaving the room. "Never fear, sir, I'll see to the gentleman's wants, and my old woman will warm the bed, for it's a nasty night to be out in. My blessed eyes, how it snows! The gentleman must have had pressing business with you, sir, to bring him out here such a night as this."

"No, my good host," replied the artist; "nothing more than a desire to be present at the tenth anniversary of the club that I have heard so much about."

The host looked astonished, and the guests felt flattered. The landlord's respect for the members of the club was augmented considerably.

"Well, well; to think of that, now," he muttered to himself. "To think that this gentleman should trouble himself to come from who knows how far off, just to be present at the tenth anniversary of *our* club, and on such a night as this, too."

11

"By the by, Mr. Hearty," said the new comer to the landlord: "I believe that's your name, is it not?"

"The same, sir; Jack Hearty, at your service, sir."

"Well, then, Jack Hearty, I have just come from foreign parts, where I have left an old customer of yours; one Mr. Rustcoin, a great friend of Mr. Oldstone's. Do you recollect him?"

"*Recollect* him!" exclaimed the landlord. "Ay, indeed, sir, do I; a pleasanter gentleman over his bottle of port or over his bowl of punch hasn't crossed my threshold since he left it. Many's the good yarn we would have together. I hope you left him very well, sir?"

"In excellent health, thank you, Jack," said the stranger. "He desired to be remembered to you."

"Thank you, sir," said the host.

"Yes; those slippers will do," said the new guest.

"Draw near to the table, my friend," said Mr. Oldstone, "for I must introduce you to the other members and guests here tonight."

"My friends," said the chairman, "this gentleman is Mr. Vandyke McGuilp, an artist from Rome, great friend of my old chum Rustcoin, whom most of you knew. Mr. McGuilp, this gentleman on my right is Mr. Hardcase, the lawyer, who will be the first to relate a story tonight. On his right is Dr. Bleedem, one of our celebrated physicians; next to him is Mr. Cyanite, professor of geology, and then comes Mr. Blackdeed, one of our eminent tragedians; next to him is Mr. Parnassus, a young poet of great promise; after him is Mr. Crucible, analytical chemist, one of the oldest members of our club; next to him, as guest tonight, is Captain Toughyarn, commander of Her Majesty's good ship the *Dreadnought*; then, next door neighbour to yourself is Mr. Jollytoast, celebrated low comedian."

The new visitor bowed to each guest at the table with urbanity, and the guests returned the salute cordially.

"Well, gentlemen," began the president, "what do you say to a bumper to the health of our new guest?"

"Hear, hear!" cried the guests, unanimously.

Each filled up his glass from the punch-bowl, and our artist's health was drunk with cheers, to which he responded in a short and modest speech. (Applause.)

"And now, Mr. Hardcase," said the chairman, after the formalities were gone through, "I think it was arranged that you should tell the first story. I hope you have one ready. I am anxious for my young friend to hear a specimen of our far-famed recitals. In this club," said Mr. Oldstone, addressing the artist, "we always esteem those stories the highest that are true, and especially if they are facts coming under the experience of the relater. What sort of story may we expect from you tonight, Mr. Hardcase?"

"The story I intended to start the club with tonight is one that I myself took part in in my younger days, and which, although I never related to any of the club before, I have been upon the point of relating a hundred times, when I have been invariably interrupted by someone else who had some other tale to relate. The story I have in store for you this evening, gentlemen, I propose to entitle 'The Phantom Flea.'"

"Ha, Bravo!" laughed the guests. "The Phantom Flea! Ha! ha! ha!"

"I assure you, gentlemen," said the lawyer, gravely, "that the narrative I am about to relate is not one to provoke mirth. It is of a solemn character, I can promise you. No one felt less inclined to laugh than I did when I was reluctantly compelled to take part in this tragedy. Though by no means a timid man, I, nevertheless, experienced a sort of cold shiver all down my back when—"

"Exactly so," said the doctor.

"And each particular hair to stand on end like quills upon the fretful porcupine," quoted Mr. Blackdeed, the tragedian.

"Belay that," roared Captain Toughyarn, from the depths of his stentorian lungs, "and make room on board for the 'Phantom Flea.'"

"Bedad, and sure I feel myself itching all over alriddy," broke in Mr. Jollytoast, assuming an Irish brogue, and scratching himself.

"Order, order! Chair, chair!" called out other guests.

"Silence! gentlemen," said Mr. Oldstone, with authority, thumping on the table; "the story is just about to commence."

"The performance is just a-goin' to begin," broke in the incorrigible little comedian, assuming the air of a showman. "Valk up, valk up, ladies and gentlemen."

"Hush! Mr. Jollytoast," said the antiquary. "Hush! gentlemen, for the 'Phantom Flea.'"

"Tremulous music, lights half down," muttered the tragedian; but he was instantly silenced by the chairman.

Mr. Oldstone gave one final authoritative thump on the table, and glanced severely at all the guests. The silence that ensued was awful, while Mr. Hardcase, after a sip at his glass and a puff at his long churchwarden, began his story in the following manner:

The Lawyer's Story

The Phantom Flea[1]

One morning, many years ago, whilst sitting idly in my chambers in town, I received a letter from baron — to come down for a few days to his country seat in —shire. It was on business he wanted me; he had got involved in some quarrel. The case was about to be brought before the court, and the baron wanted a legal adviser.

Having heard much of my abilities, as he said, he thought he could not do better than write to me at once. He regretted that business would prevent him from being at the hall on my arrival, but he hoped to return home some time the next day. In the meantime he had told his housekeeper to make up a bed for me at the hall, and had left open his bookcase, lest the time might hang heavy on my hands.

Glad of an excuse to leave town, as it was getting very hot and I had nothing to do, I took the stage, and towards the middle of the next day found myself in front of the baron's country seat.

It was a fine, stately mansion, surrounded by a moat. I crossed the drawbridge, and inquired whether the baron was at home. A respectable matron answered the door. She replied in the negative to my question.

Then, asking if I were Mr. Hardcase, the lawyer, and learning that I was, she said "The baron left word that he would be at home some time tomorrow, or the day after for certain; that in the meantime you were to make yourself quite at home, sir."

"Oh, very well," said I; "I am rather tired just at present. Leave me here among the baron's books. When I have sufficiently rested I should like to look over the house. It seems a curious old place."

"Yes, sir, it is a *very* old place," said the housekeeper. "But wouldn't you like to take a little refreshment first?"

---

1. *In the spirit world all those who have been bloodthirsty to excess inhabit the forms of fleas.*—William Blake, poet and visionary (quoted from memory).

Being then past one o'clock, and having had but a hurried breakfast, I thanked her and said I thought I could manage a little light refreshment. She then left me alone, but soon returned with a tray containing what seemed to be the fag end of a sumptuous banquet. There was venison pasty, a boiled leg of turkey, some ham, vegetables, bread and cheese, salad, raspberry and currant tart, a bottle of good old crusted port, some sherry, burgundy, etc.

Having done justice to this light repast, I rang the bell for the things to be cleared away; after which I took down a great number of volumes from the bookcase, and throwing myself into an easy-chair, I deposited the books in a heap upon the floor, and began examining their titles, and occasionally reading a passage here and there when it interested me.

The first book I laid hands on was *Fox's Book of Martyrs*, with plates showing the various modes of torture by which the early Christians were put to death. I passed on to the next. This was a book of Chinese punishments, with Chinese illustrations. I opened the book at a plate of a man being skinned alive.

Having little taste for these sort of horrors, I closed the book and passed on to the next. The third book was a description of celebrated executions, with a plate as frontispiece of a man being hanged, drawn, and quartered. "The baron seems fond of the horrible," I thought, and I took up another. This was on bull-baiting, cock-fighting, and other cruel sports. Another was a book on poisons. A sixth, on the various modes of self-defence. A seventh, a book on field sports. I put down the book for a moment and sat musing, trying to imagine to myself what manner of man the baron might be. I gazed round the room, and noticed that it was hung round by trophies of the chase—stags' antlers, foxes' brushes, intermingled with guns, powder-flasks, etc. Here and there were hung half suits of armour, belonging, no doubt, to the baron's ancestors.

Then, from musing I fell into a dose, and dreamed of the wild hunter and all sorts of curious and horrible things.

On awaking I reflected that I had not been over the house, so I went in search of the housekeeper, who asked me if I would like to see the picture gallery. Nothing loth, I followed my guide, who pointed me out the portraits of the present baron's ancestors for I know not how many generations back.

The portrait of the present baron was not amongst them. I noticed a strong family likeness running through all of the portraits, and I wondered if the baron inherited the likeness. I asked the housekeeper, and she assured me that he did in a very striking degree. On leaving the gallery, I passed through long oaken corridors, through immense chambers hung with tapestry, on which were depicted either battles or scenes of the chase.

"The baron inherits the tastes of his ancestors, it would appear," I said to the matron.

"Ah! sir," said she, with a sigh, and tried to force a smile, but it was a bitter one.

I took little notice of her expression at the time, and soon after left her, to stroll about in the garden. It was a spacious one, laid out in good taste. There were terraces, broad velvet lawns, cedars of Lebanon, avenues of yew trees, glimpses of distant hills, flower beds, luxuriant with every variety of the choicest flowers. There were broad walks and serpentine paths, oaks, beeches, elms; a lake with an island in the middle, which was reached by a rustic bridge; weeping-willows, summer-houses, and everything that could be desired. I strolled about the garden, struck with admiration every step I took at the exquisite taste with which everything was carried out, and wondered how it was that the same mind which took such delight in the horrible should possess such exquisite refinement of taste in the planning of his garden.

I doubted the garden being the result of the baron's own taste, nor was I mistaken, as I afterwards ascertained from the housekeeper. I strolled back towards the house, which I examined carefully over for the second time, then strolled out again into the garden, and so on till supper, which I took about nine o'clock.

Feeling rather lonely, I invited Mrs. Wharton, the housekeeper, to keep me company during my solitary meal. She sat down opposite to me as I commenced devouring my cold fowl and tongue, and helped myself to a glass of the baron's ale. She was an agreeable old lady, and seemed to have known better days.

"This is a curious old place," I began. "Have you any rats here?"

"No, sir, none now," answered the matron.

"Nor bugs?"

"No."

"Nor fleas?"

"No, sir,—that is to say, only one," and her face assumed a solemn expression.

"Only *one*!" I exclaimed, laughing.

"Yes, sir," said she, gravely—"only the *Phantom*; only the *baron*."

"*Phantom! baron!*" I exclaimed, bewildered. "Ah, you have a ghost story in the family, I see; but I don't think you quite understood my question," I said. "I did not inquire about phantoms, or barons; my question referred simply to fleas."

"Yes, yes; I perfectly understand, sir," replied the matron; "and I repeat that the *phantom flea* is the only flea that inhabits this mansion."

"*The Phantom Flea!*" Here I exploded. "Well, of all the odd superstitions I ever heard of, that beats them all. Really, my good woman, you should *not*—you should not, indeed, believe in such trash."

"Ah, sir," replied the matron, "it is plain to see that you are a stranger in these parts. Is it possible you have never heard of the 'baron's flea?'"

"Never in all my life before, I assure you, my good woman," I replied; "but, as it is a thing apparently well known, I should like to hear the particulars of the case."

"Well, sir," began the housekeeper, "you must know that some two hundred years or so back one of the baron's ancestors, one Sir Ralph — inhabited this mansion. The room that you will sleep in tonight was his room; the self same bed and furniture that you saw this morning were there in his time. He was not a man generally liked by those around him; in fact, it would not be too much to say that he was universally hated. No one could remember any good act or kind word of the baron's. He was cruel, bloodthirsty, tyrannical, avaricious, ambitious, and sensual. From early youth he was always allowed to have his own way, and when he came into power he was the scourge of the neighbourhood.

"There was no restraining his cruelty and malignity. Anyone who dared oppose himself to his will was put to death. He thought no more of taking the life of a peasant than one would in wringing the neck of a fowl. Maidens were carried off with impunity, and sometimes murdered; men were found stabbed or mangled to death by the baron's hounds; cottages were set fire to, and their inhabitants driven out to seek refuge where they could; robberies were committed, churches pillaged, convents sacked, monks driven out and occasionally burnt alive for pastime; nuns carried off by ruffians to the baron's hall; in short, every species of outrage and plunder conceivable. Such a state of affairs could not endure for ever. It gave rise to a rebellion. The long-oppressed people would suffer it no longer, and rose to a man. They would fain have broken into the baron's hall, and have torn him limb from limb; but the baron's myrmidons were powerful and well armed; and, cutting their way through the crowd with the baron at their head, spared neither man, woman, nor child.

"The mob, driven back, were subdued for a time; but the law interfered, though with little better success; for the first time that constables were sent to arrest the baron, he sent them back again to those who sent them with their noses and ears slit. Such an insult as this against the servants of the law could not be stood any longer. Grand preparations were made for the immediate arrest of the baron and his ruffians, with an order to raze his castle to the ground, which would most assuredly have been carried into effect, had not the sudden death of the baron rendered such measures unnecessary.

"The baron's death was mysterious. Some say he made away with himself, rather than fall into the hands of justice. Others assert that he was struck by lightning as a punishment for his many crimes. Others, that he was killed in a fray. But the story most current is, that a man introduced himself into the baron's household as servant, whose bride the baron had dishonoured, and avenged himself by putting an end to the baron's life by poison.

"However this was, testimony goes much to prove that the baron was found dead in his bed. How long he took dying is uncertain, but tradition tells that his last moments were horrible. He refused to see a father confessor, and died in his sins.

"He was succeeded by his son, a peaceful and studious youth, much beloved by the people, who did not seem to inherit a drop of the old baron's blood. In some of his later descendants, however, the spirit of the old baron seemed to reign again. When the death of the baron was made known, great rejoicings manifested themselves in the neighbourhood. Everyone wanted to know the particulars of the baron's mysterious end. Strange stories were set afloat, many of which are believed to this day. But one thing universally believed is, that, as a punishment for his sins, the baron's spirit is condemned to inhabit the form of a flea of uncommon size, which sucks the blood of all strangers who sleep in that bed. His power, however, is confined to that chamber. Other rooms are left unmolested. The marks left on the body by the bite of this fell insect are extremely large, being about the size of a wen, and the pain endures for a considerable time. I can speak from experience, for I have been bitten myself. The flea may be seen by anyone who chooses to sleep in that room. One night spent in that chamber will be enough to convince any unbeliever of the truth of my assertion.

"Many and futile have been the attempts to catch this obnoxious insect. It eludes all chase. It was not for many years after the baron's death, and until many of the occupants of that chamber had been repeatedly bitten, and all attempts to capture the offensive creature had been abandoned in despair, that the belief that the baron's spirit inhabited its fell body grew firmly rooted in the minds of the surrounding gentry.

"If, after what I have related to you, sir, you feel inclined to change your room, I shall have much pleasure in making you up a bed in another chamber, although it is against the baron's orders; for, knowing what a wretched night you *must* spend within that haunted chamber, I feel a compassion for you, sir, and all strangers that the baron cruelly hands over to the spirit of his wicked ancestor."

"On the contrary, Mrs. Wharton," I said, "I have the greatest curiosity to encounter this wonderful flea. Your conversation has been most interesting, and as it is now past ten o'clock, I don't care how soon I make his aristocratic acquaintance."

"Do as you please, sir," said Mrs. Wharton, "but if you should feel uncomfortable in the night, you've but to knock at my door, the next room to yours, and I will gladly make you up a bed in No. 12."

"No, thank you, Mrs. Wharton; I am much obliged to you all the same. I have no doubt that the baron and I will be capital friends."

"Well, sir, I wish you a pleasant night of it, I am sure," said the housekeeper, as she handed me a candle. "Goodnight, sir."

"Goodnight, Mrs. Wharton."

I walked up stairs to the haunted chamber. Having reached the landing, I entered my room and locked myself in for the night. In spite of my forced levity, I must admit that I felt a certain feeling of awe come over me upon entering the chamber once occupied by the author of so many crimes. I could not but think that Mrs. Wharton herself thoroughly believed in what seemed to me a popular superstition, but the more I reflected on what she had told me of the baron's crimes, the less ludicrous did the idea of the baron's metempsychosis appear to me.

What, after all, was there ridiculous in a flea more than in any other hideous creature? The feeling of the ludicrous in my mind was supplanted by one of horror. "There are more things in heaven and earth than are dreamed of in our philosophy," I muttered. I could not make up my mind to go to rest immediately. In fact, I did not feel in the least sleepy. I busied myself in examining the room minutely to see if there were any trap-door or sliding panel; and, tapping all the walls, expected every moment to touch some spring and for some panel to fly back, discovering a secret staircase. I examined the bed and under the bed, but could discover nothing. The baron's portrait hung over the mantelpiece. I lifted up the picture to see if there was any hole in the wall underneath, but there was nothing but good solid panel; nor could I in any part of the room discover anything suspicious. I partially undressed and seated myself in a large arm-chair in front of the baron's portrait. I was extremely interested in the perusal of his features, and had no difficulty in believing all the atrocities attributed to the original. The more I gazed at it, the more it fascinated me. I could not take my eyes from it. Somehow or other the features seemed familiar to me; I fancied I had seen them somewhere. I tried to collect my thoughts. Where had I seen them before?

Suddenly I recollected a horrible criminal, who had murdered a whole family and committed other heinous atrocities, and had been executed a year or two before. I had to plead for him at the trial, but the evidence was so strong against him, that no earthly power could save him from the gibbet. The likeness between this wretch and the portrait before me was very remarkable. This, then, was the incarnation of deep crime. These are the features that mark a life given up to every sort of cruelty, licentiousness, and depravity. The physiognomy was peculiar, and never to be forgotten when once seen. The head was round as a bullet, the hair red, short and bristly, the moustache and peaked beard of the same hue; the eyes greenish, and obliquely set in the head, like those of a cat, with an expression of the most indescribable ferocity and malice. The eyebrows red and tufted, running up also in an oblique direction, one of them being considerably higher than the other. Between the brows was a deep line. The forehead was flat, and retired from the temples in two separate peaks, that appeared to run up nearly to the back of his head; the nose was at once hooked and flat, like the bill of a parrot; the mouth was wide; the lips thin and compressed, with unpleasant lines at the corners; the chin and jaw square and massive; the neck resembling that of a bull;

the ears were unusually large, and stuck out at the sides; the complexion was florid, with two pouches under the eyes, which seemed to drag the eyes down and give them a bloodshot appearance. A deep line in the cheeks, extending from each wing of the nose to the corners of the mouth, gave to the countenance a look of cynical disdain, and completed a portrait at once characteristic and revolting. The costume was early Elizabethan, and the arms of the baron, together with his name and his age—forty-six—when the portrait was taken, were depicted with the date in the corner of the picture. For a while I sat musing. "Fit spirit," I muttered, "to inhabit the form of a flea! Heartless, worthless, bloodthirsty." I gazed at the portrait with feelings of horror and disgust. The eyes seemed to answer my expression with a look of anger.

I was unable to judge of the merits of the picture as a work of art, being little versed in such matters; but of one thing I am certain, that the painter had endeavoured to imitate as truthfully as it lay in his power all the leading characteristics of the baron's physiognomy without any attempt at flattery.

As I mused it grew late; it was now just upon midnight. I finished undressing and climbed into my bed, a high old-fashioned four-poster with heavy embroidered curtains. The baron still scowled at me from the mantelpiece, but, without returning his gaze, I set to work diligently to search for the flea. I drew back the top sheet slowly until the whole bed was uncovered. I shook the blankets and counterpane and looked under the pillow, but all in vain, not a glimpse of a flea was visible. It was a clean, well-aired bed, so, feeling now rather sleepy, I covered myself up with the bed-clothes and blew out the light, with every prospect of a good night's rest before me. But, alas! how soon was I undeceived. Hardly had I gone off into my first sleep, when I was suddenly awoke from a delicious dream with a sharp, sudden pang, like a stab or the tooth of some venomous reptile in the fleshy part of my thigh. I started up in horror, hardly able to restrain a slight shriek. The night was dark and stormy, the winds howled without, and the old mansion shook from its foundations. "The Phantom Flea!" I muttered, horrified, and reached out my hand for my tinder-box; but before I was able to strike a light, I experienced a second sharp stinging pain in the small of the back, then another in the calf of my leg. By this time I had succeeded in striking a light. Some scorpion, I thought. So, lighting my candle, I commenced a rigid search.

At length I caught sight of the vile insect. There it was, sure enough, a flea, and no mistake about it, but what a monster! It must have been the size of a coffee bean. What legs! How it hopped from one side of the bed to the other!

Well, gentlemen, I used my utmost endeavours to capture it; and here let me add that I am generally rather expert at that sort of game, having had some practice in my time; but, would you believe it, gentlemen, it foiled all my best endeavours, although I kept it in sight all the time. I was a full hour and a half engaged in this undignified chase. The "Phantom Flea" defied me to the last. What was I to do? I couldn't sit up all night hunting a flea, and yet to get any sleep with such a monster in the bed was equally impossible. Suddenly I recollected that I had a small bottle of opium in my waistcoat pocket, which I had purchased the day before to relieve a toothache that I had caught from sitting in the theatre at one end of a row of stalls, close to the door, which kept continually opening and shutting. I rose and searched for the bottle, and swallowed more, perhaps, than under ordinary circumstances would have been good for me, got into bed again, and blew out the light. The first sensation I experienced was that of a deliciously gradual dropping off to sleep, but the keenness of my senses was increased a hundred-fold. My memory and my imagination bordered on the abnormal. Every event in my life, from the cradle up to the present moment, rose before my mind in microscopic detail.

The room was dark; nevertheless, my eye, grown accustomed to the light, and sharpened by the effects of the opium, enabled me to discover every object in the room distinctly. There was the bed, the counterpane, every little tuft worked on it with painful distinctness. There was the texture of the sheets; every fibre of the blankets, and last, but not least, the "Phantom Flea" hopping about and around me, and biting me here and there at his pleasure. The opium in some measure relieved the severity of the bite, though the latter was still painful enough to prevent me from going off to sleep altogether. The sensation of delirium (for I can call it nothing else) caused by the opium seemed to increase. The room appeared to grow lighter and lighter, till it seemed to glow with a phosphoric glare.

My sight, hearing, and other senses grew rapidly more and more acute. Everything around me seemed to swell and dilate into proportions positively enormous. I felt myself grow larger, the bed grew larger, the room grew larger, the picture grew larger, and the *flea* grew larger. Larger and larger swelled the bed; larger, *larger*, and ever larger grew the flea, till it attained the proportions of a horse. I noticed that the larger it grew, the less like a flea and more human it became. At length it appeared to stop growing, and to decrease, if anything. It had now assumed the size of a man, and a form almost human. There it stood at the foot of my bed, with its arms folded on its breast, and its eye steadily fixed upon mine. How shall I describe the horror of my situation—feeling my eyes riveted on that hideous face with a preter-natural fascination? To remove them was impossible. Yet to gaze on it further was death. I can describe my feelings to nothing else than the sensation of gradually turning into stone. I felt life fast ebbing from me. My head whirled, I gasped for breath. I tried to speak, to implore for mercy, but my voice was gone. I felt my last moment had come.

The remorseless flea seemed conscious of my agony, and gloated on my sufferings, for he never took his stony eye off me all the while. Unable to move, and bathed in a profuse perspiration, I must have died in another instant from sheer agony and terror, had I not by a supernatural effort gathered up my last dying energies, and burst out in a loud, despairing yell that seemed to pierce the walls of the whole house. I felt the spell broken for the time. The fiend himself seemed startled by the sudden and preternatural shrillness of the scream, and for a moment changed the expression of his countenance. Feeling his eye no longer fixed upon mine with that fearful intensity, I dared to breathe again; but I had awoke Mrs. Wharton in the next room, and she knocked at my door to ask me what was the matter.

"Nothing, thank you," I said; "only a dream; don't be alarmed."

So Mrs. Wharton retired to her room again.

The monster who had never left me during all this time, at length spoke.

"I have summoned you here tonight, because I have need of you. I am that baron Ralph, the ruthless, whose deeds of bloodshed you have already heard of, and for which deeds he is condemned nightly to inhabit the form of a flea. You have experienced my power, and your paltry scepticism has been shaken. Listen now to me. I do not always inhabit the contemptible form in which you first saw me. In the daytime I wander to and fro on the earth, and inhabit by turns the bodies of such men whose natural propensities are in harmony with my own. Wretch! do you know that the man, who, through your in-ability to save, was executed for some few paltry murders, was none other than myself in the flesh? That it was *my* body that suffered the pain and disgrace of execution, *my* spirit that was driven back by your incapacity, to inhabit the form of one of the vilest of insects? Think not to escape my resentment. I have need of you again, it is true, but I do not ask you a favour, I command you to obey. Spirits of my order do not ask; they command and threaten, and if disobeyed, punish."

Aware of the awful power of this fell being and knowing all resistance vain, I thought it best to assume as humble a position as I could, in order to milden the severity of his look and manner—that fearful look that I had experienced only a few minutes ago, and which might kill me outright a second time. Therefore I prostrated myself before him on the bed, and in the most abject tones began.

"Illustrious flea! I will do all—"

"Irreverent varlet!" exclaimed the baron, fiercely, darting at me a glance from his evil eye that froze my very marrow. "That name is offensive to me, another such title as that, and I'll—I'll"—here the baron's face went through the most hideously savage contortions that it is possible to imagine. The baron's portrait taken in the flesh was ugly enough, but it was an ideal of manly beauty compared with the infernal aspect of this demon flea before me.

"Mercy! mercy!" cried I, gasping.

"Oh, yes, 'Mercy, mercy,'" retorted the baron, with a sneer. "Very well, then, this time, but mind—" Here his countenance again assumed a ferocious expression. "Ha! ha!" he cried. "You thought to outwit me by taking opium to deaden my bite. Fool! know it was *I* who made you buy that opium; not to make you *sleep*, but to *awaken* your dull senses to such a pitch that the gross material clay that clogs your vision might be, as it were, doffed for a moment, and that your keener eyesight might be able to grasp my form a degree nearer resembling that which I bore in the flesh, thereby in a measure removing the barrier between our beings; and each, as it were, meeting on neutral ground, to the end that you should know my pleasure and obey my commands. It was I who caused you to catch that toothache, by inspiring you to go to the theatre. It was I who so ordained the distribution of the tickets that that ticket near the door should fall to your lot, where I knew you would take cold in the tooth, being subject to the toothache. I then, by my subtle arts, caused you to buy that bottle of opium and bring it here with you. I then worried you by continual biting, till I forced you to seek comfort in that opium bottle, and now that your usually obtuse senses are raised to that abnormal state necessary to converse with beings of my order, listen, and give ear to what I have to say."

"Awful being, say on," I muttered.

"You must know, then," he continued, "that my spirit inhabits by day the body of the present baron who bears my name, though at night I am compelled to assume the ignoble shape of a flea. At this present moment my descendant lies in his bed lifeless. My spirit will animate his clay tomorrow. Call upon him early, and you will learn from him what I have not time to discuss with you now, as it is now daybreak and my power is on the wane. Farewell."

So saying, he gradually decreased in size, losing every moment more and more of the *human* element that he had assumed, and growing more and more into the likeness of a flea the smaller he grew, till he returned to the size he appeared when I first saw him, and then vanished mysteriously. The exciting effects of the opium had worn off, but they had given place to a feeling of deep depression. My head felt too heavy for me, and ached terribly; my eyeballs were as if weighed down by lead. I could not sleep comfortably, and I was too lazy to get up. I loathed my own existence, and hated everybody and everything around me. Thoughts of suicide haunted me, and I had a momentary thought of emptying the whole of the remaining contents of the bottle down my throat, and so put an end to my misery for ever. But then I bethought me of the baron; it might be the means of invoking again the "Phantom Flea."

He might be angry at being recalled, and possibly carry me off, soul and all. I turned and tossed about restlessly in my bed, and kicked the bed-clothes on to the floor. The cold grey dawn broke in at my window. I thought I would get up, so, giving one desperate spring, I found myself upon my feet. My tongue was parched, and a cold sweat matted my hair. I felt a prodigious thirst, and emptied a whole water-bottle; then I proceeded to dress, but I soon found that to shave was an utter impossibility. My hand shook as with the palsy, so I abandoned the attempt. Unshaven, unkempt, and negligently dressed, with haggard look and listless steps, I sauntered about the lonely corridors of the mansion like a restless spirit, until I heard the footsteps of Mrs. Wharton about the house. I started at the slightest noise. I was soon accosted by that worthy, who, of course, wanted to know how I had slept.

"I passed an indifferent night," I replied. "I foolishly took some opium to make me sleep, and it has given me the headache. By the by,"—I said, to change the conversation, so as to avoid being questioned, for I saw the old lady was scanning my countenance—"by the by, where did you say the baron was staying? If not too far off, I should like to call upon him; a walk might do me good."

"About five miles off, sir, in the next village, at the sign of 'The Swan,'" said the housekeeper; "as straight as ever you can go, sir, you can't miss it."

"Thank you," said I.

"Poor, poor, gentleman," I heard the housekeeper mutter to herself, as I started off, "I knew he would suffer."

I set off at a brisk pace; the sun had just risen, a silver mist was rising, and a gentle breeze somewhat alleviated the fever of my burning brow, but my legs felt weak. I tottered on for half-a-mile further; here I found a mile-stone and sat down to rest upon it. My reflections were gloomy. My recollections of the previous night were painfully vivid. My dream, my vision, my spiritual visitation, or whatever you like to call it, did not vanish upon waking, like an ordinary dream, but remained deeply rooted in my brain with fearful accuracy of detail. I recollected word for word all the monster had uttered; recalled his tone of voice, his remarkable shape—that curious and hideous blending of the characteristics of the flea with the human form, the revolting, fiendish ugliness of the *tout ensemble*, but above all, of that basilisk eye. My blood ran cold as I thought of it.

"Have I then lived to hold converse with a being of the lower world?" I muttered, to myself. "Am I awake, or is this but a continuation of the dream?" I gave my arm a pinch, a hard twisted pinch, with all my might and main, to ascertain if I were sleeping or waking, but the scene before me remained the same, and my recollections of the past night were as vivid as ever. I took off my hat to wipe my brow and let the cool breeze play with my locks and about my heated temples. I gazed at the smiling scene around me. What a contrast to the hell I bore within.

"O glorious orb!" I ejaculated, "author and vivifier of all nature, through every grade of creation, illumine the haunted chambers of my dark soul with thy golden beams; bring balm to my jaded spirit and renew the bright hope of my earlier years. Give me strength to bear my tottering limbs to the end of my pilgrimage; or, if that be not granted me, take all there is left—take my life, great orb of day! Type of my own once aspiring youth, quicken my flagging energies and breathe into me new life, new hope, new strength."

Whilst thus apostrophising the rising sun, I experienced something like the fire of my boyish days returning to my frame. I actually felt an appetite. I rose from my seat considerably refreshed, and continued my journey. I walked on with buoyant step; I had all but forgotten the adventure of the past night. If it rose up before me again at intervals, I speedily chased it from my mind.

At length I espied the village in the distance. Another half-mile led me up to the door of "The Swan Inn." It was then about seven o'clock. A raw country youth, evidently the boots, was beating a mat outside the door.

"Is the baron within?" I asked.

"Wal, he b'ain't up yet, zur," replied the youth.

"Oh, never mind," I said, "I will wait, and as soon as he is up tell him a gentleman is waiting to see him."

"Very well, zur."

"Would you like to wait here in the parlour, sir?" said the buxom landlady, who had overheard our dialogue. "The baron can't be long; he is generally up by this time, or if you will follow me, sir, I will knock at his door, and you can wait in his sitting-room till he comes out."

"Thank you," I said, as I followed the landlady upstairs, and was led into the sitting-room. The landlady knocked at the baron's door. No answer.

"Don't awake him, pray," said I, "if he's asleep."

"Oh, but the baron told me to call him early, sir."

She knocked again. Again no answer. The landlady paused a few moments to listen if he was getting up, then tapped again louder, louder still, but all was silent. The hostess ventured to open the door ajar. The baron was in bed. She entered the room. A pause, a slight scream, and the landlady came running out to me, pale and terrified.

"Oh, sir," she said, in a faint voice, "the baron—the baron—is—*dead*!"

"*Dead!*" I exclaimed. "When? how?"

"It is true, sir. Come and see."

I entered the baron's chamber. There he lay, sure enough, to all appearance dead. I touched him; he was as cold as ice. I was much struck with the singular resemblance of the defunct baron before me to the portrait of baron Ralph that hung over the mantelpiece in my chamber. It is true that the baron before me was a younger man, that he wore a shaven face instead of a moustache and peaked beard, that the livid colour of the corpse was unlike the florid complexion of baron Ralph; but the features were exact, the shape of the head, the colour of the hair and the way it grew; the same tufted red eyebrows, the right one considerably higher than the left; the same bent flat nose and tightly compressed lips, with cruel lines at the corners; the chin, the jaw, the deep line between the brows, in fact, the whole man seemed the exact counterpart of the old baron.

A horrible recollection passed through my mind. I remembered having seen the criminal before alluded to after his execution. What a startling likeness between the features of the executed criminal and those of the baron's corpse before me. I shuddered. A portion of the phantom's conversation on the preceding night occurred to me suddenly. What if—could it be that—

I called the landlady. The whole inn was in a state of confusion. The news of the baron's death had circulated through the whole village by this time.

"Perhaps," said I, "the baron may not be quite dead, he may be in a trance, he may be— At any rate, don't you think it would be best to send for the doctor, to hear his opinion?"

The doctor was accordingly sent for, and arriving shortly, was at once shown into the baron's room. The landlady and a great part of the household followed.

"Why, of course he's dead," replied the leech, brusquely, in answer to their eager questions. "Can't you see that?"

"If, nevertheless," said I, timidly, "you would not mind opening a vein—"

"I'll open a vein, if you like," he answered, bluntly; "but, I tell you, the man's dead!"

Then, taking out his lancet, he opened a vein in the right arm.

"You see now, I hope," said the leech, "that it is utterly useless; there is not a drop of blood."

"Then," said the landlady, "the baron really *is*—dead?"

"Dead! *Dead as mutton*," replied the doctor.

At this juncture the face of the corpse grew violently convulsed, his eyes rolled, the colour returned suddenly to his cheeks, and leaping from the bed with terrific energy, he seized the bolster, with which he belaboured the terrified inmates of "The Swan" right and left, knocking over the little doctor, and sending me into the landlady's lap, and the "boots" flying out of the room with a yell of terror, besides upsetting every utensil of crockery that stood in the way.

"Dead, am I!" roared the baron, "dead, eh! Where's that scurvy apothecary—that spreader of plaisters, that pill-maker, that cow-bleeder—that dared to open one of *my* veins?"

The little doctor had crept under the bed.

"And you, sir," cried he, turning upon me, "for advising him to try his filthy experiments upon me," and swinging round his bolster, sent me tottering against the wall.

"Dead as *mutton*, eh! By the blood of my ancestors, I never had such foul language used to me before. What! compare the aristocratic flesh of one descended from such a line of ancestors as mine to mutton! Ugh! *Mutton*, quotha? I'll mutton *you*," cried the baron, aiming a blow at the little doctor's head, which he caught peeping from beneath the bed.

The doctor ducked in his head, and attempted a clandestine escape on his hands and knees by the door, but was immediately pulled back by the coat-tails by the baron.

"Not so easily, young vein-opener, do you escape the clutches of the baron. Bind up my wound, Sir Shaveling, and think yourself lucky that I spare your paltry life for the vile trick which you, in your blind ignorance of this phenomenon of my aristocratic constitution, dared to practise upon me. Keep that instrument for the bleeding of cows and horses. That's more in your line than the flesh of great nobles like me."

The baron's wound was bleeding profusely. The floor was covered with pools of blood. The landlady had fallen into hysterics, and had to be carried out of the room. The leech stammered out a sort of apology and set meekly about his task of binding up the baron's wound.

"Silence!" roared the baron, "and no more prattle."

The arm being at length bound up, the doctor took his departure without further severity on the part of the baron, who had now cooled down considerably.

Whether it was the loss of blood, or what, a marked change had taken place in the baron's demeanour. He apologised amply to me for the effects of hereditary temper of which he was the victim, and invited me to breakfast. The breakfast was brought up by the landlord himself, as everyone else refused to enter the baron's apartments, saying that the baron must be the devil himself, and no one else.

"I'm afraid," said the baron, addressing the landlord, "that I frightened your good lady dreadfully this morning, eh?"

"Well, my lord," said the host, "she did take on about it a little, but—"

"I am sincerely sorry for my rudeness," apologised the baron, "but my infirmity is ungovernable. It is a disease I inherit from my ancestors; I am given every now and then to some uncontrollable burst of passion when my nerves are a little out of order, which is generally the first thing in the morning."

"Indeed, my lord," said the good-hearted landlord, with some compassion in his face, "but your lordship's sudden coming to life again after the doctor had pronounced you dead, that was what staggered us all downstairs."

"Ha! ha!" laughed the baron. "Yes; well, I dare say it did appear rather startling, but it is nothing to those who know me. The fact is, I am subject to a peculiar sort of trance, much resembling death; that also I inherit from my ancestors."

"Well, my lord, it's strange. I hope it's nothing dangerous. At any rate, I am glad to see your lordship looking so well again," said the host.

"Thank you, thank you, my good host," replied the baron.

"It would have been an ugly thing, you know, my lord, for your lordship to have died suddenly in my inn. It would have looked like foul play," said the landlord.

"True, true, my good host; I understand," replied his lordship. "I trust you'll convey my best apologies to your good lady for—"

"Oh, I trust your lordship won't mention it," said the landlord; "and if there is anything else your lordship may require—"

"Nothing, thank you," said the baron; and the landlord left the room.

I was surprised at the change in the baron's manner. Perhaps, after all, he might not be so bad as he appeared. His infirmity of temper was certainly against him. His personal appearance no less so. Nevertheless, in his better moments he appeared to possess the manners of a gentleman. I began to fancy that the experiences of the past night might, after all, have been a dream, until I caught sight again of the enormous flea-bites on my hands, which still smarted.

The baron's manner to me during breakfast was most affable. After breakfast we left the inn together and strolled leisurely towards the hall. On the way the baron made me acquainted with the particulars of his case, and I promised to do the best I could to serve him. Nevertheless, I saw at once that the baron was most decidedly in the wrong. I told him it was likely to go hard with him; in fact, I said I did not see how he could well get off.

The baron frowned, and we walked on in silence towards the hall. That very day the case was tried at the assizes, and in spite of all my efforts, the baron lost. I will not weary you with the details of the case. Suffice it that there was oppression and injustice on the part of the baron which could not be excused, resulting from a morbid belief in his own importance.

After the court broke up the baron led me in silence to the hall and beckoned me to his room, the walls of which were covered over with every sort of weapon of defence under the sun. There were pistols, daggers, blunderbusses, rapiers, broadswords, cutlasses, Malay creases, poisoned spear heads, a two-handed sword, probably belonging to his ancestor of cruel memory, and an iron bar to which were attached a chain and ball of spikes.

On entering the room he slammed the door, and turning suddenly upon me, he hissed out, "Paltry pettifogger, this is the second time that through your d—d bungling I have been brought to disgrace. Not content with hanging me once, you have played me foul a second time. But think not to escape me now," and he cleared the room with one terrific stride. (Now almost for the first time I noticed the enormous length of the baron's legs.) "Choose your weapons," he cried, "and thank your stars that I don't fell you on the spot as I would an ox."

"But—but—I don't see how you have a right to—to—I did all in my power to—" stammered I. "I don't think you ought to be offended. Reflect, my dear baron," I said. "I am sure, in your better mood, you will see the matter in another light."

"No more prating, but choose your weapon," screamed the baron.

"Really, baron," I said, "this conduct of yours is contrary to all the generally received etiquette in duelling. There are no seconds present, nothing regular. I accept your challenge, if you really cannot be brought to reason, but if I die, it must be like a gentleman, in a regular duel, with all the usual ceremony."

"Driveller! dost prate to me of ceremony? But have it your own way," said the baron. "You do not escape me this time."

"I will write to a friend of mine from town," I said. "Meanwhile, I have the pleasure of wishing your lordship a remarkably good morning."

I opened the door and made for the staircase, but, with two immense strides, the baron was at my heels.

"Take that, Sir Bungler," cried he, and lifting one of his enormous legs, lunged forth a kick upon that part of my person anatomically known as the *Glutaeus Major*, which sent me flying from the top of the stairs to the bottom, at the imminent risk of breaking my neck; but, as good luck would have it, I landed safely on my feet. Nevertheless the insult stung me to the quick.

I turned round indignantly, yet striving to master my passion, in order to preserve my dignity, and said, "baron, you are no gentleman."

With the yell of a wounded tiger, the baron vaulted with one bound from the top of the staircase to the bottom, just as my hand was on the door. I opened it and slammed it again in his face, and walked briskly in the direction of the village. I heard the door open behind me and the baron's fearful footsteps after me.

I do not know what would have become of me, if just at that moment an over-driven bull had not come to my rescue and stood between me and the baron. Seeing a man striding towards him furiously, he imagined the attack was meant for himself, and accordingly stood on the defensive. The baron tried to pass, but the bull lowered his horns, and looked menacing, so he wisely retreated to his Hall.

Arrived at "The Swan," I demanded pen, ink, and paper, and wrote to my friend in town to come to me for the purpose of performing the office of second, after which I endeavoured to kill time in this lonely village till dinner. Feeling hungry, I made a sumptuous repast and turned into bed with feelings full of revenge towards the baron.

"No more Phantom Fleas tonight," I said to myself as I tucked myself up in my comfortable little bed at "The Swan," and soon fell into a sound sleep.

And now, said the lawyer, when he had got thus far in his narrative, I must root up an old and very painful subject that occurred in my early life, and which I would fain have allowed to rest for ever.

In my earlier days, when as yet I had no fixed profession, during my travels in Italy, I became enamoured of a beautiful Italian girl. Poor Mariangela! how she loved me! That girl possessed the soul of an angel. I see her before me now, with her sweet, dreamy, saint-like eyes, and her quiet graceful step. We were never married, for I was not in a position then to support a wife. She vowed that she would never love anyone else but me. We parted, and—and—she died; died through love of me.

(Here the lawyer became visibly affected and hastily brushed away a tear-drop with his hand. Mastering himself at length, he resumed.)

On her death-bed she sent for me. I arrived just in time to catch her parting breath. When I stooped down to kiss her she hung a small relic of some saint that had been blessed by the Pope, suspended with a piece of ribbon, round my neck, and begged me to wear it for her sake, and said that it would preserve me from all harm. Poor girl! she died in my arms; I followed her to the grave and was for a long time inconsolable.

But time, that changes everything, changed me. A tender recollection of her past love only remained; the wild tumultuous passion I had felt for her while living, and the overwhelming grief I experienced at her death, had subsided. For two years I wore the relic she gave me round my neck. Not because I believed in its virtue, not being a Roman Catholic myself, but for her sake alone—in remembrance of *her*. Afterwards, however, I wore it less often, and at length discontinued wearing it altogether. I kept it still at the bottom of my trunk, between the leaves of a book.

This trunk I left in town when I went down to the baron's. The key, I must tell you, I had lost a day or two before. I was just thinking of sending for the locksmith when I received the baron's letter to come down to his place for a day or two. I left town hurriedly and the box behind me, locked—the key lost.

Ever since poor Mariangela's death, even long after I had ceased to think of her regularly, I have remarked that in those periods of my life when I was in any difficulty her spirit used to appear to me in a dream and counsel me, and being guided by her counsel, I found my way invariably out of my dilemma. When weighed down by any great grief she was sure to appear and console me.

That night when I turned into my snug little bed at "The Swan," no one was further from my thoughts than that poor Italian girl who loved me so well. My thoughts were far too full of ill-feeling towards the baron and the preparations for the coming duel to allow room for anything else. Nevertheless, I had a most remarkable dream towards morning. I thought Mariangela came towards me as I lay in bed, and reproached me for having left off wearing the charm that she had hung round my neck.

"Your life is in danger," she said. "Good swordsman and expert with the pistol as you are, you are no match for the baron with

35

either, whose skill is from the Evil One. Listen to me, and do not refuse my last petition. Wear this round your neck, and it will protect you from all harm."

Having spoken thus, she kissed me on the brow and vanished. I awoke, and would you believe it, gentlemen, I found suspended round my neck that identical relic that I left at the bottom of my trunk in town, the key of which was lost. Well, I could no longer doubt this being a spiritual visitation, so I left the relic there suspended.

In the course of the day my friend arrived. The usual ceremonies were gone through, and the meeting was to be at sundown, in a wood belonging to the baron's estate. A surgeon was also provided to bind up the wounds of the one who should fall, should they not be mortal. As I was asked my choice of weapon, I chose the rapier, having at that time no inconsiderable skill in the use of it.

The hour arrived, and we met on the spot. The baron, at the sight of me, was unable to restrain his rage, and it was with difficulty that he was prevented from breaking through every rule of etiquette appertaining to the duello. Without waiting for the customary salute beforehand, he rushed at me sword in hand at the first sight of me like a savage. The seconds interfered, and something like order was restored.

We advanced, retired, clashed swords, lunged, parried. "*Tierce, quarte, quinte, flanconade*, single attack, double attack, lunge."

The baron lunged furiously, I parried, and the baron was disarmed. Without waiting for my permission to pick up his sword, he, disregarding all etiquette, made a sudden grab at it, and flew at me again in fury. The baron's fencing was very wild. He made three or four successive desperate lunges at me, but was foiled every time. He grew more and more furious; he had never been accustomed to be thus thwarted.

I felt my hand grow lame, however. It was like fencing with Mephistopheles. To tire him out was impossible. His long wind was his *forte*. I could only try to match the baron's fury by the most guarded coolness and self-possession. For some time past I had done nothing but parry, waiting calmly for an opportunity. At length an opening presented itself. I lunged, and the baron fell, pierced right through the heart, at the foot of one of his own stately oaks. He rolled up his eyes, and after death still retained the same expression of ferocity that he wore when living.

Thus died the last baron —. With his death the line became extinct, and the property fell into other hands. Duelling even in those days was fast falling into disuse, and I had to fly the country. I travelled for many years, and at length returned home, but never from the day of the duel up to the present time have I once neglected to wear the pious relic of that poor Italian girl round my neck.

★ ★ ★ ★ ★

Bursts of applause followed the lawyer's recital. Mr. Blackdeed said it ought to be dramatised; that it would "create a sensation," and "bring down the house." The doctor shook his head gravely. The chairman, in a short speech, proposed the health of the narrator, and expressed a hope that he might be free from all such clients for the future.

"Shiver my timbers!" cried Captain Toughyarn, "if that yarn won't do for the marines. Odds, blood and thunder, if I thought anyone but a tar could have spun such a yarn as that. I tell you what it is, Hardcase, you've mistaken your calling. You were meant for the sea."

"I hope, Captain Toughyarn," said the lawyer, "you don't doubt the veracity of my statement."

"Not I," answered the captain, but with a most provoking look of scepticism, which belied his words.

"I do believe the captain's a sceptic," said the chairman. "Take care, captain, the rules of this club are severe. If any member or guest presumes to doubt the statement of any other member of the club, given out by the said member as a fact, he shall incur the penalty of being forced to drink a cup of cold water on his bended knees, and—"

"Ugh!" groaned the captain, before the chairman had finished his sentence. "Well, chairman," he said, humbly awed at the severity of the sentence, "I don't mean to say that I'll give a 'lee lurch,' and throw Mr. Hardcase's cargo overboard altogether; but the fact is I have been on shore so long, that I have got quite out of the way of shipping those sorts of goods into my hold, and it rather sticks in my tramway, but I have no doubt that another glass of grog will send it clean down, and that I shall find storage-room in my hull for that and as much more cargo as any of our messmates choose to ship this evening."

"Hear, hear," cried the guests, passing the bowl towards the captain, who, after having filled up his glass and drained it, declared himself ready to set sail.

"Another bowl, landlord!" shouted the chairman; "and whilst you are about it, you might bring up another log as well. See how the cold makes the fire burn." Then, turning to his guest, Mr. Vandyke

McGuilp, he observed, "It is lucky you arrived in time tonight for our great meeting. You have now heard a specimen of these stories, the fame of which has reached Rome."

At this moment the host returned with a fresh bowl of punch, which was received with a murmur of approbation. The landlord then stirred up the fire, and put on a fresh log. It was getting late, but that was nothing for the members of the "Wonder Club" on such an occasion as this.

"It's freezing hard tonight, sir," said the landlord to the chairman.

"Is it, mine host?" said Mr. Oldstone, rendered still more good humoured under the influence of the punch. "Then fill up a bumper and drink to the health of our club, after which you may sit down here and listen to the next story, if you can prevent falling asleep. Our first story you have missed. Oh, I can assure you it would have given you the horrors to have listened to it."

Here our worthy host filled up a glass, and, nodding his head, drank to the long life of all the members and guests, and hoped that the club might have as many more anniversaries as there were hairs in the heads of all the members put together.

This sentiment was received with applause, and the health of the landlord was drunk with three times three. He replied to it in a short, bluff, and unembarrassed speech, amid cheers; and rattling of glasses. Then modestly taking a seat at some little distance from the table, filled his pipe, lighted it, and put himself into a listening attitude.

"It is your turn now, doctor," said the chairman. "We're all waiting, and, mind, we all expect a good one. On this evening, gentlemen, each one must strive to outdo his neighbour."

"I cannot promise that I will outdo Mr. Hardcase's narrative," said the doctor, modestly, "but I will do my best to add to the entertainment of the company in my humble way."

"Bravo, doctor!" cried several voices at once.

Mr. Oldstone thumped the table and called out, "Silence, gentlemen; Dr. Bleedem will favour us with a story."

Silence immediately ensued, and the doctor began.

The Spirit Lovers

I am about to relate, gentlemen, a curious incident in my medical experience, many years ago.

When I was yet a young practitioner I had already a numerous circle of patients, out of which it will be only necessary for me to bring two cases before you this evening. The first was that of a young man of about four-and-twenty, whom I shall call Charles. He was of good family, and his parents were moderately well off. I was called to his bedside, the former doctor having been dismissed. I had had some conversation with the parents of the young man before I was ushered into his presence. They informed me that my predecessor had pronounced his disease "a rapid decline" and as incurable. But the case had other peculiarities which puzzled him. The brain, he said, was much affected.

The patient ate little, unlike other consumptive subjects, whose appetites are usually enormous. He slept much, and talked much in his sleep, but in his waking moments he was irritable and restless, and preferred being left alone all day. He could not even bear the sight of his own parents in his room. He had his regular hours of sleep, and always seemed to look forward to his hours of rest, especially to his nightly hours.

I questioned the parents as to how long he had been in this state. They told me more than a year. I inquired if any member of their family had ever died of consumption. They replied that not one, either on the father's side or the mother's, bore the slightest trace of that malady, and that for many generations back the members of both families had lived to a good old age. Neither of the parents could give the slightest account of how the disease originated.

Their son had been sent to the university two or three years before,

where he had studied hard, but without having made up his mind to follow any particular profession. They suggested that possibly over-study had sewn the seeds of the disease. He was not, as they assured me, given to dissipation.

Having ascertained these particulars, I expressed a desire to see the patient, and was shewn into the sick-room. The parents told me to prepare for a cool reception, as their son was not over partial to visitors, and especially doctors. They then retired, leaving me alone with the patient, as I had previously requested them; for it has always been my policy to work myself as much as possible into the confidence of my patients, in order to obtain more minute particulars of their case which otherwise they might be reserved upon. For this a *tête-à-tête* is absolutely necessary, as there are patients who are reserved even in the presence of their nearest relatives and friends.

The young man, as I entered, was seated in bed, propped up by cushions. He was in a thoughtful attitude, and for some moments seemed unconscious of my presence. At length, hearing my footsteps, he started, glared wildly at me, and turned his face to the wall.

"Come," I said, soothingly, "don't be frightened; I am only the new doctor. I have come to see if I can't make something out of your case. Come, turn round. I daresay we shall be better friends before long. What is this?" I asked, as I laid my hand upon a volume hidden under the clothes, and examined it. "Ah, Shakespeare!"

"Don't touch it," cried the young man, starting up with sudden energy. "I never allow my Shakespeare to be polluted by strange hands."

I was rather startled at this sudden burst of irritability from my new patient, especially in the exhausted state in which I found him, and not a little amused at the oddity of his caprice.

"You are a great admirer of Shakespeare?" I observed, after a pause.

He did not deign a reply, but fell back languidly on his cushions and closed his eyes.

"A great poet," I continued. "What insight into character! What knowledge of mankind! What a versatile genius! With what truth and exquisite feeling he portrays both the king and the peasant, the courtier and the jester! How truly he seizes the leading characteristics of the Jew and the Christian in his 'Merchant of Venice,' to say nothing of his sublime imagination in the 'Midsummer Night's Dream,' and in 'The Tempest'; the exquisite humours, too, of his 'Merry Wives of Windsor,' and then there is his—"

At this juncture my patient opened his eyes, and gave me a look that seemed to say, "Have you done yet?" and, after a pause, said aloud, "I thought you were the doctor."

"Ah! truly," said I, blushing slightly; "I am afraid, I weary you. Pardon me if my enthusiasm for your great poet has carried me away from my professional duties. But, to business. How do you feel at present?"

He eyed me with a peculiar expression, and said, "Do you really want to know?"

"To be sure I do; haven't I come—"

"You have heard that I have been given over as incurable. The last doctor was an older man than you. What do you hope to effect?"

"To effect a cure; *I* do not give you up. I do *not* think your disease is consumption. I hope in time to—"

"To what?" he asked, nervously.

"Well, to be able to serve you."

"No," he cried, "not to *serve* me, but to *cure* me."

"In curing you, shall I not serve you?"

"No. I do not want to be cured. Leave me to die, if you want to serve me."

"Oh, my dear young man," I cried, "don't talk like that. Your malady is not of the sort that you need fear death so soon."

"Fear death!" he exclaimed. "On the contrary, I seek death. I desire to die."

"What! you desire to die? A young man like you, in the pride of your youth, with the whole world before you. What can make you so tired of your life?"

"Because my life's a burden to me."

"Poor young man," I said, "can you have suffered so much! Ah," I muttered, half to myself, "youth has its sufferings as well as age."

I was young myself then, and I had suffered. I felt the deepest sympathy for my patient.

"If," I resumed, "in curing you I could make life cease to be a burden—"

"I would not accept the offer," he replied. "What should I gain by it? The grosser material part of my nature would be rendered more gross, more material; capable only of those delights that the grossest minds revel in, to the utter exclusion of those sublime visions and inspirations which visit the soul when least clogged with matter. It would be to exchange a paradise for a pandemonium; high, exalted thoughts and feelings for low and grovelling ones. No," he said; "he who, like me, has tasted both lives will hardly throw away the higher for the lower."

I was puzzled by this last speech of his. Was the brain really affected? Had I to do with a case of insanity? I studied his physiognomy for some time in silence. He would have been called decidedly handsome; and yet that is not the word. I should rather say beautiful, but the complexion was pallid and the face dreadfully emaciated. The forehead was ample, but half-eclipsed by a mass of rich, chestnut hair that hung over his head in disordered waves. The nose was Grecian; the mouth and chin classic; the eyes were large, dark, and lustrous, with an expression most unusual and indescribable.

If I may use the expression, he seemed to look through you and beyond you into space. The expression was quite unlike the vacant stare of the maniac, for the look abounded with superior intelligence, but yet it was not that sort of intelligence which men get by mixing in the world. His look had something *unearthly* in it—something of another world. I could not altogether bring myself to believe that he was mad. He would certainly have been called so by the world at large, which calls everything madness that does not come within its own narrow circle. His madness was that his faculties were too acute, his nervous system too sensitive. When he looked at me he seemed to read my inmost thoughts and answer them all with his eyes before I had time to open my mouth to give utterance to them.

I tried to reason with him, tried to show him that very good health was compatible with the most exalted thoughts, etc. But he always had an answer ready, and that, too, before the words were half out of my mouth. He was a perfect study, and I took immense interest in him. He, in turn, grew more docile and confiding, and after some five or six visits we were the best of friends.

I have said that he slept much and was given much to talking in his sleep. It was on my third visit that I had some experience of this. We were in the midst of an animated discussion, when he suddenly went off into a most profound slumber; more suddenly than I had ever before known anyone to fall asleep, and so resembling death that for some time I thought him dead. At length his lips began to move, and for more than an hour he kept up a conversation with someone in his dream, part of which conversation I committed to paper.

"What!" he exclaimed, "this is the spot appointed, and no one near.

This is the trysting tree, yonder the blue mountains, here the rocks. It is past the hour. Oh, where is she? Will she not come? Must I return to that darkness mortals call life without seeing her, without hearing one word? Oh, Edith! shake off these bonds of flesh but for one hour, if, indeed, you also have a life of clay like me, and are not all spirit. Can you not spare me *one* hour? Ah! footsteps! A bush crackles. Edith, Edith! how glad I am you have come at last. I was afraid you had been prevented. Why are you so late? What do I see—tears? Tell me what has happened. Does your father know of our meetings? But how should he? Are we not in the spirit? Come, tell me all."

Here a pause ensued, as if the lady he was addressing was speaking, during which time the expression of his face changed several times; first from one of deep tenderness, next, to that of profound melancholy. He sighed, then again a bright smile illumined his countenance. Occasionally a slight frown would cloud his brow for an instant, and his countenance bore a look of determination. At length he spoke again in earnest tones.

"Come what may, I will never leave you. Have I not sworn? Are you not mine to all eternity? We may never meet in the flesh; but what of that. Are we not happier thus? Unshackled from that fearful darkness that wars against our spirits? Oh, that we may ever live thus! Would that we could become all spirit."

Another pause ensued, and after some minutes he resumed.

"And how can your father's paltry caprices affect us—whilst we are in the spirit, how can the weapons of the flesh attack us?"

A pause, and then he said, "True, as you say, we are not always in the spirit, and then of course we must be subject to— But what is it you fear, Edith?"

Again a pause.

"Do you know," he began again, "that that is the very thought that has been passing through my mind for some time past. Oh, horrible! If one of us or both should get entirely cured, so that the doors of the flesh should close upon us for ever, our spiritual life desert us, without even the prospect of meeting in the flesh!" Here he groaned deeply. "How long will this last, this dream of bliss? It began but a year ago. If we could only escape altogether from our earthly bodies! but I feel that is impossible as yet; while I speak I feel attracted again towards clay. I am unable to resist; I feel myself torn away. I am going—going. Farewell, Edith."

The next moment he awoke. I folded up the paper on which I had been writing and placed it in my pocket; then turned to my patient. I have not given here one half of the conversation, I was unable to follow him with my pen the greater part of the time, for at times he would speak very rapidly, at other times sink his voice so low that I could not catch all he uttered.

"I am here again, then," he muttered to himself, with a groan. "When will this end?"

"You have had pleasant dreams, I hope," said I with a smile.

He looked at me suspiciously, and said, "You have heard me? Then you know all!"

"What?" I asked.

"Why, all about that——"

"I know nothing," I replied. "It is true you talked in your sleep; you have been dreaming."

"Call it a dream, if you like," he said. "I exist but in such dreams, and my waking life is to me but a nightmare."

"Pooh! pooh!" I said. "You must not take such a morbid view of things. Your brain at present is in a state of fever. We cannot expect always to be well. I'll give you a composing draught, and in time I hope——"

"Throw physic to the dogs," he replied, quoting from his favourite author. "Canst thou not minister to a mind diseased?"

"Perhaps," said I, "I might manage to do that as well, if you will bide by my instructions."

"Look here, doctor," he said, at length, "I shall be very happy to see you whenever you come, to talk with you as a friend, as long as I remain upon earth, but I refuse point blank to take any of your medicine, so I don't deceive you."

I tried to expostulate; but how can one reason with a man who wants to die, and try to persuade him to take physic, itself nauseous, but to bring him back to the life which he despises? My task was a difficult one, but I bethought me of a plan. I pretended to humour him, and took my leave, saying I would call again shortly.

On leaving the sick-room I entered the parlour, where the parents of the invalid awaited me, to hear my opinion of the case. I told them that the patient's nerves were in a most sensitive state; I had heard him talk much in his sleep; that the brain wanted repose. I told them that he had refused to take any of my medicine because he was tired of his life and did not wish to prolong it.

I then wrote out a prescription, which I told them to get made up at the chemist's. It was a composing draught which I desired them to administer in a tumbler of water, likewise pouring in some sweet syrup to hide the nauseous taste. Whenever he complained of thirst this medicine was to be given him. In this manner he would be forced to take my medicines, and might recover in spite of himself.

Before leaving the house I inquired of Charles' mother if she were aware of any love affair of her son's that might have sown the first seeds of this illness. She replied in the negative, but that she was aware that he often mentioned a lady's name in his sleep—the name "Edith."

She assured me that there was not a single young lady of her acquaintance who bore that name; that she was at a loss to conceive how he could have made the acquaintance of any lady for the last two years without her knowing it, as he had led such a very retired life since he had left the university. Truly, he might have made her acquaintance whilst at Oxford, but, then, he had never shown any symptoms of his present malady for long after.

I left the house, giving them all the hope I could, and promised to call again on the morrow. The morrow arrived, and I called again. My draught had been administered, and I thought that my patient was a degree less nervous. Whether it was my fancy or what, I know not, but it seemed to me that the invalid suspected I had been tampering with him. He said nothing, but I thought I read it in his eyes.

"How did you sleep last night?" I asked.

"Well," he replied; "but somehow I fancy that my dreams last night were less vivid."

"Not a bad sign," I observed. "Dreaming is a bad thing—sign of a disordered stomach."

"Some dreams—not all," he replied.

"No, not all; but those very vivid dreams that you allude to all proceed from a bad digestion or over-heated brain."

"Then, you set down all dreams to some physical cause?"

"Certainly," said I; "though the character of the dream will be shaped according to our waking thoughts."

"Well, yes," he replied, "generally it is so. I myself once used to have those sort of dreams. But have you never met with a patient who lived two separate existences, whose spirit during sleep wandered into those realms allotted to it; returning upon waking to the body, there to drag out a wretched existence in the world, among the hum of men, and pass his melancholy hours longing for the night, when his spirit would be again set free from its prison, to wander unrestrained through those realms of space untrodden by mortal foot?"

"Never," I replied; "and if I were to meet with a man who imagined he passed two different existences, what proof have I that his dreams are nothing more than imagination? What proof have I that he *really does* live two separate lives?"

"Proof such as you would desire to have I admit is difficult; but let us suppose a case. What would you say if, in the course of a life-time's experience, you were to find some few, very rare, cases of men as I describe, who believe, as you would say, that their spirit during sleep leaves the body and revels in a world of its own. That you were to read of some few other cases of the same sort that have occurred now and then at rare intervals since the world began, and that the written description of that abode unknown to mortal tread, were to tally in every particular with the descriptions you yourself received from some of your patients?"

"Well," I replied, "I should say, either that my patients had been reading these old legends until their brains were turned, or that it was a malady, and, like all other maladies, was manifested by certain special symptoms. Hence the similarity of the descriptions."

"I knew that would be your reply," he observed. "Doctor, doctor," he continued, shaking his head, "you have a great deal to learn."

"Have you, then," I enquired, "ever met with a man of that sort?"

"I know *one*. What should you say, doctor, if I myself was one of those men?"

"You! I should say that your imagination deluded you, that your present ill state of health is sufficient to account for any freak of the brain, however eccentric."

"Deluded mortal," he muttered. "Alas! by what circuitous paths do men persistently seek for error, when the high road of Truth lies ever before their eyes."

We discoursed upon various other topics, and I took my leave of Charles, leaving instructions with his parents concerning the treatment of their son, as I should not be able to call again for some days. I had to attend a young lady in the country, the adopted daughter of a very old friend of mine. I could not refuse to go, so I started next day by the mail.

Charles' conversation had impressed me deeply, and I meditated upon it as I sat perched up outside the stage-coach. I was sorry to leave him, for I had already felt quite an affection for him, independently of the interest I took in his case.

And who was this young lady that I was called upon to visit in such a hurry? I had never seen her, but for the sake of my friend who had benefited me in so many ways in the commencement of my career, I could not do otherwise than leave town for a short time.

I tried to picture to myself my new patient—some bread-and-butter girl with the mumps, hysteria, whooping-cough, or chicken-pox. The picture I mentally drew of my lady patient was not sentimental; but, the fact was, I was irritated at being obliged to leave such an interesting case as that in which I was engaged. During the course of my drive I entered into conversation with the driver. I asked him if he knew Squire L—. He replied in the affirmative.

"Let me see," said I, pretending not to know the squire over well, in order to draw him out, "the squire has no family, I think?"

"None of his own, sir. He has one adopted daughter, a foundling, found somewhere near Stratford-on-Avon. The squire has adopted her ever since, and—"

"What age is the young lady?"

"Well, sir, she must now be hard upon four-and-twenty, though she did not look it last time I saw her."

"As old as that!" I exclaimed. "Then she will be getting married soon, I suppose?"

"Not she, sir."

"Why not?" I asked. "Isn't she personally attractive?"

"Oh, I believe you, sir," said the coachman, enthusiastically, and turning up his eyes. "There is not a face in the whole place for miles round that can hold a candle to her."

"Indeed!" I exclaimed. "The squire is rich, too, as I hear, and I suppose she will be his heiress. What is your reason for believing that she will not marry?"

"Why, sir, she has such ill health; she never leaves the house. Folks say as how she will never recover."

"Indeed, and how long has she been thus?"

"About a year ago she was first seized; since then I have not seen her. When I last saw her wasn't she a beauty, neither!"

"I suppose this illness will have pulled her down a little. By the by, what is the nature of her complaint?"

"Well, I hardly know, sir, and that's the truth, what it is that do ail her. Some folks call it consumption, others call it something else."

"Who is her medical attendant?" I asked.

"Doctor W——, sir; lives down yonder."

"What does he say it is?"

"'Pon my word, sir, I don't think he knows more about it than other folks. Them doctors, when they once gets into a house, there's no getting them out again; and as for the good they do, they dose you, they bleed you—ay, bleed you in both senses of the word! Ha! ha! You know what I mean, sir."

I was disgusted at the vulgar contempt of this man for the noble profession of which I myself was a member, and was determined not to laugh at his low wit. I passed over his execrable joke with gravity, so as not to appear to see it.

"If the doctor knows so little about it," I said, at length, "what do the people say it is? What is the popular opinion of the young lady's malady? What are the symptoms?"

I saw by the coachman's countenance that he was rather surprised at the interest I took in the health of the young lady, and I fancy he suspected that I was a doctor.

"Symptoms, sir!" he cried. "Oh, sir, very strange ones, they say."

"How strange?" I asked.

"Well, sir, there be a good many strange reports about the squire's adopted daughter. I b'ain't a-goin' to give credit to everything I hear, but folks *do* say—" here he lowered his voice almost to a whisper and looked mysteriously, first over one shoulder, then over the other.

"Well," said I, "Folks say—"

"Yes, sir, folks *do* say that the young lady, leastways, the squire's adopted daughter, is—is—" (here he put his finger to his lips and looked still more mysterious).

"Well?" said I, impatiently.

"That the poor young lady is under some evil spell—that she is *bewitched*."

"Dear me! you don't say so," I exclaimed, with well-feigned as-tonishment.

"Yes, sir," he replied; "leastways, so folks say about here."

"How very dreadful! Poor young lady! Perhaps she is in love. Love is the only witchcraft that ever came in the way of my experience," I remarked.

"And sure, sir, you're not far out there neither; for if there's one thing more like witchcraft than another, it is that same *love*. Lor', bless yer, sir, don't I remember when I was courtin' my Poll, how I'd stand under her winder of a rainy night for hours, just to get a peep at her shadow on the winder blind, and how I'd go for days without my beer, till folks didn't know what to make of me? Ah! but I got over it, though, in time. I got cured, but" (here he gave me a knowing look) "it wasn't by a *doctor*. No, sir, it wasn't by a *doctor*," he said, with a contemptuous emphasis on the last word.

"Now, who do you think it was by, sir, that I got cured?" he asked.

"I haven't the slightest idea," I replied, dryly, disgusted at the man's manner.

"Why, the *Parson*! to be sure," he exclaimed. "Ha, ha!" giving me a dig in the ribs with his undeveloped thumb. "Yes, sir, the parson beat the doctor out and out in that ere business. He, he!"

I dare say the joke was very witty, but I was in no humour for laughing just then; yet, after all, he did not know I was a doctor, so I condescended to give a grin, a spasmodic grin like that a corpse may be supposed to give when the risible muscles are set in motion by the wires of a galvanic battery.

He then began to relate to me some of the many superstitions afloat concerning the above-mentioned lady, till I grew curious to make the acquaintance of my new patient. In the middle of one of his long stories, he pointed out to me the house of my friend Squire L—, so I descended and walked up the hill leading to his house.

Arrived there, I rang, and was shown into the parlour, and upon giving my name, was soon cordially received by my old friend. We had not met for years. He had much to tell me, and seemed very much concerned about the health of his adopted daughter, whom he loved as if she had been his own flesh and blood.

His wife soon entered, and having expressed much pleasure at seeing me after so long, began giving me the peculiar symptoms of the lady's case.

"I do not know what to make of her, my dear doctor," she said; "for a whole year past she has not been the same girl. She will not eat, nor see anyone; seems quite estranged towards us, gets nervous and irritable if anyone approaches her; sleeps much and talks much during her sleep, and frequently imagines in her dream that she is holding conversation with a young man whom she addresses as Charles."

I started. The lady and her husband both noticed my emotion, and inquired into its cause. I told them that the case of their adopted daughter so nearly resembled the case of a young man in London whom I was still in the habit of attending, that the similarity of the symptoms struck me with no little surprise.

"Indeed, doctor," said the lady. "Is it possible that there can be two such extraordinary cases in the world?"

I mused a little, and then observed, "You do not think, do you, that the first cause of this strange malady was some little affair of the heart?"

"Oh, dear no, doctor," she replied. "I am certain of it. The girl has never had the opportunity of forming the acquaintance of any young men. She has never left this village in her life, though she has often begged me to take her to London; but somehow I—"

"What! you say she has never been to London—not even for a day?"

"Never," she replied.

I began musing to myself, when I was interrupted from my train of thought by the voice of the patient calling out, in agonising tones, "Charles! Charles!"

"Edith, my love! what *is* the matter?" cried Mrs. L—, rising and leaving the room.

"Edith!" I muttered to myself. "How strange! What a strange link between the two cases." I did not know what to make of it all. However, I kept the particulars of Charles' case to myself for the present, and determined to investigate the matter closely.

"Can I see the patient?" I asked of my old friend.

"Certainly; we will go together," he said.

"Thank you, but I should prefer a private interview with her, if possible. Patients sometimes will not be communicative to the doctor in presence of others, even though they be their own relations. It is always my plan to—"

"Ah, exactly, doctor," he replied; "but I am afraid she will not give you a very warm reception."

"Oh," I replied, "as to that, I am accustomed to the very worst of receptions from some of my patients."

My friend led me to the chamber of the young lady, whom I discovered in bed, propped up by cushions, talking to Mrs. L—.

"This is Dr. Bleedem, my love," said the squire. "Now, don't be shy, but tell him all that you feel the matter with you. I shall leave him alone with you. Don't be nervous; he is a very old friend of mine."

Then, beckoning to his wife, he drew her away, and left me alone with my patient.

The first thing that struck me upon entering the chamber was the remarkable likeness my new patient bore to Charles. They might well have been brother and sister, though the hair of Edith was dark and her eyes a deep grey. The features were wonderfully alike, and the eyes had that same strange unearthly expression I have already described as belonging to Charles. Contrary to my expectations, she received me most civilly; very differently to the manner in which I was treated by Charles on our first interview. I was at a loss to account for this, as my friend had warned me not to hope for a very warm reception.

"Oh, doctor!" she exclaimed, "I am so glad you have come. Your presence brings me relief. You are the only person whose sight I have been able to tolerate for this last year and more."

I was thunderstruck. What could she mean? "Some caprice, I suppose. Perhaps my old friend has been putting in a good word for me."

"No, doctor," she said, answering to my thoughts in a manner that perfectly amazed me; "no; it is not as you think. The squire never told me until this moment that you were an old friend of his. It is not for that that I feel myself drawn towards you by some almost unaccountable sympathy; but, to tell you the truth, doctor, I have long felt the want of someone to confide in, and you are just the one; you must forgive my boldness, if it offends you, whom I should like to make my father confessor."

I smiled at the innocent want of restraint with which she uttered these words, and said I should be most happy to fulfil the office.

"Should you, doctor?" she replied. "Well, I shall be most unreserved towards you, and I hope you will return the compliment, and tell me all it is in your power to communicate."

I looked surprised, and asked, "Of what—of whom would you hear?"

"Doctor," she said, fixing upon me those deep grey orbs, with a glance that seemed to read my inmost soul, "do not deceive me; you *know* that you have been with *him*."

"Who can she mean?" I mentally asked. "Can she mean Charles?"

"Yes," she answered to my thought, "with *him*—with *Charles*. Hide nothing from me, doctor. I see you look surprised that I should know where you come from; but my senses are too keen, too abnormally acute, not to perceive that you carry about you *the particles of his being* as unmistakably as if you had been amongst roses or honeysuckles. Can I be deceived when you come to me directly from the chamber of the only man I ever loved in my life, with the atoms of his nature clinging to you? Think you that I know aught of your doings? That I have been informed as to where *he* lives? I tell you, No; I know nothing but what my senses tell me. I feel you have been with him, and whatever you might tell me to the contrary would not make me believe otherwise."

"Well," I said smiling, "I don't deny that I *have* just come from a patient in London, whose name is Charles; but London is large, and there are many Charleses."

"I do not care *where* your patient is—whether at London or the North Pole, I shall probably never come across him; in fact, I don't see that it would aid matters much if I were to. I have never seen him—that is to say, with these eyes—and probably never may," she said, with a deep sigh.

"Do I understand you to say that you have never seen this young man you talk about, and yet you take so much interest in him?"

"Never with the eyes of the body," she replied.

"How, then?" I asked.

"With the eyes of the spirit."

"That is to say," I resumed, "that this young man named Charles is but a creature of the imagination—that he has no real existence."

"Oh, pardon me," she replied; "decidedly he has an existence—a double one. A bodily one, of which I know nothing; and a spiritual one, of which I know more."

"How?" I asked. "You have never seen him in the flesh, but are yet acquainted with his spirit. Does the spirit leave his body and appear to you?"

"Precisely so."

"Oh! but these are hallucinations, my dear young lady," I said, "that patients in your state of health are frequently subject to."

"No, doctor; say not so," she answered. "It is now more than a year since, that in my dream, as I was walking alone in a beautiful garden, I met a young man, also quite alone and reading. He was of extraordinary personal beauty. He looked at me a moment and passed by. The very next evening I had the same dream—there he was again. The dream was so very vivid, that I could not believe it to be one of those ordinary dreams so common to persons suffering from indigestion. There was such a reality about the whole—the garden, the terraces, the old house—altogether had too much truth about it to have been a dream."

"And what do you think it was, if not a dream?" I asked, smiling.

"Nothing less," she replied "than a glimpse into that world so zealously guarded from our mortal eyes as to make us doubt of its existence, or, at least, to hold it as something so ethereal and visionary that we tremble even to speculate on it; but which, nevertheless, exists, has existed, and will exist to all eternity in form as palpable as the earth we this day inhabit."

I mused a little, then said, "Dreams are often very vivid; I know that by experience, but upon waking I have always been able to account for them in some way or other."

"Don't call this a dream of mine, doctor," she said. "In everything it is most unlike the dreams of your experience. Those you allude to are vivid only for one night, and disperse into air on waking. Such is not the case with my dreams. The dream of each night to me is the continuation of the dream of the preceding night, and this has been regularly going on for more than a year, each dream being crowded with a series of events such as would be sufficient to fill up a lifetime; and so vivid, indeed, is the colouring of everything in these visions, that I no more doubt in a double existence than that I am talking to you at the present moment. In awaking, too, I find, that instead of vanishing like an ordinary dream, I bear ever afterwards the strongest recollection of everything that has happened during my period of sleep."

"Indeed!" I exclaimed. "It is very strange. I am just attending a young man in London who shares your complaint. The case is a rare one; I never came across one before at all like it. The coincidence about the whole affair is so strange, too. His name happens to be Charles, and whilst talking in his sleep as they tell me you do, I have heard him mention the name Edith. Your name, is it not?"

"'Tis he! 'Tis he!" exclaimed my patient, enthusiastically, throwing up her arms and clasping her hands above her head. "I knew it, I knew it! But tell me more about him, doctor! I did not see him last night, and I was so unhappy. The night before he appeared to me less distinct than he had ever done before. Oh, doctor," she cried, in an agonising tone, "you are *curing* him, you are *curing* him!" much in the same way as she might have called out, "You are *killing* him!"

"Yes, I hope to some day. There is no great harm in that, I suppose?" I remarked.

"Oh, yes, indeed!" she cried; "you are imprisoning his spirit within his body, and I shall never see him again."

"Well," I thought to myself, "this is about the oddest courtship *I* ever heard of; but," I continued, aloud, "supposing I could cure you both; then, afterwards, you might meet in the flesh; and how much better that would be. You would preserve your health and—"

"No, no," she cried. "Do you think our joys could be half so intense, so ethereal, in a fleshly life as when walking in the spirit? No, doctor, have mercy upon both of us, and leave us to die; we shall then be all spirit."

"Charles' sentiments exactly," I muttered.

"Are they not?" she said, brightening up. "He, then, has let you into the secret of this phenomenon of his being! Oh, doctor," she exclaimed, "don't, don't, *cure him!*"

She spoke with such agony of feeling, that I could not help feeling the deepest sympathy for her, and I actually for a moment began to waver in my duties as a medical man. I began to think that, if, as it now appears, two human beings, having never met in the body, are nevertheless by some occult law of nature, permitted to hold communion with each other in the spirit as lovers, what cruelty in me to try and cut short their happy time of courtship! Would it not be kinder in me (seeing that the order of their beings differs so from that of the rest of the herd) to go against the common duties of my profession, and instead of trying to remedy the malady, to accelerate it, till it resulted in death.

"But no," I said to myself, immediately; "my reputation, my conscience. What! *I* a poisoner! No," I said; "we must all die some day, and my two lover patients must hold out in this life a little longer. Death comes soon enough for all, and then, if their spirit love was as lasting as it appeared to be intense, they might resume their amours after this mortal coil was doffed. What are a few paltry years compared with the immeasurable gulf of eternity?" Thus I mused, but suddenly I said, "You will not mind taking a little light physic, will you?"

"What! to make me well!" she exclaimed. "To imprison my spirit within my body, as you have done Charles'. But stay, if I take your physic, it will not be yet. I will wait to see if Charles is really lost to me for ever. If he does not appear again all this week, then his spirit has no longer power to wander from the body, and if he is lost to me, why should I wander about in the spirit seeking him in vain? I might just as well be cured as not."

"Very well," I said; "then, for the present it is needless to administer any medicine?"

"Not at present, doctor," she said.

I took up my hat to go, and said that I would call again soon and would bring her tidings of Charles; that I was going there straight from her.

"Stay, stay," she said. "You have told me nothing about him as yet."

"Well, my dear young lady," I said, "I really do not know what to tell you about him. Like yourself, he refused to take my medicine, and—"

"What, he refused! Then how is it that he is getting well? That he does not appear to me now? Doctor, you have had something administered on the sly. I know it. I see it in your face;" and the look that she gave me was so penetrating, that I quite quailed under it, and was obliged to admit that I had.

"And you are going to try the same trick with me. Oh! oh!"

Here she groaned, and threw herself forward on the bed in agony.

"My dear Miss Edith," I said, compassionately, "calm yourself; pray reflect. I can't, I daren't leave you to die. Be persuaded, and take only a little harmless, quieting medicine, not nauseous to the taste, and which may not have the effect of making you cease to dream."

But my fair patient was not to be persuaded, so, with hat in hand, I made another step towards the door.

"Stay, doctor," she said; "whatever you do, keep our conversation secret from the people of the house."

"Certainly," said I. "Has it not been under the 'seal of confession!'"

"True, true," she said; "and, doctor—would you mind—if you are really going to call upon—Charles, to—to—take a relic to him of me?"

"Not at all," I said. "On the contrary, I should be most happy; but—" I said, after a moment's reflection, "but—your parents—would they object, do you think?"

"Oh, don't be afraid, doctor," she replied. "I am very independent, and as for yourself, your name needn't get mixed up in the transaction."

Here she reached a pair of scissors, and severed one of her long ebony tresses, which she handed to me with these words:

"Take this," she said, "to my spirit lover, and tell him Edith sends him this in the flesh, and hopes to see him again in the spirit."

I promised I would do as she desired, and shaking hands with her, I left the apartment.

My friend and his wife awaited me in the parlour, and asked me my opinion of their daughter's case. I gave them hope of her recovery; but told them that she had positively refused to take any of my medicines, and I therefore adopted the same manoeuvre that I had adopted with Charles, and was forced to leave the medicine to be administered clandestinely. I wrote out a prescription and left the house, saying I would call again in a day or two. I took the mail that evening, and started for London. Finding myself at length arrived in the great metropolis, my first thought was to call upon Charles.

As I entered his chamber the expression on my patient's countenance was one of deepest melancholy. When he first caught sight of me I thought he looked suspicious, and was going to turn away, but as I approached him his countenance altogether changed, and grew so bright and radiant, that he did not look the same man. He had never welcomed me before in this way, and his manner puzzled me.

"Oh, doctor," he cried, in tones of the greatest joy, "is it possible you have seen her? I know you have; I can't be mistaken."

"Seen who?" I asked, smiling.

"Come, doctor," he said "you know all about it; don't pretend to ignore—"

"Ignore what?" I enquired, with provoking pertinacity.

"Oh, doctor, doctor! you'll drive me mad," exclaimed my patient. "Tell me all about her at once, and keep me no longer in suspense. Oh, Edith! Edith! I feel your presence. Come, doctor, tell me about *Edith*."

"What Edith?" I exclaimed. "Are there not many of that name? It is true I *do* come from a young lady patient whose name *happens* to be Edith. What then?"

"The same! I knew it, I knew it," he cried. "Tell me all about her, doctor; you have seen her, and spoken to her. Oh! we may yet meet in the flesh, even if she be denied me in the spirit. Did you tell her of my case, doctor?"

I nodded my head.

"I told her," said I, "that I was attending a young man whose symptoms very much resembled her own. Oh! I had a long talk with her, I assure you; and what do you think she wants of me?" I asked. "Why, she was actually unfeeling enough to ask me not to cure you; she was, indeed."

"My own dear Edith!" he exclaimed. "Of course she doesn't want me cured; and, doctor, if you would do both her and me a kindness, don't—oh, don't—cure her."

"Well, you're an amiable couple, I'm fancying," said I. "I wonder whether there are many more such loving couples in the world as you two."

"Well, doctor," he said, smiling, "have you any more news for me?"

"Perhaps I may have," I answered, mysteriously. "What should you say if she entrusted me with a present to you?"

"A present from *her*! Oh, doctor, don't trifle with me. Is it really so?"

Hereupon I thrust my hand into my pocket, and produced the lock of hair, wrapped up in a piece of tissue paper. He made a snatch at it with his long lean fingers, and tearing it open, exclaimed, "*Her* hair! I could swear to it anywhere. What did she say, doctor, when she gave this into your hands?"

"She said," said I, "'Take this to my spirit lover, and tell him Edith sends him this in the flesh, and hopes to see him again in the spirit.'"

"Bless her! bless her!" he cried, enthusiastically kissing the relic repeatedly and pressing it to his heart.

I allowed this transport to pass well over before I spoke again. At length I enquired how he had passed the night.

"Badly," he replied, sulkily.

"What! have you not felt quieter, more composed?"

"Oh, yes," he answered; "you don't suppose that I am ignorant that you have been drugging me?" he said, casting at me a look of reproach.

"Drugging you?" I exclaimed.

"Yes; did you think I couldn't taste that stuff that you got my parents to give me through all its disguise? Do you think I did not feel its influence?"

"A salutary influence only, I hope," I answered, being forced at length to admit the stratagem that I had felt it my duty to adopt.

"What you would call a salutary influence," he retorted. "But do you know," he added, almost fiercely, "that you have robbed me of those dreams that constituted the better part of my life? In fact, my *real*, my *only* life."

"I am sorry for that," I remarked. "Do you then not dream at all now?"

"If I dream, I do *but* dream—like all ordinary mortals, but my second existence is closed, I fear, for ever. I will tell you what I dreamt last night. I walked towards the entrance of a beautiful garden where I had often been in the habit of meeting Edith, and I found the gate closed. I shook it, and tried to open it by main force, when I noticed something written over the gate. I read these words, 'This is the abode of spirits untrammelled by the flesh.'

"I did not know other than that I was as much in the spirit as on any of the preceding nights, so I tried the gate again, only to meet with the same success; but this time I heard a voice calling out, 'Thy flesh hath grown upon thy spirit—the doors of thy soul are closed—hence! back to earth!' I made one more desperate effort, and called out, 'Edith! Edith!' but my voice went forth from me weak, like a voice in the distance. Nevertheless, my cry was answered. I heard Edith's voice within the garden calling out my name, but in very feeble tones. My ears were too grossly clogged with flesh to hear distinctly spiritual sounds. I was aware of Edith's presence. She shook the garden gate with her hands and spoke to me through the bars, but I saw no form. I heard only her voice.

"'Come to me,' she said, in what appeared a suppressed whisper. 'Oh, what is this, Charles? Why cannot you come?'

"Then the same unknown voice that had addressed me before spoke again, 'Spirit to spirit—flesh to flesh!' and I felt myself whirled back from the garden gate as by a whirlwind, and I awoke."

"The dream is strange," I observed. "Have you many such dreams?" I asked.

"Up to the present time, thank goodness, no; but who knows if tonight I shall be able to dream at all?"

"You will sleep all the sounder if you don't. Dreams always come when the sleep is disturbed," said I.

"Doctor, would you rob me of all I have to live for by your drugs?" he exclaimed.

"I should be sorry," I replied, "if my drugs have the unfortunate effect of robbing you of pleasant dreams; but it is my first duty as a medical man to remedy the physical ills of my patients."

"Well, no more drugs for me, that's all," he said, positively. "The next article of food I take that tastes in the slightest degree of physic I shall certainly throw away."

"In that case," I replied, "if there is no way of administering medicine to you, this must be my last visit. It is useless calling on a patient who refuses to be cured."

"Well, doctor," he said, "I shall be sorry to lose you, as your conversation serves to cheer my waking death. Of course, I can't expect you to put yourself out of the way to come here for nothing; but if at any time you are not better employed, just drop in as a friend."

"Well," I said, "I should not like to drop an acquaintance so interesting. But, the subject of medicine apart, you really must take a little more nutriment than you do."

This was what was really the matter with him. The body was worn away through insufficient diet, till the patient was in a state bordering on starvation; and this had been for a long time persisted in, as the invalid found a morbid delight in those vivid dreams peculiar to all people who practise long fasting; and so loth was he to give up his beloved dreamland, that he was ready to sacrifice life itself.

We chatted together for some time longer, and he related to me many of his dreams, which were all of a most extraordinary character. At length I got up to go, saying I would call on the morrow, and entered the parlour where the parents of the young man were seated. They asked me how my patient progressed. I told them he wanted plenty of nutriment, and, without ordering further medicine, I told them to give him plenty of mutton broth, beef tea, and other nutritious things, and to put them as close to his bed as possible, that the smell of the savoury food might awaken his appetite.

They promised to comply with my request, and I quitted the house. I had one or two other cases to attend to after that, which interested me in a much less degree, after which I returned home, and committed to paper the leading peculiarities of the cases of Charles and Edith.

In the course of the morrow I called again upon Charles. I thought he looked better. There was certainly a change in him since my first visit.

"Well," I asked, "and how did you sleep last night?"

"Oh, doctor!" he answered, "such a dream!"

"Well, come, what was it?"

"I thought," he began, "that I was again in search of that garden gate that I have before alluded to, but when I came in sight of it it was no longer distinct and tangible as on the preceding night, but misty in outline, and as I approached it seemed to recede and grew more misty, as if I saw it through a fog. The fog grew more and more dense, like an immense black cloud, and I saw nothing. Then the cloud seemed to solidify, and it turned to a solid wall of stone, and I found myself suddenly enclosed within what looked like the courtyard of a prison. I looked out for some loophole, but all attempt at escape appeared impossible. My eye soon caught an inscription on the wall, which ran thus, 'The boundary of the body.'

"'What,' I said, within myself, 'can my spirit no longer soar into those blissful realms it was wont formerly to revel in? Must I tamely submit to this imprisonment without one effort? No,' I said; 'never will I basely give in thus.' And, noticing a wide chink between the stones, I placed the tip of my foot in. I soon found another notch for my fingers. There was no one near, so, finding higher up another chink, I put the other foot in that, and after considerable difficulty and danger, succeeded in reaching the top of the wall. I found that the prison was built on a high rock in the middle of the sea, and guarded by demon sentinels.

"I looked out into the distance. There was nothing but sea and sky, and that, too, seemed so blended together as to appear all one element. In whatever direction I chanced to gaze, all was vast, infinite, indefinable.

"'Yonder must be the realms of the spirit,' I muttered to myself, as I lolled upon the summit of the prison wall. The words I uttered fell upon the ear of a demon sentinel below, armed with a long halberd. He raised the alarm, and I was forced to descend from my perch. Finding myself once more in the prison yard, I heard rapid footsteps behind me, and the jingling of keys. I turned round suddenly and beheld the jailor.

"'What is this place?' I asked, somewhat sternly, 'and why am I here?'

"'This building,' answered the jailor, 'is called *the prison-house of flesh*, and the reason you are here is that you belong to "our sort."'

"I groaned, and followed the jailor, who led me below into some horrid cell, where the daylight scarce entered. He turned the key upon me and I awoke."

"Dear me," said I, "that was a very disagreeable dream. There was nothing about Miss Edith in that," I said, smiling wickedly.

"No," he said, savagely, "and whose face do you think the jailor's was in my dream?"

"I have no idea," I replied.

"Why, *yours*, doctor!" said the young man, suddenly starting up with extreme energy, and darting a look of ferocity towards me.

"Yes, doctor, you are my jailor; it is you who have closed my spirit up in its prison-house of flesh, so that it can no longer soar together in the company of the higher intelligences. It is you who have driven me back again to earth and made me an equal of such minds as your own. *You* have robbed me of the only woman I ever loved in my life, *you*—"

"Stay, young man, one moment," I said, "and calm yourself. Is this your gratitude for the relic I brought you yesterday? If I, as you say, have robbed you of one of your lives, don't I offer you another which to a young man of your age and position is a state of existence that I can't say how many would *envy*, and which, after all, is doing nothing more than my duty as a medical man. Then, as to robbing you of the lady you love, haven't I the power of making you acquainted with her some day in the flesh, if all goes well, and I succeeded in curing you both?"

"If such a meeting should take place, do you think," he said, "that we should experience in the same intense degree those chaste joys of love, as if we were in the spirit, when our souls, unfettered from any particle of clay, are raised to that sublime pitch that we are enabled to understand the profound and lofty discourse of angels and become ourselves for the time a part of the heavenly bodies?"

"My dear young man," I observed, "life is short. If the paradise you are in the habit of entering in your dreams be indeed that place where all good souls hope to go after death, you have but to wait for a few years—"

"Wait a few years!" he exclaimed, impatiently, "when every minute spent away from *her* appears a century! It's very plain *you* are not in love."

"In the meantime," I said, "content yourself with a life of flesh like any other rational mortal."

He began to reflect upon my words, so I thought I would improve the opportunity, and, if possible, try and make him turn human, so I observed,

"I shall not be here tomorrow; I am going to visit Miss Edith. Shall I take her any message?"

"Oh, yes, doctor, certainly, by all means; that is, I'll write. Give me some paper, pen and ink."

Having handed him these materials, he sat up in bed and penned an epistle to his lady-love in the flesh, which he sealed and handed to me.

I assured him of its safety in my hands, and took my leave of him for some days, hoping to find him more reconciled to humanity on my return.

Having given the parents of Charles further instructions with regard to their son, I took my departure, and shortly afterwards taking the stage, was *en route* for my friend's country seat, where I arrived early the next morning.

"And how is our patient?" I asked, as I shook hands with my friend at the threshold.

"I fancy she sleeps sounder, doctor," he replied. "We are not so often disturbed by her talking in her sleep."

"Good," said I; "her nerves will be getting a little stronger. Can I see her?"

"Oh, yes; walk straight to her room."

As I entered, my patient was sitting up in bed, reading.

"Ah!" said I, after the customary salutations, "we are better this morning, eh?"

"Oh, doctor, is that you? I am glad you have come."

"What book is that?" I asked, at the same time looking at the title. "Ah! Shakespeare. That is Charles' favourite author."

"I know it, doctor. Oh, how often have we read it together; but now, alas!"

"Why alas?" asked I.

"Ah, doctor," she replied, shaking her head slowly, "I never see him now. You are curing him, and me, too. Of what value to me is a body in perfect health, when it imprisons within it a wounded soul?"

"Come, let me see if I can't bring some balm to the wounded soul," I said, producing from my pocket Charles' letter.

"From him?" she exclaimed. "Oh, doctor, I shall be for ever grateful to you. I dreamt I received a letter from him last night. How is he—better? Stay, let me read."

She tore open the letter and read in an undertone, just loud enough for me to hear:

"Angel of my dreams—Charles in the flesh pens thee these poor lines, greeting. How art thou, now shut from me! The doors of the body have closed upon my spirit, and I feel that I no more belong to the same order of beings as a few nights ago. For me now thou may'st wait in vain in the garden, by the trysting tree, in the wild forest, by the sea shore, in the desert, by the foaming cataract, on the bleak mountain top, or by moonlight on the crags of the wild glacier, wherever the wings of thy spirit may carry thee. I cannot follow thee. I linger in chains of clay, and languish from day to day in my prison-house of flesh, whilst thou— But, stay, perhaps the lot I bear may be thy own; perhaps the doors of the flesh may have closed upon *thy* spirit also. Oh, if it be that our souls are for ever banished from that Paradise which they have so often revelled in together! What have we further to look forward to but those earthly joys known to the most grovelling mortal? This is a melancholy prospect, my Edith, for us who remember (however, indistinctly—from the growth of that clay—over *thy* spirit perchance, as well as my own) those divine joys we experienced together when our spirits walked untrammelled from our bonds of clay and our souls melted into the harmony of those spheres which are their proper element. How the weight of this mortal coil oppresses me as I write! I can think of nothing that is untainted with the gross material nature that surrounds me. My dreams of late confirm my horrible suspicions. When, the other night, I sought thee at the garden gate, where enter only spirits untrammelled by the flesh, didst thou hear that voice that turned me away, and bid me return to earth? Oh! Edith, let us both make another effort before it is too late. Perhaps even now—"

Here the patient dropped her voice, and her eye scanned the paper in silence, from which I inferred that there was something about myself in it that she did not wish me to know; but I had heard enough. Charles wanted to persuade his lady-love to battle against all my efforts to bring her round to a proper state of health, and intended doing the same himself. Here was a regular conspiracy—two patients already all but on the point of death, had leagued together to starve themselves outright, and so baffle all the doctor's efforts to save them. Oh, it was downright suicide. I did not know exactly what to do.

"This is the last time I'll act as Mercury between two lovers," thought I.

I had a momentary thought of watching for an opportunity to get the letter into my hands, unobserved by my patient after she had finished reading it, and then of crumpling it up abstractedly, and throwing it into the fire, as it was winter and a large fire was made up in the patient's room, thinking that the impression might wear off her mind after having read the letter only once; but how might not her lover's words influence her if she were allowed to read and re-

read his letter when left alone? No opportunity, however, presented itself, for after she had finished reading it she kissed it fervently and placed it in her bosom and held it there, glancing at me rather suspiciously, as I thought, as if she read my intentions in my face; but this might have been fancy.

However, I tried what I could do in the way of argument, to show the advantage of keeping a sound mind in a sound body, besides pointing out the probability of her some day—perhaps before long—meeting her lover in the flesh, and that there was no reason why they need not eventually be happy. I talked to her much of Charles, and hoped to see her again soon, though I should not call so very often now, as my visits would not be necessary. I left her, giving instructions to her parents to administer to her all sorts of nutritious food, as I had done to the parents of Charles concerning their son.

I let some little time pass over before I called upon either of my lover-patients again. I at length called upon Charles, and found him all but recovered. Though still weak, his face had filled out considerably, and his nerves were no longer so morbidly acute, and his countenance had lost to a great extent that supernatural look that characterised it on my first visit; still, it was far from being the face of a man in robust health. I thought him silent and reserved towards me, but when I told him I had delivered his letter, and talked to him of his lady-love, he brightened up a little. I told him I should take the stage on the morrow to visit Edith.

He wanted me to take another letter, but I pleaded great hurry and escaped from the house. When I saw Edith again, she also had improved in health immensely, thanks to the careful watching of my friend's wife, who was like a real mother to her, and would *not* allow her to starve herself. Seeing her so nearly recovered, I recommended a little change of air as soon as convenient.

Upon my departure Edith managed to slip a *billet-doux* into my hand, directed to Charles; that is to say, without address, for I had not told her where he lived. We were not left alone on this interview, the wife of my friend being present all the while, so the note had to be passed into my hand clandestinely. There was no getting out of it, and I had to deliver it to Charles as soon as I arrived in town. His eyes sparkled when he saw her writing.

"Look here, what Edith says about you!" said he, somewhat bitterly. He read as follows:

Dearest Charles,

Your own true Edith writes to you in the flesh by our common but well-meaning enemy, Dr. Bleedem.

"There!" he said, "that's what she thinks of you."

"Enemy!" I cried, in astonishment.

"Yes, enemy; but well-meaning, you see, she says," he continued, in a softened tone.

He then continued to read:

The poor man thinks, no doubt, that he has achieved a great thing in bringing us privileged seers into the world of spirits back into this mundane sphere, fit only for beings of his order. Of course, what else could be expected of him? The nature of his profession, the grossness of his being, compel him to think and act in the way of grovelling mortals; but let us not be too hard upon him; he is a good man, and means well.

"There!" he observed, "you see, she is charitably disposed towards you. I don't know that I feel disposed to be so lenient."

At this odd beginning of a love-letter, and still odder allusion to myself, I fairly burst out laughing.

"Oh! laugh away," he said; "it is a fine triumph to rob two beings of the very essence of their happiness."

I had not done laughing, and he was nearly catching the infection. He observed in the words of his favourite poet, that, my lungs did crow like chanticleer, and I did laugh *sans* intermission.

He took up the letter again, and read a great portion to himself, or half aloud. I caught the following passage:

Do you remember, Charles, when, in the early days of our courtship, you used nightly to serenade me under my window in the enchanted castle, and how long it was before you knew that I, like yourself, had an earthly body that had an existence of its own? And when I told you that my parents— or rather, my adopted parents—were not in the land of spirits, but that they inhabited the same world in which, in the daytime, we ourselves were forced to vegetate; and when you thereupon asked me with whom I shared the castle, do you remember the horror, the rage, and indignation you felt when you heard that I was held captive within that enchanted castle by a horrible wizard, who tortured me and tried all his base arts to make me yield to his love? Oh! Charles, I often look back to that time. I can see the bold outline of that rude, massive building on a rock frowning on the lake below. I feel myself yet at my casement, gazing out in search of your bark, which passed nightly close to my window, and I fancy I hear your touch upon the lute reverberating through the night air.

With what horror I remember being torn from my window on that night by my captor, as I was waving my handkerchief to you on the lake. Oh! the torture I underwent within those unhallowed walls after you left me; the scenes I was compelled to witness, the oaths I was forced to hear; and then the infernal hideousness of the countenance of my demon captor!

Oh! Charles, shall I ever forget the night on which you rode up to the wizard's castle on a spirit charger, habited as a cavalier, and bearing a ladder of ropes under your mantle which you reached up to me on the point of your lance; how I descended, and you placed me behind you on your steed and galloped away; how, ere we were far from the castle, my flight was discovered, and the wizard and all his demon host mounted their demon chargers and started in pursuit of us; how they gained on us; how we avoided them for miles by hardly half-a-horse's length, until we arrived at a bridge across a river of fire, over which none but the pure in love can pass? Dost remember, Charles, how bravely thy spirit charger bore us over in safety, and how, when the fell magician endeavoured to follow us with his evil crew, how the bridge tumbled to atoms, and the demon host was swallowed up in the fiery waves? Then how, when our charger was spent, we turned him out to graze, the sun having risen; and how, having arrived at the sea shore, we found a boat, which we entered, and steered onward in search of further adventure. How swiftly, how gallantly we sailed, as if borne on by the good spirits, until we reached an island, where the inhabitants welcomed us and claimed us as their king and queen. Charles! do you remember all this? But why call up all these reminiscences? They are over now, and passed as a dream, and this hence-forward must be our life. I know nothing of your life in the flesh, my spirit lover, or what may be your social position in this world. No matter, whatever it

be, and in spite of whatever obstacles may raise themselves to our happiness in this vale of tears, remember that I am ever thine in the spirit,
Edith L—

Having concluded, he folded up the letter, kissed it, and pressed it to his heart.

"And do you remember all the details of that strange adventure alluded to by Miss Edith, as having happened to you both? Do you remember really having taken part in this strange romance in another phase of existence?" I asked.

"Certainly I do," he replied; "every particular of it."

"Strange!" I muttered, to myself. "Then these *dreams*, as we ordinary mortals would say, are really to such beings as yourself *facts*—phases of another existence," I remarked.

"Precisely so," said he.

"Then your being king of an island was no mere fantasy," said I; "but as much a fact—"

"As much a fact as that while in the flesh I am a poor devil," he replied.

"Well, I never thought I should have a royal patient," I observed, smiling.

"Ah!" he said, "now do you see the extent of the wrong that you have done me? You have robbed me of a kingdom in bringing me back to health."

"Many a sick monarch would be glad to exchange his kingdom for good health," I retorted.

This was almost my last visit to Charles. I *did* call again, but it was long after he had completely recovered.

Months passed away, when one day I casually met Charles in the streets. He had quite recovered, and was looking very well. He had much to tell me, so, as I had a little spare time on hand, we strolled into the park, and being a hot day, we sat down together beneath the shade of a tree in a solitary spot. He seemed to have grown more reconciled to humanity, having now only a dim recollection of the intensity of the joys he used to experience in his dreams. I touched upon the subject nearest his heart, and he commenced a recital of all that had happened to him since we last met. I shall endeavour to give his own words as nearly as possible.

"You will remember, doctor," he began, "that you left me without giving me the address of Miss L—" (Edith took the surname of my friend the squire, as if she were his own daughter, her real name being unknown). "I called upon you afterwards on purpose to inquire, and was informed that you were out of town. I had no one now to apply to for information, and was in despair. I did not know what to do with myself in town during the summer, so I thought I would try a little country air. I loitered about first in one country place, then in another, without any fixed purpose. I had been reading Shakespeare one day, and upon closing the book, I resolved I would take a pilgrimage to the birth place of the great Swan of Avon.

"I had never yet visited this retreat, so I started at once, and determined to put up in the village for some time. With what a thrill of delight, awe, and enthusiasm I crossed the threshold of that humble domicile! *His* foot had once crossed that same spot! Here was the window that *he* used to look out of. The identical glass, too, all carefully preserved by a network of wire. *His* table and *his* chair! There was something magical to me in that low-roofed chamber, with its old-fashioned beams.

"This, then, was the birthplace of that giant brain destined to illumine the world with the rays of his genius! Who knows how many plays had been conceived and worked out within those four walls? To me, the spot was hallowed ground. *I* could not inscribe my name on those sacred panels. It seemed almost sacrilege for me to sit down in his chair, but I did so; and begged to be left alone for a time, that I might meditate on the life and genius of the greatest of poets.

"It was not without a feeling of regret that I tore myself away from this hallowed shrine. I wandered through the almost deserted streets, and read the names over the village shops. 'William Shakespeare' here caught my eye; 'John Shakespeare' there; descendants, no doubt, of the great poet. Shakespeare seemed a common name here. I wondered whether any of them inherited his genius. No matter, it would be something to say that one was descended from so great a man, without possessing any further recommendation. I called upon a certain William Shakespeare, and inquired into his pedigree. He seemed a very ordinary sort of personage. He did not appear to know, nor yet to care much, if he were really descended from the bard or no. There was no genius about *him*. I called upon another, and then another, bearing the name of the poet, but could not discover the slightest spark of the fire that kindled the soul of the great dramatist in any one of them.

I strolled on to the church, and visited the tomb. A sensation of awe crept over me as I read the simple couplet engraved over the vault containing the ashes of the bard:

"*Blessed be he who spares these stones,*
"*And cursed be he who moves my bones.*

"I shuddered to think of the awful consequences that might ensue to the sacrilegious hand that should dare move his honoured dust. There was his effigy placed within a niche in the wall of the church, high up above the heads of the congregation, and gave the idea of being placed in a sort of pulpit. The bust was but a rude work of art, but it had the reputation of being the only authentic likeness of the poet; and, therefore, it was with intense interest that I scanned the features. I fancied that I could descry, in spite of the rude workmanship of the stonemason, certain lines about the mouth and eyes that indicated that droll humour displayed in his comedies. I stood rooted to the spot.

"Around me were the tombs of the Lucy family; close to the poet's own dust the graves of his wife and daughter. But let me hasten to the more important point in my narrative.

"After I left the church I was shown the dead of the Lucy family, and obtained permission to wander over the grounds. 'In that house,' I said to myself, 'lives the lineal descendant of that squire before whom the bard was brought for poaching, and whom afterwards he is supposed to have caricatured under the title of "Justice Shallow."'

"I wandered alone through the forest of Arden, and seemed to imbibe inspiration from the surrounding scenery. I called up scenes from 'As you like it,' and other plays. I sat down on the grass in a wooded spot, and watched the deer.

"'Here,' I thought, to myself, 'must be the spot where the melancholy Jacques moralised on the wounded deer. Yonder, perhaps, where he met the fool in the forest.' I mused awhile, and then opened my Shakespeare at the scene of Rosalind and Celia, followed by Touchstone, and became deeply engrossed.

"I might have been half-an-hour poring over this scene, when I lifted my eyes from my book and beheld coming towards me in the distance the slim and graceful form of a lady, reading a book which was bound in the same fashion as the book I was reading, and which, therefore, I concluded must be a Shakespeare. She approached with her eyes still fixed on the book. At length, as I gazed on her she closed the book, and her eyes met mine.

"'Edith!' I cried, 'do I dream still, or is it indeed yourself in the flesh?'

"She was no less surprised than myself.

"'Charles!' she exclaimed, 'how have you tracked me hither? Did you know of—'

"'Tracked you, Edith!' I exclaimed. 'I knew nothing of your whereabouts. This is the hand of Fate.'

"'Oh, Charles, is it possible!' she cried. 'To think that we should live to meet in the flesh.'

"We embraced, and strolled under the trees together.

"'Shall I awake from this,' I kept saying to myself, 'and find it also a dream?'

"We both of us began to doubt whether we were sleeping or waking. She informed me that her adopted parents, for she was a foundling, as I learnt, had taken her with them, away from home for the summer for change of air; and, as she had often expressed a wish to visit the spot where she had been first picked up by her present parents when a baby of a week old, she begged Squire and Mrs. L— to take her to Stratford-on-Avon, a place of double interest to her.

"She invited me to her house, and introduced me to the squire and his lady, who both remarked how much we resembled each other in feature. I frequented the house much, and Edith and I were in the habit of taking long walks together. It is hardly necessary to say that I was not introduced as the young man Edith used to meet in her dreams. The tale would have been too startling, and would not have been credited; and yet Edith had been so entirely under the surveillance of her parents, that it was impossible for her to have formed an acquaintance with anyone without their knowledge, so I had to trump up some story—indeed, I scarce know what—about rescuing her from a bull, just to account for our acquaintance.

"We were left much alone. Little did the parents think what an old attachment ours was; and for a long time I thought the squire looked favourably on my suit, but when matters were advanced so far that I demanded her in marriage, he drew up stiffly, and inquired into the state of my finances. I boasted of my family, but was obliged to own that as far as money-matters went, I was afraid that by my own fortune I could hardly hope to keep his adopted daughter in that style to which she had been accustomed.

"He hummed and hawed; but Edith broke in, begged and wept,

saying she had never loved before, and vowed that she never would love another. At length the squire, with some reluctance, gave his consent, but said that I must find something to get my own living, and I am consequently looking out for some mercantile employment.

"'*To such base uses must we come at last*,'" he quoted, with a sigh.

"Yes," said I, "rather a come-down from a king; but, never mind what it is, as long as it pays well."

I saw him wince at this speech of mine; his romantic nature revolted against all thoughts of making money, however pressing his needs might be.

We parted, and I called upon him about a week after, when I found he was making grand preparations for his marriage. He informed me that he had got his eye upon some appointment, but that he should have to wait. There was a certain air of sadness about his face still. He did not look like a man about to be married.

"Doctor," said he, "do you know what I have been thinking of late?"

"No," I replied.

"I have been thinking that this marriage of mine will never come off," he said.

"Why?" I asked. "Have you had some lovers' quarrel?"

"No," he replied.

"Why, then? Has the squire changed his mind, after having given his consent?" I demanded.

"No; nor that either," he replied. "I cannot myself give you my reason for the fancy—it is a presentiment. You know, 'the course of true love never *did* run smooth.'"

"Oh!" said I, soothingly, "that is your fancy; you are nervous and impatient—it is natural."

"No, no!" he said; "I am sure of it—I feel it."

"What! Have you been dreaming that it would not?"

"No; I never dream now," he replied.

"I am glad to hear it," I observed; "it is a good sign. When does the wedding take place?"

"Tomorrow was the day appointed, but it won't take place, I say. Mark my word."

"So soon! But what can have put it into your head that it will not take place tomorrow? Do you know of any impediment likely to occur between this and then?"

"No," he replied; "none for certain, but I tell you, once for all, it will not take place."

I did not know exactly what to make of this strange monomania. My suspicions were again aroused as to the brain being affected. I did not see what could happen to hinder the marriage, so I left him, after cheering him as much as I possibly could, determining within myself to call upon him as soon after his marriage as was convenient, to triumph over him and laugh at his presentiments; but this was the last time I ever saw Charles.

Shortly after this, my last, visit I was glancing rapidly over the paper at breakfast when I was shocked to see among the list of deaths the name of Charles ——, aged twenty-four. Strange enough; I had been dreaming of him much the night previous. What was my surprise and dismay when, looking lower down the column, I saw also the death of Edith L——. I looked at the date of both deaths. To my still further surprise, both lovers had departed this life at exactly the same hour— at midnight, October 12th, 17—.

"What a strange coincidence," I thought. "What strange beings both of them were! They did not appear either to belong to or to be fitted for this world. They were evidently never destined for an earthly lot together."

"The hand of providence is in this," I muttered.

I grieved much for the loss of my two patients, for I had conceived quite a fatherly affection for them both. As soon as decency would permit, I called upon the parents of Charles. The account they gave of the reason of his death caused me no little surprise. It appeared that on the eve of his marriage his mother received a badly-written and ill-spelt letter from a person who professed to have known the family a long time, begging her to call upon the writer, who was then in a dying state, and had an important communication to make.

Mrs. ——, curious to know who the writer could be, called at the address given in the letter, which proved to be a miserable hovel in one of the back slums of London. There, stretched upon a wretched pallet, lay the squalid and emaciated form of an old woman, whom, after some difficulty, Mrs. —— recognised as the monthly nurse who attended her four and twenty years ago, during her confinement.

"Who are you?" asked Mrs. ——.

"Look at me. Do you recollect me now?" inquired the hag.

"How should I? I never saw you before. Stay, your features seem to grow more familiar to me, now my eyes get accustomed to the light. Is it possible you can be Sarah Maclean, the midwife who—"

"The same," responded the hag.

"What would you of me?" inquired Mrs. —.

"I have a communication to make before I die," said the old woman. "Listen."

And she began her confession in feeble tones, thus:

"You were not aware, ma'am, that the day before your son was born, I myself was confined with twins—a boy and a girl. Being called upon the next day to attend upon you, I waited to see if your child were a male child or a female. Finding that it was a man-child, I took advantage of the agony I saw you were in, deeming that my act would never be discovered. I managed to conceal my own child under my shawl, and so contrived to substitute my child for your own."

"Wretch!" cried Mrs. —, gasping.

"Stay; hear me out. I've got more to tell," continued the hag. "Your own son died shortly after you had given him birth, through my neglect—I admit it."

"Murderess!" screamed Mrs. —.

"Bear with me yet awhile," said the midwife, "while I have still breath left to confess all. I wished that one of my children should do well in the world, and I adopted the stratagem I have just confessed to you.

"As for my other child, being a girl, I was anxious to get her off my hands as soon as possible, so I left her at the foot of a tree near Stratford-on-Avon, where I myself was born."

"What have I to do with all your other crimes, wicked woman?" exclaimed Mrs. —. "They rest between yourself and your Maker. Spare me further confession."

"Stay awhile yet," said the old woman, in still feebler tones. "My second crime concerns you perhaps in scarce a less degree than my first. My daughter, as I heard afterwards, was picked up by a certain Squire L—, and, having no children of his own, it is likely he will make her his heiress."

"What!" cried Mrs. —; "then Miss L—, who is engaged to my son—at least to—to is, in fact, your—your daughter? Then they are twin brother and sister!" and Mrs. — fell back in hysterics.

"Wretch! Infamous woman!" cried Mrs. —, scarcely recovered from her fit. But when she gazed again at the withered form before her, behold the evil spirit had left its tenement. Sarah Maclean was no more.

When Mrs. — returned home, she communicated the mournful tidings to Charles and Edith, who were together at the time—tidings which, of course, put a stop to their union.

They both received the news in a state of stupefaction. Neither wept. Their grief was too deeply seated to give vent to itself in tears. They could not, after having loved each other as they had loved, look upon each other in the light of brother and sister, and as their union was impossible, they agreed that it would be better to part at once and for ever. They embraced and parted, each vowing never to love again. That night both were stricken with a violent fever, and on the night of October 12th, at the midnight hour, the spirits of both lovers were released from their mortal tenements. Let us hope that they are now at rest!

★ ★ ★ ★ ★

Two years after the death of Charles and Edith, finding myself in the neighbourhood of my old friend Squire L—, I called at the house. He was glad to see me, as usual; but I thought he looked very much aged. The death of his adopted daughter, whom he loved tenderly, had been a great blow to him. I should not have liked to touch upon a subject so painful, had he not broached the matter first himself, and asked me if I had heard of the circumstances that led to the death of Edith and her lover. I replied that I had heard all from Charles' mother.

"And who do you think that Edith and Charles turned out to be?" he asked. "Why, lineal descendants of the great bard of Avon," he said.

"Is it indeed so?" said I.

"Yes," he replied; "after the death of my poor Edith I was curious to know something about her real mother. I made inquiries into her pedigree, and the report I heard from more than one quarter was— well, it is a long story; and, at some future time, when we are not likely to be interrupted, I may relate it to you. Suffice it to say, that the descent of Charles and Edith may be distinctly traced from our great Bard, William Shakespeare."

"Strange," I observed. "It is not impossible that some of the great poet's genius might have run in the veins of Charles. He always im-pressed me as a young man of great intellect. He might have been something had he lived."

"Oh, yes," replied my friend; "I am certain of it. He was a very promising young man; and there was Edith, as full of genius as she could be, poor child. I tell you, doctor, it was marvellous what that girl had in her."

"Oh, I believe it," I said. "There was something extremely intelligent in her expression, if I may use the word; perhaps I ought to say, intellectual and poetical. Well, genius, though seldom inherited from father to son, rarely dies out of the family altogether, but often, after lying dormant for generations, breaks out again in some form or another, like certain diseases."

"Yes, doctor," said my friend; "I have observed the fact myself, and how seldom do we find genius unaccompanied with disease. Do you know, doctor, I often thank Heaven that I am no genius?"

Containing Mr. Parnassus's Poem

The Glacier King

At the conclusion of Dr. Bleedem's narrative he was highly complimented by his audience, and various were the comments upon his recital. The chairman declared himself unable to decide as to which of the two stories related that evening was the more marvellous.

The host of the "Headless Lady" vowed he had never heard such a tale in all his life before, though he knew a good story or two himself. Mr. Oldstone proposed the health of the doctor, which was drunk accordingly, amid cheers. He responded to it in a short speech, when the old Dutch clock in the corner struck one. The president rose and addressed the club thus:

"Gentlemen, we have listened to two most interesting stories; but time flies—the clock has announced the commencement of another day. I regret that, on account of the length of the first two narratives, we shall be prevented from hearing a story from everyone; yet I should be loth to break up this very pleasant meeting without hearing *one* more recital. I propose, however, that, in consideration for some of our worthy guests—the gallant captain, to wit, and our comic friend here, who, as you see, gentlemen, appear somewhat overwhelmed under the all-inspiring influence of the punch— (laughter)—that the next narrative be of shorter duration than the two preceding.

"According to order, the next tale ought to proceed from Professor Cyanite."

Then, turning towards the professor, he inquired if he had a story ready that would not take too long in the recital.

"Well, chairman," said the professor, "the fact is that I had prepared somewhat a lengthy one for our meeting. At present I can't think of one sufficiently short to wind up the evening."

77

"In that case," said the chairman, "perhaps Mr. Blackdeed will be able to favour now."

Mr. Blackdeed begged to be excused. He said he could not think of one at all. He hoped, however, to have one ready for the next evening.

"Dear, dear!" said the chairman; "this is really a very bad state of affairs. Has no one some short story ready? Mr. Parnassus, cannot you favour the company?"

The young poet, blushing slightly, replied, "I thought of bringing before the company this evening—or, rather, last evening, I ought to say—a curious little incident out of my own experience, which occurred to me when travelling in Switzerland a few years ago. I have put it into verse in the form of a ballad. It is not long, and if it will not weary the company, I shall be most happy to sing it."

"A song, a song!" cried many voices at once. "Bravo, Parnassus! Hear, hear!"

"The title of the ballad I am about to sing to you, gentlemen, I propose calling 'The Glacier King.'"

"Good," said the chairman. "Silence, gentlemen, if you please. A song from Mr. Parnassus."

A dead silence ensued, and the poet, after clearing his throat once or twice, began in a clear, rich voice the following ballad:

The Glacier King

In youth, when I mid mountains roamed, full well I can recall
That fearful night. The pale moonlight shone on the glaciers tall.
I wandered from my chalet's hearth (the world was locked in sleep),
But something on my bosom made my soul a vigil keep.

I wandered on, I recked not where, for I was sad of mood,
Until upon the basement of a glacier grim I stood.
The moon peeped out behind the clouds, the scene was strange and
*   weird—*
Like sheeted ghosts those icy rocks above me now appeared.

I cared not if I lived or died; my soul was sunk in gloom.
I'd little left to live for then; I almost sought my doom.
"We die but once," I inly said. "Death's certain, soon or late,
And I would just as lief it came, as still protract my fate."

I crunched the snow beneath my feet, and little recked of fear;
I trod the giant pinnacles (the night grew dark and drear),

Yet onward recklessly I strode, nor cared which way I went,
Until across this sea of ice appeared a mighty rent.

A horrid chasm, with below the torrent's deafening sound,
But with the madness of despair I cleared it with a bound.
A little onward still I stood (the scene was weird and grand),
A wondrous cavern wrought in ice by Nature's playful hand.

Its dripping arches overhung the cataract beneath,
Its pendant massive icicles appeared like dragon's teeth;
And lost in contemplation of this fearful yawning cave,
I deemed its chilly arches the recesses of the grave.

Anon the cave appeared when moonbeams would its depths illume,
A fairy hall of diamond, anon, a ghastly tomb.
And as I mused in fantasy, forgetting half my woe,
I wondered whether elves or ghouls their revels held below.

My blood ran chilled within my veins, a tremor shook my frame,
As, mingled with the torrent's roar, unearthly voices came.
Awhile I listened breathlessly, as louder still they grew;
The icy cave's inhabitants for ever nearer drew.

But one deep voice above the rest, in stern commanding tone,
That echoed through the cavern's walls, cried, "Silence, and begone."
Then, terrified, I scarce had time upon my feet to spring,
When, robed in icy majesty, there stood the Glacier King.

A mantle of the drifted snow bedecked his regal frame;
Upon his head a crown of ice, his sceptre of the same,
His hair and beard were icicles, his visage stern and pale,
His eyes like glacier caverns sunk, with look that made one quail.

With terror rooted to the spot, with fright uprose my hair,
While on me, as in wonderment, he fixed an icy stare.
At length he ope'd his lips and spake, in deep sepulchral tone,
"What seekest thou, stranger, in our realm, a night like this alone?"

I know not what I answer made, with voice below my breath,
When nearer, with majestic stride, he came, and thus he saith—
"Thou 'rt welcome to our palace cold; it is full many a day
Since one of thy mortal race hath wandered past this way."

He led me kindly by the hand. But, oh! that hand of ice.
I felt benumbed all over, but he held me like a vice.
Then with his sceptre tapped a door, which opened with a bang.
While through the cavern's icy halls infernal laughter rang.

He led me down by steps of ice, hewn in the solid rock,
And halting at a portal, with his sceptre gave a knock.
The door of ice was opened by a figure grim and grey,
That bowed in deepest reverence, then onward led the way.

We entered then the hall of state, where stood the icy throne;
The courtiers on our entrance bowed as if to gods of stone.
Their hair hung dank about their forms, the wildest ever seen;
Their raiment dripping icicles, their bodies of sea green.

Then out and spake the Glacier King, "Make haste and bring a light;
A mortal from the outer world will sup with us tonight.
Let supper be in readiness at once without delay."
The menials made obeisance, and hastened to obey.

Then soon the hall of banqueting we entered, when, lo! there
A lofty cavern lighted up with phosphorescent glare;
A ghastly light from out a lamp suspended from a height,
That shed upon the icicles its dim funereal light.

The table was a slab of ice, the dishes they were cold,
And when they were uncovered I shuddered to behold,
For some were human corpses that had perished in the snow,
Or in the glacier's crevices had met their fate below.

My heart then sank within me, and I from the table turned.
The guests all looked in wonderment, that I their dishes spurned.
The King then turned upon me. "Though our dishes you decline,
You must not leave this hall tonight before you taste our wine."

He bid a menial near to fill a goblet to the brim,
And as he filled a ghastly smile played o'er his features grim.
The King then raised it to his lips, and first a draught drank he;
The giant goblet carved in ice he handed then to me.

I seized the beaker in my hand, and raised it to my lip;
And cautiously I tasted it, although 'twas but a sip.
I laid the crystal down in haste, as horrified I stood.
The liquor that the goblet held I found was human blood!

The King of Ice he marvelled, and his brow grew grave and stern,
His eye would seem to ask me, "Dost thou thus my favour spurn?"
I trembled, for I noticed when the icy monarch frowned
The reflection of his countenance upon the court around.

Each drew a pointed icicle from out an icy sheath,
They wore as daggers at their sides—for fear I scarce could breathe—
And brandishing them high aloft, while as their hands they clenched,
They vowed that such gross insult should not pass unavenged.

"Ho! sheath your daggers," quoth the king. "Once more our guest
    we'll try.
Base mortal! if thou still refuse to drain yon goblet dry,
Then dread our fell displeasure, for by our crown we vow,
The King of Glaciers ne'er is mocked by mortals such as thou."

I seized the goblet once again, and in despair did quaff.
Now through the banquet hall resounds a wild unearthly laugh.
The nauseous fluid seemed to burn like fire through my veins
I felt intoxication stealing o'er me for my pains.

I fell down in a stupor, know not how long I lay,
But when my eyes were opened 'twas past the break of day.
The King and court had vanished, but around me I descried
A troop of tourists, who that morn the glaciers would bestride.

They asked me how I came there, how I could be so mad,
Alone to scale the glaciers, upon a night so bad.
I told them shortly all my tale—all I had got to tell—
About the awful Glacier King, down in his icy cell.

They smiled, and said it truly was a very fearful dream;
But I vowed all that had happened like truth to me did seem.
They asked me to point out to them the grotto that I saw.
I gazed around me, and behold the grotto was no more.

Whether it was dream or not, I know not to this day;
'Tis strange the grotto in a night should all have thawed away.
And when I spoke about the cup I quaffed the cave beneath,
"That was my brandy-flask," quoth one, "I forced between your
    teeth."

"Else you had perished in the snow, in truth, you looked far gone.
'Twas by the greatest chance on earth we found you here at dawn.

I thought you dead, but still I plied my flask, and, as you see,
It has proved worthy of its name, immortal 'Eau-de-Vie.'"

I thanked them for their courtesy, but when I strove to rise,
No muscle of my rigid frame could I, to my surprise,
As much as put in motion. My bones seemed on the rack,
And to my chalet's fire-side had to be carried back.

'Twas long ere I recovered my wonted life and strength;
The tourists oft would visit me, and we grew friends at length.
And the day of my recovery, to mark the grand event,
I started in their company to make a great ascent.

My mountain days are over now, my friends in other climes;
But when we meet together we talk of bygone times.
But still the name of Glacier for ever doth recall
The horrors of that fearful night, within that icy hall.

And at their friendly tables I'm often asked to dine.
They order "Vin du Glacier," as well as other wine,
And ask me if it tastes as well, as o'er their wine they sing,
As that from out the cellars of H.M. the Glacier King.

Hardly had the poet concluded his lay, when the cheering and
clapping of hands that ensued half-deafened all present; that is to say,
with the exception of two individuals—*viz.*, the worthy captain and
our friend the comedian, who had been deaf for some time past, under the kindly influences of the punch.

To say that the health of the poet was drunk with three times
three would be unnecessary. We leave that to the imagination of the
reader. Not only was that conventional ceremony gone through, but
the chairman, after a short complimentary speech, proposed that a
crown of laurels should be made and the young poet crowned there-
with there and then.

The poet modestly interposed, but the command of the president,
especially on such an occasion as the present, was not to be recalled.
John Hearty, of the "Headless Lady," was sent outside, snowing hard
as it was, to gather some laurel from a bush which grew close to the
inn, and the poet was crowned with all due honours. There were two,
however, who did not witness the imposing ceremony. Who these two
were we will leave our readers to guess.

The fumes of the punch had thrown the ideas of these two worthies into another channel, and the reverie into which they had fallen was so deep as to render them perfectly unconscious of all that was going on around them.

The captain was the first to recover from his meditations.

"Ease her! Stop her!" he cried, awaking with a yawn.

Then, glancing round at the company, his eye first caught sight of the poet's brow crowned with laurels.

"Odds bobs, messmate!" he cried, "what the deuce have they been doing to your figurehead?"

"Ah! captain," said one of the members, "you do not know what you have lost. You've missed a song."

"Missed a song, have I? Well, I thought someone must have been singing; it came in my dream. But what, in the name of Davy Jones, has Mr. Parnassus been taking. Why, one would think he had been taking a glass of prussic acid, to break out all over laurel leaves like that."

"That," said the chairman, "is the crown awarded to genius. Mr. Parnassus has this evening—or, I should say, this morning—favoured us with a poem."

"Humph!" said the captain, who was not of a poetical nature himself.

"Yes," continued the chairman, "a poem; the work of his own pure brain, for which he has been rewarded with the crown that now adorns his temples, a crown of no intrinsic value, as you perceive, like the bejewelled diadem of royalty, but which, nevertheless, has been sought after by minds no less ambitious in the early days of ancient history, when the love of honour alone was a deeper incitement to the soul than the mere love of worldly pelf, and when once obtained, was guarded as zealously—"

Here our comic friend showed some signs of returning animation. He stretched, yawned, and, rubbing his eyes, gazed round upon the company in bewilderment. He also fixed his eyes on the laurel crown, and so ludicrous was the expression of wonder on his countenance, although he did not utter a word, that the whole company was thrown into an immoderate fit of laughter, which completely drowned the end of the chairman's sententious speech. The poor little comedian got most unmercifully chaffed by each of the company in turn, being asked gravely by one what his opinion was of the last story; by another, whether he liked the punch—whether it was strong enough for him. By another wag he was offered a penny for his thoughts; while another insisted upon hearing the story he had been thinking of all that time, etc., etc. The little man answered good-humouredly to all their bantering, when the president once more thumped the table.

"Captain Toughyarn," he began, "you have been guilty at our meeting of falling asleep in the middle of a story, and of being so engrossed in your state of—of—What shall I say, gentlemen?—of lethargy, as to be totally unconscious of a most spirited song that ensued. You have raised our curiosity, however, by telling us that the song entered into and formed part of your dream. We would fain hear your dream, as some slight expiation of such gross violation of etiquette."

"What will he say to me," thought our comic friend, "if he doesn't let the captain escape?"

"Hear, hear!" cried several voices at once. "By Jove, you're in for it too, Jollytoast."

"Well, chairman," said the captain, "I'm sorry I've broken through discipline; but when a man has got grog stowed away in his hull—"

"Exactly so," said the chairman; "but for all that the company must hear your dream."

"Yes, yes!" shouted the company.

Captain Toughyarn's Dream or
The Mermaid Palace

Come unto these yellow sands
—Tempest

Well, messmates, I don't know whether I am sufficiently clear up aloft to recollect all the details of my dream; but hold hard a moment, perhaps I can. Ah! yes; I remember now.

I thought I was on board my good ship, the *Dreadnought*, which was bound for Timbuctoo. I was seated in my cabin, making an entry in the log, when I was aroused by a noise of shouting on deck. I thought I would go and see what was adrift; but hardly was I out of the cabin when, in the twinkling of a bowsprit, I found myself pinioned.

The crew were in a state of mutiny, and headed by the first mate. I was speedily lashed to the mizen, when Ned Upaloft (that was the name of the first mate), presenting a brace of pistols at my face, called upon me to yield.

"Avast, there! Ned Upaloft," I cried; "and you, Jack Haulaway, with the whole gang of you, and tell me what the devil is the meaning of this mutinous conduct."

"No more palaver, but yield," he cried.

"Never!" I answered.

"Then you're a dead man," he said.

"Fire!" said I; "you may take my life, but never will I yield up my power to a pack of mutineers."

His finger was on the trigger, and the next moment I expected to be my last.

I must mention that the whole of that day the weather had been extremely sultry. A storm arose suddenly, and the ship pitched and rolled tremendously. All the crew were in liquor, and the helm was

deserted. At the moment I expected it was all up with me a terrible flash of lightning struck the barrels of the pistols, which went off of their own accord, luckily missing me.

Ned Upaloft was struck blind. The crew were sobered for a moment.

"Behold," said I, reaping advantage from the confusion, "behold, how Heaven rescues her own. So may it go with all mutineers. Look up aloft," said I (a flight of Mother Cary's chickens just then passed overhead.) "Look! has that no warning? What are those but the souls of departed mariners, who have come to beckon you to your doom?"

A terrific clap of thunder almost instantaneously followed the flash, and drowned my last words. The crew looked irresolute as to whether they should renew their attack or throw down their arms and yield themselves as mutineers; but they were roused by the voice of Jack Haulaway, the second mate, who cried out,

"What! are you scared at the thunder and this man's words? Ho! there; reef the main-top-gallant sail."

The crew looked up aloft and hesitated, for the top mast threatened to snap every moment.

"Come, look sharp, or in two minutes we shall all be scudding under bare poles. What! you're afraid? Cowards that you all are. It will have to be done. I'll go myself."

And up went Jack Haulaway; but hardly had he taken in a reef, when the mast snapped, and main-top-gallant sail, Jack Haulaway, and all were blown far away into the sea.

"Behold the fate of your second commander," said I. "Look to yourselves now, for your time is not far off."

The waves were now so enormous that the vessel was soon on her beam ends. Smash went the bowsprit as it struck against a rock; crash, crash, went one mast after the other, until we were literally scudding under bare poles. It was difficult for the sailors to maintain their equilibrium, and several fell overboard. I looked for the first mate. He had disappeared.

Some of the sailors clung to the fragments of the vessel and tried to pray, others supplied themselves with grog, till they lost all consciousness. One of the men came forward to me, and, unloosing me, begged my pardon; said he bore me no malice, and if he hadn't been in liquor, he would never have joined the gang.

We all shook hands, for we deemed our last hour had come; and so, indeed, it had for most of us. In another moment the vessel was dashed against a rock, filled with water, and went down.

Some made for the lifeboat, others for pieces of floating timber. The storm still continued with increasing fury. The sky was black as pitch, and the waves the size of mountains. Planks, hencoops, and other fragments of the wreck were floating about in all directions. Most of the crew, if not all, must have been swallowed up by the waves, for, as I looked around me, I saw no one. As for myself, I kept afloat on a cask of grog, and thus I was left to the mercy of the winds and waves. Up one wave, down another, still I held on to my cask of grog, out of which every now and then I'd take a drop, just to keep out the cold; then, replacing the bung, remounted my cask, and was contented with whatever direction the waves chose to toss me. The lightning flashed and the thunder growled around me.

It was for all the world like being inside an immense big drum, and Davy Jones drumming outside. As I was being dashed to and fro by the merciless billows, I thought I heard, mingled with the dying tones of the thunder, the sound of a harp and singing. Could it be fancy? I listened again. No. I was quite sure this time my ears did not deceive me. The notes grew more and more clear, the voice more and more distinct. Yet, who could it be? There was no land near for hundreds of miles. It could be no mortal harper that touched those chords. I looked around me in wonderment, but saw nothing. At length I was carried to the top of a tremendous wave, and as I was sliding down the other side of it astride my cask of grog, I perceived coming towards me from the opposite wave a female form, beautiful as Venus, and naked to the waist.

Good Heavens! it was a mermaid. Yes, there could be no mistake. Her golden tresses fluttered in the breeze, and every now and then I caught a glimpse of a large dolphin-like tail of a greenish hue, that, at every movement she made, gleamed like silver. We could not help meeting each other; so, as I was always gallant towards the fair sex, I saluted her. Heavens! What eyes! What teeth! What features! But above all, her smile.

Gentlemen, I assure you her beauty was divine. Talk about sentiment! But words are wanting to express even the thousandth part of her charms. Enough, gentlemen, that all that is innocent, virtuous, and heavenly, was expressed in that smile she gave me.

"Angel of Beauty!" I exclaimed, "whatever your name, your parentage, your birthplace, I vow—"

"Toughyarn, Toughyarn," said a voice within me, "don't make an old fool of yourself. Mermaids are deceitful and dangerous, however beautiful, as you will find out to your cost before long. Think of your age, your position. Is it likely you can excite a genuine passion in any maid? For shame, sir. How can you appear romantic in her eyes, astride a grog cask. Only reflect a little."

But I would not reflect. I stifled the voice within me, and, abandoning myself to the impulse of my passion, pressed my hand to my heart, and was about to burst out afresh, when the fair one, fixing her large deep blue eyes upon me—deep as the Mediterranean in a calm—with a supernaturally winning smile, addressed me thus, in tones to which the softest music was discord:

"Welcome, Captain Toughyarn, to our haunts. Welcome to the Mermaid Grotto of pearl and coral, to my father's palace. It is long that we await you. We have heard much of your exploits by sea, and we are all impatient to make the acquaintance of a hero so illustrious."

"What!" I cried; "you have heard of me and expected me, O fair one?"

"Yes, captain, our Sybil has prophesied your arrival here, and your visit to our palace. Oh, she told me many things about you that she has seen in vision. The mutiny of your crew, your first mate struck with blindness when about to take your life. The loss of your second mate while reefing a sail. Your release by one of the crew, after having been bound to the mast; the wreck of your vessel; and, finally, our meeting, which tallies in the minutest particulars."

"What!" I exclaimed, in extreme astonishment, "all this she saw—even the grog barrel?"

"All—everything," replied my charmer; "but follow me, and lose no time; we all await you below."

So saying, she beckoned to me with the most bewitching smile, and floundered away from me, lashing her tail playfully as she went, and touching the chords of her harp, sang so sweetly, so divinely, some submarine ditty about fairy palaces, halls of coral, and fair mermaidens, that all resistance was vain.

"Don't be weak, Toughyarn," said the voice again; "resist her wiles, be deaf to her song."

But I was deaf only to the voice that warned me.

"Divine enchantress," I cried, "I will follow you wherever you go."

A wave now dashed me forward till I found myself by her side.

"Are you really willing to accompany me?" she asked, with a gleam that made me feel—I don't know how.

"To the utmost corners of the earth," I replied.

"And even to the depths of the ocean?" she asked.

"Even there," I replied. "Anywhere, anywhere with thee, for *I love thee.*"

The murder was out. She heaved a sigh, and her head sank on my shoulder.

"Take care, Toughyarn," said the voice; "be warned ere it be too late." This was the last time the voice spoke to me. It *was* too late.

"And do you really love me?" she asked, gazing up into my face, her large blue eyes filling with tears.

"With all my heart and soul," I replied.

"And are you prepared to give me a proof of your love?"

"Any proof you may desire, my angel," I answered. "What is it?"

"I mean," she said, "would you be ready to make a *very great sacrifice?*"

"Anything," I replied; "anything for thee."

"Generous mortal!" she exclaimed, and she sobbed aloud.

The sight of beauty in tears always moved me. I was deeply touched at this outburst of grief on the part of my charmer, and did all I could to soothe and comfort her. I put my arm round her delicate waist; she offered no resistance, so, clasping her to my breast, I—I—well, gentlemen—I kissed her. The lightning played around me; the thunder crackling, threatened to break the drum of my ear, but I saw nothing, I heard nothing; I was unconscious of everything around me in that long loving kiss.

My lips seemed glued to hers. I thought I should never be able to tear myself away. I felt her heart beat violently against my waistcoat. My blood tingled in my fingers and toes with the intensity of my passion. I no longer felt cold, for I bore a fire within.

When I at length removed my lips from hers, with a prodigious smack, she fell fainting in my arms. It was as if her whole soul had been poured forth in that one kiss, and there was none left to re-animate the frail form. I sprinkled some of her native element in her face, and she recovered.

I petted and caressed her, clasped her again and again to my breast, while she clung round my neck, confessing her love for me, and begging me never to desert her. Oh, the rapture of those moments! She vowed that I was all in all to her, that she had never loved before, and never should again; that she was mine, body and soul, and that if I ever ceased to love her, she should die.

She called me her own dear Toughyarn, her hero, her "beau ideal," her lover, her husband. She said that I was her master, and that she would be my slave for life.

I vowed that I was unworthy to pick off the seaweed that adhered to her tail. At the word "tail," she heaved a deep sigh, and, glancing at my lower extremities, burst into a fresh flood of tears. I was unable to account for these weeping fits, to which she seemed subject.

"Some female caprice," thought I; "nothing more."

"What ails thee, my beloved?" I said, tenderly. "Say why, O bewitching enchantress, do those pearl drops continue to pay their tiny tribute to the great ocean?"

"Oh!" she cried to herself, clasping her hands and looking upward, "I feel the sacrifice is *too* great. It will cost him dearly; but has he not promised?"

"Promised!" I muttered. "What is this sacrifice, I wonder, that she requires of me? What can it be but always to live with her in her own home, under the sea. When once my soul is united with hers," I reasoned, "we shall be one being. I shall be able to live under the water as well as on *terra firma*. And what have I to make me wish to return to land? I am a widower without family. I've no fortune, in fact, I am all but a ruined man, and I feel anxious to begin a new phase of existence. The sacrifice, after all, is not so great. What does it matter to me where I live, as long as I can bask the livelong day in the sunshine of such beauty?"

I felt that that long ambrosial kiss, the intensity of which had so exhausted my beloved, had imparted to me a new life. I no longer dreaded or believed in the possibility of being drowned. I felt an intense desire to behold the wonders of the deep, and visit those palaces of coral and mother-of-pearl that I had so often heard of, so seizing my beloved by the waist, I exclaimed,

"Come, O joy of my soul; lead me to the hall of thy father. Let us plunge into the turbulent billows. I thirst for thy element. I feel irresistibly drawn down by some new power that has come over me."

"Follow me, then, my beloved," she said, and with one splash disappeared beneath the waves.

To kick away my grog cask and plunge in after her was the work of a moment. I dived down, down, down, till I caught up my charmer, and we both dived together side by side. Down, down, down, deeper, deeper, and deeper, still we dived through forests of seaweed, startling away all sorts of curiously formed fish and sea monsters in our rapid course.

I thought I should never get to the bottom. At length, after long continued diving, I thought I descried gleaming through the waters, the mother-of-pearl roofs and pinnacles of various edifices; nor was I deceived, for as I dived deeper, I could distinguish a great city, built in a wild, weird, grotesque style of architecture, thoroughly new to me, yet grand in design, far above human conception.

There were castles on rocks, both the rock and the castle being formed out of one immense piece of coral, either white or red. The rock was hollowed out by nature, and natural staircases of the same material branched off in different directions, and led to the castle above. There were grottoes of mother-of-pearl, bridges of clustering and festooned coral, intermixed with common rock, and overgrown in parts by large quaint sea plants, which hung down in long creepers, entangling and festooning themselves, crossing and recrossing each other, and communicating the upper part of the city with the lower, the town being built partly on hills, and partly in the valleys.

Immense pits and hollows in what in other cities would have been the road, appeared to lead to some part of the city below. Crowds of the inhabitants were seen emerging from these grottoes, and disappearing through others. Several were seated in chariots of mother-of-pearl and turtle-shell, drawn by some hideous sea monster. There were mermen, bearded and muscular, bearing in their hands tridents; troops of mermaids of every conceivable variety of beauty, from the blue eyes and flaxen hair of the north, to the dark, Oriental type. Gigantic zoophytes and sea anemones opened their petals at us from every parapet. Music and singing was heard everywhere, and the submarine grottoes echoed with the strains of fair mermaidens. Groups of dancers surrounded us as we descended, twisting their lithesome bodies into all sorts of elegant and fantastic attitudes; beautiful *mer*-children sported with the most hideous sea monsters it was possible to conceive.

The city seemed wealthy, the inhabitants contented, and yet there was little or no sign of industry amongst them. All the houses and palaces were evidently formed by the hand of nature, save where here and there a window or a mother-of-pearl roof or pavement betrayed manual skill. Money, as I ascertained, was an article unknown to the submarines. They had few wants, and lived peacefully among themselves.

As my fair bride and I swam through the streets of this great city together, my appearance attracted great curiosity. The children were frightened, and darted away into some grotto hard by. I heard an old white-bearded merman, who had, doubtless, seen a great deal in his day, call out, "A landman! a landman!"

I began to feel fatigued after diving so long, and was greatly relieved when my companion halted in front of a large portico with pillars of the most delicate pink coral, and said, "This is my father's palace."

The *mer*-princess (for her father was no less than a king), instead of knocking at the door, ran her fairy-like fingers over the strings of her lyre, and wrung from its cords such a wild and unearthly strain, that it seemed like the distant wail of souls in purgatory.

The door was opened by an immense shark, standing on the tip of his tail. He opened and shut his huge mouth at us by way of salute, as we entered the hall, which was paved with mother-of-pearl, inlaid with pale coral and turtle-shell. My fair one conducted me through many passages and corridors, the roofs and walls of which were covered over with every sort of curious and beautiful shell found under the sea, till at length we entered the dais chamber of the king, and I was introduced to his majesty, and to his serene consort, who both received me graciously.

Formalities over, a richly liveried *mer*-attendant announced that the royal sea-serpent, harnessed to the state carriage, awaited their majesties' pleasure. The *mer*-king affably offered me the use of his carriage, which I gladly accepted. Their majesties, Lurline, and myself descended the stairs, and passing the portal, stepped into a magnificent car or chariot, formed of mother-of-pearl and turtle-shell, the wheels being of gold and embossed all over with the most exquisite precious stones. The coachman, or charioteer, was a stout merman, with a trident, with which he began to goad the enormous sea-serpent, who, rearing and plunging, bid fair to upset us all. However, the skilful driver, drawing the reins, made of strong seaweed, studded with pearls, kept him in abeyance. We then visited all the chief temples and other public buildings, and his majesty's parks and hunting grounds, chatting all the time pleasantly with my beloved Lurline, and after having spent a most enjoyable day, we returned towards evening to the palace.

It was the dinner hour. About a hundred harps from below struck up a lively air, in lieu of a dinner bell.

"Captain Toughyarn," said the king, "will you take down the Princess Lurline?"

I bowed, and offered my arm, and we swam into the dining hall. It was a long and lofty apartment, with festoons of white and red coral pendent from the arched roof. The walls were ornamented with choice shells in patterns, and the floor covered with a matting of plaited seaweed. The furniture was of mother-of-pearl and turtle-shell.

His majesty headed the table; his royal consort, who had come down dressed for dinner in necklaces of immense pearls, sat opposite to him. Other members of the blood royal, as well as some distinguished guests, were also present. We were waited upon by sea monsters, who handed round large open shells in their mouths, which served as plates.

A saw-fish brought me a knife and fork, a porpoise changed the plates, a dolphin entered with the larger dishes, and a young whale handed round the vegetables, which consisted of different sorts of seaweed. The dinner was chiefly of fish, varied with albatross and sea gull, the first course being oysters, by way of whetting the appetite.

The king was pleased to ask me about my adventures, so I entertained the whole dinner table with a recital of them. The queen smiled benignantly on me, and the beautiful Lurline gazed into my face with an expression of the most undisguised admiration.

I felt myself quite the lion of the day, and had the conversation all to myself. During the repast a bevy of fair mermaidens swam round and round the hall, and over our heads, pouring forth divine melodies on the harp.

Towards the close of the meal his majesty entered into the particulars of his own family history, and the great deeds of his ancestors, which I shall not weary your patience, gentlemen, by retailing.

The dinner being at an end, we left the apartment, and the sea monsters, after devouring everything that was left, cleared away the plates. We strolled into the garden, which was filled with every imaginable variety of sea plants. Some grew up like palm trees and tree ferns, others were trained up against a wall, while others hung gracefully over the veranda of the palace, after the manner of creepers. Large shells, filled with sand, served as flower pots, and contained, as his majesty assured me, plants of extraordinary rarity. I forget their crack-jaw names.

A sword-fish acted as head gardener; he was digging away with his proboscis as we entered, and a saw-fish was raking the flower beds.

It was already evening, and was getting dark. The king ordered the saloon to be lighted up, when two lusty mermen brought the lamps, which they hung in the corners of the apartment, and which consisted of shells, to each of which were attached three chains of pearls, the bowl of the lamp being filled with those phosphoric *animalcula* that are to be seen at night round the prow of a vessel when the keel disturbs them as it ploughs its course through the ocean.

The saloon being lighted, musicians were called. They were of both sexes; sturdy mermen, with gongs and sea horns; those of the gentler sex with harps. I was asked if I could dance, and replying that I could after the fashion of my country, the music struck up a merry tune, and a number of fair sirens insisted on me joining in the dance.

The dance commenced; it was a curious step, consisting of a wriggle of the upper part of the body, and a splash with the tail. They formed a circle, each taking hold of the other's hand, closing and widening several times; then letting go of hands, each dived down head foremost, their fingers touching the ground, flapping their tails upwards.

They went through all sorts of fantastic steps, which I tried hard to imitate, and my failures were the cause of much merriment. I was asked whether I would favour them with a dance of my country, so I danced the hornpipe. With this they were delighted, and wanted it repeated. I had to dance it again, and again, to please them.

Refreshments were handed round by the same sea monsters, and the evening wound up with games—hide and seek, blind man's buff— and other amusements.

The queen said she was glad to see me enjoy myself so much. One bewitching young siren, fixing her dark eyes upon me, and then looking down with a sigh, said it was pleasing to see such a great hero as I was condescending to take part in their humble games. Another hoped that I was in no hurry to leave them, as she was looking forward to many such pleasant evenings. A third mermaid wished that she had been born with legs, in order to learn the hornpipe. A fourth hoped I should sleep well after my fatigue.

The party at length broke up, and as I was the lion of the evening, I stationed myself near the door to shake hands with all the pretty mermaids as they swam out of the saloon. I gave a gentle squeeze to each, and I am certain that if not all, at least the greater part of those young ladies, went to bed in love with me that night. But what of Lurline? I must not forget *her*. The fact was I did not like to be too pointed in my attentions, lest it should excite suspicion, for as yet her parents knew nothing of our attachment, so I appeared rather to neglect her than otherwise.

Poor child! she retired to rest unhappy that night, fancying that I had become estranged towards her. I had no opportunity for an explanation, and after quitting the saloon was shown to my bedroom by a *mer*-servant girl.

The walls and ceiling of my bed-chamber were covered over with handsome shells, the floor inlaid with mother-of-pearl and coral, over which was a carpet of variegated seaweed, plaited in a pattern. The bed posts were inlaid with mother-of-pearl, agate, lapis lazuli, and other rare stones. The mattress was of very soft sponge, and the counterpane one broad piece of seaweed.

Having undressed, I blew out the candle; that is to say, I smashed the *animalcula* inside the shell that the servant girl brought me in lieu of a candlestick, and tucking myself up I tried to sleep, but was haunted all night by the bright eyes of Lurline.

Towards morning I fell into a light sleep, from which I was roused by the dulcet tones of a harp at my door and the enchanting voice of Lurline singing. I leaped from my couch, donned my clothes, and welcomed her with a kiss on the sly.

"Cruel one!" she said, "I thought you had ceased to love me."

"*I* cease to love thee, sweetest! Never!"

"You are quite sure you love me, then?" she said. "And you will never desert me?"

"Desert thee! my angel," said I. "Do you think I could be so base?"

"Hush!" she whispered. "Here comes mamma," and she dived downstairs.

"Lurline, Lurline," cried her majesty, who had overheard every word of our conversation. "Lurline, come here; I wish to speak with you."

Up swam Lurline again, pale with fright. She entered her mother's room, and the queen turned the key. I heard the mother's voice within speaking angrily, and half-an-hour afterwards Lurline left the chamber, sobbing.

I came forward to soothe her, but she motioned me away, and put her finger to her lip. I dived after her downstairs, resolved to hear the worst. It seems her mother had scolded her for flirting; said she was too young to marry; that I was too old for her; that she knew nothing of my family; and that she must not fix her affections upon anyone who was not of royal blood.

"Here, then," thought I, "among this simple primitive people, there is as much aristocratic pride as in our more civilised countries."

What was to be done? Relinquish Lurline for a foolish piece of barbarous pride. I couldn't and wouldn't. There was nothing left me but to speak to his majesty; assume as much dignity as I could and boast of my pedigree.

At breakfast I thought both the king and queen cold towards me, but I appeared not to notice it, and talked away fluently about my country, my family, and insinuated, rather than said outright, that I was of royal blood.

Their manner towards me grew by degrees less frigid, and after breakfast I followed his majesty to his dais chamber, and proposed for his daughter's hand. He demurred for a long time, but I declared that in my own country I, too, had been a king; that I had been driven from my throne by my rebellious subjects; that, growing disgusted with ruling, I had sought refuge from *ennui* in a life of adventure.

His majesty, like his people, being of a simple nature, believed all I said, and left me, saying he would think about it and talk to the queen. I saw him from the window shortly afterwards in earnest conversation with her majesty in the garden. I burned to know the result of their interview.

In the course of the day one of the queen's mermaids-of-honour informed me that her majesty desired to speak with me. I entered into her presence trembling.

She accosted me thus, "Captain Toughyarn, his majesty has already acquainted me with your proposal, but before we give our consent to a marriage with our daughter, even after your assertion that you are of royal blood, we must know you a little longer. Marriages are not to be contracted in a hurry. You did very wrong to engage our daughter's affections without first consulting us in the matter. It was an insult to our royal self. However, let that pass; it is too late now. My daughter seems thoroughly to have set her affections upon you. I have lectured her severely for her imprudence; but the matter seems to have gone so far, that I fear to break her heart if I peremptorily refuse to give my consent to this marriage. If my daughter will take my advice, she will, upon reflection, break off this match. You'll excuse me, Captain Toughyarn, for saying that I think your age a decided objection."

"As regards my age, your majesty," I said, "the men of my country get grey and bald at thirty, though they maintain their healthful vigour to a prolonged period. I myself am thirty-six." (I would not say that I was sixty-three.)

Her majesty looked incredulous, and then a momentary smile crossed her features, as if she were having a joke all to herself, but she stifled it immediately.

"There is another thing, Captain Toughyarn," said her majesty, "that perhaps you may not be aware of. Marriages between your race and ours are extremely rare. When they occur some sacrifice is always expected on the part of the gentleman, just by way of proving his love," and she glanced at my legs as she spoke. I did not quite understand her meaning.

"Sacrifice—sacrifice," I said to myself. "Ah! yes," said I, aloud; "your majesty does not wish that your daughter should leave her house and visit my country. Is it not so?"

"That is part of the conditions, but not all," said her majesty.

"And what else might your majesty be pleased to exact from me?" I asked.

"Well," she said, with a smile and a second glance at my legs, "we should like you—we expect you to—to—to become in fact, like one of us—to conform—"

"Oh, quite so," I said, without as yet catching her meaning thoroughly; "to conform—yes—certainly—to all the customs of the country I have adopted."

"To *all* of them, mind?"

"Yes."

"Then you consent to this trifling sacrifice. You have no objection to—to be operated upon?"

"Operated upon!" I cried in astonishment. "What?—How?—I don't quite catch your majesty's meaning."

"Well, Captain Toughyarn," said her majesty, "if I *must* be more explicit, the fact is, that legs are out of fashion here, only tails are worn in this country. If you really wish to marry our daughter, you must submit to an operation."

"W-h-e-w!" whistled I, the real nature of the sacrifice dawning upon me for the first time. "So that is your meaning!"

"Precisely. Do you refuse?"

Now, I always prided myself particularly on my legs. In my youth they were the admiration of the sex; even now they are far from contemptible, and to give them in exchange for a tail was of all things the furthest from my thoughts. I did not know what to answer. At length I asked, "And this operation—how is it performed, your majesty?"

"Oh, it is simple enough," was the reply. "A surgeon is called, who amputates the lower extremities; a dolphin or other large fish is procured, which, after being killed, is cut in half, and the tail half of the fish is bound to that part of your body still suffering from the operation, until the parts unite, and the transformation is complete."

"I am infinitely obliged to your majesty," said I, "but I hope you will pardon me if I refuse to comply with this last condition. Legs such as mine are extremely prized in my country; in fact, they are only to be found in those of the blood royal, and I really could not consent to part with such a very strong mark; indeed, perhaps, the only mark of royalty about my person."

"Then you refuse?"

"Absolutely," said I, bowing.

"In that case," said the queen, "I must talk to his majesty, to see what can be done."

The queen rose. I bowed, and left the apartment.

Shortly afterwards I heard the king's voice in great wrath, calling out, "What! he won't sacrifice his legs? Did you say he *won't*? *Won't*, indeed! I'll let him know who the *mer*-king is. He comes here uninvited, wheedles himself into our daughter's affections, and then his love is found wanting at the proof. He won't even give up his hideous legs, and wear a respectable tail for *her* sake. By my trident, he shall for *mine*. I'll tail him. Here, Thomas!" That was the name of the shark that opened the door for us. "What ho! Thomas, bite off that insolent stranger's legs this instant. Come, make haste, and lose no time about it."

I happened to be looking out of my bedroom window at the time, which was open. At these words I plunged through the casement and struck out upwards. I had not proceeded very far—though in all my life I never struck out as I did then—when I heard the palace door open and the splash of the huge monster behind me. I struck out upwards, upwards, ever upwards, but the immense fish was at my heels with the rapidity of lightning.

Truly, I thought my last moment was at hand. With the energy that despair alone gives, I struck out so frantically, that even the shark had hard work to keep up with me, but I was fast getting exhausted.

What should I do when completely so? There seemed no hope for me.

"While strength lasts, I'll use it," said I, to myself, and struck out more desperately than ever, but the shark gained upon me, nevertheless.

At length, after repeated exertions, my head appeared once more above water. Once more I felt the fresh breeze on my bald pate.

"Thank heaven!" I cried.

There was a vessel in sight, not far off. I hailed her, bawling out with all my might and main, still swimming furiously. The shark was now nearer than ever. He had already turned on his back, preparatory to biting off my legs, and the ship though she had noticed my distress, and was coming fast to my rescue, was not sufficiently near as yet to save me.

I felt the tip of the monster's nose against my shoe. I lunged out a tremendous kick, which ought to have sent several of its teeth down its throat; at any rate, it sent him backward about a foot. Meanwhile, I struck out more fiercely than ever, but the brute recovered itself and was at me again.

My strength was now quite exhausted. How I managed to hold out so long puzzles me now. I was about to sink from sheer exhaustion. In another moment my legs must have been off, had not one of the officers of the ship thrown out a rope, which I clutched eagerly, and being speedily hauled on deck, the monster was baulked of its prey.

Whilst yet dangling in air, before my feet had time to touch the deck, I heard a "bang," and, looking behind me, to my intense relief, I saw the corpse of my dread foe bobbing up and down in the waves, and staining the water with his blood.

"So much for Thomas," thought I.

The sailors were just about to lug it on board, when at this juncture I awoke.

Lucky for me that my flight was so precipitate. If *she* had crossed my path at the last moment I thoroughly believe the very sight of her sweet face would have made me consent to the operation. Poor Lurline! But what is the use of giving way to sensibility, gentlemen? And, as to losing one's legs, it is bad enough to lose them in an engagement for the honour and glory of one's country, but to have them bitten off by a shark, or amputated by a *mer*-surgeon, at the caprice of a *mer*-king, and a fish's tail substituted in lieu thereof, is a thing that Toughyarn can't quite stomach.

Supposing me to have been weak enough to have submitted to the operation at the tears and entreaties of Lurline, it becomes a very different matter when my limbs are exacted as a forfeiture, and imperiously demanded by an infuriated parent.

Toughyarn may be as weak as a child in the hands of a pretty woman, but he won't be *forced* to anything by the greatest tyrant that ever existed.

★ ★ ★ ★ ★

"Bravo, Toughyarn!" cried all the company, with one voice.

This enthusiasm was as much in praise of the sentiment that the captain had wound up with as for the story itself.

"I knew the captain wouldn't be beaten in a yarn by the best of us," said Hardcase, "although he did find mine rather difficult to swallow."

Cheers and rattling of glasses followed, and the captain's health was drunk with due honours, after which the chairman rose and addressed the company thus:

"Most honourable and august members and guests of the Wonder Club, you will all allow that the gallant captain has amply expiated his offence. There is, however, an individual present who has been guilty of the same offence as the captain, and who has not yet undergone the penance expected from him by our club."

All eyes were turned towards the little comedian who blushed and laughed.

"Need I point out that individual, gentlemen?"

Cries of "No, no!"

"Now, Jollytoast, for your turn, old boy," said the tragedian.

"Hear, hear!" cried other members.

"Gentlemen," continued Mr. Oldstone, "our time is short; the clock has already struck two, and I have observed more than one yawn from amongst the company. It will be my painful duty to dismiss this genial meeting, but I cannot conscientiously do so without first performing an act of justice to the company. I, therefore, sentence Mr. Jollytoast to a comic song before our meeting breaks up." (Cheers and laughter. Cries of "Hear, hear," and "Now then Jollytoast; a song, a song—Jollytoast for a song!")

The little gentleman, thus addressed, begged for a moment's reflection, and then broke into a very merry ditty with a chorus, in which all had to join. There was plenty of acting and grimace in it, with here and there a part spoken, and any amount of "tooral-looral" in the chorus.

The song being ended, our comic friend was much applauded, and the chairman, in a short speech, expressed himself satisfied with the expiation, and, wishing all the company a "good night," and many more such genial meetings, was about to retire, when Captain Tough-yarn called out, "Avast! there, chairman. You are never going to dismiss the crew without splicing the main brace first!"

"True, true, captain," said the president; "besides the health of our sublime warbler, Mr. Jollytoast, has not been drunk yet. Fill your glasses, gentlemen, and drink to the health of Mr. Jollytoast."

Shouts and yells ensued, during which our comic guest's health was drunk with three times three, to which he responded in a short and laughable speech that called forth more cheering.

"And now, gentlemen," said the chairman, "after having spent the tenth anniversary of our club in the company of mermaids, sea monsters, ghouls, spirits, and phantom fleas, how can we do better than wind up this honourable meeting by joining hands and singing that song composed by one of our members—now, alas! no more—to be sung at the inauguration of the Wonder Club?" The proposal was received with applause, and all the company joining hands, our host included, sung the following ditty:

Song of the Wonder Club

As we join hand in hand
Let us sing to our band,
And lift up our voice in a ditty;
May memories well stored
E'er enliven our board
With the wondrous, the weird, and the witty.

Let each thirsty soul
Round the merry punch bowl
Drink deep to our brotherhood's founding,
And loud be the cheers
That resound in the ears
Of the member with tale most astounding.

Round the merry Yule flame
May our band of the same
Meet year after year in their niches,
And list as of yore
To our tales by the score
Of phantoms, wraiths, goblins, and witches.

Then our song's jocund sound,
When our nectar flows round,
Sure Olympus was never so merry.
Right jovial our crew,
Whate'er be the brew,
Whether brandy, port, whisky or sherry.

Now whate'er befall,
Here's a "goodnight" to all,
May Queen Mab with her train cheer our slumber;
And with one last toast,
Let us drown every ghost,
Or goblin, or ghoul, in a bumper.

The song at an end, a last bumper was drunk by way of a nightcap, and each gallant member or guest walked, or staggered, as the case might be, off to bed.

"Ho, steward!" cried the captain, to the landlord; "douse the glims, and show the passengers to their cabins. Where have you slung my hammock?"

Our host provided candles for each of his guests, and bidding them all "goodnight," gave a yawn, and followed the example of the rest.

The Artist's First Story

The Headless Lady

The morning following the saturnalia was cold and bleak. Without it was snowing hard, and the windows of the old inn were covered with frost crystals. Breakfast was late, few of the members of the club having yet risen, apparently not yet recovered from the effects of the previous evening.

The landlord exerted himself to make the interior of his inn as cheerful as the gloomy state of the weather would permit. A large log crackled on the hearth, and the breakfast table teemed with all the delicacies that the inn could boast of; coffee, toast, hot rolls, eggs and bacon, ham, chicken, tongue, and fresh butter. One by one the guests made their appearance. They seemed to have slept well, for they looked none the worse for their last night's carousal.

The last to enter the breakfast room was our fresh arrival, Mr. Vandyke McGuilp. He presented a very different appearance to any of the rest. He was pale and haggard, and his hair hung disordered over his eyes.

"I'm afraid you have not slept well, Mr. McGuilp," said Mr. Old-stone. "What is the matter? It surely can't be the punch, for you drank less than any of us last night. Why, I don't believe you drank more than a couple of glasses the whole time; but perhaps you are not accustomed to these orgies, and a little upsets you. Look at us—seasoned old casks all of us—we are as jolly as ever. As for myself, I never felt better in all my life."

"Oh, it is not that," replied our artist; "but I feel somehow I passed an indifferent night."

Dr. Bleedem felt the pulse and looked at the tongue of the new guest, and pronounced him a little feverish, but said that it would soon pass over.

"My blessed eyes!" cried the captain, "if the gentleman doesn't look as scared as I felt when the shark was at my heels last night. What say you mine host?"

"Well, Captain," said the landlord, "if I might venture a remark, the gentleman looks as if he had had a visit from the *headless lady*."

McGuilp started.

"Why do you start, sir?" inquired Mr. Blackdeed, who alone had noticed the action, his eye being ever open to anything of a dramatic effect.

"A little nervousness, that is all," replied the artist. "I feel far from well this morning."

"I assure you, your action was quite dramatic," said the tragedian. "Oblige me by repeating it. Thank you; I'll practise it before the glass this morning. It will just do for my tragedy, when the wicked baron, who is in the act of carrying off a lady by force, is suddenly checked in his career by the appearance of the spirit of her brother, whom he has murdered."

"Ha! What's that all about?" cried Oldstone, who had pricked up his ears at something resembling a story, while the rest were gossiping on indifferent matters. "You must act us a scene out of that tragedy, Blackdeed; remember, we had no story from you last night."

"Breakfast is ready, gentlemen," said the landlord.

The guests flocked round the table and commenced their repast.

"By the by, landlord," said McGuilp, as that worthy was about to quit the room, "you give your inn a curious name. Is there any origin to it?"

"Well, sir," replied the landlord, "it was my grandfather, or great grandfather, who gave it that name—I'm not sure which."

"But—but, is there no origin to it?—no legend connected with—"

"Oh, as to that, your honour," said the landlord, "folks used to say that this house was haunted by a lady without a head; but that's a long time ago. I don't exactly recollect the particulars of the story, but I have heard my father say, when I was a youngster, that he had seen her; but it's five and thirty years come Michaelmas that this inn has been in my hands, and I never see anything of the sort, sir. No, sir; depend upon it, she don't 'walk' now, sir. Even in my father's time her visits used to be rare, though my grandfather used to tell me lots of stories about her when I was a child."

"Do you remember any of those stories?"

"Not now, sir. I only remember hearing say that the lady was a nun; but for what offence she was beheaded I can't exactly call to mind now."

"Perhaps I might be able to refresh your memory," said the artist. "What would you say if I really had had a visit from the headless lady last night?"

"You, sir!" exclaimed the landlord in great astonishment. "You don't mean to say that you really *did see*—"

"The headless lady. Yes, I do; I mean to say that I had a visit from her last night."

The landlord opened his eyes and mouth with a look of awe. The guests remained as if petrified. The captain's red face grew a shade less so. Mr. Parnassus became livid. The tragedian's hair stood on end. Mr. Oldstone looked a few years older, while the countenances of the whole company betrayed various grades of wonder and consternation.

"Ahem!" coughed the chairman of the previous evening, at length breaking silence. "Perhaps you would not mind telling us about your experiences of last night, Mr. McGuilp? I am sure we are all most curious to hear something about this mysterious lady. I have never met anyone yet who could say that they had seen her, though I have heard over and over again that she used to 'walk.'"

Thus entreated, our artist proceeded as follows:

Well, then, after I left you, gentlemen, last night, before I retired to rest, in looking round my apartment, I was much struck with an old portrait, painted in a very early style, of a lady in a nun's dress. In spite of the hard style of the period, there was something in the face—a sort of resigned melancholy—that interested me exceedingly. Still it was little more than a passing glance that I bestowed on the picture, for I felt very sleepy, and more inclined for bed than for criticising works of art. I accordingly undressed as quickly as I could, blew out the light, and in two minutes was fast asleep.

I could not have enjoyed more than a quarter-of-an-hour's repose, when I was suddenly awakened by what felt like a cold hand pressed upon my forehead. I started up, and tried to call out, but could not raise my voice above a whisper. I looked in the direction in which I expected to find the person who had awakened me, but could see nothing.

All was pitch dark around me, but I heard, or thought I heard, a deep sigh as I strained my ears to catch some sound of the intruder.

"Who's there?" I called out, in a husky whisper; but I received no reply.

Beginning to be alarmed, fancying that some dishonest person had entered my chamber to rob me, or else that it was someone of the household given to walking in their sleep, I sat up in bed and peered into the darkness.

As I listened I distinctly heard a low moan of such piteous anguish that it made my flesh creep and my hair to stand up.

"Who could it be?" I asked myself. "Perhaps some person of unsound mind in the family whose habit it was to walk at night, and lurk about the bed-chambers."

The thought was anything but a pleasant one. Who knows what form this madness might take? Mad people are not to be trusted. I trembled to think what the intent of my visitor might be. Was he armed? I tried to reach out my hand for my tinder-box, but such a supernatural terror pervaded my whole frame, that my limbs were paralysed, and I remained sitting up in bed, as if rooted to the spot, without power to move a finger.

At length, not being able to bear this suspense any longer, I bethought me of striking terror into my visitant, and though carrying no arms about me, my object was to alarm the stranger into speaking, so I called out in husky tones as loud as my voice would permit me, "Speak, or I fire!"

But no answer was given. What was to be done? I could not carry my threat into execution, having no weapon. I could not even move from my post for fear, I felt the cold perspiration streaming down from my temples, my whole frame shook, and my teeth chattered together.

It was something more than mortal fear that I suffered; it was as if I were in the presence of some supernatural being. Gradually I became aware of a dark form, apparently that of a woman, close to my bed. My eyes had grown accustomed to the darkness, and I could distinguish the various objects in my bed-chamber with greater facility.

I riveted my eyes on the figure, but all I could discern was a long black robe and two white hands. I looked for the face, but in vain. It seemed covered up, for the shoulders merged into the darkness.

Soon, as if to aid my vision, a sort of pale blue light spread a halo around the figure, and grew gradually brighter, setting it off in relief. I could now see the whole figure distinctly. I looked for the head. Oh, horror! *It was wanting.*

I shuddered, and felt an intense desire to scream, but my voice was gone. Had I then really lived to see a ghost? Was there, then, some foundation for the strange name given to the inn? I had never heard from my friend Rustcoin that it was reported haunted, and I most assuredly should have heard about it if he had had any knowledge of it.

Perhaps it was a thing not generally known; perhaps its appearance was not usual, and it only appeared at intervals to certain privileged beings. Was I one of those beings? I asked myself. Perhaps so. It might have something to communicate. I would address it, but my tongue clove to the roof of my mouth, for now I saw distinctly that the head I had missed was carried under the left arm of the figure.

I marked well the face; it was extremely beautiful, and I thought I recognised a likeness to the old portrait I had been looking at; but oh! how far short that old piece of painted panel fell of the original; if, indeed, it was ever intended for a representation of the lineaments I now gazed upon.

I made a second effort to address it, but as I opened my mouth to speak I heard another most audible moan from the headless figure. I was awed, but that intense fear which I experienced when I became aware that some stranger had entered my chamber had all but vanished now that I was *certain* that I was in the presence of a denizen of the spirit world.

Awful as this certainty was, it seemed to fade into insignificance when compared with the terrible feeling of doubt I had before experienced. I now felt comparatively relieved; so much so, indeed, that I even found room in my heart for pity—that one so young and so beautiful as she appeared to be should have suffered such a cruel and ignominious death. At length, in a low and subdued tone, I addressed the figure.

"Spirit, whate'er thou art or wert, whether of good or evil, whether from the regions of the blest or the haunts of the damned, speak! Declare thy mission."

A hollow moan proceeded from the trunk of the headless figure, and the eyes in the head held under its arm rolled upwards with a look of despair, while in tones low, solemn, yet sweet, it spoke, the lips vibrating, though the voice came from the neck.

"I am the spirit of one who, dying in mortal sin, am doomed to perpetual unrest. Beheaded for my crimes in this world, I wander nightly round this spot, the scene of my infamy. Here where this house now stands once stood the convent whose walls imprisoned me while yet on earth. Forced into a life of seclusion for which I had no calling by a relentless parent who, deeming that his daughter's alliance with the man she loved would sully his illustrious name, I was compelled to utter vows with my lips against which my heart revolted.

"I could not join in the pious oraisons of my sister nuns, for while my knees bent and my lips moved my spirit was elsewhere. Day after day I languished within my prison walls, mechanically going through my duties with the rest, but to all outward seeming with devotion, for not one of them knew but that I myself had chosen that calling.

"None knew then what I bore within. I made no friends, sought no confidant. When I confessed, my confessions were always of a vague sort, for I was reserved on that one point which, if confessed, would have been regarded as the most heinous crime.

"At length our father confessor, who was an old man, died, and a new priest took his place.

"Holy Virgin! it was my lover. He had discovered my whereabouts, and, with no holier object than the desire to see me again, he had entered into holy orders, and by stratagem contrived to enter our convent."

Here the figure gave a deep sigh, and paused. The face writhed, as if struggling with itself, whether it should proceed or remain silent. The pause was agonising, but I wished to hear more.

"Proceed," I said.

Another deep sigh ensued, and she continued.

"Mortal," she said with evident reluctance, "you will despise me when you have heard the full extent of my crime. No matter, I am not what I was—I can bear it. Know, then, that I fell. Ay, blush for me, hate, loathe, despise me as thou wilt. Those holy walls which re-echoed for ages with nought save the prayers and the chanting of pious nuns, were doomed to hear the whispered words of fierce passion and to witness scenes that must for ever leave a stain upon their fair memory.

"Enough, our intrigue was discovered, and I was sentenced to death. I was beheaded secretly, yet even blood could not wash out the foul stain from my soul, and I have ever since been doomed to eternal pangs of remorse."

"What!" I exclaimed, "and had your lover no knowledge of this?"

"He had, and furious at the news, he came by night and set fire to the convent. The building was razed to the ground, and every nun perished."

"And your lover," I asked, "what became of him?"

"He died shortly afterwards. I was permitted to see his spirit but once, and then he was torn away from me for ever. It is that which grieves me most, for I know not what fate is reserved for him.

"Heaven grant that his state may be happier than mine. Oh, how willingly would I bear the weight of all his sins, so that his portion might be in the region of the blest. I would then bear my doom without a murmur, even were my sufferings ten-fold."

"And with this charitable feeling towards the author of thy ruin, canst thou possess a soul so black as to merit eternal punishment?" said I.

"Alas!" murmured the spirit, "when we die in mortal sin our doom is sealed, yet I would fain hope still that before I quit this state of purgatory and am consigned to eternal flames that the prayers of others—"

"I understand; it was with that object, then, thou soughtest me— that I might pray for thy soul?"

"It was," replied the spirit; "and also for my lover. Oh, let me not pray in vain. Tell me thou wilt pray for me."

"Spirit," I answered, "I am not of thy creed. I am a Protestant. Our church holds all prayers for the dead useless."

"I know it; but it is an error. Pray, nevertheless. Thou comest from Rome, and wilt shortly return thither. Bid the pious monks and nuns there pray for my soul, and for the soul of my lover."

"Spirit, thy request is granted, and if my own weak prayers may serve in any way to relieve thy torments, they, too, shall be added."

A smile of the most ineffable sweetness and gratitude, more eloquent than words, spread over the face of the decapitated. She pressed my hand fervently with her pale, icy-cold fingers, and gradually faded from my gaze.

When she had vanished, it was already daybreak. Sleep had deserted my eyelids, and as I tossed restlessly in my bed I kept wondering to myself whether what I had seen and heard could be a dream, or whether I really and truly had held converse with a ghost.

The rest of the time, with the exception of a short doze I took previous to rising this morning, I spent in prayer for the release of the soul of the headless lady from purgatory, and likewise that of her lover.

★ ★ ★ ★ ★

I leave the reader to imagine the sensation our artist's spiritual visitation excited at the breakfast-table before the members of the Wonder Club, whose thirst for the marvellous and supernatural was insatiable. Second and third-hand ghost stories are common enough, and are generally taken for what they are worth; but here was the case of a ghost story told by the ghost seer himself, who had seen and spoken to the ghost only the night before; in the very house, too, in which they had all been sleeping. Then, added to that, was the manner of the narrator, which alone bore the stamp of truth on it. The quick roll of his eye, when he was describing the excited state of his feelings at the time, the involuntary shudder, and the furtive glance which he from time to time would give over his shoulder; all signs of a nervous system that has received some great shock—to say nothing of his worn and disordered appearance, as might be expected in a man that has seen a ghost.

All this enhanced the power of his words immensely. Then there was the strange fact to be borne in mind that no one had informed him that the house was haunted. No one could say that his imagination had been unduly excited by any story concerning the house previous to his going to sleep. He had retired to rest calmly, without any fear of a spiritual visitation. And how could it all be a dream? For the landlord now distinctly remembered that all our artist had related was exactly what had been told him by his grandfather. Various were the exclamations of wonderment from the guests at the breakfast-table. They gazed with awe on the narrator, then at each other, then at the narrator again. Our artist had won the esteem of the whole club.

Breakfast being finished, our friends drew round the fire, and the landlord left the room, looking grave and shaking his head. McGuilp's strange adventure had furnished food for comment for two or three hours afterwards. The whole forenoon nothing was talked of but the ghost.

At length a lull occurred in the conversation, and someone recollected that it was Professor Cyanite's turn to tell a story. At that moment our host's pretty daughter, Helen, a blooming girl of sixteen, entered with the lunch.

Our artist was enraptured with the golden hair, blue eyes, and rosy cheeks of the maiden, after the swarthy beauties of Italy; but, above all, with her innocent, modest, and half-bashful manner.

"Well, Helen," said Mr. Oldstone, "has your father told you about the ghost?"

"Oh, yes, sir," replied the girl, her merry expression changing suddenly to a look of awe; "he did frighten me so; I am sure I shall never be able to sleep again in this house."

"This is the gentleman who saw the ghost, Helen," cried one of the other members, pointing to our artist.

The maiden turned and saw a fresh face in the club. Our artist was the youngest, by many years, of any of the other gentlemen present, besides which he was decidedly good looking. He gazed into the eyes of the girl till the poor child blushed crimson and looked down abashed.

"Ho! ho! Helen, my girl," said Mr. Crucible, one of the oldest members of the club, "you don't blush like that when you look at us old fogies—what is the matter, eh?"

A general laugh ensued, much to the confusion of poor Helen, and our artist himself felt not a little confused at having produced such an impression on the girl in the presence of so many others of his own sex.

"What ho! Helen, bring another log; we're freezing," cried Professor Cyanite, changing the conversation, much to the relief of the girl, who was glad to escape from the banter of the club by quitting the room.

Our guests began their repast of cold meat and pickles, bread and cheese, and home-brewed ale. After they had finished the daughter of the landlord re-entered with a large log, which she placed on the fire.

"That's right, my girl," said Mr. Oldstone, drawing his chair up to the fire; "now bring us pipes."

The girl left the room, and soon returned with a bundle of long clay pipes, already waxed, which she distributed amongst the company, receiving a chuck under the chin from one; a gentle pat on the cheek from another; from a third, a stroke on the head; from a fourth, a squeeze of the hand; a fifth placed his arm round her waist; while a sixth pretended to kiss her, but no further harm was done. Our artist placed a chair for her next to himself, round the fire, and asked her if she were fond of hearing stories.

The maiden blushed and smiled and said that she was.

"Bravo, Helen," said Mr. Oldstone; "remain with us and hear a fresh story. Professor Cyanite is just going to favour us."

A circle was formed round the fire; Helen seating herself modestly by the side of the artist, while the professor, sitting back in his chair, and stretching out his legs towards the fire, stroked his ample forehead, and with a puff at his pipe, commenced the following story.

The Geologist's Story

The Demon Guide *or*
The Gnome of the Mountain

Some twenty years ago, when I was on a scientific tour in the mountains of Switzerland with a friend of mine, who travelled with the same object as myself, a strange incident occurred to me, which I have never been able satisfactorily to explain. We journeyed in each other's company daily, each carrying with him a geologist's hammer and a light travelling bag slung round one shoulder, for the purpose of collecting specimens of various minerals, fossils, etc., that we might find during our march.

We jogged along merrily enough together, each day bringing home some rare specimen or other. We were both in full vigour of health, and both capital climbers. Mountain air and exercise had given us marvellous appetites, and I never remember being in better spirits in my life. As we were not pushed for time or money, and were on a scientific expedition instead of what is called a pleasure trip, it was less our object to scour large tracts of country than to stroll leisurely through the district, making observations by the way.

Travelling, therefore, both with the same object, and not obliged to hurry onward, we had nothing to try our tempers, as ordinary tourists have, who travel in company and usually fall out with each other by the way because one with short wind can't keep up with his longer-winded companion.

Nothing, perhaps, is more trying to the temper than being obliged to keep pace with a well-trained mountaineer if you yourself happen to be out of training. To see him striding on ahead with the most perfect ease and enjoyment, whilst you are toiling and sweating, and puffing and gasping in the rear, parched with thirst and ready to drop with fatigue; perhaps knee deep in snow, plunging about like a porpoise, in the frantic attempt to keep up with your well-trained companion.

Why, the treadmill is a joke to it! How you curse your folly for coming to visit such barbarous places, and how you internally vow never to leave home again. How inconsiderate of your companion to leave you so far behind, as if you did not belong to his party. He seems to ignore you, and you feel the slight. He ought to keep pace with you, not you with him, you think.

How you hate him for his rude health and long wind; and should he so far forget himself as to add insult to injury by bawling after you to "come on," and not "lag behind;" or call you by some such name as "slow coach," "stick-in-the-mud," or other choice epithet, oh, then it is not to be borne. Your ire is raised beyond due bounds. You could stab him if you only had him near enough, and a weapon handy.

If any of my friends who content themselves with taking their daily walk of a mile or so on level ground fancy that this is an exaggeration of the state of a man's feelings when the body is tired out and the nerves on the stretch, I recommend him to try a trip in some mountainous district when out of training, and to choose as companion some well-trained son of the mountains.

As I observed before, gentlemen, my friend and I were not wont to fall out in this way with one another, and we took our journey very easily, chipping out a fossil here and a crystal there, conversing the while on secondary and tertiary formations, volcanic eruptions, alluvial deposits, debris, quartz, and marl, mica, slate, talc, calc, etc., etc.

Thus we journeyed on together day after day for weeks, until we found that the face of the country changed suddenly. Two mountain ranges branched off almost at right angles from one another.

My friend and I resolved to separate, and each to explore in a different direction, and to meet again in about a fortnight.

We accordingly parted, and I commenced exploring a wild track of mountainous country alone. Charmed with the wild beauty of the scene, as well as interested in its geological structure, I suffered my footsteps to lead me onward until hunger stole upon me. I had eaten nothing since the morning, and it was now getting late. One day at home without food is bad enough, but it is not to be compared with a day spent in the mountains, walking and climbing all the time.

I looked out for a chalet, but there was none visible. Meanwhile it grew dark, and I found myself benighted. There was not even a shed to rest under, so I was obliged to repose my weary limbs upon the cold, damp, rock, with such shelter from the night air as the dark pine trees afforded.

It was a strange, wild, scene the spot where I encamped. The spectre-like pines stretched forth their weird branches, drooping with bearded moss, like phantom Druids invoking a curse over this scene of desolation. The moon, peeping fitfully through the black clouds, lit up the glaciers on the mountain opposite. Here and there was a great pine torn up by the roots, or over-hanging the abyss below. Immense clumps of rock, grown over with dank moss, were interspersed through the dark pine forest. A small stream trickled over the large stones, pursuing its zigzag course till it reached the valley below.

The howling of the wind and the occasional thunder of the avalanche from some neighbouring mountain lent a kind of terror to the scene, which I should have enjoyed, had I been in a more comfortable frame of mind. But, with the gnawing pains of hunger and the horrible feeling of doubt as to whether I should ever meet with any traces of civilisation where I might recruit my wasted energies, the beauty of the spot was shut from me, and I found it only a cold, damp, disagreeable retreat.

It was yet early in the night when I took up my quarters here, but it was dark and cloudy, and I put up at this place, despairing of finding a more hospitable lodging, on account of the darkness, besides which I was tired out. I had reposed in my uncomfortable quarters for, it might be, two or three hours, though without sleeping, when the clouds began to disperse and the sky was calm and serene, the moon bright and clear, so I thought I would leave my camping place and venture a little further, in the vague hope of finding some hospitable chalet where I might obtain fire and food.

I was now considerably rested from my fatigue, but the pangs of hunger grew ever more intense. I wandered on and on, till the pines grew less thick, and a wide extended view opened before me, when I fancied that I descried afar off in the valley a light. My heart began to revive. As I strode onward I saw below me a small lake, over which frowned dark toppling crags. The moon shone brightly over all.

Still keeping the distant chalet in sight, I could think of little else than the meal which would await me on my arrival; but while glancing casually over the lake illumined by the moonbeams, and the cliff that overhung it, my eye was suddenly arrested by an object, apparently a human being, clambering up a height that I should have imagined inaccessible to any mortal man. It literally overhung the lake.

At first I thought my eyes deceived me, but as I looked I was more and more convinced that it was a human being performing this feat. I had heard much of the daring of the Swiss mountaineers, but this beat anything I ever heard of, for the cliff, besides over-hanging, was comparatively smooth, being of slate, and there appeared nothing to hold on by.

"Could it really be a human being?" I asked myself. If so, it was so hideously misshapen as hardly to deserve the title. In spite of my hunger, I panted awhile in breathless anxiety to observe the course of this creature.

"Surely some madman," thought I, "tired of his life."

Every moment I expected to see his foot slip and to hear a splash in the lake below; but no, the being, whatever it was, crawled steadily upwards like a huge spider, till it gained the summit of the cliff. I then lost sight of it. A few steps further on led me to the spot the climber had reached, when soon among the lengthened shadows of the pines, I descried a shadow which was not that of a tree.

I approached, and as the moon lit up the object in my path, I beheld a sight that made my blood freeze to look upon. It was one of those hideous cretins which inhabit the valleys of all mountainous countries.

I started, and the idiot, who gazed at me vacantly at first, seemed to have sense enough to be aware of the impression he had made, and to take a fiendish delight in the effect that he had produced. The aspect of this being was the most frightful of anything I had ever seen in human shape. He could not have exceeded four feet in height, but the breadth of his shoulders was such as to make his figure a complete square. His neck was short, and his head, which was enormous, was covered over with scant sandy hair. The complexion was ghastly; the lips thin and livid, the nose flat and spreading, and the eyes, which were an immense distance apart, pale green and fishy; the face was round and broad, and though generally idiotic in expression, was lit up at times with a look of intelligence, mixed with the most preternatural cunning and malignity. The muscular development of the upper part of this strange figure was prodigious, and the arms were so long that the fingers all but touched the ground, but the legs were extremely short and misshapen, the feet being monstrous. His back was round as a camel's, and from his throat down to his waist hung a huge goitre, which gave a still more disgusting look to his *tout ensemble*; added to this, his ears were large and shaggy, his fingers short and stunted, the palms of his hands hard and horny. He was dressed after the usual fashion of the Swiss peasantry in that part of Switzerland, but his clothes were so patched and tattered, that the masterpiece was barely discernible.

I gazed for some moments in silent horror at the spectacle before me, when the monster blocking up my path clapped his hands suddenly on his thighs, and burst into a loud discordant laugh, exhibiting two rows of black, uneven teeth. My blood curdled as the echo of those fiendish tones broke on my ear. I recoiled, but, mastering my fear, I said in his own native tongue—or, rather, in better German than is spoken among the peasantry—"Well, my friend, does my appearance amuse you? Are strangers so rare in your country that they are found worthy of so much notice?"

The idiot gazed at me awhile with vacant stare, then pointed to his mouth, to signify that he was dumb.

"Poor wretch," I muttered to myself; "and yet he seems to understand a little."

I thought I would ask him by signs where he lived. I read by his eye, which suddenly grew intelligent, much to my surprise, that he understood my question, and he answered by gestures, which seemed to say, "My home is here, there, and everywhere. On the black mountain top, in the pine forest, by the still lake—anywhere where there is earth and sky."

"Poor wanderer," thought I; "houseless, like myself, and yet how infinitely more contented. Who knows but that that stunted form may contain the soul of a philosopher."

"Idiot," I said, with all possible meekness in my outward bearing, "I am hungry. Can you lead me to a chalet where I may get food and shelter?"

He nodded his head.

"Bravo!" said I. "Lead on."

The dwarf gave me a peculiar look, which I understood to mean, "What will you give me if I show you the way?"

"Oh, don't be afraid," said I; "I'll pay you well; only make haste; I'm starving."

I put my finger in my waistcoat pocket to make him comprehend that I was willing to reward him, but he glanced contemptuously at my gesture, and, thrusting his hand into his pocket, he brought out a handful of good-sized gold nuggets, which he threw towards me with a disdainful air.

I was amazed, and seeing them glitter in the moonlight, I stopped to pick them up. At this the creature burst out again into a loud laugh. I felt somewhat abashed at this reproof of my covetousness from one who evidently despised filthy lucre himself, but I consoled my conscience with the thought that I looked upon the nuggets more from a geologist's point of view than from a miser's.

"Where did he find the gold?" I asked myself. "Could it really be a great philosopher who stood before me, who despised the yellow metal, or was it an idiot who did not know the value of it?"

These reflections of mine were silent. Nevertheless, the cripple gave me to understand with a nod of his head and an unmistakable look in his eye, that he very well understood what they were worth to such men as myself; but with another gesture he expressed that for himself he was above it.

"Indeed," said I, "then what would you of me, if not gold?"

He gave me a malicious smile, and nodded his head slightly, but I understood not the gesture.

I was impatient, and wanted to put an end to our mummery, so I said, "Come, lead on; I am hungry. Since you despise gold, I suppose you will do so much for me as an act of friendship?"

He grinned from ear to ear and nodded.

"It is well," said I, and I followed my guide.

We began slowly to descend the mountain, my guide running nimbly on in front, then standing still at intervals and beckoning to me. This he continued to do until we arrived at the foot of the mountain, and I remember feeling an irresistible and unaccountable impulse to follow my guide more quickly than before.

As the steel is attracted to the magnet, so I felt irresistibly attracted towards the monster. It was as if he possessed some strange magnetic power over me, for whenever he lifted up his finger to beckon to me I felt it impossible to resist following him.

I thought the feeling might be fancy at first, and I attributed my quickened pace against my own will to the impetus given by the steep declivity of the mountain, but afterwards I found that it was exactly the same on level ground.

We walked on further, till we found ourselves at the foot of a glacier, where stood the chalet which I sought.

I knocked and entered, and was welcomed by the owner of the hut, a middle-aged and portly dame with a goitre that hung over her breast, and some young children with incipient goitres.

I told the hostess that I was a hungry traveller, and asked her to give me the best that she had in the house.

Whilst waiting for my supper I warmed myself by the fire and scrutinised the inmates of the cottage. The children seemed very healthy, and not bad looking, if they had not been all disfigured with the family goitre, which they all inherited in a greater or less degree. They seemed to be great friends with my guide, gambolling around him and buffeting him unmercifully.

At length my supper arrived, consisting of poached eggs, cold sausage and ham, Swiss cheese, stale bread, and some sort of spirit drunk in the mountains. Having concluded my repast, I lit a pipe, and, drawing up my chair to the fire, entered into conversation with mine hostess.

"This is your son, I presume?" asked I of the landlady, pointing to my guide.

"No, sir," she replied; "he is only a poor cretin that I have taken in out of charity, as the children are fond of him. They say in these parts that it is lucky to have an idiot in the house, so, having none in my family, I took in this poor afflicted being; though, as to being lucky, all the luck which I've known since—"

The hostess suddenly stopped in her conversation, and her face became locked and rigid without any apparent reason.

I looked in the direction of the cripple, and observed his glance fixed on the hostess. It was a glance which nearly took my breath away. No wonder the landlady paused in her conversation. It was as if he possessed the gift of the evil eye. The magnetic influence he had over her completely closed her mouth.

Curious to know whether the landlady was really under a spell, I resumed.

"And this unfortunate, besides being idiotic, is he also deaf and dumb?"

The landlady seemed to awake suddenly, as from a dream, and replied, "Alas! yes, sir; no one has ever heard him utter a sound, or even—"

Here she paused again, and again I noticed the creature's glance fixed upon her.

"It is very strange," I observed, following up the conversation, "for I myself this evening have discoursed with him by signs, and so far from being idiotic, I must say that I found him very intelligent."

"Ah, yes, sir," she rejoined; "and if you should want a guide to-morrow, you could not do better than take him. No one knows the mountains here better than he."

"Indeed," I replied; "then he cannot be altogether an idiot."

"Well, as to that, sir, I fancy at times he is more knave than fool. Indeed, I cannot quite make him out. He is an odd being. No one hereabouts knows who his parents were, or how he came in these parts."

Again the landlady ceased suddenly, as before, and I noticed again that the creature's eye was fixed upon her.

"What a very mysterious personage," I resumed, affecting not to notice the magnetic spell the worthy dame appeared to be under. "I am interested in this odd creature. Tell me more of him."

Mine hostess was unable to reply.

"Why do you pause?" I asked. "Why do you not answer?"

The creature's eye was upon me now, and I experienced a curious sensation, as if my voice was suddenly taken away from me, that I had no power to move a limb; in fact, that I was completely in the power of this horrible imp; but rousing myself, I determined to combat against this spell, and I succeeded in stammering a few words with the utmost difficulty. But that fearful eye was again upon me, and my tongue was completely tied; my limbs grew stiff and paralysed, and so I remained for some minutes, till the eye was removed.

"What can this strange feeling be which has just come over me?" I asked. "I never felt so in all my life before."

The cretin's eye vacillated between me and the dame, as if to forbid further conversation. Feeling tired, and not caring for further discourse, as well as glad of an excuse to escape from my friend, whose mysterious power over myself I had already experienced and therefore could not deny, I thought I would take rest until the morning, so I asked for a candle, and was shown into a small chamber with a heap of straw in one corner of it. I partly undressed, and fell asleep.

Thus I reposed till an early hour in the morning, though still dark, when I was suddenly awakened by a terrific snore. I started up, and remained in a sitting position. A pause, then again there was a long, deep-drawn, unmistakable repetition of the same. I fixed my eyes on the spot whence the sound proceeded, and perceived, as well as the darkness would permit, a heap upon the floor in the opposite corner of the apartment.

Who could it be? I was about to strike a light to satisfy my curiosity, though I had but little doubt it was my friend of the previous evening, when the sleeper, to my surprise, began talking in his sleep; and my ill-favoured friend, it seemed, was dumb.

My hand was arrested in the act of striking a light, as the speaker began talking loud and fast and in a very peculiar strain. I was curious to hear more of his conversation; accordingly I refrained at present from striking a light, as the sound might awaken him, and listened attentively.

I wondered much what could be the subject of the sleeper's dream. I grew more and more puzzled at his words. It is impossible for me to give you one hundredth part of his conversation here, even if time permitted; for his utterance was so rapid that he would have outstripped any shorthand writer.

Some part of his strange colloquy, however, I have retained, as I fancied that in it I found reference to myself.

"Fools!" he cried with vehemence; "I tell you the prize is sure. I have him in my power, he *cannot* escape me. Ye who prize blood rather than gold, make ready the chasm to receive him. He is one of those fools who delight in danger, and he will follow me. What think ye? He seeks chasms and grottoes for the insane pleasure of burdening himself with the dross which we beings of a higher order tread under foot. Crystals, fossils, shining stones, the ore of different metals, especially gold and such trumpery, are trifles that his mind (if such it may be called) revels in.

"Do you not believe me, my friends? Ha! ha! I wonder not at your disbelief; ye whose sublime philosophy is nourished in the peaceful bowels of the earth, and who are therefore unable to comprehend how there can exist an order of beings so totally degraded and so approaching the brute, nay, so far surpassing even the brutes themselves in the grossness of its appetites, as to yearn for the very stones which form the pavement and the walls of our subterranean palaces.

"Ye, my friends, who never issue from your cells to visit that outer world, because, forsooth, your eyesight is not formed by nature to endure the glare which illumines the surface of this globe, how is it possible that ye should believe that there exist without intelligences so stunted and depraved? But I tell you, my brothers in philosophy, that this fool belongs to a race of maniacs, who have long attempted to invade our peaceful shores, and even succeeded so far as to penetrate nearly to the roofs of our dwellings—let us be thankful that their frames are not suited to endure our genial element below—with much labour, and for the sole purpose of obtaining metal or some such rubbish out of which they form—

"Tush! I do but waste time in attempting to enumerate the countless uses to which these madmen turn our paving stones. When ye are more at leisure, if ye are content, I will relate to you some of the incredible absurdities of those insects which crawl upon the outward surface of our globe.

"At present, my brother gnomes, we have a great work before us; our wants must be satisfied, and we must adopt the means to satisfy them. We thirst for blood, and we must have it. This fool loves to feast his eyes upon gold, and gold he shall see by the stratum. He but barters his blood for gold, after the fashion of his own vile race. What else can he expect from us?

"It is not often, my friends, that we have a feast of blood. Only now and then when some stray traveller falls into a crevice or impudently approaches too near to the craters of Vesuvius and Etna, till he gets suffocated by the fumes and falls senseless into our maws.

"Happily for us, we are not so constituted as to need sustenance to the extent of those gross gormandisers of the upper world who, would you believe it, my comrades, find it necessary to devour food three or four times a day.

"Ah! well you may open your august eyes at the mention of a vice so brutally preposterous. Thus it is to be sons of clay. We, who are more finely organised beings, of an essence more ethereal, are content to allow ages to pass before we indulge our appetites with a full meal; yet we, too, my brethren, need sustenance sometimes.

"Again we are suffering from the pangs of hunger, and we must be satisfied. Patience, my fellow sages and students of those sublime and abstruse sciences ignored by the gross intellects of our reptile neighbours, patience, for tomorrow I bring you a feast of blood. I have brought you blood before, and I will do so again. It is for this that I have taken upon me the base form of one of the vilest among their own vile race.

"My own comely shape by which I am known here below is ill-suited to brook the atmosphere of the surface world; therefore, partly to excite compassion, and consequently disarm suspicion, I have adopted a loathsome disguise, through which even ye, my friends, would fail to recognise me. At this moment, while I am speaking, the filthy clay that for your sakes I shall don tomorrow lies in the chamber of the victim.

"I am so far able to free myself from it as to speak with you in the spirit, but I much fear that the sympathy which to some extent must exist between my spirit and the fulsome mask that awaits me in the world above, may so influence the organs of the foul body as to cause it to correspond audibly to the voice of my spirit, and so alarm the victim in whose chamber it sleeps, and scare him into flight.

"Therefore my discourse must be brief. There is no time to be lost. At once ye must commence to stir up the internal fires in this earth's centre, and cause a powerful earthquake. The external crust which these mortals inhabit must crack and gape into chasms. I will lead him into the mountains tomorrow when he will be your prey; till then, farewell."

No sooner had the orator concluded his harangue than I began to feel a curious sensation. It was as if the floor on which I had been lying were lifted up under me, and I felt myself rolling from side to side, much in the same manner as if I were at sea. This motion continued and increased, and was accompanied by a low rumbling sound. After a time this grew louder, and I heard an explosion, and then a heavy crash, as if the mountains were being riven asunder, and were now toppling headlong into the valleys, sweeping away whole villages with a force inconceivable.

The whole chalet rocked like an open boat in a storm. I was panic struck, and trembled in every limb. It was then really true all that I had seen and heard; it was no disordered dream. The gnomes were really at work.

Louder and louder grew the rumbling. Crash followed upon crash. All the inmates of the chalet were aroused, and screams of women and children resounded from every quarter. I sprang to my feet, hurriedly donned my coat and boots, and rushed out of the hut, but my fiendish companion was at my heels.

Upon gaining the outside of the cottage I found the face of the country much changed. Huge crags had been loosened, and tumbled quite close to us. Many chalets had been completely crushed under them, and as far as the eye could see all was one scene of desolation.

The terror and the consternation of my poor hostess was pitiable. She gathered her children together as a hen gathers her chickens under her wings, and remained stupefied with despair.

As for myself, having escaped the danger of being crushed alive, my only thought now was to escape my tormentor in the best way I could. The earthquake was at an end, so I strode on in the direction I had followed on the previous day, taking advantage of the momentary absence of the dwarf, who had entered the hut for some purpose or other, and imagined for a moment that I should not be overtaken. Alas! vain hope; hardly had I proceeded for ten minutes, when I heard steps behind me, and lo! there was the hideous elf running after me on all fours, his physical conformation rendering this mode of progression the easiest. I started, and my blood ran cold.

"What do you want?" I asked, angrily, still striding on.

But it was useless. Raising himself on his short legs, he beckoned to me, and I immediately felt myself spellbound.

"Follow me," he signed with a gesture.

"I do not want a guide," I replied. "I am neither in search of crystals, fossils, nor of shining stones; no, nor even of gold."

"Never mind," he seemed to say; "come all the same; I will show you what the earthquake has done."

"I am much obliged to you; but I have seen enough of the earthquake, and I repeat I do not want a guide."

"I do not want your money; I will follow you for friendship," he appeared to say.

"Not even for friendship," I said; "I prefer to walk alone."

"What!" he intimated, "when you can get a companion for nothing?"

"Don't you see, my good man," said I, "that your presence is a bore to me—that I'd rather be alone?"

"Nevertheless, yesterday evening you were glad enough of a guide, and I asked you for no reward for my trouble," he seemed to say with his eye.

"It is false," I replied; "I did not want a guide. I could have found the hut myself."

"That is ungrateful," he said, in his dumb manner. "Did you not ask me?"

"If I asked you," I replied, "I did so for the sake of not passing you without a word; besides, I offered you money, and you refused it. I won't be under any obligation to you," said I. "Here, take your nuggets; I want them not," and I threw them at him. "I'll have nothing to do with one who feigns to be dumb in the daytime, and yet can talk well enough at night."

The cretin gazed scrutinisingly at me for some time, as much as to say, "Ha! ha! my friend, you have overheard my discourse. I thought as much, but no matter; escape me if you can."

He then walked rapidly on in front of me with his short legs, every now and then beckoning to me with his long arms, and I immediately felt myself impelled by a power not my own, and found myself forced to follow the wretch in spite of all my efforts.

"I will not, I will *not* follow you like a victim to the altar," I cried, straining every nerve to control myself. "Vile gnome, thou shalt *not* feast on *my* blood!"

The fiend nodded his huge head slowly with a complacent smile, as if to say, "We shall see, we shall see."

On, and still on, up, further up the mountain, through thick pine forests and gigantic clumps of rock the demon guide led his unresisting prey. Breathless, footsore, over the most impassable places the relentless fiend magnetically dragged me after him; at a rate, too, that thoroughly surprised me; until, to my horror, I found myself close to a deep chasm formed in the rock by the late earthquake.

The demon halted, and now speaking for the first time since our walk together, he asked with a malicious smile if I desired any fossils or any gold, observing that all sorts of curiosities were to be found down there. He then made a strange gesture with his hand towards my face, and I suddenly perceived I was under a spell.

I had no memory of anything that had happened up to that time. I bore no malice against my guide; on the contrary, he appeared to me my best friend. He did not even seem any longer ugly in my eyes, and when he asked me if I would descend into the chasm, I replied cheerfully.

"Yes; but how shall we manage it?"

"I have brought a rope on purpose," said my friend. "Bravo!" said I.

He then began to unwind a long rope from his waist, and adjusted it underneath my shoulders.

I then descended gradually, my companion holding the rope and letting it out by degrees, until I had descended a very considerable distance, when he fastened the other end to a stump. I then began chipping out various geological specimens, and experienced an intense delight in my novel situation.

Soon, however, while busily occupied in extracting a bone of an ichthyosaurus, I was interrupted by a cry of many voices from below.

"Secure the victim! Down with him, down with him! Our feast of blood is at hand."

Then followed a hungry roar, as of wild beasts unfed. The charm was broken in an instant, and I awoke to a sense of my awful position. To drop my hammer and clamber up the rope as fast as I could was my first step; but what was my horror, when, on raising my eyes aloft, I descried the fiend in the act of deliberately cutting the rope. How fortunate I happened to look upwards just at that moment.

The rope was already half cut through; in another moment I must have been launched into the abyss, to be devoured by the bloodthirsty monsters below. There was no time to lose; I was desperate, so thrusting one foot into a chink in the walls of the chasm, I looked about for another, then for some projecting stone to grasp hold of, and thus by slow degrees, at the imminent peril of my life, I climbed up until I gained the ledge of the chasm.

It was a terrific struggle for life. The rope was of immense length, and, deep as I had descended, there was yet an immeasurable gulf below me. The darkness of the chasm prevented the gnome above from seeing his victim, though I could see him well enough. When he severed the rope he knew none other than that I had already been precipitated into the maws of the gnomes below. When, therefore, lacerated and exhausted, I reappeared at the top, the utmost consternation and chagrin were visible in the features of the wretch. Too astonished, perhaps, to think of working another charm upon me, the ogre pounced upon me like a tiger on his prey, and a terrific tussle ensued—a tussle for life and death.

I soon found I was no match for my misshapen, but powerful, adversary. I was soon worsted. Every moment I expected to be my last.

"Can the Almighty allow the fiends to triumph over His own?" I asked myself, in my dying moments.

I offered up a short prayer, and gave myself up for lost. Suddenly a crash. A huge mass of rock above me had loosened. The demon let go his hold to save himself, but it was too late.

The deformed body of the cretin lay crushed beneath the weight of the enormous fragment.

I myself escaped with but a slight graze on the head and shoulder. Had I been one whit less active, I must have shared the fate of my guide. For a moment I stood rooted to the spot, stupefied, bewildered; then, offering up a prayer of thanksgiving for my miraculous salvation, I departed on my way rejoicing.

The last sounds which rang in my ears were the voices of the hungry gnomes, calling out, "Give us our victim; we famish."

But I heeded them not, and continued my journey with a buoyant step. I had a long and tedious walk before me. At sundown, however, I reached the hotel from which I had started.

My friend, of course, had not arrived, as I had returned before the time specified. I know not how it was, whether from the effects of over-fatigue or excessive fright, but I was seized immediately upon my arrival with a prolonged illness. A leech was sent for, the best that the mountains could produce, and after feeling my pulse and looking at my tongue, shook his head gravely. He asked me the symptoms of my case, and to what I attributed it. I told him the story that I have just retailed to you, gentlemen; but he only shook his head again, and said that I was in a high state of fever, that these ravings were but the offspring of delirium, that I had been deluded by my senses, etc. But I knew better, for previous to meeting with the monster I had never enjoyed better health in my life.

★ ★ ★ ★ ★

Need the reader be told that at the conclusion of this narrative the professor was greeted with murmurs of applause from his gratified audience?

"Well, Helen," said our artist, to his fair neighbour, "what do you think of the professor's story?"

The maiden blushed, and smilingly replied in a low voice, that she liked it very much, and then added:

"And are there really those horrid what-ye-call-ums that eat up poor gentlemen all alive?"

"So the professor says," replied Mr. Oldstone. "You would not doubt his word, would you?"

"Oh, no, not for a moment, sir," said the girl; "but how dreadful; I'm sure I shall dream horribly tonight."

"Oh, no, you won't, my dear," said Mr. Crucible. "Don't be afraid;

and, I say, Miss Helen, don't you think you could tell us a story? I am sure Mr. Blackdeed, who comes next on the list, will yield his turn to you."

"Oh, certainly," said the tragedian; "only too happy; besides, it is not every day our club is honoured by a lady."

"There now, lass," said Captain Toughyarn, "if I may be allowed to put in my marling spike, that's the prettiest little compliment you've shipped this many a day. Come, sail along. What! afraid to set sail alongside big ships like ours? Bah! When I was a little craft of your tonnage I did not want so much towing when asked for a yarn."

"The captain's nautical language confuses the young lady," observed Mr. Hardcase.

"Come, don't blush like that, Helen," said Dr. Bleedem, "or I shall think you've got the scarlet fever, and shall be obliged to bleed you."

"Fairest of thy sex," said little Mr. Jollytoast, going down on one knee before the maiden and placing his hand on his heart in the manner of a stage lover, which added to the girl's confusion ten-fold; "say not nay, prithee, say not nay."

"Come, Jollytoast," said Parnassus, "see you not that she will not be courted by importunities. Give the muse time for inspiration."

The members desisted from further persecution, and a slight pause ensued, which was broken by McGuilp, who, squeezing the maiden's hand, whispered, "For my sake, Helen."

The girl blushed deeper still, looked down, and a subdued sigh might have been noticed by the observer.

At length she looked up imploringly, and said, "But what story shall I tell? I know none."

"Oh, nonsense! Come, think," said various members at once.

The girl appeared thoughtful for some moments, then, after giving a half-bashful smile at our artist, turned towards the company, and said, "I will tell you one that my grandmother told me when I was a little thing, if you would care to hear it."

"Too delighted, Helen," said several voices.

The maiden, blushing slightly, and looking down, timidly began her story.

The Landlord's Daughter's Story

The Pigmy Queen: a Fairy Tale

Once upon a time—I think, in Germany, grandmother said that it happened; but I am not quite sure; perhaps it never happened at all; but if it did, it was very far off, and a long time ago, that there lived a very wicked king, who, to increase his power, had leagued himself with the evil one, and used to practise witchcraft. All sorts of witches and wizards were encouraged at his court, and the land soon became insufferable. Many wealthy citizens being persecuted by the malice of these creatures, fled the country.

It happened one day, however, in the very midst of his crimes, that the bad king died, and was succeeded by his son, who proved in every respect the very reverse of his father. He was a good man, of a peaceful and amiable disposition, and who had received an education far superior to that given generally to the laity at that time.

He had married lately a foreign princess of great wit and beauty, and on ascending the throne his first act was to rid his realm of all the witches and wizards which had infested it in his father's time. He threatened with death all those who should be found in the land after ten days.

These tidings were received with murmurs of disapprobation by all these wicked people, who would fain have wrought a charm upon the king to kill him, if they could; but the king, being a good man, was under the protection of the good fairies. Nevertheless, the populace were delighted at this determination of their monarch's, having known nothing but oppression and persecution under the reign of the late king.

A few days after the good king had given out his stern edict he was seated on his throne, with his consort beside him, when he was informed that a poor woman without desired to speak with him.

The king, ever open to compassion, imagining it to be some poor widow oppressed by an unfeeling and dishonest tyrant, who sought redress for her wrongs, ordered her to be admitted into his presence. The guards accordingly made way for her, and a wild, ragged, squalid, and malignant-looking beldame prostrated herself at the monarch's feet.

"O king," she pleaded, "thou who art great and mighty, have mercy on the poor and houseless, and cease to persecute those that do thee no harm. Know that I am queen of the witches, a race much patronised by thy late father of blessed memory, and who were accounted worthy to dine at his table and be his constant companions."

To which the good king replied, "My father's reign is over. Another and more virtuous king now rules the land. My father encouraged the evil, I the good. Ye have heard our order; our word is irrevocable."

Then the hag prostrated herself before the queen, and begged with much fervour that she should intercede with the king for her, that he might milden her sentence.

But the queen replied, "I have no other will than that of my husband, whose sole desire it is to benefit his country by exterminating the wicked. If I granted your request I should be an enemy to my country."

Then the witch queen, rising to her feet and standing erect, spake to the queen and said, "For this inclemency I curse both thee and thy husband; and thy firstborn daughter whom thou shall shortly bring into the world shall be a dwarf, and shall know much tribulation."

At these words the queen was seized with great grief, and the king's ire being roused, he commanded his guards to conduct the hag from his presence. Hardly had she departed when a bright light filled the palace and the queen of the fairies appeared in a chariot drawn by butterflies, and assured the king and queen that the blessings they should enjoy as a reward for not granting the witch's request should counterbalance the curses of the witch.

"Alas!" cried her majesty, "then the witch's curse cannot be annulled?"

"Not entirely," quoth the fairy queen, "but it can be so modified that you shall feel it but little. The witch has declared that your daughter shall be a dwarf, and dwarf she shall be; and that, too, of so diminutive a stature, as not to exceed a span in height. Nevertheless, I will bequeath to her extraordinary beauty and talents, and she shall reign long over a contented people. Great adventures she will have to go through first, but her good judgement will cause her to surmount all obstacles. Furthermore, ye shall have nothing to regret during your lifetime than that your daughter's stature is not equal to that of other mortals."

With these words the good fairy disappeared.

In due time the queen was brought to bed of a female child, so tiny that it was hardly the length of the first joint of the queen's forefinger, but withal of such surprising beauty that the fame thereof spread throughout all the land.

The child grew and increased each day in beauty, until it reached its full growth of one span in height.

About a year after the birth of the young princess the queen was again confined of twins, both girls, rosy and healthy of the average size of babes.

As the three sisters grew up their mother did her best to instruct them in those duties which should fit them for good princesses, as well as good wives and mothers, when a fever then raging through the land—probably part of the witch's curse—carried off the good king and queen almost at the same time, when the eldest princess was scarce eighteen, and the three children were left in charge of a guardian.

Now, as there was no male issue, the Princess Bertha (the name of the firstborn) had every right to the throne. This she knew, nor ever deemed that her right would be disputed; but her younger sisters, who were neither so good nor so beautiful as their elder one, were suddenly seized with envy, and began to plot together in what manner they could secure the crown for themselves. They had never loved their sister nor each other, but they both agreed that the rightful heiress was to be deposed, while each of the twin sisters vaunted herself most fit to govern the country.

Neither of them had the least intention of yielding the crown to the other, though both saw the necessity of wresting it from the lawful heiress, as they said it would be absurd to permit such a farce as a dwarf queen to rule over them. Now, this led to a very hot discussion, which the Princess Bertha, who was concealed from them in some nook in the chamber, happened to overhear.

This envy of her sisters grieved her very much. She herself was not ambitious, and had her sisters been good to her, she would willingly have ceded the crown to them, but seeing their envy, her just indignation was roused, and she was determined not to be thrust aside because she was little of stature, so striding majestically up to them, and drawing herself up to the full extent of her tiny height, she angrily accosted them.

"How is it, sisters, that envy has filled your hearts, and that ye meditate an act of injustice? Know ye not that I am your lawful sovereign? The crown is mine; I will yield it to no one."

"Pooh!" cried both the sisters, with a laugh; "you could not wear it."

"No matter," said Bertha. "I will have one made on purpose."

"You!" answered one of the sisters. "Shall we have a dwarf to reign over us?"

"What has my stature to do with my lawful right to the crown?" quoth the elder. "Think you that I am an idiot as well as a dwarf? Have I not abilities equal to yours—nay, superior. Come, don't let me hear any more of this silly bickering, or I shall find means to punish you both."

These big words, proceeding from such a small body, and from one, too, who had never showed herself of an imperious disposition, but had hitherto allowed herself to be trampled upon and set at nought by them without a murmur, half-startled the twin sisters, and half-provoked their mirth.

They were enraged at such words being used towards them by one whom they thought fit to despise, and knew not what to answer, so they only looked at one another.

Now, there was something in that look which told Bertha that her sisters would make very little to-do about silencing her for ever, if she did not remain quiet; and being so small a personage, to murder her and conceal the murder would be a matter of small difficulty, so she prudently withdrew. But no time was to be lost; one of her sisters might be proclaimed queen if she did not engage the people on her side. So, wending her tiny steps to the foot of the palace stairs, she hid herself behind the hall door.

Now, in the hall were two serving men, who were discussing as to which of the twin sisters should wear the crown.

"Of course," said one, "the poor little dwarf princess won't have a chance."

"Why not?" said the other. "She is the firstborn."

"True," said the first; "if she had her rights, but you'll find that some day she will be found missing, and not likely to turn up again."

"What! you don't mean to say that—"

"Hush!" said the other, putting his finger to his lips.

Now, the Princess Bertha had heard enough of this conversation to make her wary, and perceiving that one of the serving men had his hat on and appeared about to leave the palace, she managed to creep unseen behind his chair, and climbed up into his pocket. Shortly afterwards the serving man rose up to go, and left the palace.

Then the pigmy princess, whilst snugly ensconced in the man's pocket as he walked along the street, began to reflect what should be her next step.

"Within the palace," she said to herself, "all is scheming and envy. I am easily put out of the way when they once get me. I must escape far from the palace and put myself under the protection of the people. At any rate, I'll first have a peep at the world without."

So, thrusting her little head out of the man's pocket, she looked to the right and the left, and found herself in the middle of a large square. There was a great crowd of people, who were looking at a puppet show. The serving man whose pocket she was in also stood still to look. She, too, seized with curiosity, strained her head out of the pocket to take a peep at the puppets.

A play was being acted in which two puppet knights were fighting for the love of a fair lady. A sudden thought struck her. She would join the puppets and mix in the play; it would be a way of showing herself to the public. So she stole out of the serving man's pocket, and taking advantage of the people's absorbing interest in the play, crept stealthily over their feet, till she came to a box full of puppets on the ground. The uppermost puppet in the box was a lady, gaily attired, probably the very lady for whom the puppet knights were fighting, so she laid herself over the body of the doll, so as to be taken by the man when he wanted her, instead of the usual puppet.

The very next moment the showman, who now had to bring the lady on the scene, reached down his hand without looking, and seizing the princess in lieu of the wooden doll, brought her upon the stage.

"Cease your broils," shouted the pigmy princess in her tiny voice. "Is it thus that noble knights waste their precious blood for the love of a woman? Is not the love of a woman at her own disposal—to be granted to the man she pleases? Will she necessarily love the victor, or will he have the arrogance to think that he can conquer her heart as he could conquer a foe? Cease, madmen, and spare your blood to grace the battlefield, or to defend the rights of woman. Ye are not too plentiful, my noble knights. The realm has much need of ye.

"Wrongs enough ye have to redress. What say ye to the grievous wrong they are trying to do the Princess Bertha, by pushing her aside, who is the firstborn, because they deem her too small to take her own part? But ye noble knights, who love justice, will assert her claim to the crown throughout the kingdom, and defeat the insolent champions hired by her envious sisters, who would defraud their own royal sovereign.

"Proclaim throughout the land that ye will have none other to rule over you but the rightful heiress—the Princess Bertha."

After the princess's harangue, the showman, who had long dropped the other puppets in amazement, believing that none other than a fairy trod his stage, stood with his eyes and mouth wide open, knowing not what to do. The spectators were in ecstasies at so beautiful and so natural-looking a puppet, while the crowd increased ten-fold.

The serving man in whose pocket Bertha had hidden herself had never seen the princess, for he was not one of the servants of the palace; besides which, the diminutive princess was usually hidden from the vulgar gaze, the family being rather ashamed of her than otherwise; but one among the crowd, who happened to have seen the princess once or twice on rare occasions at the palace, cried out, "By my troth, that is the Princess Bertha herself, and none other! How comes it that she is made a puppet of in this man's vile show? Citizens, I arrest this man for high treason!"

The little princess, seeing the showman in danger, said to the gentleman, "No, worthy sir; do this man no harm, seeing I came here by my own free will, without his knowledge, for the purpose of making the country acquainted with its future sovereign."

The gentleman pushed his way through the crowd, and was about to lay his hand on the princess to bring her back to the palace, when a monkey near at hand, also the property of the showman, and who happened at that moment to be loose, seized the diminutive princess in his arms, and clambering up the side of a house by the water spout, was soon out of sight.

Now, when the news of this catastrophe reached the palace, the twin princesses were delighted that harm was likely to befall their elder sister, so that their right to the throne might be no longer disputed; nevertheless they ordered a strict search to be made for the body of the little princess.

Two parties, each headed by one of the princesses, started in different directions to search for the missing sister, but for a long time nothing was heard of her. Wearied at length with long search, the Princess Clothilde, one of the twins, gave out to her followers that she had found the body of her elder sister, but that it was so far decayed that she could not permit anyone to see it; so, making believe to wrap up the body of the princess with a handkerchief, she carried it under her cloak and returned to the city, shedding false tears as she went.

Having arrived at the palace, she ordered a coffin to be made just large enough to contain the corpse she was supposed to have found, and when it was ready she filled it with rubbish and ordered it to be interred with due honours.

Now, at that time there were two factions, one voting for the Princess Clothilde and another for her sister Carlotta. It was decided, therefore, that each should choose a champion, and she whose champion should prove victorious should rule the land.

Great were the preparations for this grand spectacle. Two stalwart knights, the stoutest and the ablest that the land could produce, each of whom had gained great reputation for feats of arms, faced each other to decide their cause. The day had arrived for the combat, and the jousts were crowded with all the great people of the land. The combatants appeared, and charged at each other furiously, but the good fairies who had already prophesied that the Princess Bertha should reign, willed not that either of the champions should win, and they caused a thick mist to rise between them, by which means they could neither of them see the other; nor was the sound of their horses' hoofs audible.

The spectators, finding that nothing could be decided on that day, went away discontented, and the fight was deferred till the next day. Again the combatants appeared in the lists, and no obstacle seemed likely to interfere with the combat; but at the moment they commenced to charge at one another the good fairies, through their art, rendered their horses so ungovernable that each knight had enough to do to preserve his seat, and this continued all day.

A second time the spectators were disappointed, but they insisted upon the champions making a third trial. The third day arrived, but with no better success, for this time the fairies struck both knights and both horses with paralysis, so that neither could move an inch, but stood looking at each other all day, like two fools.

At first the people laughed at so droll a sight, but at length getting impatient, they heaped showers of abuse upon the two champions, calling them fools and cowards to be afraid of one another. Other champions at length took the place of the former, but the good fairies again interfered, using all sorts of impediments, so that neither could vanquish the other, and this lasted for many days, until the people despaired of ever witnessing a fight again.

Let us now return to the Princess Bertha. The fright that she experienced at finding herself in the grasp of this horrid monkey caused her to swoon away but on recovering her senses she found herself on the top of a tree in the midst of a forest, still in the monkey's grasp. It was out of her power to escape, so she thought she would try and ingratiate herself with her captor, so she said, "Good monkey, do me no harm, for I am a king's daughter and the rightful heiress to the crown. When I am queen I will grant you any boon you ask."

"Agreed," said the monkey; "I will hold you to your promise, for I am not a common monkey, but an enchanted prince, forced to wear this loathsome form through the malice of the witch queen in the reign of the late king, because I would not wed her daughter."

"Alas! poor monkey," said the princess, "and how long art thou doomed to wander about the earth in this disguise?"

"Until the death of the witch queen," said the monkey, "when I shall resume my customary shape."

"Ah," said the princess, "there is then hope that I may yet attain to the stature of my fellow mortals, for I, too, am under her curse."

While thus discoursing together a passer-by, perceiving the monkey in the tree, but without seeing the princess, aimed a stone at the poor ape with such force on the back of its head, that it fell senseless to the foot of the tree. The princess deeming the animal dead, grieved much for it, and called after the man who threw the stone, scolding him; but her tiny voice was unheard, and the man was already far off.

Left alone on the top of a tree in the middle of a forest, what could she do? She began to look around her, and on the next branch she saw a crow hatching her eggs.

"Good crow," she said, "I am a king's daughter, have pity on me and carry me on thy back to a stream, for I thirst."

"I will carry you thus far," said the crow, "if you promise to grant me a boon when you wear the crown, for I am not a common crow, but an enchanted queen suffering under the evil spell of the queen of the witches."

When the princess had promised to grant her request the crow suffered her to mount on her back, and away she flew till she came to a winding stream, where she left the princess, saying, "I must now return to my eggs."

The princess having quenched her thirst, began to reflect upon the step she should next take. She knew not which way to wander, and did not care much, as long as it was far away from her sisters. She knew that the good fairies protected her, and believed in their promise that she should be queen. Whatever hardships she might have to encounter she made up her mind were for her good. All day long she wandered by the side of the stream, over the rough stones, with her tiny feet, subsisting on berries and roots, and thus she wandered for some days without adventure.

At length, one day, having arrived at the top of a high cliff which overhung a lake, and which she had ascended to see the country that lay before her, her dress caught in a thicket, and she heard the sound of horses' hoofs behind her. It happened on that day that her two sisters had joined a hunting party and passed by in that direction.

The rest of the party passed over without observing her, but her sister Clothilde, who was behind the rest, suddenly caught sight of the little princess's shining robe, and dismounting, came up to her, saying, "So I have found thee at last, minx; but think not to live to prove my tale false," and with that she spurned her pigmy sister with her foot, so that she fell over the cliff.

A stone which she dislodged at the same time fell into the water with a splash, and Clothilde, fancying that it was her sister who caused the splash, and that she was now hidden for ever at the bottom of the lake, rode off, rejoicing that she had rid herself so cleverly of her hated rival.

But the Princess Bertha, instead of falling into the water, was caught half-way in the web of an enormous spider, who made towards her as if to devour her; but she said, "Good spider, harm me not for I am a king's daughter, and when I am queen I will grant thee whatsoever boon thou askest."

"I will remember thy promise," said the spider, "for I am no common spider, but an enchanted prince, and a victim to the malice of the witch queen."

Thereupon the spider seized her gently with its legs, and letting out its thread, descended carefully with her to the bottom of the cliff. Then the spider left her, and she was once more alone on the brink of the lake.

Presently she heard the sound of a woodcutter's axe on the opposite bank of the lake. She would speak with the woodcutter, and tell him her tale; perhaps he could help her, but how was she to cross? She looked around for a moment, and saw some water lilies. One of the leaves was detached and seemed floating slowly on by itself. This she managed to reach, and it was sufficiently strong to support her light form; then, spreading out the scarf that covered her shoulders towards the wind for a sail, she was slowly wafted to the opposite shore.

Now, as she was about to land, it happened that her foot slipped and she fell into the water, uttering a slight scream. The woodcutter, who was resting from his work, had his eyes fixed on the lake, and perceived with surprise the pigmy princess sailing towards the shore. When, therefore, he heard the scream, small as it was, he rushed down the bank and seized her slight form in his huge hand. The princess, however, was already insensible, but the good man wrung her clothes dry and kept her in his bosom until she should recover. Now, during her swoon the queen of the fairies appeared to her in a dream, and told her that the woodcutter was the man she was destined to marry and to go at once with him to a cave hard by where lived a holy hermit, whom she had already commissioned to marry them.

Then, leaving her a magic wand which changed any object she touched into whatever she pleased, she disappeared, enjoining her to use her own judgement in everything.

Upon this she awoke, and found herself still in the woodcutter's bosom. Now, the woodcutter was a young man of a stature approaching the gigantic, immensely powerful, but very ugly, very clumsy, and very stupid. At the first sight of him the princess recoiled, and could not make up her mind to take him for a husband; but then she thought that the fairies must know best what was for her good, so she reversed the generally received order of etiquette and made him a proposal of marriage.

The young man simpered, scratched his head, and looked very sheepish; but having heard the princess's story, and being assured by her that the fairies had ordained it so, he turned away his head, blushed, and accepted her.

Then the princess, finding the magic wand beside her, waved it over her head, and instantly converted the peasant's ragged clothes into a suit of mail, his axe into a lance, a knife that he wore at his side into a sword; while the tree that he had just felled, she converted into a magnificent charger. She then bade him mount and place her within his helmet, close to his ear, so that she could give him any instructions that might be necessary without being observed by anyone.

Then asking Hans (which was the name of the transformed wood-cutter) whether he knew where the hermit lived whom the fairy had mentioned, and receiving an answer in the affirmative, she bade him put spurs to his horse, and in a short time they arrived at the mouth of the cave. The recluse rose to meet the man in armour.

"Good day, fair son," quoth the holy man. "What would'st thou of me?"

"Holy father," said the knight, "I have come to get married."

"And the fair bride?" asked the hermit.

"She is with me."

"With thee! I see her not."

"Here, holy father, here," cried the princess, emerging from the helmet of Hans. "I am the Princess Bertha, and have been command-ed by the fairies in a dream to call at thy cell with my betrothed that we may be joined together in holy matrimony."

"I know it, O illustrious princess," said the hermit, with deep rev-erence; "and doubt not that I shall discharge my duty. May it please your royal highness to enter the abode of the humble?"

"Dismount!" cried Bertha in the ear of her betrothed, suddenly, as if to wake him up, for the simple youth looked as if he intended to remain on the horse's back all day.

Hans dismounted clumsily, and nearly tripped himself up with his pointed iron toes.

"Now, then, tie up the horse to a tree and enter the cave, and don't look such a fool," said the princess.

Hans entered the cave, and placed himself in front of the rude altar, having unclasped his helmet and deposited his bride on a large stone near.

The hermit lit candles, opened the mass-book, and the ceremony began. As the moment for putting on of the ring drew near, a faint and distant music, together with a perfume like incense, seemed to fill the cave. Then followed a bright sunbeam, through which swam troops of fairies. Then the distant sound of trumpets was heard, and the troop made way for the chariot of the fairy queen, who, stepping out of her car of mother-of-pearl and precious stones, and standing upon a cloud of incense, handed Hans the wedding ring, and bestowed a benediction on the happy pair.

It was no easy task for Hans' clumsy fingers to place so small a ring upon so tiny a finger, but at length by the aid of a needle brought to him for the purpose he accomplished the feat, and the marriage ceremony over, the knight and the lady rode off in the same fashion as before.

Now, it may be thought by some, perhaps, that these two were ill matched, but that only shows how the whole world may be deceived by appearances, for they were most admirably mated. It is true they had little in common with each other, but for that very reason in this case, at least, they pulled well together. Bertha was physically weak, but then Hans was strong. Hans was as stupid as an owl, but the princess was as clear sighted as an eagle and as cunning as a fox. Bertha possessed the brains and Hans the brawny arm. Each was a type of those two items which go to make up the most perfect human being—mind and matter.

In this case the husband was not the head of the wife, but the wife the head of the husband, and a very clear little head it was, too. The princess was ever concealed in her husband's helmet, close to his ear, to give him sage councils, which he, as you shall hear farther on, often had occasion to put into practise by his superior physical strength.

The world would have chosen for Hans some rough daughter of the soil, as stupid as himself, and as nearly as possible of his own dimensions; but this sort of wife, however well she might have suited Hans in his former contented existence, would never have raised him into the hero that he afterwards became.

The humble woodcutter, beneath his rough exterior, had hidden seeds of greatness which were destined to be developed in a new soil. Our knight and his lady did not profess to love each other very much, just because they were married; indeed, how should they upon so short an acquaintance; but that was not necessary, for love is one thing and marriage another, as all the world knows. Enough, that each had need of the other at present.

Now, the first thing to be done was to ride to the city, and for Hans to proclaim the right of the Princess Bertha to the throne; and should any other champion come forward for either of the twin princesses, it was meet that they should do battle for their cause.

"Therefore, Hans," said the princess, "ride quickly to the town, and proclaim my rights. Pass over yonder hill where stands a ruined castle."

"Let us not pass thither, fair princess," said Hans, "for yon castle is inhabited by a terrible wizard, who has lived here since the reign of your highness's grandsire, who, you will have heard, rather encouraged these sort of people than otherwise, and whom no power can force to flee the country, for as soon as the king's guards approach the castle he enchants them into rocks and fir trees."

"Oh, oh! we will see about that," said the Princess Bertha. "So this man is a dangerous character. I do not intend to allow any dangerous person when I am queen. Come, we must subdue this man."

"But—" remonstrated Hans.

"But me no buts, Sir Shaveling," quoth the princess, "but do my bidding. Must I lend thee courage as well as wit? Onward, I say."

Hans could ill brook being called a coward, and that, too, by a woman—such a little woman, too—so, crossing himself, he put spurs to his horse and ascended the hill till he arrived at the gate of the castle.

"What do *you* want?" said the wizard, suddenly making his appearance at the window.

"Say," said the princess in the ear of her husband, "that you have come in the name of the Princess Bertha, our future queen, to bid him flee the country."

Hans cried out in a loud voice as he was instructed by his spouse. The wizard answered with a loud laugh, and descended the staircase.

Now, the princess knew that evil charms availed not against good ones, so, touching her husband with her wand, she thus made him proof against any magic power of the wizard.

"Wait a bit," said the magician, descending; "you will be no harder task to manage than the rest have been, I'll warrant," and he proceeded to draw a circle on the ground and to mumble a spell.

"Enough of this mummery," said Hans, at the instigation of the princess. "Prepare to leave the country at once, or you die."

"These words to *me*, you churl!" cried the wizard, pale with rage. "Dost know who I am?"

"I know, and I defy you—both your arms and your spells."

Then the wizard, mortified at finding that his charm failed upon Hans, entered his castle in great wrath, put on his armour, and came forth mounted on a black charger with fiery eyes, and ran at Hans furiously with his lance, but the lance was shivered into splinters against the magical armour of Hans.

The wizard then seized his two-handed sword, and Hans seizing his, a terrific combat ensued. At length Hans smote off the wizard's head at a blow, and the bleeding carcase dropped from the saddle. At the death of the wizard his fiery charger was instantly changed into a fir tree, and his castle into a rock.

"On this spot," said Bertha, "I will erect my palace," and waving her wand over the rock, a magnificent palace arose where had stood the ruined castle of the wizard, made of gold, silver and precious stones, with windows, each pane of which was a sheet of diamond.

Hans had hardly recovered his surprise at his unexpected victory over the wizard, when he turned his head and observed the magnificent palace that the princess had magically erected. He stood aghast, with his eyes and his mouth wide open, and seemed beside himself with amazement.

"Onward, you fool; don't stand gaping there; onward towards the town."

Hans clapped spurs to his horse, and halted not until he arrived at the gate of the city.

Then entering, he stood in the middle of a large square where there was a great crowd of people, and receiving instructions from the princess, called out to the populace: "I proclaim the Princess Bertha the rightful heiress to the crown. Whoever would depose her and set another on the throne in her stead, let him come forth and do battle."

Then some of the crowd cried out, "The Princess Bertha is dead; we have seen her funeral. Who art thou, that speakest so boldly?"

"I am the champion of the Princess Bertha, eldest daughter of the late king, and whosoever says that she is dead, lies."

So saying, he lifted his tiny spouse from his helmet with finger and thumb, and showed her to the people. Then a great commotion arose. There were some among them who recognised the princess, and admitted her right to the throne. Others said nay; that it was a puppet, and voted for the Princess Clothilde. Others, again, shouted for the Princess Carlotta.

Presently the two first champions appeared who had fought together—one for Clothilde, and the other for Carlotta, and they both called out, "We ignore your Princess Bertha, for it is well known that she is dead. In vain you exhibit your dwarf or puppet, for we have seen her funeral."

"Then," said Hans, at the dictation of Bertha, "it is false; the body was never found, but one of her intriguing sisters, anxious to usurp the crown, gave out to her followers that she had found the body, and ordered a mock funeral."

"Thou liest, thou liest!" shouted the two knights, both at once.

"Let it be put to the proof," said Hans. "Let the coffin be disinterred, and if the body be found therein I will lose my head on the spot where I stand; but if the body of the princess be not found therein, then shall ye, the champions of the two usurpers, lose *your* heads."

"It would be sacrilege to disturb the dead," said the knights. "We cannot agree to the proposition."

But the people called out, "It is well said; 'tis a fair trial."

The two knights began to remonstrate, but their voices were drowned by the herd, who wished the matter settled by the disinterment of the body.

When the commotion had ceased a little Hans lifted up his voice, and said to the multitude, being instructed, as usual, by his spouse, "It is the pleasure of the Princess Bertha, whom you now see before you, that she be taken instantly to the presence of the arch-priest of this city, who has known her well from infancy, and who baptised her. He, as you all know, citizens, is a man of good repute. Should he recognise the Princess Bertha, let her have her rights; but if he says it is another like to her, let the coffin of the supposed defunct be opened publicly, that all may be satisfied."

"Sacrilege, sacrilege!" cried the knights.

"No, no!" cried the populace; "the stranger knight has well said. It is most fair. To the arch-priest, to the arch-priest!"

The crowd made room for Hans, and conducted him to the palace of the arch-priest. When the good man saw this great crowd in front of his palace he came out to demand the reason, and was informed that the Princess Bertha, whom all believed to be dead, had returned to the city with a champion who was ready to maintain her right to the crown, provided that the arch-priest himself, who knew her well, should testify to her identity.

"Show me this champion," said the priest.

Hans then rode up, and holding in his hand the diminutive princess, placed her in the hands of the arch-priest.

The crowd pressed hard together while the aged priest took out his spectacles and examined the tender form minutely.

"In good sooth," he exclaimed, "it is the Princess Bertha and none other. My fair princess, what treachery has been at work to deprive thee of thy rights?"

"You know me then, holy father?"

"Know thee, daughter," quoth the old man, tenderly. "Methinks it were difficult to make a mistake."

"You hear then, O people," cried the little princess, straining her feeble voice to its utmost pitch, till it resembled the squeaking of a fife; "you hear that the venerable arch-priest has recognised me."

"Ay, ay, your royal highness; long life to you, and welcome to the throne!" cried the populace.

Then a great cheering arose.

"Long live the Princess Bertha, our rightful queen!"

But some of the faction for the Princess Clothilde called out, "It is false; she is dead and buried, we will not be imposed upon by this man and his dwarf."

"The arch-priest recognises her," cried others. "The arch-priest dotes; he is mistaken," cried they for the Princess Clothilde.

"Let the coffin of the princess be exhumed!" cried the crowd, and they appealed to the priest, who consented that the coffin should be opened in the presence of all the people.

"Where is the undertaker?" cried one of the crowd.

"Here!" cried a voice.

"Let him come forward."

Then the crowd made room for the undertaker, and one amongst them asked him if he had placed the late princess in the coffin with his own hands.

He replied in the negative.

"Who closed the coffin, then?" asked the former questioner.

"The Princess Clothilde herself," answered the undertaker.

"That seems suspicious," said another; "she also is said to have found the body, which she concealed in her cloak and allowed nobody to see."

"Because," answered one of the faction, for Clothilde, "because the body, being already in an advanced state of decay, she was unwilling to make a disgusting exhibition of the remains of her sister, who she so dearly loved. We are witnesses of her emotion upon finding her sister's body."

"It is false," cried Hans; "the Princess Clothilde is a hypocrite and an usurper, and has plotted to obtain the crown for herself."

"Treason, treason!" cried the faction for Clothilde. But those in favour of the Princess Bertha applauded the words of Hans, and cried out, "We shall see if the remains be in the coffin."

After waiting some little time longer, the coffin was exhumed and given into the hands of the arch-priest, who, standing upon the balcony of his palace, opened the coffin with his penknife in the presence of all the crowd, and found therein nothing but cinders, which he emptied into the street below.

"I hope now, citizens, you are convinced that foul play is at the bottom of it all," said the old priest.

"Ay," cried the crowd, "most vile treachery—down with the Princess Clothilde; we will have none to reign over us but the Princess Bertha."

"Stay a moment," shouted the champion for the Princess Clothilde. "What was there in the coffin if not the body of the Princess Bertha?"

"Nothing but dust and ashes," answered the arch-priest.

"A sign that decomposition has already taken place," responded the former. "That is no proof that the princess Bertha was not buried in the coffin."

But the crowd laughed him to scorn, saying that it was scarce a fortnight ago since the princess was missed, and that it was impossible the body should have decomposed so rapidly.

The arch-priest then gave his word of honour to all present that he had found nothing in the coffin but cinders from the grate.

One of the crowd below picked up a cinder which had fallen from the coffin, and cried out, "The holy father speaks the truth, for the coffin contained nothing but cinders of burnt wood."

Then the champion for the Princess Clothilde, fearing that all were siding with Bertha, called out in a loud voice, "Long live the Princess Clothilde!"

But the crowd hissed, and showed signs of disapprobation.

Then the other champion for her twin sister called out, "Long live the Princess Carlotta!" but he, too, was hissed.

Then spake out Hans.

"Whoever objects to the Princess Bertha being queen, let him do battle with me."

Hans then threw down his gauntlet, which was immediately picked up by Clothilde's champion.

Our little princess took refuge once more in her husband's helmet, and whispered in his ear to keep his lance steadily directed towards the breast of his foe, and then, touching him with the wand again, she rendered him proof against all mortal harm.

The adversaries charged together, and so violent was the shock with which Hans came upon his foe, and so accurately did he direct his lance, that the deadly weapon pierced through the massive breast plate of his enemy and came out at his back.

Hans, whose natural strength was terrific, and which was increased ten-fold by the magical touch he had received from his spouse, whirled the dead champion at the point of his lance two or three times round his head, and then flung the body to an incredible distance over the heads of the crowd.

The champion of the Princess Carlotta, seeing the fate of the other champion, would fain have drawn back, for he thought Hans could be none other than the foul fiend himself.

But the crowd cried out to him, "Thou, too, votest for the Princess Carlotta."

"Ay," he was constrained to say.

"Do battle for her, then," said Hans.

Carlotta's champion sullenly laid his lance in rest, and aimed at a portion of Hans' vast body which seemed least protected; but the point of his lance got entangled in the shirt of mail that Hans wore beneath his plate armour without doing further injury to him, while Hans' lance pierced through the left eye of his foe, and passing through the back of his skull, helmet and all, pinned him to the ground, whilst his horse galloped off through the crowd.

Now, the news of the return of their sister and the defeat of their champions soon reached the ears of the twin princesses, who knew not how to contain their rage; but the Princess Clothilde, the more wily and wicked of the two, bribed her followers with large sums of money to feign to vote for the Princess Bertha, and thus make friends with this stranger knight, and invite him into their houses, to offer him a cup of wine after the fatigue of the combat, which, when unobserved, she commanded them to drug, and as soon as he was insensible he was to be carried off to prison and loaded with chains, care being taken to secure the Princess Bertha at the same time.

Hereupon all those who had formerly voted for the Princess Clothilde commenced to shout, "Long live the Princess Bertha!"

But the little princess, suspecting treachery—for she recognised the faces of the men who now shouted for her as being the same as before shouted for her sister—warned her spouse not to receive any man's hospitality but the arch-priest's, telling him that if he disobeyed her command it might cost him his life.

Hans promised to obey, but when he saw so many well-dressed gentlemen of the court come forward to offer him their congratulations and invite him so cordially to their houses, being very simple and unsuspicious, he forgot the warning of his spouse, though she did all in her power by pinching and biting him to make him remember, and he accepted the invitation of a certain lord, imagining his spouse's vehement urging to be nothing more than the bite of a flea.

"Fool!" cried the princess, "you will ruin both yourself and me;" but Hans paid no attention, for he was hungry and thirsty.

The great lord who had invited Hans to his mansion possessed all the polished manners of a courtier, though he had a very black heart, and easily working himself into Hans' affections, he locked his arm within the arm of Hans, and led him to his home.

"May I also have the honour of entertaining Her Royal Highness the Princess Bertha?" asked the nobleman.

"Oh, yes," said Hans in his simple manner; "she is inside my helmet. I'll bring her, too. You see, she being small and I being large, it is the only way we can discourse together."

"Ha! ha!" laughed the nobleman; "an original idea. By all means let me have the honour of entertaining my princess."

Hans was charmed at the affable manners of the nobleman, and arrived at the mansion, took a seat at the lord's table, where he was introduced to other men of high rank, who all congratulated him on his prowess, and expressed their delight at having made his acquaintance.

A meal was speedily prepared, and wine handed round.

"Drink not," whispered the princess. But Hans, deaf to all counsel in the presence of so many genial companions, accepted glass after glass, until he was in a state bordering on intoxication. Now, Hans was a good man, and a true, but he had one small failing, which was an inclination to tipple.

He could never refuse a good glass of wine when he was among boon companions. He had also a most ravenous appetite, and afforded the other guests much amusement by the clownish manner in which he devoured his food, as well as by his brutal stupidity and broad peasant's brogue.

When the wine had loosened his tongue a little he soon informed the nobleman of his former condition, saying he was no knight of the court, but a humble woodcutter, and would take no notice of the signs made to him by the princess to keep quiet (who now, by the by, was seated on the table before him, Hans having unbuckled his helmet) but went on eating and drinking, and chatting and laughing, in a manner ill-suited to his dignity as champion, to say nothing of husband to the princess.

The Princess Bertha was treated with the respect due to her rank, and was pressed to partake of something, but she refused, pleading no appetite.

When the host observed that the wine had got into Hans' head, he motioned to some of the guests to engage the princess in conversation while he administered the drug.

Then, taking a paper containing a powder from his pocket, he emptied it into a goblet of wine which he offered to Hans.

But the princess, who observed this, said to the host, "May it please your lordship to drink first this toast—'to the prosperity of our kingdom.'"

The nobleman looked confused, and stammered out that he hoped that Her Royal Highness would excuse him, as he, a humble individual, could not think of tasting the cup before so illustrious a guest.

"Then you refuse to do me this small favour, my lord?" said Bertha.

But before the host had time to reply Hans had already grasped the goblet greedily and drained it dry. The effect was not immediate, but after about twenty minutes Hans fell back in his chair in a state of the most perfect insensibility.

"I am afraid," said the host, "that your Royal Highness's brave champion has partaken a little too freely of the contents of my cellar. It is an accident that is apt to befall the best of us. I am sorry for his state, though I cannot but feel it a compliment to my wine."

The princess answered not save by a look of scorn. Then, fearing that the nobleman would offer to remove her to another room while he procured men to remove the helpless body of her spouse, as well as secure her person, and bring her, in spite of herself, into her sister's power, who was sure to make away with her secretly, she touched herself with her wand, and instantly she became invisible.

The lord searched the chamber in every corner, for his first object was to make himself master of the person of the princess, but failing in finding her, he next began to unbuckle Hans' armour, and examined every plate as he stripped him of it in his careful search for the tiny princess. He grew more puzzled than ever at not finding her, and ordered the other lordlings to search the house. This they did for an hour or more without success, when, fearing that Hans might awaken from his trance, he ordered a litter to be brought, upon which he securely bound our champion.

The helpless knight was then borne upon the shoulders of four strong men, and carried to the common prison, where he was fettered hand and foot, and left in a dungeon, deep, damp and chilly, being in a state of unconsciousness all the while. The princess, however, though invisible, followed her husband. If she had chosen, she could have rendered him also invisible, and spirited him away out of harm's reach, but she would not.

"No," she said to herself, "let him reap the fruits of his folly. He will learn better by experience than by my precepts. I will not come forward to help him until the last."

Now, when Hans was left alone in his cell—that is to say, alone save the invisible presence of his spouse—it was already getting late. The effect of the potion was to last for five hours, during the whole of which time—and who knew how much longer—the princess was doomed to breathe the damp air of a dungeon and to wallow in the filth therein, shivering with cold; without a fire, without her supper, and frightened to death lest the large rats that infested the prison should make their supper off her or her husband; but she recollected the wand.

The first thing she wanted was a light, for it was pitch dark, not merely because it was night but because the dungeon was underground. Feeling a stone at her foot, she touched it with her wand, and it became a candle, so brilliant as to light up the whole cell perfectly; but what should she do for a fire? There was no fireplace or stove, no place where the smoke might escape.

"With this wand, I shall want for nothing," she said, and touching the wall of the prison, that part of it was instantly converted into a magnificent fireplace, with a chimney and a most comfortable fire.

She proceeded to warm herself, but soon she felt there lacked something. She was hungry, so she touched the ground, and instantly there arose a little table spread with a white tablecloth, and a little chair just big enough for herself. Still, there was nothing on the table as yet, save empty plates, with knives and forks, but at that moment she noticed a great rat gnawing her husband's toe. She hastened to drive it away, and in doing so touched it with her wand, when it became a roast hare.

Then, touching a stone, it became a loaf of bread. A piece of bottle glass that she found on the dungeon floor became a bottle of wine; and finding there were no vegetables, she changed a blue-bottle fly into a dish of spinach; a spider into some turnips, and a handful of earth from the floor into some salt, after which she proceeded to carve.

Having partaken sufficiently of the first course, she changed the remains of the hare into an apple tart, and the vegetables into different sorts of fruit. Thus she obtained all she required.

Having finished her supper, the princess waved her wand, and the supper table, with everything on it, chair and all, disappeared through the floor; then, seating herself by the fire, she waited for her spouse to awake.

In about three hours her worse half opened his eyes, and stretching his gigantic limbs, gazed about him in stupefied astonishment.

"Where am I?" he asked, with a yawn.

"Where thou deservest to be," answered the princess, with severity, drawing herself up to her full height. "A pretty position, I ween, for the queen's consort—drugged and cast into prison! Maybe that another time thou wilt pay more attention to my words; but the worst has not come yet. Thou art to be handed over to the malice of my two sisters. Who knows in what manner they may reek their vengeance? If thou escapest with thy life, thou wilt be fortunate.

"Prepare, then, for thou hast brought all this on thyself by despising my counsels. What! is a man like thee to be at the head of the realm? *Thou*, with thy brutish appetite, thy dense stupidity and deafness to the voice of wisdom? A pretty example to thy subjects, forsooth! Or thinkest thou that the strength of thine arm alone will suffice to govern the kingdom? I tell thee, brainless boor, that whatever your besotted notion of a king may be, it is a post that is no easy task to fill, and woe to him who aspires to the title and is not able to discharge the duties belonging to it.

"Knowest thou not futurity will judge thy action, that thy name is destined either to honour or disgrace the page of history? That a king must not only be brave, but wise, just, good, merciful, temperate?"

"Enough, O royal spouse, most august princess," answered Hans. "Enough for the present; but tell me first how I came here, and next how to get out again, and for the future I will always listen to thy counsels, though allow me to observe that it was thy will to make a king of me rather than mine own; therefore, if thou hast hit upon the wrong man, methinks the blame is thine. And I had known when I was an humble woodchopper that to be a king I must bear this splitting headache, lie in a dungeon full of rats, to be hanged perhaps on the morrow, besides having to kill so many good hearty fellows just because they happen to differ a little in opinion from your Royal Highness, I should have said, 'The devil take all the kings and kingdoms in the world; I'll e'en abide here and chop wood.'"

"Hush!" cried the princess, with asperity, "and offend not our royal ears with such clownish sentiments. It is but natural that thy rude nature should rebel against counsel that is intended for thy good. It is to be hoped, however, that with time thou mayest be brought to a right view of the great destiny that thou hast to fulfil.

"I confess that had I not been specially commanded in a dream by the queen of the fairies to take thee and raise thee to the throne, I should never of myself have chosen so clownish a helpmate."

"Well, for the matter of that," said Hans, "dreams are things that I don't often trouble my head about, as I never had one come true in my life. Many is the time I've dreamed I had my pocket full of gold, and waking in the morning, devil a *groat* have I found within it; but maybe it is not so with you princesses, who are a different sort of grain to us poor beggars; and perhaps fairies appear to you in dreams and tell the truth; but whether that is or is not, I know not, being no scholar."

"Well, Hans," said the princess, "thou art not far wrong in not trusting to every dream, or in believing there are certain privileged individuals to whom dreams are given as a warning, as consolation, or as prediction of good fortune; but thou oughtest no longer to doubt, after what thou hast seen and gone through; that thou thyself since thy nuptials hast been under the protection of the good fairies.

"Has not everything gone right so long as thou didst hearken to my voice; and did not thy good luck desert thee solely when thou didst refuse to listen to my warning?"

"Well, wife," said Hans, "I believe thou art about right; d— me if I'll ever be such a fool again."

"Hush, sir!" said his spouse. "No oaths in the presence of royalty, if you please. Such language befits not the mouth of a king."

"Well, well, have it thine own way," said Hans. "I'll try to improve, only let me have a little sleep now—I am tired."

"That's right, husband mine," said the princess, seeing that her husband was more docile; "I do not quite despair of thee yet. Thou mayest be the right man after all. The fairies know better than I. Sleep, and arise tomorrow a wiser man. Yet another thing thou must bear in mind, however, thou must try to unlearn that horrid peasant's brogue of thine. Dost hear?"

"Ay, that will I, royal spouse," replied Hans, in a brogue as broad as before. Then, turning on his side, was soon fast asleep. The princess, however, slept not a wink that night; the excitement of the day and the thoughts of what might possibly occur on the morrow kept her wide awake, and thus she remained until the morning, when she was suddenly alarmed by the sound of footsteps, and four men entered. Bertha instantly made herself invisible again. The foremost of these men advancing, and shaking Hans roughly out of his sleep, informed him that it was the pleasure of the princesses that he should be brought instantly before them. Hans started up, and would have been violent, but his chains prevented him.

"Where is the princess?" asked he, looking round him.

"What princess?" asked the man.

"The Princess Bertha—our future queen, and my lawful wife," replied Hans.

"The Princess Bertha!" exclaimed one.

"Your wife!" laughed another.

"Why, the man's mad, or else is not quite sober yet," cried a third.

"Stay," said the fourth; "it is possible he has got the dwarf princess concealed about his person. So much the better, we shall get them both together, and divide the reward between us. Let us search him."

"Ha! is that so?" said the first.

A rigid search was made on the person of Hans, but they found not the princess.

"Hold there, ruffians!" cried Hans. "Ye shall do the princess no harm. Do you hear; for, besides being your rightful queen, she is my wife."

A general laugh ensued. Hans was no less puzzled than the men themselves at her disappearance.

"Where can she be?" quoth he. "All last night she was watching beside me, like a true wife, and now—"

"Come, the fellow is dreaming still, or else trying to befool us," cried one of the men, at length. "Let us hasten with him to the princess."

Hans was then conducted into the palace, and led into an amphitheatre, where the late king was wont to listen to stage plays, singing, recitations, and such like.

The theatre was crowded, and in a conspicuous place he noticed the Princess Clothilde and her sister Carlotta.

"Welcome, Sir Peasant Knight. Welcome, Sir Woodchopper," said the princesses, mockingly.

"We have heard of your great deeds of yesterday, Sir Knight," said the Princess Clothilde. "Surely such bravery deserves a reward."

Then, turning to one of the men who accompanied Hans, she added: "Give the brave knight the reward he merits."

The men had previously been instructed how Hans was to be treated, so one of them proceeded to strip him to the waist, whilst another took from behind a column a cat-o'-nine-tails, with which he belaboured the naked shoulders of our knight with such force that he drew blood at every stroke, while the spectators applauded and the princesses laughed.

Hans bore his flogging without wincing, though his back was streaming with blood. The Princess Bertha was with her husband all the while, though invisible. She was touched at the cruel spectacle, and her blood rose in indignation against her sisters, yet she would not yet come forward to assist her husband. He had been in the wrong, and he must take the consequences of his folly. She pitied him from her heart; she admired, too, the fortitude with which he endured such pain and indignity; but she had his good in view. She knew that, as a child is taught to know better another time by one good flogging, so her husband, who was nothing but a child in mind, must be cured by the same remedy.

"The loss of a little blood, as our leeches say, is good for the health occasionally," remarked Clothilde. "Besides, as your knighthood is well aware, a knight, whose trade it is to shed blood, must not wince if now and then a little of his own is shed."

"How thinkest thou, Sir Knight," asked Carlotta, "that a back *sanglant* would look in thine escutcheon?"

These, and such like gibes were thrown at Hans, who treated them all with silent contempt.

At length Bertha, observing by the countenance of her spouse that he had had enough, thought it high time that the tables should be turned, and the spectators punished for their barbarity, so she whispered thus in her husband's ear:

"I am with thee. Now that thou hast suffered the consequences of thy disobedience, take thy revenge upon thine enemies."

So saying, she touched his fetters with her wand, and they snapped.

Hans needed not this prompting. Finding himself free, his suppressed wrath having increased his natural strength to that of a Titan, he sprang up the steps of the amphitheatre, and seizing the throat of the Princess Clothilde with his right hand and that of her sister with his left, he squeezed them with such force, that it was a wonder both were not killed outright. However, they certainly would have been, had not one of the lords, whom Hans recognised as the same false lord who had invited him to his house, and afterwards drugged him, instantly interfered.

Hans left go the throats of the princesses, who fell, to all appearances, dead, and who did not recover till long after, and, seizing the sword of the false lord, which he had drawn against him, he snapped it in two across his knee, and threw the pieces into the arena. Then, seizing the lord himself by the collar and by the seat of his hose, he flung him with such violence over the heads of the people, that he fell headforemost after his sword, and his brains were dashed out.

Shouts of "Murder!" and "Treason!" were heard on all sides.

"Seize the miscreant!"

The four men who had led Hans before the princesses came forward, and would have secured him, but Hans, brandishing in one hand a piece of his broken chain of great weight, broke the skull of the foremost, the back of the second, the ribs of the third, and the shins of the fourth.

Some few others now attempted to seize Hans, but there was something so terrible in his aspect as he furiously fought his way through the crowd, knocking down one with his fist and another with his chain, that they prudently drew back, and every spectator took refuge in flight before the ungovernable fury of Hans.

Then the Princess Bertha, making herself again visible, ordered Hans to carry her to her two sisters, who had just recovered consciousness. Standing upright in the palm of her husband's hand, she addressed them thus:

"Are ye not ashamed of yourselves to treat a brave knight in this spiteful manner? Mean spirits that ye are; but ye are rightly served. Nor is this all; there is more in store for ye. Your ambitious scheming is seen through, and the good powers protect the right. Ye shall live yet to see me crowned, together with this man, whom I now declare to be my husband. The coronation will take place tomorrow, in spite of all your puny schemes. Farewell!"

The two princesses were so enraged at the words and bearing of their little sister whom they had persecuted, that they knew not what to reply, but turned red and pale by turns, stamped their feet, bit their hands, tore their hair, and screamed.

"Let us go to the arch-priest," said Bertha, to her spouse. "Go just as thou art, half-naked and bleeding. All the world shall know how these princesses treat brave knights."

So saying, the Princess Bertha left the amphitheatre in the hand of her gigantic husband, leaving her two envious sisters behind, foaming with rage.

Hans hastened through the streets, his back covered with weals and streaming with blood, towards the palace of the arch-priest. The people recognised him as the knight who had vanquished the champions of the twin princesses on the day before, and asked him how he came in such plight.

Then Hans, being instructed by Bertha, answered thus:

"Good people, you all see in me the champion of the Princess Bertha, who is ready to shed his last drop of blood for her sake; and these wounds that you see have not been inflicted in a fair fight, but by treachery. After I vanquished the two champions of the twin princesses several lords of the court came forward to congratulate me on my success, and invited me into their houses. I, contrary to the orders of our most august princess, whom I now hold before ye (cheers from the populace), and who, more wily than I, suspected treachery, contrary to her orders, I trusted too easily to false appearances, and accepted the hospitality of one of them. He invited me to his house, gave me to eat and to drink, and when I had well eaten and drunk, he drugged my cup, and cast me into a dungeon underground, where I remained all night, and was fetched away this morning, loaded with chains, only to be brought into the presence of the two usurping princesses and flogged before the whole court.

"But it pleased the good powers to loosen my chains, and I have given some few of them their deserts. Follow me, all ye that love justice, and proclaim the right of the Princess Bertha to the crown."

"Long live the Princess Bertha, our rightful queen," cried the mob.

"Prince Hans, our rightful king," cried the princess. "I here declare in the presence of all men that I am already married to this brave knight!"

Tumultuous cheering ensued this speech of the little princess, and shouts of "Long live King Hans and Queen Bertha" followed them until they arrived at the palace of the arch-priest. Hans knocked at the door. The servant who opened it started back in surprise and horror at the half-naked and bleeding figure of the visitor.

"What do you want?" he asked, rudely, as yet not noticing the princess.

"I want the arch-priest. Who else did you think I wanted," responded Hans, equally roughly.

"The arch-priest is not at home to everyone," said the menial, haughtily. "What's your business?"

"Come, let us in immediately, and don't stand prating there. I am the Princess Bertha," said the dwarf princess.

"I crave your Royal Highness's pardon," said the servant, bowing low. "I did not observe you," and he allowed our pair to enter without further opposition.

"What is all this?" exclaimed the arch-priest who came to meet them. "My little princess, with her champion naked and bleeding!"

"Holy father," said the princess, "we wish to be crowned tomorrow. See that preparations are made for the occasion."

The arch-priest bowed to the ground.

"Your Royal Highness's will is law. Is there no further obstacle to the coronation?"

"None; and if there were, I'd conquer it as I have done the rest. See that my spouse and I are crowned tomorrow in presence of all the people," said the princess.

"Your spouse!" exclaimed the arch-priest. "I knew nothing of it. He is not what he seems, then—he is of royal blood?"

"Royal blood or not, he is my lawful spouse, and he is to be crowned," said the princess, firmly.

"But, my dear princess," answered the priest, "if he is not of royal blood, how can I?"

"Enough," said Bertha. "I have the warrant of the queen of the fairies that he is to be my partner in life. Here is my certificate of marriage."

And she produced a paper five or six times as big as herself, which she handed to the priest.

The priest opened it, and glanced through it.

"What!" he exclaimed. "Then he really is of royal blood. I see. What is this paper enclosed? Ha! a pedigree." And he began to read, "Prince Hans Wurst, son of King Blut Wurst, lost in early youth and picked up by a woodcutter, with whom—"

"You see," said the princess, "how the fairies befriend me. This second paper must have been placed here by their hands, for this is the first time I have set eyes upon it. Are you content with the information therein contained?" asked the Princess Bertha.

"Perfectly, your Royal Highness," said the arch-priest, bowing.

"Tomorrow, then, it must take place, father," said the princess.

"Without delay," replied the priest. "But, tell me, what on earth brings His Royal Highness Prince Hans here in this pitiable plight?" Bertha then began to recount the misadventures of her knight and the spite of her envious sisters, the detailing of which filled the poor old priest with horror.

"But, at any rate," said he, at the conclusion of the narrative, "let the prince's wounds be healed. Send for a surgeon."

"A surgeon! Bah!" cried the princess. "Behold, sir priest, what one favoured by the fairies can do," and thus saying, she touched her husband's back with her wand, and it instantly healed so that none could see even the slightest scratch.

"Gramercy!" quoth the arch-priest; "I never before beheld such a miracle. Thou art indeed favoured of the higher powers."

"Does that surprise thee, holy father? Behold another wonder," said Bertha, and she touched the back of Hans a second time with her wand, and instantly her semi-nude champion was covered from head to foot in an elegant royal dress, composed of a crimson velvet tunic, half-way to the knee, and trimmed with ermine, and silken hose of a buff colour.

A gold-hilted sword, in the form of a cross, hung by his side, within a bejewelled scabbard, likewise a dagger. A chain of massive gold about his neck, and a graceful barrette, with a white ostrich feather, which was fastened by a huge diamond. The arch-priest started back several paces, rubbed his eyes, and, looking first at the princess and then at Hans, and then at the princess again, he took her in his hand, and whispered in her ear that he hoped it was not witchcraft, and being assured by Bertha that it was not, he smiled, and congratulated Prince Hans on his improved appearance.

Hans, suddenly discovering that he had undergone a change, called for a mirror, and was shown into another chamber, where there stood one large enough for him to look at himself at full length. Our prince began to admire himself, and to cut all sorts of capers, at which the arch-priest laughed heartily; but Bertha reproved her spouse for his levity, and told him such antics did not become a king.

The prince immediately ceased his tricks, and taking leave of the arch-priest respectfully, left his palace with his little wife in the breast of his tunic.

As he opened the palace door, he saw standing at the gate his own charger, gaily bedizened. The animal had been sent to await him at the arch-priest's palace by the fairies. Hans mounted, and proceeded to show himself to everyone through the streets of the city, while the crowd shouted, "Long live King Hans and Queen Bertha!"

Now, Bertha knew her twin sisters too well not to suspect them of treachery up to the very last.

"It is certain," said she to herself, "that they have sent spies after us. They will not rest until Hans, at least, is killed."

Looking round in the crowd, she spied a man whose face pleased her not, and who glanced furtively at Hans. She observed, too, that he carried a long rope with a slip-knot over his arm. Her natural penetration told her that danger would proceed from that quarter, so, touching her husband's neck with her wand, she said:

"Be as hard as iron and as immovable as a rock."

They rode on together till they came to a large square, when suddenly the man with the rope, watching his opportunity, threw the cord over the heads of the people, so that the slip-knot fixed itself round the throat of Hans, and the man pulled with all his might and main to throttle him and to drag him from his seat; but instead of accomplishing his object, the rope did no more harm to Han's neck than had it been the trunk of a tree, while the horse and his rider proceeded as before, dragging the man behind after them; nor could he leave go the rope, for the princess had wrought a charm on him, and thus he was dragged through the city in the sight of all men, hooted and pelted by the crowd as he was dragged along.

As for Hans, he felt the rope no more than had it been a spider's web. The report of the strength of Han's neck spread throughout all the land, and all declared that that alone was sufficient to qualify him for the crown, accordingly, on the following day great preparations were already made for the coronation, which was to take place in the cathedral of the town.

The doors of the church were crammed with the equipages of all the lords and ladies in the land, amongst which were the carriages of the Princesses Clothilde and Carlotta, who had arrived, each with an escort of armed men, to prevent the coronation of their sister, but the mob was so violently in favour of the Princess Bertha, that the escorts were beaten back. The little princess, however, gave orders that her sisters were to be admitted, so the twin princesses took their seats to witness the ceremony.

Now, a man had been bribed by them to be close to the person of the prince all the time, and the moment the crown was being placed upon his head to stab him in the back; but Bertha, still suspicious of treachery, looked around her and saw the man, who was just in the act of assassinating her husband, when, waving her wand in time, she converted his dagger into a venomous serpent, which twisted itself round his body, and bit him that he died.

Great was the uproar and surprise at this scene, and the crowd were ready to tear the twin princesses to pieces; but the arch-priest commanded them to forbear, and the ceremony proceeded without opposition.

Suddenly a soft music was heard throughout the cathedral, and a perfume as of incense arose. Then a sunbeam from one of the upper windows in the church revealed an innumerable multitude of little fairies, two of which carried a little crown between them, just big enough for the head of the pigmy queen.

The multitude was struck with awe and the two sisters filled with fury at the sight; but the ceremony passed off quietly. Nevertheless, the twin princesses, dreading the mob, stepped hastily into their respective carriages, and drove back to the palace.

When King Hans and Queen Bertha drove off in their carriage, which, by the way, was made by the fairies themselves for the occasion, the mob was half-blinded by the brilliancy of the jewels with which it was inlaid, and our new sovereigns were cheered by the crowd till they arrived at the palace door.

Now, the two princesses, instead of yielding up the palace to the rightful owners, had ordered the door to be barricaded and entrance refused to the royal pair, which, when Bertha discovered, she immediately waved her wand in front of the palace, and changed it into a prison filled with gloomy cells, and the gay clothes of the people within into the squalid garments of prisoners, while the golden bracelets of the princesses became manacles for their wrists, and their garters fetters for their feet.

Then, waving her wand in the direction of the prison in which her husband had been confined, which stood not far off, it became a magnificent palace, equal, if not superior, in grandeur to that which she erected upon the ruins of the wizard's castle, so that all wondered, and shouted, "Welcome to Queen Bertha, and down with the twin princesses!"

The man who had attempted the life of Prince Hans with his lasso on the day before was publicly hanged with his own rope on the roof of the prison where the two princesses now languished as an example to all rebels.

After the wicked princesses had been imprisoned for a week the tiny queen released them on condition that they should flee the country and not show their faces again. The sisters heard their sentence in sullen silence, and quitted the country shortly afterwards, amid the curses of the crowd, and established themselves in a foreign land, where, out of spite, they gave themselves over to witchcraft, and leagued with the queen of the witches, who was also exiled there, to work all sorts of spells upon their sister from afar; but they all failed, as the pigmy queen was too powerfully protected by the fairies.

King Hans grew in wisdom every day under the sage counsel of his spouse, till at length his subjects bestowed on him the name of "The wisest and the bravest king living."

In proportion as Hans' intelligence and good manners improved, grew the love of Bertha for her husband. They soon knew how to appreciate and respect each other, till at length there was not a more loving couple in the whole world.

About a year after King Hans and Queen Bertha had ascended the throne a war broke out between his and a neighbouring country. The latter was the same land where the wicked princesses had fled into exile, and this was to be the seat of war.

One day, as the queen was seated in the boudoir of the palace in a pensive attitude, while her husband was putting on his armour, previous to departing for the war, she was startled by a sound of chattering, screeching, and the fluttering of wings. As she was about to ring the bell for the servant to inquire the meaning of this strange noise the door opened, and an ape and crow entered, followed by a large spider, which, making towards the queen and bowing low, cried out, "A boon, a boon! O gracious queen, according to thy promise."

And immediately the little queen recognised the ape that had escaped with her from the hands of the showman and carried her to the top of a tree, the crow that had carried her down again and left her on the banks of a stream, and the spider that had saved her life by catching her in its web and carrying her safely to the bottom of the precipice, when her cruel sister Clothilde thought to rid herself for ever of her rival by precipitating her into the lake below. She remembered that she had promised a boon to all three when she came to be queen.

"A boon, a boon!" chattered the monkey.

"A boon, a boon!" screeched the crow.

"A boon, a boon!" whispered the spider, whose voice was less strong than the other two, being an insect.

"What boon do ye ask?" demanded her majesty.

"Change us to our proper forms again!" cried all at once. "We have heard that thou possessest a fairy wand. Disenchant us, O queen, and give us back our natural forms."

Queen Bertha then waving her wand over the head of each, they suddenly resumed their respective shapes. The ape and the spider became two handsome youths, while the crow took the form of a comely and dignified matron in the habiliments of a queen. Each of the two youths recognised the other, though after a lapse of many years, as his lost brother, and rushed into each other's arms.

The venerable lady who had hitherto figured as a crow, but who was neither more nor less than a queen herself, recognised in these two youths her long lost sons, and they, in their turn, recognised the late crow as their mother, and fell upon her neck and kissed her. The old queen wept for joy, and knew not how to thank Bertha for what she had done.

"O favoured of the fairies!" pleaded the mother of the two princes, "think me not bold if I further trespass on thy benevolence and crave another boon."

"Ask, and it is granted," quoth the smaller queen.

"I have yet another son and I know not what has become of him— my eldest boy—also three daughters, whom the queen witch has metamorphosed into a bat, a toad, and an owl. Let me set eyes again on my eldest son, if he, indeed, be living, and, prithee, O gracious queen, disenchant my daughters."

"It shall be done," responded the pigmy queen, and waving her wand, there immediately flew through the window, which was open, an owl and a bat, the owl bearing in its beak a toad by the leg, which it immediately dropped on entering the royal boudoir, and the three stood in a row before Bertha.

"Obnoxious beings," said the pigmy queen, "resume your respective forms."

So saying, she waved her wand over each, and they were suddenly converted into three beautiful maidens, who immediately recognising their mother and their two brothers, fell into their arms and devoured them with kisses.

At the same moment that the three unsightly objects made their appearance at the window the door opened, and in walked—who? Hans, clad in complete armour, and the old queen recognised her lost eldest son. Hans remained stupefied at the group before him; then, when everything was explained, he wept upon his mother's neck, and embraced his brothers and sisters.

But Hans had little time to lose; his army was about to march, so taking a hasty farewell of his relatives, he placed his diminutive spouse within his helmet, as was his wont, and mounted his charger. His two younger brothers, Otto and Oscar, were determined to follow him to battle, so Queen Bertha changed two black pigs that had strayed into the palace garden, and were uprooting the plants, into two fiery war horses, nobly caparisoned, and the three brothers started for the war, while their mother and three sisters waved their handkerchiefs after them until they were out of sight, and uttered prayers for their safe return.

Now, this war had been brought about by the evil spells of the queen witch and Bertha's two malicious sisters, who, wishing to avenge themselves on their pigmy sister, caused the monarch in whose country they lived to pick a quarrel with King Hans, which should lead to a war, by which they hoped to be the gainers. But Hans and Bertha were in favour with the good fairies, and the luck was, as usual, on their side.

The foreign monarch's city was besieged, and many put to the sword. The king himself, together with the witch queen and the two wicked sisters were taken prisoners. The witch queen was burnt alive publicly, as a punishment for her many sins, and the twin sisters imprisoned for life. Queen Bertha was naturally of a benevolent disposition, and would have pardoned her sisters, but her prudence conquered this feeling, and she deemed it expedient to put it out of their power to do harm to anyone by shutting them up in prison, where, after languishing for some years, they died still impenitent.

After the death of the witch queen the spell which she had wrought upon Bertha while yet unborn was broken, and the pigmy queen took suddenly to growing, and increased each day six inches in height, till she reached the stature of an ordinary full-grown woman.

She preserved her surpassing beauty till her death, and lived to bless her husband with a family of twelve children.

Hans' two brothers returned unhurt from battle, and lived with their mother and sisters in the splendid palace that Bertha had raised on the spot where had stood the wizard's castle.

King Hans lived to a good old age, and died a good man and wise monarch.

★ ★ ★ ★ ★

It would be in vain to describe the enthusiasm that prevailed as Helen concluded her fairy tale. Any story that partook at all of the marvellous was sure to meet with thorough appreciation, whoever might be the teller; but when the sunny dreams of fairyland were shaped into words by lips so rosy as those of our host's daughter, Methuselah himself might have felt his blood boil in his veins.

All the old fogies of the club felt their youth suddenly restored to them, and it was all they could do to keep themselves from falling prostrate at the feet of the fair story-teller. As for our artist, he had lost his heart long ago. Here was a pretty to do! As for Helen, I'm afraid that she had caught the complaint. What was to be done? Well, never mind at present; perhaps the dart may not have struck very deep.

But here comes our host, who, roused by the boisterous cheering of the guests, has come to call away his daughter to her meal. And high time, too, unless he wishes all their heads to be turned by this bewitching enchantress.

The eulogiums on Helen's beauty, manners, and powers for story-telling lasted until dinner time, and such an impression had her story and manner of telling it made upon all, that no one felt inclined either to relate or listen to another, and the club actually retired to rest that evening without a story.

The Tragedian's Story

The Haunted Stage Box

The following morning was bright, clear, and frosty. At an early hour two of our guests were to leave the "Headless Lady" by the mail for London. These two were Captain Toughyarn and our comic friend, Mr. Jollytoast. Each had urgent business on hand, and the other members of the club had risen to see them off.

Breakfast had been laid for these two worthies; their companions seated themselves at the same table, and chatted with them whilst waiting for the stage-coach.

"Well, captain," said Mr. Oldstone, "after you return from your next voyage, you'll visit us again and have another dream over our punch like that last one of yours, won't you?"

"Ay, ay, messmate," replied the captain; "you may be sure of that. That is to say, if we are all still in the land of the living. I'd come, even if I had no other inducement than the bright eyes of our host's pretty daughter."

"Avast there! captain," said Mr. Jollytoast. "Remember the mermaid! Think of Lurline! Take care, lest Helen should prove even more dangerous."

Just then the horn of the stage-coach was heard in the distance, and in a short time the horses were at the door. Our two travellers took their seats, after having been repeatedly invited to return, and some jovial sallies having passed between our host and the driver over a stiff glass of grog, the coach started, and was soon out of sight. After their two friends had departed the rest of the club set out together for an hour's stroll before breakfast, to enjoy the fresh morning air, walking all of them abreast, and taking up all the carriage road.

The way was long and lonely—not a soul stirring, and the landscape as far as they could see covered with snow; but the sky was cheerful, and the little birds sang overhead. Our club felt exhilarated by the nipping air, and discoursed by the way on divers subjects, until Mr. Oldstone, whose appetite for stories was insatiable, said that he saw no reason why Mr. Blackdeed's story that was to come next should not enliven their walk. The proposal was seconded, and Mr. Blackdeed, finding himself loudly called upon, began his story thus:

I must begin, then, gentlemen, by informing you that my family name is not the one I bear at present. It is many years since I dropped that. My father was of good family, and possessed a large estate in —shire. I was an only son, and should have inherited my father's estate, had not a rascally uncle of mine cheated me out of it.

I was looked upon as a lad of great promise by my fond parents, and from earliest youth seemed destined for the stage; for as far back as I can remember my greatest delight was to see a pantomime. I was more precocious than the general run of children at my age, for at an age when few children have begun to read I was already manager of a toy theatre. This taste of mine grew with my growth, and was encouraged by my parents—probably because they saw it was an innocent amusement and kept me out of mischief.

At ten years old I began to write plays, in which I used to act myself and invite my schoolfellows to act with me. This rendered me very popular at school, both with the boys and with the masters, and I won many a prize for public speaking and for learning by heart long passages from Shakespeare and other poets.

At fourteen I grew ambitious, and published a book of plays under my own name, which, unluckily, was cut up unmercifully by the critics. This was mortifying enough, but added to this I had to bear my father's displeasure for having published the book under his name, my parent believing it a great disgrace for a son of his to write books or plays. So he gave me a severe reprimand, and from that time forth thought it his duty to discourage my taste for the drama. But nature will have her own way, in spite of whatever obstacles parents, and friends place in her path, and at fifteen I yearned for the mysteries of the "green room."

I had secretly, but no less determinedly, set my heart on following the stage as a profession, and one day my father took me into his study, and said it was high time I should make up my mind what profession to follow. I replied that I had made up my mind already what profession to follow. I told him that I intended to be an actor.

167

At this he told me to get such ideas out of my head as soon as possible, that he would never allow a son of his to disgrace his name by associating it with the stage.

I repeated my determination. He grew furious, and after beating me, locked me up in my room and ordered bread and water to be brought to me by a servant. This treatment, he told me, was to last until I had come to my senses. However well this mode of proceeding might have answered with a youth of less spirit, it did not answer with me. Even an ordinary boy of fifteen is no child, and I at that age was equal to a man of twenty.

I felt the indignity of this treatment as an excessively sensitive organisation would. I refused to touch either the bread or the water, and meditated an escape from the paternal roof, never to return.

Now, it happened that at that time there was in the village a band of strolling players, who had hired a barn to act in. These I had been in the habit of seeing act every evening, till my passion for the stage was augmented to an intense degree.

The players were to leave on the morrow. Here was an opportunity! I would wait till the evening, escape by the window of my chamber, and offer my services to the manager. I looked down from my window into the garden, to ascertain if I could venture upon a leap; but it was much too high for me, yet there was a ladder against the wall, though not near enough for me to reach.

What was I to do? I tied sundry pocket-handkerchiefs together, which I wetted. I then tied an ornament that served as a paper weight, being rather heavy, and holding one end of the wet handkerchief in my hand, I threw the heavy end towards the ladder, which it caught, winding itself round one of the rungs so tightly that I was enabled to draw it towards me and place it just under my window, ready for the evening.

The evening came. I waited till my parents were at supper. This was just about the time that the evening's performance would be at an end. I donned my worst clothes, and tying up some necessaries in a handkerchief and taking a walking-stick to carry the bundle across my shoulder, I opened my casement and cautiously descended the ladder till I found myself in the garden.

There was yet another obstacle to be overcome; the garden wall had to be scaled, for the gate was already locked. The wall was high, but after much exertion and many falls, I scrambled up—I hardly know how—and leapt down the other side into the road. I found that I had ripped up my coat behind and damaged the knees of my small clothes.

In this plight I made my appearance before the manager. He looked at me from head to foot, scrutinisingly; asked me my name and what I had been bred up to. I gave him the name I bear at present, and said that I had never been brought up to any trade, but had always had a taste for the stage.

"Humph!" he muttered, observing that I spoke better English than himself or his company, "you appear a youth of some little education—eh?"

"I trust that will not unfit me for your company?" I said.

"On the contrary, young man," he said, "we are in want of educated actors; but what brings you in this pitiful plight?"

"The frowns of fortune," I observed, laconically.

"Ah!" he observed, with a smile; "I understand. Well, what can you do?"

"My *forte*," I replied, "is high tragedy."

"Ah! I dare say," said he, satirically, "and I've no doubt you'll tell me that Macbeth, Hamlet, and Othello are your chief characters."

"Precisely so," I replied; "that is just what I mean to say."

"I thought so," he said. "My dear young man, you're stage-struck like many others at your age. All you youngsters, when you begin, fancy that you are going to leap over the heads of us old experienced actors with a bound; but in everything you must begin at the beginning, and you will have to serve your apprenticeship at acting as well as anything else."

"Serve my apprenticeship!" I muttered to myself, indignantly. "*I*, the son of a gentleman, serve an apprenticeship!"

But I held my peace, as it did not suit me to quarrel with the manager at the onset.

"You must content yourself at present with small parts," said the manager, "such as a page or walking gentleman, or, being yet very youthful looking, you might take a female part."

The latter part of the manager's speech offended my dignity, but I said nothing.

"Come," said he, "let me see what you can do. Give me your idea of Hamlet. Begin with, 'To be, or not to be.'"

I accordingly began at the well-known passage, and recited it all the way through.

"Not so bad, by jingo!" said he. "Bravo! I did not think you were such a clever fellow. Now do the dagger scene in Macbeth."

I then went through that with equal success, and received very high praise from the manager, who engaged me on the spot. I gave out a hint that I had eaten nothing all day, and was very hungry, so the manager invited me to supper. I made the acquaintance of all the other strolling players—a queer lot—who looked at me askance, doubtless because they saw I came of a rather better stock than they themselves, and probably they speculated on what they could make out of me.

Early the next morning we all started for London, and my *debut* was made in a low London theatre, where I took the part of a young lady carried away by brigands. In the next piece I acted a page, in the next a lover, and so on. But I soon grew discontented with this small theatre, for I longed to show myself to the educated public, so I left my first manager, and sought an engagement in some more fashionable theatre.

Here I had to act a fairy prince in a pantomime. The pantomime was a great success, and drew many spectators. At the same time that the pantomime was going on, I had to act a page in one of Shakespeare's plays. I was now seventeen, and both tall and well grown, and possessed at that time—I think I can afford to say so now, gentlemen, as I am verging at present towards "the sear and yellow leaf"—a figure and a face that were the envy of the whole company.

Well, gentlemen, I improved fast in my profession, and one evening when the play of Romeo and Juliet was being acted at the theatre, the actor who should have taken the part of Romeo was indisposed only a few minutes before the curtain drew up. There was no one else in the company but myself who was sufficiently up in the part to take his place, so I offered my services, and they were accepted.

Now, Romeo was one of my favourite characters, and I had studied the part carefully; but the manager knew nothing of my talents as yet; in fact, he confessed to me afterwards that he was very doubtful as to the success of the piece that evening.

When the curtain drew up and the piece proceeded, I fancied I noticed signs of discontent among the audience at not finding the usual Romeo, but as I went on with my part the applause was so great that I felt as if my reputation were established for life. In fact, I completely eclipsed the actor whose part I had taken, inasmuch that the public refused to hear him again in that part, and the manager allotted his part to me.

This led to great jealousy between us. We quarrelled, and I made this the excuse for leaving the theatre, being anxious to appear in a still more fashionable one. I sought an engagement in one of the largest theatres in the metropolis, and as I already had some fame, I was engaged at once. The manager had seen me perform himself, and promised me when Romeo and Juliet should be acted again in his theatre that he would give me the part of Romeo. They happened to be acting Hamlet then; and the part of Laertes was allotted to me. I acquitted myself with much *eclat*, and a long and favourable criticism appeared in the papers afterwards.

One evening I took the part of Hamlet, the usual actor not being able to perform, and acquitted myself so well that the papers were full of the wonderful young actor. From this time my name began to be famous. I received a good salary, dressed fashionably, and entered into the best society. Nevertheless, I was aware of the prejudice that the world has against an actor, however celebrated he may be, so whenever I went into society, I dropped the name of Blackdeed, and resumed my own rightful one. Many, however, on being introduced to me remarked how much I resembled the celebrated young actor Blackdeed; but it was not for some time afterwards that it was generally known that we were one and the same person. One evening, as I was entering a ball-room, I noticed that when my name was announced some confusion took place. As I entered, who should come forward to meet me but my father, whom I had not seen for three years. He advanced towards me, more in sorrow than in anger, and addressed me in tones in which pride and natural affection strove for the mastery.

"We meet at last, sir," he said; "I leave it to your conscience to imagine the state of anxiety into which you have thrown your poor mother and myself by your cruel conduct. I would fain have overlooked the whole as a boyish freak, had you returned home of your own accord and sought my pardon; as it is, what can I say to you for having disgraced my name?"

"Disgraced your name, father! How?"

"Yes, sir; disgraced my name, by associating it with the stage—a name untainted and highly honoured for many generations back."

"Indeed, sir," I said, "I never yet heard that talent or genius could disgrace a name. However, aware of your prejudice against the stage, I have dropped your name, which might otherwise have become famous, and act under a fictitious one."

"Humph!" said he, somewhat pacified that his name had escaped disgrace. "And what may be your theatrical name?"

"Blackdeed," said I.

"What! So you are the celebrated young actor everyone talks so much about," said he. "Well, well, you have been very foolish and very wrong, but if you consent to leave this life and return home with me, all may yet be well. Come," he said coaxingly.

"Father," I said, "my course is mapped out. I have chosen my profession, and I must follow my true avocation. The voice of nature is stronger than yours. Seek not to battle against my destiny."

My father, though immensely disappointed at my determination, would not, I believe, have cut me off, but dying suddenly, intestate, his estate was seized by his brother. This led to a law-suit between my uncle and myself, which lasted until nearly all my father's fortune was squandered away. I never got a farthing. Thus ever since I have had nothing to depend upon but my profession for a livelihood.

It now began to be rumoured abroad in society that I was none other than that very Blackdeed whose acting had created such a *furore* in the world. It also began to be said that I was the heir to an immense fortune, out of which I had been swindled by an unprincipled uncle. I met those who knew my family well, and my misfortune procured for me the sympathy of many. I possessed a still greater interest in the eyes of the world now, and I found myself a greater lion than ever.

On one occasion after I had been acting Romeo at our theatre I donned my dress clothes and dropped in late at a friend's house where there was a ball, and here I made the acquaintance of a certain family who resided not far from my father's house and knew my father intimately. The family consisted of an elderly gentleman, his wife, and three daughters.

The two elder sisters were very ordinary young ladies, such as one is sure to find in every ball-room. They were neither pretty nor ugly; their manners conventional, their conversation flat and insipid. When talking to one they appeared to be thinking of something else, and their answers were generally in monosyllables.

The youngest daughter, however, differed much from her two eldest sisters, both in mind and in features; so much so, indeed, that I imagined for some time that she must be their step-sister, but this was not the case, as I found out afterwards. Maud—that was the name of the younger—was by far the cleverest really of the whole family, and

yet she was looked upon as a ninny by the rest. She had more originality in her than either of her two sisters, as I soon observed from her
remarks; but she was also more retired, and preferred to hide her light,
as it were, under a bushel. It was only now and then that I could catch
a glimpse of it, but when I did so it was most brilliant.

Without being strikingly beautiful, her face had that in it that cap-
tivates more than mere beauty. The expression was ingenuous and
pensive, at times melancholy. When in society she never seemed like
one of the herd, or to take the slightest interest in what was going on.
She went through her dancing mechanically, and always seemed in the
clouds, or, as her sisters would say, "wool-gathering."

It was easy to see from the first that no very sister-like feeling existed between the two elder sisters and their younger one. Even the
parents preferred their two elder girls to their youngest daughter.

The fact was that they—none of them—understood her; she was
not of their order, and they set her down as rather wanting. If she
was scolded for anything and she bore the rebuke with patience,
this was set down to indifference and want of feeling, when my
own experience of her character was that she was the most sensitive
creature that I had ever met with. If, as was often the case, she fell
into a reverie in company, it was called sulkiness, and if when asked
to perform on the piano, she meekly obeyed in a sort of languid
manner peculiar to herself, it was called unwillingness to oblige; yet
when at the instrument her touch was so soft and full of feeling, her
voice so clear and modulating, that it seemed as if her whole soul
was poured forth in the piece.

Nevertheless, neither her parents nor her sisters appreciated her
playing, or found in it anything more artistic or soul-stirring than in
the performance of other people. She was never thanked or applauded
by her family for any service or kindness of hers towards them, but often upbraided for selfishness when her dreamy nature would cause her
to forget the wants of others, while in reality she was one of the most
unselfish beings on this earth. How many mistakes might be rectified,
if the different members of a family would take the trouble to study
each other more accurately!

Maud's nature was reserved to a fault; she did not care to shine,
and this was put down to incapacity. Whether it was she felt she could
if she chose, and in so doing utterly eclipse her two elder sisters, and
consequently incur their envy, or whether it was an excess of modesty,

I know not. One thing is certain, she possessed fine talents, and those, too, of an uncommon kind. Her health was delicate, and her parents, perhaps attributed her peculiarities to the state of her health, while her two sisters, without allowing any such excuse, looked upon her as a downright fool.

She was snubbed on every occasion, and kept as much as possible in the background. It will be understood that all these observations of mine were not made in a single evening. It was not until we grew intimate and I had been repeatedly invited to the house, that I found out how matters stood in the family. I could not help feeling nettled at the deliberate way in which poor Maud was put on the shelf by her elder sisters, and I felt it my duty, as much as good manners would permit me, to take her part, and pay somewhat more attention to her than to the two elder daughters.

This preference I saw was observed, and not looked upon very favourably by the parents, who, I began to find out, had marked me for one of the elder girls. I saw plainly through their schemes, and heartlessly amused myself at their discomfiture while I paid my attentions to Maud. During the summer I was invited to stay at the country seat of this family, and it was here that our intimacy ripened. Here I observed the fine points of Maud's character, in spite of all her reserve.

Without being regularly in love with each other, a sympathy had grown up between us which by others, I have no doubt, was regarded as love. We appreciated each other's talents, and esteemed each other's characters.

The family had repeatedly seen me act, and Maud, more than any of them, seemed to appreciate my acting, while I was equally charmed at her skill on the piano and on the harp, and with her singing.

"I do not know how it is, Mr. Blackdeed," she said to me one day when we were left alone together in the garden, "but you are the only person I know who treats me with respect, or, indeed, like a rational being."

"Indeed," said I, feigning not to have observed the way in which she was treated by her family. "How so?"

"Oh! you know very well how I am treated at home. I have seen the surprise on your face whenever my sisters snubbed me, and saw that you felt how unfair it was. You will not pretend that you never observed it."

"Well, Miss Maud," I replied, "your penetration is such that I cannot do other than confess that *I have* observed it, and that I was very much surprised at it. I have often wondered what the reason could be."

She answered with a slight sigh.

"No one seems to understand me. From childhood I was ever different from the rest. I seem to live two distinct beings—one with my family, and before the world, and another in my own thoughts.

"You will have observed my silence when in company. I am aware to what it is generally attributed; but the fact is, that I have so little in common with my sisters I feel that if I were to give utterance to my ideas I should not be understood, but be considered more mad than they think me at present; hence my silence. I never knew anyone but you who thought even in the slightest degree like myself, and therefore to you I feel less inclined to be reserved than to others; in fact, with you I feel it impossible to be reserved at all.

"It is as if you had some power over me to draw out my ideas—to draw me out of myself. All my life I have longed to know someone; to have some friend who was unlike the rest of the world, and more like myself, who could understand me, and to whom I could pour out my thoughts, and feel that they were not poured out upon a desert soil."

"Do you know, Miss Maud," said I, "that from the very first I saw that you were quite different to any other young lady that I had ever met with? But far from regarding you in the light that I know your family regard you, I conceived an immense respect for you as a being of a higher order than the generality of young ladies. There was much, too, that puzzled me in your character. I was convinced that you could not but be aware that your abilities were above the ordinary, and it surprised me much that you should care so little about showing them, or even asserting your right against the—the tyranny, if I may say so— of your sisters."

"Well, it is my nature," she said. "What is it to me if they *do* have their own way in everything. I do not think it a matter worth disputing about. I do not live in their world, nor they in mine."

"And do you not long to make yourself better understood to your sisters?" I asked, after a pause.

"I should like to," she replied; "but that is impossible."

"Why impossible?" I asked. "Have you ever tried to do so?"

"No; but from my knowledge of their characters it would be useless." She paused, and then added, "Do you know that I sometimes

175

wish that I were better suited to this world than I am? My nature is so very peculiar that perhaps you would laugh at me were I to tell you some of my peculiarities."

"No," said I; "I do not think I should laugh at any peculiarities of your nature, whatever they might be. Your nature is one to study gravely and reflect upon, not to laugh at."

"I mean," said she, "that my temperament is subject to certain phenomena that many, perhaps *you*, might call hallucinations. I have never confided this to anyone before, fearing that I should be ridiculed or perhaps placed under the hands of some ignorant doctor."

"Indeed!" I exclaimed. "I am curious to hear of what sort these phenomena are. I take an immense interest in natural phenomena, especially that sort connected with the temperament of individuals."

"Well," she answered, "as you encourage me so far, I do not mind telling you some of those most common to me. Ofttimes when I am alone, either in my chamber or walking in the fields, a sort of dizziness comes over me, and I seem to be in the midst of a bed of flowers. When I try to pluck one they instantly vanish, and the dizziness likewise disappears. At other times I have seen before me a wreath of stars, which lasts for two or three minutes, then also vanishes. I have seen, too, distinctly in the daytime the faces of certain relations of mine, long since dead, and at night I occasionally start out of my sleep and see human forms bending over me, and sometimes they speak to me."

"It is very strange," I observed. "And have you never been able to attribute these visions to any nervous excitement, or to any natural cause whatever?"

"No; on the contrary, they generally appear when I am most calm."

I told her I had heard before of similar phenomena during, or even a long time after, a serious illness, and that I thought in most cases they might be attributed to an over-excitement of the brain, brought on by indigestion or other causes. She told me that she had never had any really serious illness in her life, though she admitted that she was constitutionally delicate. We then went into a metaphysical discussion, which was interrupted by the rest of the family, who came to meet us in the garden.

"I am sorry we have disturbed your *tête-à-tête*," said one of the elder sisters, quizzingly. "It must have been quite a pleasure to have been concealed behind the summer-house and listened to your intellectual conversation."

These words to a stranger would have conveyed nothing but a sort of merry banter, nor was there more conveyed in the tone, yet I, who had studied the nature of the speaker well, thought I discovered an undercurrent of sarcasm in the word "intellectual," as if she was perfectly sure that no conversation between us could be intellectual.

"There is many a true word spoken in jest," I replied. "I assure you that our conversation *has* been *most* intellectual. Miss Maud's ideas are so lofty, that it is really quite an effort on my part to follow her," said I, with a smile, though I really meant what I said.

"I wish she would let us have the benefit of them," said the other sister, laughing, imagining, of course, that I had spoken satirically. "She never favours us with any of those lofty ideas."

"No?" said I, affecting astonishment. "Then I must be a favoured individual. Miss Maud's case is, however, not without parallel. Many of our greatest minds have been most reserved and unassuming. It is a characteristic of genius to be retired, though, if I had the abilities of Miss Maud, I am sure I should be too vain to keep them secret."

This was uttered with a sincerity of manner on my part that checked the laugh that might have arisen from the sisters, and they were silent. The mother looked at us both, first at one and then at the other, in amazement, as if she half-believed me, and scrutinised Maud very narrowly, as if she fancied she must either be a great fool or very deep.

In the course of the afternoon the lady of the house took me aside and asked me if I were in earnest in my eulogium of Maud's intellect.

I replied that I was decidedly.

"What a strange girl it is!" she exclaimed. "She never seems to take any interest in anything or anybody around her. In fact, we none of us can make her out. What do you think now is the reason of this strange reserve towards her own kindred?"

"Well, madam," I answered, "if I must tell you my real opinion, her nature is an uncommon one, and can only live in the society of other uncommon natures. Her silence I attribute to an excessive sensitiveness, which not rarely accompanies genius, and which proceeds from a consciousness that she is not easily understood."

"But surely, Mr. Blackdeed," said the lady of the house, "one would expect that she would open her heart to her own flesh and blood, rather than to a comparative stranger like yourself."

"The idiosyncrasies of temperament, madam," said I, "are difficult to explain. The mere accident of relationship will not necessarily give a similarity of disposition. Occasionally we do find one in a family totally unlike the rest, and therefore misunderstood by them. The reason why Miss Maud takes no interest in what is conventionally termed society is that she feels above it. She pants, as it were, for a higher atmosphere. For this reason she prefers lone rambles and the contemplation of beautiful nature, with no companion save her own thoughts, to the artificial society of the ball-room, with its insipid conversation.

"She evidently lives completely in a world of her own, into which she will admit but very few. To judge from her conversation, she seems excessively well read, and acquainted with authors who rarely form a part of a young lady's education. You must have observed that she reads very much. Indeed, I was perfectly astounded at her research, as well as the originality of her remarks."

"Ah!" sighed the mother, "she is a very odd girl. It is true that she is always reading. I have seen some strange books, too, in her library, but to tell you the truth, Mr. Blackdeed, neither myself nor any of the family ever thought for a moment that she really had anything in her. Her sisters look upon her as a perfect ninny."

"A great mistake," I observed; "and if you will take my advice, you will try to understand her better. It may be difficult at first to get into her confidence. It is a nature that requires great sympathy and encouragement and if once ridiculed at any idea she expressed, which to you might appear strange or wild, you may be sure that she will close the doors of her confidence upon you once again and for ever."

At this moment the master of the house came to meet us, and inform us that dinner was ready. At dinner time I was seated opposite Maud. She was thoughtful and dreamy as usual all the while, and when addressed by any of the family would start as if out of a dream.

This peculiarity of hers was not taken notice of either by the family or the servants, who were accustomed to her eccentricity, and the dinner passed off without any conversation worth recording. In the evening we assembled again to take a dish of tea together. Maud was still silent and pensive, and while the others were conversing together, I could not help admiring the calm, intellectual serenity of her countenance.

I fell into a reverie, my eye being fixed upon her with intense interest, when to my surprise and horror, she suddenly fell back in her chair and became as one lifeless.

"Maud! my dear, my dear!" exclaimed her mother, "what can you be thinking of, to fall asleep like that in company," while her two sisters, between whom she was sitting, began to shake her, but to their surprise she felt as rigid as a corpse in their hands, and appeared as insensible.

"Mamma!" cried one of them, now really frightened. "Send for the doctor."

Someone went to fetch a glass of cold water, but as I never assisted any lady before in such a predicament, and not knowing exactly what to do, I did not offer my services until I was asked to support Maud, who was falling off her chair, when I rushed suddenly to her aid, and seizing her by the shoulders, replaced her on the seat. My hands had no sooner touched her than she again awoke, and opening her eyes sleepily, gazed about her wonderingly.

It would seem as if my will that she should recover were sufficient, for I touched her so gently that it was impossible the mere touch could have awakened her out of the deep magnetic trance I had unwittingly sent her into.

"How do you feel now, dear?" said her mother. "What can be the meaning of this swoon? Has it ever happened to you before?"

"No, never."

"I must consult a doctor about it," said her mother. "It may be the beginning of a series of fits, and must be looked into."

Wonderments on all hands were expressed as to what could be the origin of this unexpected swoon, but I saw from a look Maud gave me that she was aware that it arose from my influence over her. Maud and myself alone were in the secret, but I was more cautious for the future, and dared not look too fixedly at her, for fear of bringing on another trance. We spent many happy days together while I was staying at this country seat, and I enjoyed much of Maud's charming conversation. But soon I was recalled to London to continue my theatrical career, so I took leave of the family, and started with the stage for London.

Hamlet was to be acted at our theatre, and it so happened that a famous actor of ours had died, and the part of Hamlet was allotted to me.

In the middle of my part I could not help wishing to myself that Maud were present to see me act. The wish was intense; nor was it mere vanity that prompted it, but I really had a sincere respect for her opinion, and she was that sort of girl who would have told me to my face of any defect in my acting she noticed, for she was a merciless critic.

I rather longed to hear my acting severely cut up by her than to receive unqualified praise, although I was sure that praise from her lips would be unfeigned.

The memory of Maud's face haunted me throughout my part, but so far from being an impediment to me, I fancied I acted better than usual, and I was anxious for Maud to be present that I might hear her candid opinion of my performance afterwards. I was in the middle of that scene where Hamlet strains his eyes into space after his father's ghost when I noticed the figure of a lady seated in one of the boxes near the stage which up to that time had been empty. Surprise at seeing a lady alone whom I had not noticed before so near the close of the piece caused me to look again.

Good Heavens! it was Maud herself. What could she be doing in that box alone? Not even dressed for the theatre, but wearing the identical dress I had seen her last in, as if she were at home. I started, in spite of myself. She seemed to heed no one, for her eyes were constantly fixed on me. Her appearance there I did not attempt to account for, but I felt a thrill of delight that my acting was being appreciated by one at least.

I inwardly resolved at the close of the last scene to wrap my cloak hurriedly over my theatrical dress and rush out to meet her before she stepped into her carriage, but I was not in time, so I undressed and leisurely returned home.

A few days afterwards I met the medical attendant of the — family in the street. I inquired after the young ladies and especially Maud.

"It appears they are in London," said I.

"Indeed!" replied he. "Then it must be very lately, for it was only on the tenth, in the evening, that I was called for to attend upon Miss Maud, and they did not say anything about coming to town."

"On the tenth!" exclaimed I, in amazement, "you say you saw Miss Maud?"

This was the very evening I had seen her at the theatre.

"Yes; on the tenth."

"Are you sure?" I asked.

"Perfectly," he said. "In the evening, at about half-past nine."

"At half-past nine, on the tenth!" I exclaimed. "Why, she was at the theatre at that hour. I saw her."

"Impossible!" said the doctor. "You must have been mistaken; someone like her, perhaps."

"No, no, doctor," I firmly asserted; "I tell you she was in a box near the stage while I was acting Hamlet. I was as near to her as I am to you now; it is impossible that I could be mistaken."

"But I tell you, you *are* mistaken, most grievously," said the doctor, somewhat warmly. "I give you my word of honour as a medical man and a gentleman that I attended Miss Maud at her own country house on the tenth instant, at about half-past nine in the evening."

"Then it must have been her ghost I saw, that's all," said I. "And do you know, doctor, that the most strange part of it all was, she was perfectly alone in the box, and not dressed for the theatre, but wore the very same dress I saw her last in? I marked her well, and wondering to myself what brought her there unaccompanied and in such plain attire. It is true, she is a little eccentric, but then her parents, I thought, would have looked after her sufficiently to prevent such a breach of etiquette. Really, doctor, I don't know what to think of it."

"Come," said he, with a smile, "come, confess you are a little smitten with the young lady. You can't quite get her out of your thoughts, even while you are acting. She has made a great impression on your over-sensitive brain, and at the time perhaps your nerves were a little unstrung from over study or over excitement about your part, or else"—here he relaxed into another smile—"are you quite, *quite* sure you did not take just a *leetle* drop of *something* upon an empty stomach, just to screw yourself up to the right pitch?"

And here he laughed heartily.

"Upon my honour, doctor," said I, "I am not in the habit of having recourse to stimulants. I assure you—"

He interrupted me with a hearty laugh, and said, "Ah! you actors are sad dogs."

I smiled and then after a moment's reflection said, "By the way, doctor, for what were you called to attend upon Miss Maud? I hope she is not dangerously ill. What is her complaint?"

"Well," said the physician, gravely, "I am afraid it is somewhat serious. She had a fit that appeared to me to be cataleptic. It is the second she has had it seems. It lasted for some considerable time, and when she awoke she complained of a weight over her eyeballs and an inclination to sleep, with a pain down the whole right side of the body. She felt extremely nervous, and asked for a fan, with which she begged me to fan her powerfully, and afterwards to change the movement, so as to cause the current of air to pass her face in a transverse direction. This I did, after which she declared that she had recovered."

I was startled at the doctor's relation, but said nothing, for I was now more convinced than ever that my intense desire for her to be present had influenced her magnetically, and had been the means, though unwittingly, of withdrawing her spirit temporarily from the body. But what would have been the use of my declaring my suspicions to such an old-fashioned fogey as this worthy doctor? I should only have been laughed at, so I held my peace.

"Well, doctor," said I, after we had walked on together for some time in silence, being occupied with my thoughts, "if you have nothing else to do in the evenings, now that you are in London, I should be glad if you would drop in at our theatre to see me act. This evening I am going to act Romeo again. If you have any spare time, I can give you a box-ticket."

He thanked me, and said that as he was free that evening he would gladly accept my offer, so we parted.

The evening arrived, and when I made my appearance on the boards I noticed my friend the doctor already in his box. His appearance put me in mind of the conversation we had had in the morning, and, do what I could, I was unable to get Maud out of my head all through the piece. I certainly *did* long for her to be present, though I tried not to wish too strongly, lest I should bring on another magnetic trance. I glanced towards the box where I had last seen Maud. It was occupied by two gentlemen, and Maud was not there.

As the piece proceeded, however, I forgot my caution, and an intense desire to see her again, which I could not restrain, came over me. Shortly afterwards, glancing casually towards the same box, which was just opposite the doctor's, *I perceived Maud, dressed as on the evening before.*

I was horror-struck, for I knew now that I saw her spirit for certain, and that the body was nearly a hundred miles off. The two gentlemen in the box did not seem aware of her presence, while she looked neither to the right nor to the left, but seemed thoroughly absorbed in the piece. Her apparition there on that night was not of such long duration as on the evening of the tenth, probably because I was frightened at what I had done and wished her spirit back to its earthly tenement.

When I looked again towards the box after a quarter-of-an-hour

Maud was no longer there. At the conclusion of the play I undressed hurriedly, and sought my friend the doctor among the crowd, but I could not find him, so I strolled into a supper room hard by, just before returning home, and there at a table I saw my friend.

"Hullo! doctor," said I, "so you have come to refresh yourself after the fatigue of seeing me act, eh?"

"Why, you see," retorted he, merrily, "your capital acting has quite given me an appetite."

After one or two complimentary speeches on his part, I took my seat by his side and gave my orders to a waiter.

"Doctor," I said, after a pause, "I saw her again tonight."

"Who?"

"Why, Maud, to be sure."

"Bah! I'll tell you what it is, young man, you want bleeding."

Pulling out his lancet, he wanted to bleed me on the spot, but I refused to be bled.

"Nonsense, doctor," said I; "I haven't any more blood than I know what to do with. I tell you I saw *her* as distinctly as I see you now. She was in the box opposite yours where those two gentlemen were, but she did not seem to belong to them."

"Well," said he, "I saw those two gentlemen in the box opposite mine, and I can take my oath there was no one else there."

"Mark my word," said I, "when you return to — and call on that family, you will be informed that Maud has had another fit. This is the 15th. Mark the day and the hour, and if she has not, I will lose my right hand, or I will give you permission to bleed me."

"What connection is there between her having a fit and your imagining that you saw her at the theatre? If she was at the theatre, I must have seen her as well as you, and if she were in a fit this evening, how could she be at the theatre?"

I pretended to be convinced by his arguments, but forbore to explain myself further, merely adding:

"Well, we shall see—if you hear Maud has had a fit on the evening of the 15th, at about the same hour as the last one, you will let me know, will you not?"

"Oh, certainly."

At this moment the waiter returned with my supper, and the conversation took a different turn; but after we had finished and were returning home, he urged me again to be bled or to try a little change of air, as he observed that my nerves were evidently out of order. Having arrived at the corner of a street, I shook hands with my friend, and we parted. It was about a week after our parting, on returning from a walk I found a letter on my table. My servant told me that an elderly gentleman had called and enquired if I were at home, and receiving an answer in the negative, he had asked for pen, ink, and paper, and left me the following lines:

My Dear Sir—
Since I saw you last I have received a letter from Mrs. — begging me to return as soon as I conveniently could, as Maud had had another fit on the evening of the 15th, between nine and half-past—the very day and hour, you will remember, you fancied you saw her in the box opposite mine. I am not a believer in spiritual apparitions, and therefore cannot set this down to anything more than a very strange coincidence. I called at the house of Mrs. — and saw the whole family. When the lady of the house had told me about Maud's fit, I afterwards related to her, in the presence of the young lady herself, the curious circumstance of her fancied appearance to you in the stage box. Maud listened with great attention, and seemed to take more interest in my recital than the rest did, for afterwards, taking me apart, she asked me many questions about you; when I had seen you last, how you were, etc., etc. I returned to town yesterday, and as you asked me to let you know if your prophecy came true, I have left you this note. Till we meet again,—
Yours very truly,
John Merrivale

How I triumphed inwardly on the perusal of this letter! I placed it in my pocket, and taking my hat and cane, I left my lodgings and walked about the streets with a buoyant step, hoping to meet Merrivale, just to crow over him for disbelieving my vision. I would have called upon him, had I known his address, but I saw no more of my friend—at least, for some time afterwards. It happened that on that very evening a piece was being performed at our theatre in which I did not act, and I thought I would be a spectator for once in a way, so, from caprice, I took the very box in which I had seen Maud. On entering the box I experienced all the awe and veneration of a pious devotee when he kneels at some holy shrine.

"This place has been visited by Maud's spirit," said I to myself, as I shut myself in. "This is the very chair she used."

I seated myself, and the curtain drew up. It was a melodrama, if I remember rightly, which was acted that night, but I was so occupied with my thoughts about Maud, that I really cannot say with certainty what piece it was. The audience applauded every now and then, so I suppose it took well. As for myself, I had fallen into a reverie of which Maud was the subject.

That stage box had for me a certain sanctity and purity since the first time I had seen her there. Whether it was that on this evening I had not my part to think of and so felt my mind open to other thoughts than those connected with my profession, or whether this hallowed spot awoke in my breast certain feelings, I know not, but certain it was that never had Maud so thoroughly taken possession of my thoughts as on that evening.

I attempted to analyse my thoughts. What was it that I felt for Maud? What was it that made me think more of her than of other girls? And why did I think more and more about her every day? I hardly knew myself how to answer these questions. Was it—could it be—no—*love*, that I felt for her? No! it was not that; at least, if it was, it was not like other men's love. It was a feeling far purer, far loftier than falls to the lot of ordinary men's experience. I thought that the world did not—never did, nor ever could contain another Maud. She was different to the rest of her kind. *Her* beauty, *her* talents, *her* beautiful nature, could never excite in me such a vulgar passion as that which the world calls love. The thought never entered my head to make her my own, and I was content to worship her at a distance.

I began to wonder to myself if Maud could be aware of the strong impression she had made upon me. I even dared to hope, though humbly, very humbly, she might not *quite* have forgotten *me*; that there was still a spare corner in her memory—I had nearly said *heart*—left vacant in which I might crave a home.

Did she, perhaps—here an electric shock ran through me at the very thought—did she feel for me *exactly* in the same way as I felt for her? Oh, rapture! and I tried to persuade myself that she did, for the thought comforted me.

"Ah, Maud, Maud," I muttered to myself, in the midst of my reverie.

At that moment I heard the door handle move.

"Confound that box-keeper," muttered I. "What can he want, coming to disturb my meditation?"

The door opened, and I turned my head to see who it was. Gentlemen, will you believe it? It was Maud, again dressed exactly the same as before. I started, and my blood ran cold, my hair stood on end, my teeth chattered, and my knees knocked together. I essayed to speak, but my tongue refused to give utterance to what I wished to say. I was then in the presence, nay close to, a supernatural essence bearing the lineaments of Maud, whose body I knew for certain to be at her country seat, nearly a hundred miles away.

The figure gave me a friendly look of recognition, and seated itself. I fancied it offered me its hand, but I was too dumbfounded to accept it, and remained stupefied. At length this excessive feeling of terror began to wear off, and I ventured to say, in a low tone, broken with emotion, "Maud, is it really you? Speak."

"William," said a voice proceeding from the lips of the figure, but which sounded as if it came from a long way off, "William!"

And there was the deepest pathos in the tone. It was the first time I had been called thus by Maud. When she was in the body she always called me Mr. Blackdeed. I waited for some moments to hear if the voice would say more.

After a long pause it spoke again, and said, "You called me. Wherefore?"

"Called you, Maud!" said I. "I called you not."

"The concentration of your thoughts has had the power to command my spirit from afar," said the figure.

"Is it so?" said I. "And can you not battle against such commands?"

The figure replied not, save by a look, which seemed to say, "When you command, no."

I understood the look, and felt flattered by its meaning, but knew not how to respond, so I was silent for some moments.

At length I said, "Maud—if I may call you Maud—tell me, do you suffer much when withdrawn from the body?"

"Less out of it than in it," was the reply.

"How so?" I asked.

"You know how I stand with my family," she said.

"True, true," I observed; "and this must cause you great pain. However, I hope in time—"

"Never, never," she replied with a sigh.

"Oh, why not? Do you not wish to live happily with them?"

"Oh, how willingly!"

"Then let me see if I cannot make matters a little smooth for you. Perhaps—"

She shook her head doubtfully, and said, "I feel as if I did not belong to them nor they to me; in fact, I feel as if I never belonged to anybody, nor ever should."

"And never should!" exclaimed I. "Why, you do not mean to say that—that—you never intend to marry?"

"I fear I should make but an indifferent wife."

"Why so? I am sure you possess qualities that many married ladies might envy. Of course, you would require a husband who understood you and was able to appreciate your virtues."

"You flatter me," she said. "Nevertheless, you will see that I shall never marry. Mark my words. I was not born for it. Do you know," she said, lowering her voice, and speaking in a solemn tone, "that of late I have had a strange presentiment that my end is not far off."

"Now, really, Maud," said I, "pray do not talk like that, for I sincerely hope that nothing more serious than a little temporary indisposition has given rise to such a presentiment."

"My health of late has been, if anything, better than usual. I do not think this presentiment can be reasonably accounted for in that way. At other times when I have felt at all poorly such a thought has never occurred to me."

I merely shook my head and said that I hoped she would not encourage these presentiments.

"William," she said, "remember my words; I shall not live till the year is out."

I did not know what to answer, and gazed upon her in astonishment for some minutes, when suddenly her face grew agonised, and she manifested symptoms of impatience.

"What is it, Maud?" I asked. "What ails you?" She seemed to have difficulty in answering, but I fancied that I understood the words, "I am drawn to the body; let me go."

And rising suddenly from her chair and gasping, she made for the door, but disappeared from my sight before she had time to reach it.

I remained stupefied at the figure's sudden disappearance, as well as at the whole occurrence of the evening. I knew not what to think. Had I been dreaming? No. This was not the first time, either, that I had seen her. I had been holding converse with no less a being than Maud's ghost; her own pure and beautiful spirit, drawn by my art from the body while yet breath remained.

A horrid thought struck me. Perhaps I had detained the spirit too long away from the body. Perhaps there was no one in the house to wake her out of her trance. I reproached myself for not foreseeing the mischief that I might do, and returned home from the theatre that evening with Maud more than ever in my thoughts.

Next morning when I awoke, whether from the excitement of the previous evening or from a cold caught by walking home in the rain, or both combined, perhaps, I found myself in a high fever. I was compelled to remain in bed, though I was averse to sending for the doctor until some days later, when I found the fever grew rapidly worse.

A doctor was sent for—not my friend Merrivale, as I knew not where he lived—and he attributed my illness to over-study and want of proper exercise. I merely mention my illness to tell you a dream which occurred to me during a portion of it. I thought that I was transported to realms of enchantment, and that whilst the most beautiful scenery imaginable lay before me, I heard in the distance soft strains of music and singing, which gradually drew nearer and nearer to me.

The atmosphere seemed to fill with a delicious perfume, and looking upwards, I descried a troop of angels, bearing one with them who seemed lately of this earth. The angels gradually descended, and left the figure they carried with them at my feet, whilst they flew upward. I instantly recognised in the figure before me the features of Maud. She was dressed in a long robe of white, and, with an expression in her countenance too beautiful and too unearthly to describe, she spoke these words:

"Farewell, William; we meet again," and vanished.

I awoke, and the dream remained impressed upon my mind for a long time afterwards.

Recovering at length from my illness, I resumed my duties at the theatre, where I was received with immense applause after my long absence, and continued my career with enthusiasm on my part and admiration on the part of my audience. Night after night I would go through my part, and week after week and month after month passed away, and I neither heard nor saw anything further of Maud since our strange meeting in the stage box—*viz.*, on the 31st of December.

Sometimes a violent desire to see her again would seize me in the midst of my part, and I would glance furtively towards the haunted spot, half expecting to see her, but I never saw her again from that day to this. The dream I had had concerning her during my illness often recurred to me, and I wondered whether it really was a revelation or only an ordinary dream to be accounted for by the state of my health at the time.

I had seen no more of Maud's family, neither had I again met our common friend the doctor or any other friend of the family from whom I might learn the state of Maud's health, or whether she were dead or alive.

A year or two passed away, when I was invited by some friends of mine to spend a week or so at their country seat, not very far from the seat of Maud's family. I took the stage, and was put down at a country inn, from whence I had to walk about a mile-and-a-half to reach my friend's house. It was early in the morning when I arrived at the inn, and not being in a particular hurry to reach the house, thinking that the family might not yet have risen, I sauntered leisurely along the carriage road, halting occasionally and looking around me. The whole scene—the air itself—seemed to call up memories of Maud.

Absorbed in a reverie, I wandered on until I found myself at the gate of a cemetery, which I mechanically entered. I had passed the same cemetery often before in my walks with Maud. What a picturesque old place it was! Filled with old crumbling monuments with quaint epitaphs and overgrown with rank grass and weeds.

It was one of Maud's favourite spots for meditation, as she told me. It was so perfectly solitary—overlooked by no houses and shut out from the gaze of passers-by with thick yew trees and cypress. Then, when you entered at the gate, what a silence reigned within! I love those grand old melancholy retreats, and so did Maud. Here the rich and poor of the surrounding villages for miles around were buried. I passed by the elegant marble tombs of the wealthy and the humbler grassy mounds of the peasantry. My thoughts were filled with the shortness of human life, the vanity of its noblest pursuits, and the equalling, never-sparing hand of death.

Even the bracing morning air and the merry sunshine were insufficient to dispel thoughts like these, for the spot had a solemnity of its own about it. The abode of the dead is at all times sacred to us, even when we find it in the heart of a populous city, amidst the bustle and

189

stir of daily life; but how much more is it sanctified when we discover it in some rural and secluded spot ungrimed with the smoke of factories, unbroken in upon by rude voices from without, and the mossy stones and overgrown weeds and brambles of which even the hand of the trim gardener has not disturbed.

I seated myself upon an ancient tomb, and gazed around me. Here lay a knight of old, there a lord of the manor; yonder some poor rustic whose humble grave of turf bore no record of the name, age, or sex of its occupant, what its owner's deeds had been on earth, whether fruitful or unfruitful. Close beside it rose a stately tombstone of white marble with a long inscription. "Doubtless here lays some rich landowner," I thought, "whose supposed virtues are here recorded in full."

I was too far off to read what was inscribed, but the tomb was a new one. It was not there when Maud and I took our rambles together, and I recollected all the most important gravestones. I rose and advanced a few steps, when I suddenly halted a few paces from the tomb, and recoiled in horror. I was seized with trembling, my heart sank, and I felt my brow covered with a cold sweat. The letters on the monument swam before my eyes. I brushed away a tear as I read the following lines:

Sacred to the memory of
Maud E—n
Youngest daughter of George E—n of —
who departed this life the 31st of December, 1750,
aged 21 years

Then followed one or two verses from the Bible.

"Oh, Maud, Maud!" I cried, in an agony, and throwing myself on her grave, I wept bitterly.

"What says the gravestone? 'On the 31st of December,'" said I to myself. "Good heavens! That was the very evening on which I saw her spirit last in the stage box!"

I had drawn her soul away from her body for too great a length of time. *I* then was the cause of her death. Poor Maud! She was right in saying she should not live the year out, but I little thought that when her spirit hurried from my presence on that fatal night that it was then about to leave the body for ever.

I felt like a murderer. The thought that one so good, so innocent, and so talented should meet with her death through one so worthless as myself galled me. My agony was insufferable. "Oh, Maud! would that we had never met!" I cried aloud, for now, but, alas, too late, I began to feel the consuming fire of an intense love for her that in her lifetime was as yet undeveloped; added to which were the stings of remorse for my own careless, if not wicked, conduct.

I felt now that she had loved *me*. Why had I not come forward before to crave her hand? Could I not see that she loved me, though she confessed it not? Fool that I was! Could I not have been happy with her and made her happy? What was it that made me draw back? I know not. There was something about her which awed me, and kept me aloof.

Then, again, was I in a position at that time to support a wife? Had I the right to come forward? No, I answered myself, and this thought consoled me somewhat, but had I not already allowed myself to be carried away by a passion that had engulfed both her and myself?

Love, grief, and remorse struggled in my breast for the mastery. I wept aloud, and kissed the cold gravestone fervently. I know not how long I might have been thus, for in my anguish I took no count of time, when I was suddenly aroused by a footstep behind and a voice.

"Mercy on us, who is this?" said the stranger.

I turned, and beheld my friend Merrivale. Whilst taking his morning's walk as usual he had been attracted by my lamentations, and curiosity led him to enter the cemetery.

"Why, what the—I say—what! Is that *you?*" he said, as I looked up abashed in the midst of my grief, and knew not what to reply.

"Come, come," said he. "I understand all, I saw all from the beginning. I am not surprised, you know, with one of your temperament, but do you know, young man, you might catch your death of cold, indulging your grief in the morning dew on a cold gravestone. You must be—really, my dear sir—you must be insane."

"Doctor," said I, "we may meet another time, when I may have more to say to you. For the present leave me. I arrived here early this morning, having been invited to a friend's house. It is time for me to make my appearance. Till we meet again, farewell. And, doctor," said I, "you will keep this matter secret, eh?"

"Very well," said he, with a smile which seemed to me forced in order to disguise his emotion, for I noticed that he turned away his head suddenly, shook my hand, and walked away hurriedly.

We had both of us left the cemetery, and about half-a-mile further on led me to the door of my friend's house.

I tried to assume an air of indifference before my friend, and discoursed on various topics; nevertheless, he noticed that my hand trembled, and that I seemed distracted. I said I had been a little out of health lately, and was glad of a little change of air.

"My doctor, Mr. Merrivale," said he, "will be here today to look at the children. If you would like to see him—"

"Thank you, thank you; but I hope it is nothing worth mentioning."

In the afternoon Merrivale arrived, and I managed to find an opportunity of speaking with him alone. I inquired after the family E—n, and was informed that Maud had died suddenly in a trance, and he had been called too late. That her two sisters were engaged to be married. That Maud had spoken much of me before her last fit, and had given out some strange mysterious hints of a certain power I had over her, and nothing could induce her mother and sisters to believe otherwise than that I had cast an evil spell over her.

He added that her father was more reasonable, and did not believe in those things.

The family would be sure to hear of my arrival in the village, therefore I resolved to call on an early opportunity. I did so, and was well received by Maud's father, he having been intimate with mine, but by the mother and sisters with rigid coldness. They did not even offer me their hand. I expected this, but nevertheless felt it my duty to call. I made some slight allusion to Maud's death in as delicate a way as I could, but was checked in the midst of my remarks by scornful glances from the mother and sisters.

I left the house, and I need hardly say that this was my last call on that family, although the master of the house wrung my hand cordially, and said he should be always glad to see me when chance led me to those parts.

I returned to my friend's house, where I tried to divert myself with a week's shooting. I frequently met my friend Merrivale. We used to take walks together sometimes. In one of our rambles I recounted to him all the particulars of the evening of the 31st of December, when I had last seen and spoken to Maud in the spirit at the theatre.

He marvelled, but was silent.

★ ★ ★ ★ ★

By the time the tragedian had finished his recital, our friends had arrived at the door of the inn, where their host's pretty daughter waited to receive them.

"Well, Helen, my dear," said Mr. Oldstone. "Is the breakfast ready? We have had a long story, and we are all very hungry."

"Yes, sir," answered the maiden; "everything is on the table. I'll run and fetch the eggs. I put them in to boil when I saw you coming in the distance. The toast and rolls are hot, and all in order."

"Bravo! Helen, bravo!" said Professor Cyanite, rubbing his hands.

"By my troth, Helen," said our artist, "if I wanted an appetite your bright eyes would be enough to give me one."

Helen blushed and smiled, and skipped lightly away to see after the eggs.

"Ah! here is a breakfast fit for a king," said Mr. Crucible, as Helen re-entered with a tray.

"And all made with her own fair hands, too, I'll warrant," said McGuilp.

"What makes you blush so much of late, Helen?" asked Mr. Hardcase.

"Oh, what a shame to tease the poor child," said Mr. Parnassus, with tenderness.

"Ah! Helen," sighed Dr. Bleedem, "your health and rosy cheeks are worth all my drugs."

"'I would I were a glove upon that hand, that I might touch that cheek,'" quoted the tragedian from his favourite "Romeo and Juliet.'"

"Order, order!" cried various other members at once.

At that moment our host entered to call away his daughter, so Helen was spared further banter.

As the meal proceeded the company began to dispute who should tell the next story. Of those present who had not yet entertained the company with a tale were Mr. Crucible and Mr. Oldstone. One of the two *must* tell a story, as the club decreed, but as each of these gentlemen wished to lay the burden of the story upon the shoulders of the other, nothing seemed likely to be settled.

Accordingly, after the breakfast things had been removed dice were called for, and it was agreed that whoever should throw the highest should tell the story. Our host soon returned with the dice-box, and remained to see which of the two gentlemen should throw the higher number.

Mr. Oldstone seized the dice-box, and shaking it well, threw double five. It was now Mr. Crucible's turn, so taking the dice-box from the hand of the first thrower, and rattling it twice or thrice, he threw the number twelve.

"Now then, Crucible," said Mr. Oldstone, laughing, "no shirking, but let us have the story at once."

"What! so soon after breakfast!" exclaimed Mr. Crucible, "and before we have had time to digest the last properly."

"I hope you will excuse my presence here gentlemen," said Mr. Hardcase, "for I have a case to attend to."

"Now really, Hardcase, that's too bad," ejaculated Mr. Oldstone.

At this moment a servant arrived hurriedly at the "Headless Lady," to call away Dr. Bleedem to see a patient.

"Really, gentlemen," said the doctor, "I am very sorry, but business *is* business."

"Business! business!" exclaimed Mr. Oldstone, in horror at such a word being uttered within the sacred precincts of the club. "Business! Ugh!"

Professor Cyanite, too, had a great scientific work which he was getting ready for the press, and begged also to be allowed to withdraw.

"Well, gentlemen," said Mr. Oldstone, "this is really very provoking. I cannot think what ails you all this morning. Since our club is reft of three such staunch members, there seems nothing else to be done but to defer the story until the evening, when there will be no excuse for anyone to be absent."

This was agreed to, and the remaining inmates of the "Headless Lady" began to while away the time each after his own manner. Our artist began a portrait of the landlord's pretty daughter. Mr. Blackdeed, who was only here for the holidays, sat to work to finish a tragedy that he had begun. Mr. Parnassus composed an ode. Mr. Crucible retired to his chamber to try some chemical experiment, and Mr. Oldstone, finding himself deserted, had nothing left him to do but to look over his cabinet of curiosities.

Let us return to our artist and his model. How happy they both are! Both of them young and good-looking, and left all to themselves. With what inspiration the hand of the painter glides over his canvas, and how the face of the pretty Helen brightens up every time the artist refreshes his memory by taking a peep at her from behind his easel. There is no affectation in the expression or the pose of the sitter, it is quite easy and natural, and beautifully simple. She does not seem conscious she is sitting for her portrait.

Every now and then, after working in silence for some twenty minutes or so, McGuilp breaks the monotony by some pleasing remark or question, to which the maiden replies charmingly. Sometimes she in her turn will ask him questions about Italy, and whether the country and the people are the same as in England.

"No, Helen," McGuilp replies; "not the same. Italy is warmer, the sky bluer, and grapes grow in the open air along the road side. The people's faces are darker and their language more musical than ours. They are all Roman Catholics; but, alas, the government is bad, and the country is infested with brigands, who attack travellers in the mountains and sometimes keep them as hostages till their friends can be sent for to pay any ransom they may choose to ask, in default of which their victims are tortured and maimed in the most inhuman manner."

"Oh, what horrid wretches! I was just going to say, before you told me that, what a paradise Italy must be to live in! But I don't think I should like to live there now."

"Well, these are drawbacks, I admit," said McGuilp, "but, nevertheless, Italy is a very charming country. Fancy a land where every peasant makes his own wine—good wine, and cheap, too. What merrymakings they have, too, on their feast days, and how picturesque their costume!"

"Ah! do tell me how they are dressed. I should so like to know."

"Would you, Helen?" said McGuilp. "Then, as the sitting is now at an end, being past twelve o'clock, I will let you look over my portfolio. You will find some studies that I have made both of men and women in the costumes of the Roman peasantry."

"Oh, do show them to me," exclaimed Helen, in delight. "I am so curious to see what they are like. Did you say it was past twelve o'clock? I began my sitting at nine, and it does not seem to me more than half-an-hour that I have been here."

And I have no doubt she spoke the truth. Happy moments are short. Alas! how rapidly time glides away in youth, and how provokingly long it appears when we have most reason to wish it should pass quickly. As Helen was engaged in admiring the studies and sketches of McGuilp our host knocked at the door to ask if his daughter could be spared, as her mother wanted her aid in the affairs of the house.

"Oh, certainly," said McGuilp; "but I must have another good sitting tomorrow."

"Very well, sir. May I be permitted to look at the portrait?" asked the landlord.

"You may look," replied our artist; "but I warn you the likeness is not striking at present."

"Gramercy, sir!" exclaimed the landlord, in ecstasy; "if it is not my girl herself already!"

"Ah! my good host, wait until I have had some half dozen sittings or so, and then look again," said McGuilp.

Our landlord then looked approvingly over our artist's portfolio, and said, "Ah, sir, it is a noble art."

Helen was delighted with her portrait, of course, and equally so with the contents of the portfolio. McGuilp complimented her upon her sitting, and Helen disappeared for the present.

At one o'clock Helen reappeared with the lunch, and those members of the club who remained at home met again over their frugal meal. They whiled away the time until the evening with politics and a rubber at whist.

At length the village clock struck the dinner hour, and all guests were present. The dinner passed off merrily, and all awaited the story anxiously. Our host and his daughter were invited to hear it, so having filled their pipes and stirred the fire, Mr. Crucible, finding himself loudly called upon, took a sip at his port and began his story.

The Analytical Chemist's Story
The Spirit Leg

Being left an orphan at an early age, I was consigned to the care of a bachelor uncle, one Admiral Broadside, who instructed me almost entirely himself until I reached the age of twelve. I was then sent to school, where I went through a routine of learning taught to boys at that time, and though I was backward in many things when I first entered the school, I was a persevering scholar, and soon left behind me many boys who had the start of me. I thus made enemies, and being of a retiring disposition, owing to my previous education, I made but few friends.

But let me return to my uncle. I have the liveliest recollection of the old man with his weather-beaten face, his deep-set eyes, and over-hanging black eyebrows, resembling a moustache rather than the feature we usually see in their place. Well I remember the sheen and the lustre of that rubicund nose, sprouting with grog-blossoms, the iron-grey hair, and long pig-tail; his spectacles, with glasses as big as a crown piece, his cocked hat, his uniform adorned with medals, and his hobbling gait—for he had lost his right leg in an engagement, and used as a substitute a wooden one. How well I can call to mind his nautical language and his merry laugh; but, alas, I remember too well also his angry frown, and the sundry thwackings that I got with a "cat-o'-nine-tails," when I had "offended against discipline."

From an infant he tried to instil into my young mind the glories of a sea-faring life, and what a grand thing it was to fight for the honour and glory of one's country. He told me that he had great interest in the navy, and if I turned out a worthy nephew of his, he would get me on in my career, and that he hoped I should never disgrace his name by showing the white feather and turning landlubber.

He tried to influence my youthful imagination with stories of

sea-fights, the capture of pirates, the manners and customs of foreign countries, the merry crew on board, etc. He would cut out boats for me from blocks of wood, and would rig out and launch them in a fish pond in a garden behind his house.

Up to a certain period in my youth my uncle's nautical stories and his promises of pushing me on in life, if I answered his expectations, fired my ambition, and I could talk of nothing else than of going to sea.

My uncle having no children of his own, looked upon me as his son, and said that I was just the sort of boy for him. He would praise me to his friends and before my face, but his eulogium of myself lasted only during the time I lived with him—namely, before he sent me to school, for at school a great change came over me, and my uncle noticed with regret upon my return for the holidays the growing coolness in me towards a sea-faring life; in fact, that my tastes had begun to develop themselves in quite another direction.

Away from the influence of my guardian, I had dared to breath in a new atmosphere, and to find out that there were other walks in life quite as noble, and to me much more fascinating than that of the sea. The term "landlubber" conveyed no disparagement to my ears now. I merely saw in it the venting of the spleen of an egotistical and narrow mind. How paltry that class of men must be which speaks with disparagement of all others who do not happen to be within its own narrow circle.

I was ashamed of myself for ever having been led away by such false opinions, and had many a hot dispute with my guardian about his illiberal notions. Now, the admiral had a temper of his own; he was not a man accustomed to be thwarted. He had made up his mind that I was to go to sea, and to sea he was determined to send me, whether I willed it or no.

I was now about fourteen, and since I had been away from home I had imbibed strong notions of independence. I did not see that any man had a right to dispose of me as he thought fit. I felt myself a free agent, and my youthful blood rose at the cool way in which my uncle thought to bend me to his will. Had I not the right to seek my own walk in life? Was I to be baulked of my true avocation because I was told that my interest lay elsewhere? Interest! Bah! I despised interest.

My uncle promised me that if I went to sea he would leave all his fortune to me, as I was his heir, and if I refused, he would not leave me a *groat*. What then? I had a small income left me by my father when I should come of age, which was enough to keep me like a gentleman. What did I want with the old admiral's money? I was not going to sell myself for filthy lucre.

It was whispered that the old man had amassed a considerable fortune, and I should be called a fool by the world to quarrel with him. But was my will to be bought with gold? I was grateful to him for what he had already done for me, and I never wished to quarrel with him; but when I saw that he expected as a proof of my gratitude I should humour his whim by sacrificing my highest ambition in life to follow a profession I now really cared nothing about, I felt it my duty to rebel against my guardian and choose my own course.

I felt myself born for something better than a sea-faring life. The sea might be very well for those who had a taste for it, or for those who were fit for nothing else. Besides, sailors are generally such ignorant people, and I flattered myself that I had a mind to cultivate and resolved to devote myself to study.

My hobby was science, and the branch I was chiefly anxious to excel in, chemistry. I believe the first thing that fired my imagination to pursue this delightful science was the reading a book lent me by a friend, entitled, "Lives of the Alchemists." From this I learned how many clever men had devoted their lives and fortunes in pursuit of the philosopher's stone. I do not remember reading any of them actually *did* make gold; but the perseverance and energy of these men! There was something sublime in a man of means giving up the wealth and luxury of his position to follow science. How I loved to read of these persevering sages, of their trials and disappointments, and how, heedless of all vicissitudes, they still pursued to the last with unflagging energy that science that they alone lived for. I had no doubt that in early times there was an immensity of superstition mingled with their science.

Nevertheless, thought I, is it possible that so many clever men should have wasted their whole lives in study and have been just upon the point of discovering the secret if there were really nothing in it at all? I inquired of a chemist in our town whether he believed in the possibility of making gold. He told me that he did not; but then a learned man with whom I once conversed said that he was of opinion that it *was* possible, but added that if the secret were discovered it would certainly be valueless.

I preferred leaning towards the opinion of the learned man who believed in the possibility of making gold out of baser metals, and resolved to give the study of my life to the discovery of the secret without letting others know what I was striving after.

It happened that the chemist of our town whose opinion I had consulted as to the probability of success in alchemy sent his son, with whom I was rather intimate, to the same school as my guardian had put me at. He was a lad of my own years, and shared my taste for study. Having much in common, we soon struck up a warm friendship, which lasted for many years; in fact, until his death, some fifteen years back. I may assert that he was the only friend I ever had in my youth, for I was a reserved lad, and did not court friendship. He, too, was reserved, and sought no other friend but myself.

We were always in each other's company, and used to be nicknamed Castor and Pollux by the other boys. They could none of them understand why we two withdrew ourselves from the rest and refused to join in their games, and they wondered much what we found to talk about one to the other. We were both looked upon as unsociable, and accordingly disliked.

We both of us had high aspirations, and each of us felt the value of his existence, and that high honours awaited him in posterity, if not in this life, provided that he made the best use of his abilities. We might each of us have been about fifteen, when we swore an eternal friendship, and likewise to keep secret from others the nature of our studies. When I returned home from school for good—being then about seventeen—my uncle the admiral was in despair at finding me more than ever confirmed in my views of a studious life, and said I had disappointed his hopes, and that I need henceforth hope for no help from him.

A gentleman who visited my uncle, and who seemed to take an interest in me, seeing that I was a young man of some promise, advised me to go to a German university, and recommended to me the university of Jena.

He took upon himself to remonstrate with my guardian upon what he called his harsh treatment of myself, and told him that he had no right to force me against my true calling, but his words were as wind in the admiral's ears, for he was as obstinate as a mule.

"Do you mean to tell me, sir," said the admiral, "that my boy can't be made a sailor of, if he is only properly brought up?"

"Yes," said his friend; "it is precisely that point I wish to discuss. I deny that we are all born alike; and if you force this young man to go to sea you will make a bad sailor of him when he might have done honour to his country in another way."

"Boys mustn't be allowed to go just any way they like. They must learn discipline and obedience. I tell you that it is to his interest to go to sea. He is my heir, and if he conducts himself properly he may hope to be pushed on in life as long as I live, and inherit my fortune at my death. If he refuses, I shall cut him off, so he knows what to expect."

"I sincerely regret your harsh determination," said the gentleman, "for I really consider your nephew a young man of great promise. He is studiously inclined, and in every way shows that the sea is about the very last calling for which he is destined. Why should you try to waste his young life in a profession which he is unfit for?"

"Unfit for!" exclaimed the admiral. "Unfit for! In my time there was no talk of a lad's being unfit to serve his country at the bidding of those in authority over him, unless he was a cripple. Is not my nephew strong and well built enough for the sea? Why should he be unfit?"

"Not physically unfit," said his friend. "I do not doubt for a moment his physical capabilities, but if he has formed other tastes, and feels himself called in another direction, why—"

"Nonsense, sir, nonsense! about his feeling himself called in another direction. He ought to feel himself called where his interest lies, to say nothing of his duty towards those placed over him," said my uncle.

"But you wouldn't make a slave of the boy?" said his friend.

"I only wish to call him to his senses, to make him do that which is best for himself. Am I to yield to a mere boyish whim, for which he himself would be sorry later in life? And as to his having no taste for it; he was full of it whilst he lived under my roof, before he went to school. It is only since he left me that he has got these new-fangled notions and hoisted the white feather."

"I do not see that it is any sign of cowardice to have changed his opinions since he was under your roof. Since then his mind has become more enlarged, and he is better able to see what he is fit for than when he had received no other instruction than your own. Since then he has made acquaintances—"

"And pretty acquaintances he has made! About the only acquaintance that he has is the son of a d—d apothecary, who happens to be at the same school. Do you think I can't see from whom he has picked up his sickly notions? Should I be doing my duty to my brother's son were I to aid him in his insane hobby of turning apothecary? To allow one of *my* family, one of my own flesh and blood, to make pills and spread plaisters for a living, when he might be boarding the enemy's fleet and shedding his blood for the honour and glory of his country? Why damme, sir, it's not manly, I'll be hanged if it is."

"Because he may have formed some acquaintances with this apothecary, doesn't necessarily show that he intends to turn apothecary himself. He says that he wishes to devote himself to the study of chemistry. Surely there is nothing disgraceful in that! Perhaps his determination may not be quite fixed as yet. He wishes to go to the university, where he will receive the education of a gentleman, and after a few years of study he will be enabled to settle down in that walk of life which suits him best."

"In the meantime he is wasting the flower of his youth in moping study, whilst he might be earning his laurels at sea."

"Life, my dear admiral, is a playground on which numbers meet to play at a vast variety of games. You have won your laurels at sea; let the poor boy earn his in the game he most delights in. We are not all born alike."

"Bah! Laurels gained at pills and poultices. Much good may his laurels do him. If he is wise, he will forget at once his low acquaintances, awaken to his real interest, and take a cruise with me. I have no doubt that after a time I shall set him to rights again."

"And if he refuses to go?"

"Oh!—then—then—why, he may as well begin to mix drugs at once, and the sooner the better."

"You mean that you would cut him off."

"Ay, that I most decidedly should."

"Now, my dear admiral, don't you think it would be kinder, as well as the best way to save the honour of your family, to try and prevent him from following the apothecary's business by doing what you can to aid his studies, that he may choose some other gentlemanly profession besides the sea, since he seems to have taken such an aversion to it?"

"No, no; my determination is fixed. If he does my will I will help him in what way I can. If he will not, neither will I help him in anything. He knows what he has to expect, either the sea and my portion when I die, or pills, poultices, and beggary."

"I much regret your stern decision, I must say," said the gentleman, and here the conference ended.

I was well aware of the admiral's decision, and that nothing on earth could move him; and as I was equally determined not to go to sea, I informed him how I had decided.

"Well, then," he said, "from today you are no longer nephew of mine. Follow your own silly inclinations, but don't hope for any help from me."

I considered myself turned out of the house, so I quietly packed up my things, and without taking leave of my uncle, I called upon my uncle's friend, the gentleman who had shown so much interest in my cause and explained how I was situated. I told him that I had money left me by my father, which I could not touch until I came of age. In the meantime I might die of want, as my uncle had refused positively to call me his nephew any longer. Therefore I begged him to be kind enough to lend me a sufficient sum to complete my studies at a foreign university, and I would repay him when it lay in my power.

My uncle's friend was a man of means and of a generous disposition, and not likely to see me go down thoroughly in the world, granted my request. I left my native town without letting my uncle know, and departed for Germany. I found my way to the university of Jena, where I entered and commenced my studies.

My first step was to perfect myself in the German language, to accomplish which I took lessons, visited the theatre, and went into society. The romance that seemed to attach itself to the life of a German student had long inflamed my youthful fancy, and I entered a "chor," or company of students, who distinguish themselves from others by their own especial "tricolour," which they wear in a ribbon across their chests and round their caps, and from ordinary mortals by their otherwise fantastic way of dressing themselves.

The novelty of this life, rather than the life itself, charmed me; for though I was delighted with the freedom and good fellowship amongst these young men, I was not a youth naturally given to excess, and I soon found that a little of this sort of life went a long way.

Nevertheless, at the beginning my fondness for the study of human nature in all its phases induced me to take part in all the manners and customs of my companions. I joined them at their *kneipe*, drank and sang with them, smoked with them, fought with them. I never refused a challenge, and sometimes even provoked a duel. I was never behind hand in any midnight brawl. I wore high boots and enormous spurs; gambled, betted, serenaded, played practical jokes, and soon got the reputation of a *flotter bursch* or rowdy fellow.

As every German student has his *liebchen*, I, too, had mine. A fair Teutonic damsel of good family deigned to smile on me, and there was much talk at one time in the little town of Jena about Fräulein von Hammelstengel and the handsome Englishman being *verlobt*.

People will talk at all times, and when news is wanting—what so easy as to invent? All the inhabitants of the town of Jena thought that they had a right to know and to talk of my private affairs, and seeing that I was of a reserved disposition and that they were not likely to extract much from me by pumping, it began to be rumoured abroad that I had certain grave reasons for maintaining secrecy, and in a very short time it was reported that I was a great "my lord," travelling in disguise for political purposes, and that I possessed a fortune of countless millions of pounds sterling.

This interesting discovery soon reached the ears of the parents of the already-mentioned young lady, who, by the way, had other admirers besides myself, and I could not without vanity at that time fairly consider myself the favoured one. Nevertheless, from the time the report of my fabulous riches spread throughout the whole university town I suddenly found Fräulein von Hammelstengel thrust in my way in the most obtrusive manner.

If I went to the theatre she was sure to be blocking up the doorway as I entered. If I was invited to a party, she was sure to be there. If I went to a public beer garden, there she was again; in the streets, in church—everywhere.

At the time I speak of I had but little experience of the world, but that little sufficed for me to see the trap that was laid for me. I was amused at the farce played before me, but disgusted with the actors, and resolved to withdraw myself.

Now, Miss von H. was a very fair specimen of the German upper classes. Besides being pretty, she could cook, knit stockings, do every sort of household work, had a very nice voice, and was a very excellent performer on the pianoforte. She was amiable, and possessed all the qualities of a good housewife. I may even confess that she was not quite indifferent to me at this time, but when I saw that her parents were making a bait of her to catch me, I was awed at the hook, and meditated escape.

I therefore prepared to undeceive the family as to the state of my finances, giving out that I was only a poor student who, unable to make both ends meet in my own country, had retired to the continent to live cheaper. This I confided to the young lady herself, and it was evidently soon after repeated to the parents, for a marked change in their behaviour soon manifested itself towards me, which was not only what I expected, but what I wished for. However, after a time it was reported in the town that I could not be as poor as I pretended to be, as it was remarked that I always paid my bills—a somewhat rare occurrence among German students—that I was always well dressed, lived well, had given wine parties, and had books expensively bound.

Now, when the von Hammelstengels heard this last report, they began again to believe in all that they had been told of me at first, and rather than let their prey escape so easily, they resolved to make another effort, and commenced to weave their meshes around me again.

In vain I repeated that I was only a poor student, and could not hope to marry. I saw that I was not believed, and was persecuted more than ever with attentions. Mrs. von Hammelstengel grew so amiable, that I was quite alarmed. Her husband so cordial and obsequious, that I grew disgusted. The *fräulein* herself so languishing and sentimental that I saw that there was nothing open for me but flight, so informing them all that important family affairs had called me suddenly back to England, I bade them a hasty farewell, and shut myself up in my own lodging for a time.

Now, this stratagem was discovered by the brother of Miss von Hammelstengel, an officer in the army. He met me about two months after I had taken leave of the family, and having ascertained that I had been in Jena all the time, and had never mentioned to anyone else my intention of returning to my country, he came to the conclusion that my retirement was nothing but a "ruse" to free myself from the clutches of his family.

He could not let me slip without playing his last card, which was to frighten me into marriage if possible. With this object he managed to pick a quarrel with me, asking me if I thought it was behaving like a gentleman to excite hopes in the breast of a young and innocent girl, and then absconding, saying that he could not see his sister pining away day by day without taking her cause in hand, etc.

There was nothing left me, he said, but to marry his sister or to fight him. My decision was soon made. I told him that I would never be forced into marriage through fear of a wound, and I resolved to fight him.

An officer in the army is the only grade of man that a German student deigns to fight with. All others are beneath his notice. Now, as my adversary was an officer, it was considered no degradation on my part to accept the challenge, so weapons were provided, compliments exchanged between seconds, and the adversaries met.

The offence towards his family was seen in such a grave light by my foe, that instead of the ordinary method adopted by German students—the use of the customary leaden collar, and pads to protect the more vital parts—nothing would satisfy him but a duel with the sabre, without pads and bandages.

This is the most terrible challenge, save that with the pistol, but I did not shrink from it. I left a letter directed to the gentleman in England who had lent me the money to pursue my studies at the university in the hands of my second, to be posted in case of my death, and hastened to meet my adversary. The fight was short, though desperate. My adversary fell severely wounded in the arm. Parties tried to hush up the matter, but of course the town was soon full of it. The story of the duel was variously told. Some said that I had vanquished the captain, and others that he had vanquished me; but the truth soon oozed out.

Fräulein von Hammelstengel subsequently married an old count, who was supposed to be rich, but who proved afterwards not to possess a penny.

But to return to myself. Disgusted with my experience of human nature, and of womankind in particular, I set to work now more diligently than ever. Bade farewell to my "chor," and gave up rioting and revelling, and wrote to my school friend the chemist's son to come and join me in my studies. I also wrote a letter to the gentleman who had kindly furnished me with funds to continue my studies abroad, and in due time I received the following letter:

My Dear Charles,
I am delighted to hear that you have at length settled down again to earnest study. I hope you will not get into any more scrapes, or another time you may not get off scot-free. Duelling is a very wicked and a very silly practice, and does no credit to either party; therefore I hope you will never seek a

quarrel, but do all you can to steer clear of pugnacious persons. You have now been more than a year at the university, and you write so seldom that you leave me in the dark as to what progress you have made during your stay. I wish you would write oftener, as I am very much interested to know how you are getting on. Now for a bit of home news. Your uncle the admiral, shortly after your departure, took to himself a young and pretty wife. I am afraid, however, instead of the happy home he contemplated, he sees too late that he has done a foolish thing. She is a desperate flirt, and rumours of such a nature are afloat in the town, that I should not be surprised if before long he sues for a divorce. He has never been the same man since you left, and looks considerably older. The disappointment that he felt at your determination to go your own way instead of his has been indeed a great blow to him. I constantly remonstrated with him on his views of your conduct towards him, but you know how obstinate he is. He grumbles that you left his house in a huff without even taking leave of him, but he has never had the curiosity to ask what has become of you, and hasn't an idea that I know of your whereabouts. "I called at your friend's the chemist's yesterday. His son told me that you had written to him advising him to join you in Jena. He would be delighted to go, and I do not think his father is averse to sending him. He is a superior lad, and I am not prejudiced enough to advise you to cut his acquaintance on the mere ground of his having been born in a humbler sphere of life than yourself. The admiral may have his prejudices, and to a certain extent I agree with him; that is to say that one ought rather to seek acquaintances within his own class than out of it. Still, when we meet a man of superior mind in a class a little below our own, I see no reason why we should draw the line of society too tightly. I must now leave off, and hoping that you will take care of your health, as well as improve in your studies,—I remain, yours very truly,
Edward Langton

Here was news indeed! My old bachelor uncle—he who when he was merry used to laugh at the foibles of the fair sex and ridicule married men—had himself been betrayed into marrying one of those frail beings he professed to despise. All the experience of his long life had vanished like smoke before the sunshine of his charmer. He had been dazzled with her eyes, and had taken a step in the dark, and found himself, too late, in the quagmire of remorse.

Poor old fool! I sincerely pitied him.

"This comes," said I to myself, "of turning nephews out of doors. Had you, instead of trying to bend the iron resolve of your nephew to your own poor old obstinate will, assisted him in his very laudable determination to follow science, you might yet have lived and died a bachelor to your heart's content. But console yourself, my uncle, St. Anthony was tempted by a fair demon before you. Now you have learned a lesson, although it has come somewhat late in life."

Although I deeply sympathised with my guardian's mistake, I could not do otherwise than feel that he fully deserved this punishment for his treatment of myself. How absurd and arrogant of a man, to persist in bending another to his own selfish will! Are we free agents, or are we not?

But enough of this. My uncle had sinned, and he was punished. He had imagined his charmer an angel, and found after all that she was but mortal like the rest of her sex, a poor, weak woman. He could hardly ever have been besotted enough to fancy that she had married him for anything else than his money, but what will not a man do to obtain the idol of his affections?

Perhaps it was not mere blind passion that had induced him to thrust his neck under the yoke. It might only have been pique. He would show his nephew that he could live very happily without his companionship, and this was the way he showed it.

I mentally drew a portrait of my aunt. A dashing, reckless girl, determined to have her own way in everything, running up dressmakers' bills, driving about in her carriage to spend her days in visiting and frivolity. Ambitious of pleasing every man but her husband. Dragging her poor old wooden-legged spouse after her to balls, operas, and concerts, or else leaving him at home, perhaps poorly, whilst she was enjoying herself in some crowded assembly, surrounded by a troop of young gallants, encouraging their attentions and making game of the poor old fool she had cajoled into marrying her. I imagined her pretty, witty, vivacious and with a temper. A thorough incapacity for the management of a household, vain, extravagant, frivolous, heartless, calculating.

Such was the mental picture I had drawn of my young aunt. How

I could imagine her of an evening—if she ever stayed at home with her husband in the evening—yawning over the admiral's long nautical stories, sighing and pouting when he asked her to bring him his slippers, or rather his slipper, for he had but one. Turning up her nose as she mixed his grog for him or lighted his pipe. Shuddering when the old man caressingly touched her dimpled chin, and pleading fatigue that she might go to bed early to be alone and dream of some handsome young lieutenant she had met at Mrs. So-and-So's ball.

"Well, well," said I to myself, "I will not triumph too long over your fall, uncle, lest some day the like may happen to myself, which Heaven forfend."

I tried to imagine myself with a wife like my aunt. I, a scholar, a searcher after the philosopher's stone, with a gay young wife always out at parties, a family of neglected children at home, breaking in upon my studies and smashing my crucibles and retorts, tearing up my valuable MSS, turning my laboratory into a nursery, and profaning my hours of study with their crying and squabbling.

"No," said I, "it shall not be. I will live single. A scientific man is wedded to science."

After the letter I had received from my friend Langton, the opinion I had formed of womankind was somewhat of the lowest. I imagined that all women were alike, and the dread I felt lest I should fall into a trap myself, induced me to shut myself up more than ever. I built a laboratory and fitted it up. I pored over my books, fasted, slept little, and sought as much as possible to reduce matter into mind. I resolved to give myself wholly up to the study of the transmutation of metals, nothing doubting that some day if I persisted in my labours I should be rewarded by the discovery of the philosopher's stone. I paid no visits, neither received any. I had seen enough of dissipation, and was now resolved to make up for lost time. A sudden change had come over me. I was no longer the *flotter bursch* that the year before swaggered, booted and spurred through the streets of Jena, foremost in the midnight revel, dauntless at the duel, guilty of every species of extravagance and excess. I had become the haggard and emaciated student of the dark arts, nervous in the extreme, shunning company, and the nature of whose studies was a mystery to all. Slovenly and smoke begrimed, daily and nightly I poured over my crucibles, trying all sorts of experiments and suffering many disappointments, denying myself the common necessaries of life, that I might expend my small income in instruments and articles wherewith to pursue my science. Absorbed in that one pursuit, I quite forgot the world without, forgot that I was of the same clay as my fellow mortals, lost all sympathy for the rest of my kind, neither sought any from them. My whole mental energies were concentrated on that one topic—that of making gold. Nor was it avarice that induced me to make gold the object of my pursuit. Nothing, I assure you, but the pure love of science prompted me in my studies. I had already made several curious discoveries. I was on the eve, or thought I was, of discovering the great secret, when owing to excessive fasting and want of sleep, my health broke down. Being originally of an iron constitution, I deemed in the pride of my youth that I was proof against any fatigue of mind or body until actual experience taught me that there were bounds even to my powers of endurance.

As I had not for a very considerable time to set foot beyond the narrow walls of my cell, and my mental faculties were thoroughly engrossed with study, my system required but slight stimulant. A cup of milk and a roll in the morning and a leek in the evening was all I required to keep soul and body together. Nay, latterly I confined myself to a slice of bread and a glass of water, and this lasted me all day for more than a fortnight. This scanty food was brought me by an orphan boy, who was deaf and dumb, whom I had engaged as my servant, as being better able to keep silence as to the nature of my studies.

Each day I fancied brought me nearer and nearer towards the discovery of the grand secret, when Nature, long trampled upon, rebelled, and positively refused to hold out any longer. My form was reduced to that of a skeleton, objects swam before my eyes, my brain reeled, and I repeatedly fainted for want of nourishment. My hand trembled, my mind lost its energy, and I was no longer fit for study. I found that I had overtaxed my strength, and saw the necessity of taking more food.

One morning when I felt so debilitated that I really thought my last hour was come, I ordered my servant to make me some broth. He had scarcely left my laboratory to obey my orders when a peculiar sensation came over me. I am as certain as I am of my own existence at the present moment that I was then in a waking state, though what I am about to relate to you now may appear to some like a dream. I felt—if I may so describe my feelings—that I did not belong to myself, or, as if my spirit were entirely free and independent of my body. It was a feeling as of a bounding elasticity, as if neither the walls of my cell nor any other material objects were impediments to me, and that I was capable at will of soaring into realms of space, and of conversing with intelligences of an immeasurably higher order than those of our mundane sphere, and of perfectly understanding discourses that in the body I was perfectly sure would be beyond my comprehension.

I remember that on this very morning I was seated in a high-backed arm-chair of carved oak, in a reflective mood. My crucibles and retorts strewed the laboratory in the greatest disorder. I was too weak to study or even to rise from my chair, when suddenly upon raising my eyes towards the opposite wall of my laboratory, the scene seemed changed, and instead of the bare wall before me I saw the mouth of a large cave, through the innumerable arches of which I could see to a great distance, for the interior seemed lighted up as with fire.

Now, I know that I was perfectly unable to rise from my chair, yet it appeared to me that I rose, and with firm step entered the cave.

It was dark and very chilly. I gazed around me for a moment and shuddered when I discovered at my side, my eyes being now accustomed to the light, the form of an old man, bald-headed, and with snowy locks and beard. His brow was high and his eye clear and beaming with wisdom and benevolence. His form was upright and his step firm, and he wore a tunic with ample folds and of a sad colour.

At first I started and looked at him wonderingly, as if to ask him who he was. He answered to my thoughts affably. "I am your guide. You have courted our intimacy, and sought to become our equal. Come with me, and I will initiate you into our mysteries and show you the lot for which you have so long been striving."

There was something so inviting in the old man's manner, something so charming in the calm and dignified look that superior intellect invariably gives, that I could not but comply, and following my guide, I was conducted through long labyrinths of arches in silence, until I reached the centre of the cavern, when I found myself in a vast hall formed by nature, or roughly hewn out of the natural rock, and illuminated by torches.

Here I saw a number of tables, and at each table sat one man. They appeared to be all engaged in chemistry, for each man had before him his crucibles and other instruments. So absorbed did they all seem in their work that not one of them noticed our entrance, although we were talking loud enough for all to hear and our voices re-echoed through the cavern.

I tried to catch the eye of some of them in order to salute them, and perhaps to enter into conversation with them, but no one looked up.

I felt somewhat chilled at this reception, as it seemed to me that they must have heard us, and purposely avoided looking up. My guide, who could read all that was passing in my mind, responded to my thoughts.

"Be not grieved at their apparent want of civility, for they do not even see you. These spirits see nothing and hear nothing but what is immediately before them and connected with their pursuits. All you see here are alchemists. In your terrestrial globe their sole delight was in the endeavour to make gold. To this end they voluntarily imprisoned their spirits in one channel in order to concentrate the force of their intellects towards the object of their pursuit.

"The development of their intellects alone at the expense of everything else that is human, was their desire in the world; their intellects alone, therefore, after death remain engrossed in their one pursuit to all eternity, and they are both deaf and blind to all else."

"And will this be my lot?" I asked of my guide.

"That depends upon yourself," was the reply. "Your spirit is not so entirely separated from your body as to make your doom irrevocable. In whatever state you quit the world of the body, in that state the spirit remains to eternity. If the state of these spirits pleases you not, there is time to set your affections on another.

"Anon I will show you another class of alchemists. These that you have seen are spirits who strive to make gold from love of science. Those I will show you now are those who have the love of gold for their aim, to which they make science subservient."

My guide then conducted me through a long dark corridor of arches until we reached another hall lighted up in a similar manner to the first. Here were a number of spirits, each likewise occupied with his own crucibles and apparatus, and paying no attention to those around him. The hall and the instruments used by the spirits of this second hall differed little from those of hall the first, but the faces of the men were different.

In the second hall the faces were less dignified and the skulls were broader, each of them having a preternatural protuberance like an egg at the temples, whilst the crown of their heads was flat. The heads of those of the first hall were higher, and their bearing more philosophic.

"I do not like the faces of those men," said I to my guide. "I dislike the expression of greed depicted on their countenances. Remove me from hence."

"I will now show you another order of spirits, also alchemists in their way, since gold is their pursuit," and here he led me down a dark subterranean staircase, damp and cold, which I descended with difficulty on account of the slipperiness of the steps.

"This is no place for you," said my guide, "as I observe by your cautious footsteps, yet many are they whose haste to enter at yon door makes them rush down head foremost, regardless of the slime, and at the risk of breaking their necks."

By this time the hand of my guide was on the door, which he entered, leading me after him. I immediately found myself within a large and elegant hall, lighted up with the light of day, with columns and pavement of marble. Here was a crowd of men divided into groups, and discussing business. Others hurrying and bustling, jostling each other in their haste, as they traversed the hall. The physiognomy of these men was decidedly material. Sharp and shrewd many of them, but for the most part of that cold, stolid, matter of fact sort that defies you to read beyond the surface.

As business and business men had little charm for me, my scrutiny of the spirits in this hall was less minute than my observation of the spirits in the two previous halls, and my guide, observing an expression of weariness in my countenance, said:

"I see these spirits interest you not. These are merchants, and men of business, who have made the acquisition of gold their chief delight in the world, without using it merely as a means to an end; but let us pass on."

We then entered a hall adjoining. Here was to be seen a long table, at which numbers were gambling. The faces of some of these were truly hideous; others merely simple. It was easy with half an eye to discern the dupe and the sharper. Faces indicative of the most sordid avarice jostled others of trusting simplicity. I saw to what class these spirits belonged, and, sickened at the sight, my guide led me by the hand and withdrew me from the hall.

On leaving the gamblers we next found ourselves in a beautiful garden with terraces, fountains, beds of the choicest flowers, with a sunny landscape beyond. In the centre of a velvet lawn was a motley group of dancers, singers, and players on musical instruments. The dancers were of both sexes, and many of them fair to view. They seemed to whirl round in the giddy dance with true delight.

"These, at least," I said, "are happy. How they seem to enjoy themselves! Who would not be happy in the midst of such a beautiful scene?"

"These, my friend, are but deceptive joys," replied the sage, with a sigh. "These, you see, are those who in the world have made pleasure the sole aim and object of their lives, and who, on entering the world of spirits, still retain their former tastes."

I watched the group of dancers for a time; at first with pleasure, then with indifference, and lastly with a feeling akin to disgust mingled with pity. Dancing and merry-making is all very well as an interlude to hard work, and doubtless did good both to mind and body, but when I reflected that this trivial amusement had been the sole occupation of their lives in the world, and would continue to be so to all eternity, I turned away with a sigh. The whole scene seemed to me less beautiful than before, though I could not observe that any change had taken place in the landscape, and an intense feeling of weariness came over me, with an inclination to yawn, which my guide observing, said:

"So you have soon become disenchanted with your realms of delight."

"You are right," said I; "lead me from the scene." Turning my back on the dancers, I followed the old man, who led me over hill, down dale, through thicket and bramble, discoursing all the while the states of various classes of spirits after death, till we reached a thick forest of old gnarled trees. Flanking the forest ran a river of molten gold. I stood upon the edge of a rock and looked down upon the river. Here I descried a number of naked forms of both sexes bathing in the stream and splashing each other with the liquid metal.

"Who are these?" I asked.

"These," said my guide, "are those who in the world found gold without seeking it, and possessing it in abundance, knew not how to make use of it. Their sole delight was in wasting it. The same passion remains with them after death."

I fell into a reverie.

"Is it possible," thought I, "that these people have nothing at all to do with their money? Could they be in ignorance of the poverty that surrounded them whilst in the world? Even if they were selfish and did no good to the rest of their kind, is it possible that they had no private way of enjoying their worldly goods?"

"The spirits here in the world wasted their fortunes, but the ruin of one fortune is the foundation of others, as you will see anon," said the sage.

He then pointed out to me some men, miserable looking and wretchedly clad, who were crawling on their hands and knees in search of nuggets of gold that the wanton bathers had thrown in a liquid state on to the shore, where it had cooled. Each of these wretched men had a bag which he filled with lumps of the yellow metal, and when it was full, carried it on his shoulders, tottering under its weight, till he reached his home.

"Neither do these men know the use of gold," said my guide, "for they are misers, and their sole delight is to collect gold and to worship it, without doing good to themselves or others."

My curiosity was roused at this strange sight, and I followed these men with my eyes, as a wide plain stretched itself out, and I being on elevated ground, could see to a great distance, for I wished to see how far they could stagger under their enormous weight. No dwellings appeared near at hand, and yet I was surprised to notice that one after the other these men suddenly disappeared. Many of them had started about the same time laden with their sacks of gold, and not one of the many was visible to me now on that broad open plain. Where could they have all gone?

"I will tell you," said my companion, answering as usual to my thoughts. "These spirits, fearing lest their houses should be broken into and pillaged, burrow under the ground, where they can keep their riches in security. They seldom show themselves in the daytime, but come out of their holes at night like the owl in search of plunder. In the world they lived by stealing, cheating, and getting money under false pretences, and this is their lot after death. Their subterranean dwellings are paved and lined with gold, yet they are always wretched, for they know no other delight than to amass gold for its own sake."

I grew melancholy as I reflected on the lot of these men.

"At least my lot will not be with them," I said to myself. "I hope it cannot be said of me that I worship gold. If I have made the converting of other metals into gold the study of my life, it was not for the sake of the yellow metal, but from the pure love of science like those philosophers of the first halls."

"True," said my friend, in reply to my meditations, "and yet methinks their lot pleased you but little. The study of science for the sake of science and without other object, is little better than the grubbing of gold for the sake of gold. Think you not that a man's life ought to have a little higher aim?"

"Certainly," said I, "that our studies may be useful to others, that our discoveries may benefit mankind to the end, that we may become more civilised, more intellectual, more virtuous, more moral."

"If then," replied the sage, "you admit this to be the true end of the life of man, why do you persist in following the one study of converting baser metals into gold, which, if the secret is once made known, could not be of the slightest service to mankind at large, whilst you would only reap the selfish and vain satisfaction of having discovered the secret, whereas the precious time that has been wasted in this useless study would have been better employed in experiments that might tend to discoveries beneficial to the whole human race."

The argument of my venerable guide made a deep impression on me, and I reflected a moment.

"Is it possible," thought I, "that all my life has been a mistake. Have I mistaken mere vain and selfish ambition for that pure love of science that dignifies and elevates the human mind? No," I answered to myself, "not exactly; and yet I have been mistaken in studying alchemy; for surely we ought to consider the end of whatever study we pursue, which end ought to be in some way or other useful to mankind at large. Now, supposing, after having wasted the energies of a lifetime in pursuit of the philosopher's stone, I had at length discovered the secret, it could only benefit myself, and my aim after all was no higher than that of those wretched spirits whose lot I shrank from. You are right, O sage. I will no longer waste my time and health in a fruitless study, but henceforth devote myself to something that may benefit my fellow creatures."

"You are fast growing wise," said the sage, replying to my thoughts; "keep to that resolution, and the comfort you will experience from the consciousness that you have devoted your life to the welfare of your race will be the true alchemy, for it will be spiritual gold."

My heart yearned towards the kind old man at these words, and in an ecstasy of affection and reverence as well as joy at having discovered the error of my life, I embraced him, begged him never to leave me, but be ever with me—to guide me in wisdom; to be, in fact, a father to me, and I would follow his counsel as a son.

The kindly sage smiled benevolently on me, and replied:

"My son, our lots are different; at least, for the present. Recollect that you are yet in the body, whilst I have for many ages back been all spirit. We must shortly part; you will return to the body until you are called from thence, whilst I must hasten to the society of spirits to which I belong. Till then, however, I will be your guide, and give you what instruction I may in spiritual things."

I thanked him, and expressed my regret at having to part from him so soon, and hoped we should meet again when our conditions became the same. I then begged him as my time was short, to show me the lot of spirits of a higher order, saying:

"You have shown me those who have sought gold from the love of science and those who have sought it from greed. Also those who, having gold, knew not how to use it. Now show me the lot of those who, born wealthy, have made the best use of their wealth."

"My son," said the sage, "those spirits are few in number and belong to a higher sphere. One direct from earth as yourself enters with difficulty within that holy region. However, follow me."

Then there appeared to rise from the ground a sort of mist, which thickened until it became a small but dense cloud. Upon this my guide alighted, leading me after him. We both of us trod the cloud beneath our feet, upon which we made no more impression than if our bodies had been made of the same ephemeral substance as the vapour we trod. The cloud then commenced to rise, and slowly wafted us high in air, carrying us over trees and mountains as we discoursed together by the way. Moving upwards, yet not straight and suddenly, but describing wide circles in the air, as if we were ascending a winding staircase, we found ourselves, after a time, in the midst of a large dense cloud, and our motion ceased.

By degrees the mist seemed to clear away, and I beheld a curious phenomenon. I stood firmly, as if upon the solid earth, yet when I looked above me the earth appeared over my head, whilst the sky seemed under my feet.

"What is the reason," I asked, "that in this planet or aerial dwelling of spirits, the laws of nature are reversed?"

"Your vision only is reversed," replied my guide, "because not being as yet entirely freed from the body, your spirit savours too much of clay to be in harmony with the spirits of this sphere. Everything in the spiritual world is a type, and has a hidden meaning. As the sky is a type of heaven, so the earth we tread is a type of material things. The reason you see the earth above your head and the sky beneath your feet, is that you as yet place material things above spiritual things. It is difficult for you, as a mortal, to do otherwise, and therefore your vision is distorted. I can, however, while I am with you, communicate a portion of my being to you, sufficient for you to see objects as they really are."

He then touched my forehead, grasping my temples between his finger and thumb, when a new sensation came over me. It seemed as if I had been suddenly lifted with the rapidity of lightning a mile or two higher in the air, although my guide assured me that I had never moved from the spot I was standing on. I appeared to breathe more freely, and experienced a most exhilarating feeling of buoyancy, with an intense and boundless expansion of mind.

The sky was now above my head and the earth beneath my feet, as in our world. I found myself surrounded by a beautiful landscape that would baffle all my descriptive powers to give any adequate idea of. Trees, beautiful and curious, bearing fruit of gold, silver, or precious stones, and of ferns that I had never seen in the world. Hills and valleys of rich luxuriance, crags, waterfalls, lakes with islands, magnificent palaces of the purest white marble in a style of architecture truly sublime. Human forms, surpassingly beautiful, of both sexes and of all ages crossed me at intervals, from blooming and laughing infancy to hoary but hale old age, each stage of life bearing a marked beauty of its own. Everyone seemed happy, and no one idle, although the occupations of some were of a quiet, meditative sort.

Philosophers discussed theories among themselves or taught wisdom to the young, who listened attentively. Children romped or indulged in amusements suitable to their age. Lovers passed and repassed, discussing together in earnest whisper. Here and there a solitary poet composed an ode or landscape painter plied his art. The more I gazed on the scene, the more I became enraptured, for all was sunshine and content.

"How different," thought I, "is this to those false delusive joys that I have just witnessed in the lower world of spirits, and which I, in my besotted ignorance, mistook for a paradise!"

Then my guide turning towards me said:

"I perceive that you are enchanted with this scene, that the beauty around you surpasses your wildest imagination, and that you could never desire a paradise more delightful. These are those who in the world were born rich, or, at least, if not rich, used the little they possessed to relieve or promote the happiness and welfare of their kind, denying themselves luxuries or even necessities in order to enlarge the field of their charity, counting the dead pleasures of wealth as nothing in comparison with the satisfaction they derived from rendering happy their poorer neighbours. These are the angels of the lowest heaven, but there are higher joys than these, which neither you nor I may ever be permitted to witness."

So enraptured was I with all around me, that I hardly listened to the words of my guide. I yearned to converse with some of the inhabitants of this paradise, but a feeling of shyness, owing to a consciousness of inferiority, held me back.

The inhabitants even invited me to discourse with them, for they looked on me kindly, as if waiting for me to address them. Maidens of most heavenly beauty gazed upon me with sweet looks of chaste innocence. Lovely children seemed about to seize me by the hand to lead me away to play, but on approaching nearer to me and perceiving that I was not of their heaven, scampered off half-terrified. One or two hospitable persons came forward and offered to take me into their houses, and to show me some of the public buildings, but my guide observing that a giddiness had seized me, owing to the excess of delight I experienced in things so new to me, explained to them that I was yet a mortal only temporarily withdrawn from the body, and that a longer stay in this region might prove dangerous to me, as he had been commissioned to let me return shortly. My conductor then waved his hand courteously to everyone by way of farewell, the good spirits also returning the salute while we descended more rapidly than we had ascended, and all around me became as before, a thick cloud. I felt nigh fainting with a singing in my ears, but this vanished by degrees the farther I left the paradise behind.

At length my senses being sufficiently recovered, I gazed around me; all was mist still, but every now and then I observed certain curious phenomena, visions which appeared and disappeared. Sometimes it was a garden or a building, sometimes an animal, a solitary tree or flowers. I heard strains of music, voices, laughter. Sometimes a rose or other flower fell at my feet, and immediately vanished; sometimes a toad or other reptile fell near me, and likewise vanished. Sometimes birds of prey or fierce animals were seen striving with one another. Then again, fragments of distant landscape appeared and vanished.

None of these apparitions lasted beyond a few seconds.

Then turning to my guide, I said:

"Tell me, O sage, what is the meaning of all these appearances?"

To which the old man replied:

"These are all signs and symbols of things which in your world have no visible nor tangible existence, their essence being purely spiritual, yet which, nevertheless, in their own atmosphere—the spiritual world—have a visible existence of their own. These are the thoughts of mortals yet living in your world.

"We are fast approaching your earth, and therefore these appearances become visible. The more beautiful of these visions, such as the flowers, landscape, and singing birds, are the representations of the pure thoughts and desires of the good; those of the less pleasing sort, such as the toads, adders, serpents, bats and owls, signify the evil thoughts of the wicked, and correspond to revenge, hatred, lust, murder, fraud, and the like.

"Where these wild beasts and reptiles appear in great numbers in the spirit world, and are seen combating one with the other, it is a sign of war on earth."

"But tell me why," I said, "I hear the sound of music yet see no musicians, and hear the sound of voices yet see no one?"

Then my companion answered me: "The murky atmosphere through which we are now passing is also an inhabited world. The spirits of this world are invisible to you because you are not altogether freed from the material veil which obscures your vision, and that veil thickens the nearer you approach earth. The thoughts of mortals become visible to you here because you yourself are a mortal, but the thoughts of the purest mortal on your earth cannot arrive at the same pitch of sublimity as the thoughts of the meanest of disembodied spirits of this world, and therefore the spirits themselves are invisible to you, although they are far inferior to those you have just visited."

"Then why could I enter the angels' lower paradise, and yet am not able to see these inferior spirits?" I asked.

"Because," replied my instructor, "your spirit then received sufficient light from contact with mine to enable you to see them. I could also let you see these, but why desire to see the lot of ordinary spirits after having seen those of so far higher an order? It might remove the impression, which I presume you wish to retain. Besides our time is short, for we are near touching earth."

"True, true," I said hurriedly, for another vision suddenly arrested my attention. "Tell me, O my guide, what is the meaning of yon strange sight?" And strange sight it was indeed! For it was the vision of a human leg clad in the knee-breeches of our time, and walking about by itself.

"That," replied my preceptor, "is a portion of the body of some spirit not as yet freed from clay, and for that reason it is made visible to you. Our spirits on first leaving the material world are an exact counterpart of our terrestrial bodies, being an essence filling every part and particle of our earthly frames, from which they receive their stamp. The body itself does not rise again as some of your world vulgarly believed, but the spiritual body its counterpart, while the earthly covering but contributes its dust to your globe's surface."

"Then the vision I see is a portion of a human soul about to leave its earthy tenement?" asked I.

"By no means," replied the sage. "The owner of that limb has yet some years of material life before him, although, I observe, he is aged. The reason that you see but the leg and not the rest of the body, is that that portion of the physical body is wanting. You cannot perceive his corporeal body because you are now in the spirit, and the spirit can only see that which is spiritual, as likewise the material eye only that which is material. You are sufficiently spiritual to see spirits who are yet encumbered with clay, but not enough so to see spirits perfectly disembodied. On the other hand, being withdrawn from the body, you are not yet sufficiently material to descry material bodies."

"Then in fact," I observed, "the vision that I see before me is the spirit leg of someone who in my world has lost his material leg?"

"Precisely so," the sage replied, "for mortals live in two worlds at the same time; in the material world as to their bodies, in the spiritual world as to their spirits. I should imagine," added he, regarding the vision fixedly, "from the way in which it seems to approach you that it belonged to some friend or relation of yours. Have you no relation in the world who has lost a leg?" he asked.

"A relation who has lost a leg?" I exclaimed, for instantly my uncle, the admiral, flashed across my mind.

"Exactly so, your uncle, the admiral," he replied, reading my thoughts.

There was an individuality about the limb that from the beginning seemed familiar to me. It was a right leg, too, the very leg that my uncle had lost. There could be no mistake about it.

Then said I to my guide, "I recognise the leg, sure enough, but is its appearance now a sign that he is near me in the body?"

"If not so, at least in thought," responded the sage.

By this time my companion told me that we had already arrived on earth, and said that he must now leave me, so we embraced, and he vanished from my sight. Then the mist around me suddenly cleared away, and I was surprised to find myself once again in my laboratory, seated in the same old carved arm-chair, and surrounded by several persons.

Well, gentlemen, amongst those persons I instantly recognised a face long familiar to me. It was my uncle's!

Poor old man! He had dreadfully changed. His iron grey hair had become perfectly white, his black eyebrows "a sable silvered." He stooped very much, and the muscles of his face were drooping and flaccid, while his ruby nose had lost its fine rich colour and faded into a sickly ashen hue. The individual next to him I recognised at once as our common friend, Mr. Langton. Then I saw a strange face which I concluded must be the doctor. There was also my deaf and dumb boy, who had not long brought up my basin of broth, as it was still steaming, and he was awaiting my recovery.

Little more remains to be told. My poor uncle, as our friend Langton had prophesied, had been obliged to sue for a divorce, shortly after which his worthless partner eloped with a paramour. The whole sad occurrence preyed upon the old man's mind, and brought on a dangerous illness, from which, however, he recovered. During his illness he had spoken much of his nephew, and on his recovery the doctor had recommended him a change of scene to divert his mind. As he had expressed a wish to see his nephew once more before he died, his friend Langton had offered to accompany him. The doctor also formed one of the party, and they had travelled together to Jena as an agreeable surprise for me.

It is needless to add that all former differences were forgotten, and that my old uncle resolved never to make a fool of himself again. He even encouraged his nephew's studies, and gave his sanction at length that my friend the chemist's son should join me in my studies. My health rapidly improved under careful treatment, and I never saw any more visions. I quite gave up alchemy, and applied myself to other branches of chemistry. Nevertheless, my studies had not been quite useless, as in my search after the philosopher's stone, I had made several very curious discoveries in science, and my name soon became famous throughout the university.

My uncle's illness had wrought as great a change morally as it had done physically in him. His nature was completely changed. His treatment of me was now of the kindest. He seemed even to respect me for the perseverance I had shown in my studies and to be ashamed of his former narrow-minded notions. He remained with me at Jena until his health and my health had completely recovered, when I accompanied him to England, where I once more saw my friend, the chemist's son, whom I subsequently took out with me to Jena, where we pursued our studies together for some three years, after which we both returned to England, where I took up my quarters at my uncle's house.

The admiral lived a good ten years after his illness, and died at the good old age of ninety, leaving to me his entire fortune.

An Interlude

On the conclusion of Mr. Crucible's narrative that gentleman was highly complimented on his tale by each member of the club in turn, especially by Mr. Oldstone. Our worthy host, owing to a strong potation he had imbibed before the commencement of the recital, more than once manifested symptoms of dropping into the arms of Morpheus, but was prevented from doing so each time by the opportune administration of sundry pinches of snuff from Mr. Oldstone's snuff-box.

If there was one thing this gentleman never forgave, it was a man going to sleep in the middle of a good story; he, therefore, as soon as the narrator had finished, felt it his solemn duty to remonstrate with our host severely upon his want of good breeding, to which the worthy man replied in a humble apology to all the company. As for his daughter Helen, she was attention itself throughout, and with the exception of Mr. Oldstone, was the loudest in praise of Mr. Crucible's recital.

"Well, Helen," said one of the members, "what do you think of the last story?"

"Oh, I am delighted with it," exclaimed the girl in ecstasy. "How I wish it had happened to me! I should so like to have a vision of that sort."

"Would you my dear?" said Mr. Crucible, "then I hope that if ever you see the Paradise I saw that you may remain there, for there you belong. You are too good for this earth."

"Now then, Crucible, none of your nonsense," said Mr. Oldstone. "Is that the way you talk to young ladies? I'm surprised at you. Look how you have made the poor girl blush."

"Don't be jealous, old boy," retorted the last narrator, "but give us another story. This is your turn."

"Yes, yes!" cried several voices at once. "Mr. Oldstone for a story! Hear, hear!"

"Really, gentlemen," said Mr. Oldstone, "it is so soon after the last, and as it is now getting somewhat late, I would fain put off my story for another time, and spend the evening between this and bedtime in some other way. Suppose we all fill our glasses. Perhaps someone may recollect a song."

"Agreed!" cried all the guests at once, "but who's to be the songster?"

"Can't you favour us, Helen?" asked Mr. Parnassus.

Helen declared that she could not sing, that she did not know any songs.

"Come, come, Helen, that's all nonsense," said the doctor, "I've heard your voice before now warbling away when you thought no one was listening to you."

"Ay, ay," said our host, "you are right, sir, she *can* sing when she likes as pretty a little song as ever you'd wish to hear, though I say it, that shouldn't."

"Come, Helen, don't be shy, sing away my girl," said Hardcase.

"Let us make a bargain, Helen," said McGuilp. "If *you* will sing a song, *I* will. There, you cannot refuse."

The girl's face brightened up as she stole a glance at our artist, and thus urged, began in a clear and sweet voice the following ditty:

The Nightingale

The nightingale sang to her love the rose,
One night when the moon was shining,
The earth was hushed in still repose,
But a heart with love was pining.

Two lovers through the misty air,
Beneath the trees were strolling,
A gallant and a lady fair,
A bell in the distance tolling.

"Beloved, hear'st thou that distant wail,
That sad and mournful knelling?"
"Sweetheart, 'tis but the nightingale,
That her tale of love is telling."

"No, no, 'tis not the nightingale,
I feel a dire foreboding,

The night spreads o'er her dusky veil,
Our joys of love corroding."

"Nay, loved one; banish idle fears,
The moon is bright and beaming,
Seek not to drown thy joy in tears,
When thy star above is gleaming."

"See here this flower," (he plucked a rose),
"How beautious is its blossom.
Wear this for me, for it but grows,
To deck thy snow white bosom."

Then out and shrieked the nightingale,
"Oh spare, oh spare, my lover.
Too late!" she cries, with dismal wail,
Beneath the greenwood cover.

"Ah me!" outshrieked that bird of night,
"My love is gone for ever,
But vengeance waits thee, cruel knight;
Thou from thy love shalt sever."

Too true, alas! the night bird's curse,
For 'neath the trees did hover,
An envious wight with arquebus,
T'await his rival lover.

Scarce had the gloomy prophecy
Died on his ears unheeding,
When the foe a poisoned shaft let fly,
And the knight fell pale and bleeding.

A lady mourns her love deceased,
Her eyes in death are rolling,
The distant tolling knell had ceased,
But again the knell is tolling.

"Thank you, Helen, thank you; very well sung," said several voices at once.

"It is a fanciful and mournful ditty," said Parnassus, "but the tune is good."

"It is, indeed, somewhat melancholy," said McGuilp. "Have you no other, Helen?"

"I did but bargain for one," said the girl, smiling.

"True," said McGuilp, "and now you want to hear one from me, eh?"

"Precisely so," said Mr. Oldstone. "Keep him to his word, Helen. Don't let him shirk off."

"Now, Mr. McGuilp," said several voices at once, "we are all waiting."

"Well, gentlemen," began the painter, "if you will permit me to retire—"

"Retire!—Oh, nonsense!" exclaimed Oldstone, Crucible, and others simultaneously. "Why you never mean to back out after having—"

"No, gentlemen, nothing of the sort, I assure you," said our artist, "I was only going to ask leave of the company to retire a moment to my chamber to bring down an article indispensable to the song I am about to sing."

"I believe he is going to sing in costume," said Mr. Blackdeed, "and that he is going in search of some 'property.'"

"No, nor that either," said the painter. "The song I shall sing to you this evening, gentlemen, is an ode that I composed myself to a skull which I found among some ancient ruins in Rome, and out of which I have made a drinking cup. As this is a drinking song, in which the cup is often alluded to, it will be necessary that the goblet itself be present."

"By all means," said several members.

"Let us see the precious relic," said the antiquary. "These things are quite in my line."

"And mine too," said the doctor.

Our artist left the apartment and returned with the relic, which he placed in the centre of the table for all to admire.

"There, Helen," said he, "that cup was once a man's head, who laughed, sang, and told stories, too, I've no doubt, like the best of us."

"And you use it to drink out of!" exclaimed the girl, in extreme disgust. "What a horrible idea."

Mr. Oldstone put on his spectacles and bent over the table attentively to examine it. Dr. Bleedem took it up, tapped it, looked at it all over, and declared that it was different in form to the skulls of the present day, observing that it was evidently of great antiquity, as the enamel had worn away. The bone, he said, was of great thickness.

The object of general curiosity was handed round the table from one to the other. At length Mr. Blackdeed took it up, and striking into a Hamlet-like attitude, quoted at full length the well-known passage:

"'Alas! poor Yorick! I knew him, Horatio; a fellow of infinite jest, of most excellent fancy,' etc., etc."

Applause followed the quotation.

"The song! the song!" cried others, impatiently.

"Composed by himself; mark that, gentlemen," said Mr. Parnassus. "A brother poet! Hear, hear!"

The company then drew themselves eagerly round the table, while our artist filled the human goblet to the brim, and after taking a sip from it, stood up, and holding it aloft, sang in a clear rich voice the following words:

Lines to a Skull

Stern relic of a bygone age,
What changes hast thou seen ere now?
Wert thou a warrior or a sage,
And did the laurel deck thy brow?
Wert of Imperial Caesar's line,
Or poet inspired with art divine?

Whate'er thou wert in days of old,
Whate'er the deeds they sing of thee,
Though ne'er so great and manifold,
Thy crown as a cup shall serve for me.
Here from they soul's deep-vaulted shrine,
Quaff I the blood of thy native vine.

And while it braces every nerve,
Hail! to Bacchus and Venus, too,
The gods that thou wert wont to serve,
In days of yore, to me be true,
As I lie 'neath the shade of the clustering vine,
Merrily quaffing the red, red wine.

Wast thy hand steeped in blood Achaean,
Whilst fighting for thy purple land,
Wert thou patrician or plebeian,
Or fell thou by th' assassin's hand,
Did'st thou in arms thy foes outshine,
Or did thy foe's arm conquer thine?

Or in the crowded Coliseum,
Did'st fall to glut the beasts of prey?
Wert thou reared in the athenaeum,
Or were thy haunts among the gay?
Now from thy skull on the Palatine,
I drink to thee and the muses nine.

On the banks of the Tiber's yellow tide,
In the mighty days of ancient Rome,
Perchance thou ruled'st in all thy pride,
O'erlooking thy seven-hilled home.
Thus I muse as at noonday I recline,
Quaffing the juice of the Roman vine.

Now, peace to thy Manes and farewell,
This toast to the quiet of thy remains,
I quaff from out thy hollow shell,
That once was filled with Roman brains.
In the land of the cypress and the pine,
Some future bard may drink from mine.

★ ★ ★ ★ ★

At the end of our artist's song he was unanimously cheered by the members of the club, and highly complimented upon his poetical skill, especially by Mr. Parnassus, who voted that he should be crowned with laurel. Mr. Oldstone eagerly seconded the proposal, but McGuilp modestly declined the honour. However, our worthy host, Jack Hearty, was sent out once more in the snow to gather laurel for the brow of the new poet laureate, in spite of our artist's modest protestations. He returned shortly afterwards with a branch of laurel, off which he first shook the snow, and then deposited upon the table. Mr. Oldstone quickly converted it into a wreath, and decreed it should be placed upon the songster's head by the fair hands of the pretty Helen. The decree was greeted with cheers, and Helen, blushing deeply and smiling, placed it on the head of the newly-discovered poet, our artist receiving it on bended knee amid the cheering of the club. McGuilp having risen from his knees, took his seat again at the table by the side of our host's pretty daughter, then rising to his feet and raising the skull aloft, he proposed the following toast in these words:

"Gentlemen, I propose the health of the 'Wonder Club,' and that of our worthy host and his fair daughter, our guest, to be drunk by every member present solemnly and devoutly from this goblet."

More cheering, during which McGuilp took a sip at the funereal chalice, and then passed it on to his neighbour, who did the same, each member in his turn sipping and nodding round to the rest.

When the skull had been the round of the table, it was then passed on to our host, who hoped that the company would excuse him, but that his lips had never yet been contaminated by dead men's bones, and he hoped they never would be.

Persuasions and remonstrances from the members were alike vain, for neither our host nor his daughter could be persuaded to touch the sacrilegious relic.

In order not to give offence to the company, our host proclaimed his willingness to drink the toast out of a clean glass. This was at length agreed to, and the worthy man rose, and in a short bluff speech, thanked the company present for having drunk his health and that of his daughter. A clapping of hands followed our host's speech, and then Mr. Crucible, being the eldest member, returned thanks on the part of the club.

At that moment the hooting of an owl was heard outside. Helen turned pale, and instinctively drew nearer to our artist.

"Why, Helen my girl!" cried the doctor, "how pale you are. What are you frightened at?"

"Do you not hear?" said the girl. "It is the cry of the owl; they say it is a sign of death in the house."

"Come, Helen," said Hardcase, "you must not be superstitious; those things are all nonsense."

"Oh, no, I can assure you—" began the girl, when Mr. Oldstone broke in.

"I say, Mr. Poet Laureate, look how your fair companion trembles at your side. Cannot you think of some lay that might cheer her spirits and dispel her fears? Just try."

"Well," answered he of the laurel crown, "talking about owls, I once kept a pet owl myself, that I captured one night in a nook under the arches of the Coliseum. He was a great favourite of mine, and used to perch on the top of my easel when I was at work, and watch every movement I made. I composed an ode to him. If you would like to hear it—"

"Oh, by all means," promptly answered Oldstone.

"In that case, Jack," said McGuilp, addressing our host, "you will oblige me by getting my mandolin. I mean that musical instrument that you will find in the corner of my room upstairs, just by way of accompaniment."

Jack Hearty left the room, and returned soon with the instrument.

"Ah, now we shall hear some music," said Oldstone rubbing his hands, and by this time Helen seemed to have forgotten her fears, and her eyes glistened in anticipation.

Our artist then ran his fingers lightly over the instrument by way of prelude and began the following ditty.

Ode to an Owl

Grim bird of Pallas old,
For what purpose yet untold
Wert thou cast in such a mould?
Speak, declare!

Though thou utterest not a word
As thou gazest on the herd,
I scarce can deem thee bird,
Such thy air.

There thou stand'st, a ghastly sight,
Sworn enemy of light,
Thou ill-omened bird of night,
'Neath the moon.

The charnel's dusky hue
Is lovelier to thy view
Than the clear cerulean blue
Of the noon.

As my task I daily ply,
Every movement thou dost spy,
From my easel perched on high
Gazing down.

Thou look'st so wondrous wise,
With those round mysterious eyes.
What unearthly glitter lies
In thy frown.

Once with thy friends so gay
Thou did'st turn night into day,
And while seeking for thy prey
Round would'st prowl.

Now from out thy ruined hall
In the Coliseum's wall
They nightly miss thy call,
Oh, my owl!

A captive now, alas!
Thou for aye art doomed to pass
Thy life far from the mass
Of thy race.

Like Stoic thou dost stand,
Exiled from his native land,
With that look so sage and grand
In thy face.

Were Pythagorean lore,
Current now as once before,
In the classic days of yore,
I could swear,

That the spirit of some sage,
From some dark and mythic age,
In thy body found a cage
Or a lair.

And once more on Earth was sent,
To retrieve a life misspent,
Till his crimes he should repent.
In that form.

But hereafter might arise,
After penance to the skies,
Where bliss awaiting lies
His reform.

My lamp burns low. Farewell.
Thus ends my verse's spell.
And now thy mournful yell—
Fearful din—

May commence, my eyeballs ache,
For my couch I now must make,
I to sleep and thou to wake,
May'st begin.

★ ★ ★ ★ ★

Immense applause greeted this last ode of our artist's, and the health of the new poet laureate was proposed by Mr. Oldstone and drunk all round, after which our artist returned thanks in a humorous speech which called forth much laughter from the other members, and much clapping of hands and rattling of glasses ensued. Glasses were then re-filled, and after a little more pleasant conversation the party broke up for the night and each retired to his solitary bed-chamber.

The Antiquary's Story
Lost in the Catacombs

The next morning broke dull and cheerless. It had been snowing hard all night, and was snowing still, and so murky was the atmosphere that the club was obliged to breakfast by candle-light, and indeed continued to burn candles till early noon.

Our artist was in despair about the weather, for he reckoned upon a long sitting from his fair model, and, under the circumstances, painting was impossible, so he wandered gloomily about the inn like a wild animal in a cage. Breakfast over, a discussion arose as to what should be the order of the day. Some voted for cards, others felt inclined for chess, yet no one felt a very strong longing for any one thing in particular. It was one of those melancholy days when a man really does not know what to do with himself. Some yawned and stretched themselves, others gazed gloomily out into the darkness, until someone suddenly recollected that it was Mr. Oldstone's turn to tell a story, so without more delay, chairs were drawn round the fire, Jack Hearty was called for to put on a fresh log, pipes were lit, and Mr. Oldstone forced into an arm-chair and pressed to begin his story without further preface.

Our host was invited to remain, but he excused himself on the score of business. Helen was also called away to help her mother in household affairs; but this, of course, the club could not hear of, so after some little parley, she was reluctantly permitted to keep the club company, as one of the members observed it would be hard indeed to deprive the club of Helen in such weather, as her face was the only sunshine they were likely to get all day. Helen smiled somewhat confusedly at this broad compliment, and then accepted a seat placed for her between McGuilp and Parnassus.

The company drew nearer to the fire, one of the members giving

a preliminary poke at the log, while Oldstone, after tapping his snuff-box and taking from its inside a copious pinch of snuff to clear his memory, threw himself back in his easy-chair, and folding his hands, commenced his story thus:—

When I was in Rome, many years ago, with my friend and brother antiquary, Rustcoin, well-known to most of you gentlemen, and especially to my friend Mr. Vandyke McGuilp. We had put up together during the early part of our stay in a large Hotel in a fashionable quarter of the city.

We were both young then, and furnished with ample means for travelling. It had been the dream of my youth to visit the eternal city, and here I found myself, free for the first time in my life to wander about to my heart's content among the venerable ruins of antiquity, the history of which had so interested me from my boyhood.

Being neither pushed for time nor money, having a comfortable little income left me upon the death of my parents, I never could make up my mind to follow any profession in particular, and having from my youth upwards always had a passion for antiquarian lore, I resolved to make it the study of my life. Rustcoin was similarly situated to myself, and we have always pulled wonderfully together. Not a day passed but some interesting ruin, church, or picture gallery, was explored, a minute description of which was immediately entered into my diary with a view to a grand archaeological work which I intended for the press, and which was afterwards published.

We knew the Vatican by heart, St. Peters, and all the chief churches. Had visited the Capitol, the Forum, the Palace of the Caesars, the Coliseum, the baths of Caracalla, of Titus, of Diocletian, the Pantheon and other antique temples. One sight, however, I had not yet been to see, and that was the catacombs. They had always had, from my boyhood, a great fascination for me, those dark, dank, mysterious subterranean labyrinths excavated by those pious enthusiasts, the early Christians, to shelter themselves from the persecutions of their pagan tyrants. Little did their oppressors imagine, I presume, when first a few straggling fanatics assembled clandestinely under the dark arches they had hewn for themselves out of the solid rock to carry on their devotions undisturbed by candle-light, that that little sect would one day fill the wide world with its followers to the utter extinction of the old pagan superstitions.

How strange is destiny! Religious faith proved too strong for tyranny. Persecutions and martyrdoms were of no avail, for still the faith increased. The very victims of the faith, too, the holy martyrs magnified into heroes after death, as if in defiance of the old creed.

Well, gentlemen, these facts are as well known to all of you as to myself, yet such were my reflections as I drove off one morning to visit the catacombs of Saint Sebastian. But I anticipate. Rising one morning filled with the idea of exploring these subterranean burial grounds as far as they extended, though for twelve miles those indefatigable early Christians have undermined the eternal city, I breakfasted hurriedly, calculating on my friend's company, but Rustcoin happened to have business on hand that day, and could not be persuaded to go, so I determined to start off alone.

A little before starting I accompanied Rustcoin down one of the by streets to make a call, and whilst, waiting for him to return, I amused myself by looking into an antiquary's shop window. There were some ancient Roman coins, some rusty Roman armour, pieces of Etruscan pottery, antique lamps and fragments of statuary. As I stood gazing at these curiosities for some considerable time, the antiquary bowed me in, giving me to understand that I was at liberty to look over the contents of his shop without being obliged to buy. He saw that I was an Englishman, and evidently had an eye to business.

He showed me some fragments of Roman tombs bearing a portion of an inscription, some bronze pans, and other instruments used for sacrifices, some spearheads, some ancient mosaic, etc., etc. I was soon attracted by a plate of antique seals, and was poring over them with a lens.

"Ah, *signor,*" said the man, "I see you appreciate these gems of art. That ring that you are looking at now was found entire in a place underground, where the vestal virgins used to be buried alive when convicted of unchastity."

"What will you take for it?" I asked.

"Well, considering that it is such a fine gem of art, sir, I could not ask less than four hundred *scudi.*"

"Four hundred *scudi!*" I exclaimed. "Why, that is four thousand *pauls,*" said I.

"Precisely so, *signor.*"

"Come, come," said I, pretending to be more knowing than I actually was. "I see you take me for an Englishman. Well, if I am an Englishman, I am one who understands the value of these things, for I have had dealings before in things of this sort."

Now, I had not the slightest idea of the prices that these articles fetched, but knowing that it was perfectly necessary to beat down an Italian in a bargain, I took it for granted that he had asked just double, and said, "Come, now, without wasting time in further parley, I will give you the half of what you ask—two hundred *scudi* and not a jot more," (being 40 pounds sterling.)

"Impossible, *signor*," said the man.

"Oh, very well, then," said I, "I wish you a good morning," and I made towards the door.

"Stay, *signor*," said the shopman; "let us say three hundred and fifty *scudi*; it is dirt cheap, and if I were not in immediate want of money I would not let it go at such a price."

"No," said I, walking out of the shop; "you know my terms; if you agree to these, so much the better for you, if not, *Addio*," and off I walked.

I had got about half way down the street when the man ran out after me. "*Signor*, only three hundred *scudi*; this is for the last time, think of that! It is a sin to let such a bargain slip."

"No, no," said I, "not even for two hundred and ten. I have said two hundred *scudi*, and I even grudge that, yet if you will take it—"

"Not even for two hundred and ten!" repeated the man. "*O Gesu Maria!*" added he, slapping his forehead.

"You seem anxious to get rid of it, my friend," said I, half-quizzingly.

"No, *signor*," replied he, "I can assure you it cuts me to the heart to part with such a gem, but I am a poor man with a large family, and I want money, otherwise I would not sell it for three times the amount."

"Well, then, if you want money," said I, dryly, "the best thing you can do is to assent to my terms, for I shall certainly give no more."

He seemed to reflect a little, and then with a shrug said: "*Ebbene*, as the signor wishes; but it is a dead loss to me; *you, signor*, are the winner, not I."

So I paid him the money, and walked off with the ring on my finger the same that I wear to this day, gentlemen. Here it is. There is no doubt that it is a very excellent specimen of Graeco-Roman art, and is most elaborately cut. I have not the slightest doubt, however, that I paid enough and more than enough for it, for as I followed the man with my eyes, I noticed an avaricious chuckle on his face, as an Italian shopman may be supposed to wear at having bamboozled an Englishman.

By this time my friend Rustcoin returned. I showed him my purchase, at which he went into raptures. I told him that I wished to visit the catacombs that morning, and therefore could not accompany him further. He advised me to wait till the morrow, and that we should go together, but I had inwardly vowed that morning that go I would, and nothing should prevent me; so telling Rustcoin that we should meet at dinner, I hailed a carriage and drove off to the church of St. Sebastian.

It is a comparatively modern church, built upon the site of the ancient basilisk supposed to have been erected by Constantine, and consecrated by St. Silvester, was renewed by the Pope San Domaso, and since repeatedly restored, being at length rebuilt in the year 1611.

On my arrival I found several carriages waiting outside. I entered the church, and there was a party of about a dozen English people, who had likewise come to visit the catacombs.

I joined the party, and we descended a flight of steps, each of us bearing in our hands a taper, or rather tall, narrow candle. We were conducted by a lean, emaciated monk, who looked as if he had lived upon nothing but by inhaling the damp air of the catacombs. As we descended, the first object shown us was a bust of St. Sebastian by Bernini, over the tomb of the saint, and near was an altar under which was interred the body of St. Lucine.

As we walked along single file through these long dark corridors, the roofs of which were every now and then so low that we were obliged to stoop, we were shown the graves of saints and martyrs who had been entombed within the walls, every now and then arriving at some little chapel, in the walls of which three or four popes had been buried.

The place where the altar had stood was also carved in the rock. Here we came across a tomb with an inscription, there upon some rude drawings on the wall by the early Christians, representing various sacred subjects.

Impatient at having to stand still and listen to the explanation of the monk who accompanied us and to hear the questions of this knot of English people, I felt an incontrollable impulse to strike out for myself into some new track, not meaning to content myself with the mere fashionable route shown to foreigners.

I considered that I had not come there merely to have a peep at these subterranean vaults, for the sake of being able to say when I returned to England that I had seen the catacombs, but intended whilst I was about it to investigate these mysterious haunts thoroughly and conscientiously, for the sake of discovering, if possible, some inscriptions or other relics worthy of note that I might describe in my great archaeological work, and thus hand my name down to posterity.

The investigation of some unknown region, especially if accompanied by a spice of danger, has always been with me a passion. I longed to be able to do something that nobody yet had done. I could not but be aware of the danger of my resolution to explore these dusky labyrinths without a guide, yet I prepared myself in a measure against a contingency, carrying in my pocket an extra roll of paper, in case that which I bore in my hand should come to an end, and a tinder-box.

Besides this, I had filled my pockets with bread, partly in case of extreme emergency, to sustain life, and partly to drop in crumbs behind me as I went to mark the way. I had commenced dropping my breadcrumbs from the very beginning and making slight excursions by myself, then turning back to join the party of English.

Once or twice the monk called me back, and as I went and returned several times, I suppose no notice was taken when I really did strike out in an unbeaten track. I took an opportunity of starting when a stout English female was assailing our ascetic friend with trivial questions in wretched Italian.

Whilst public attention seemed engrossed I started off with my taper through a long and apparently interminable passage, which I was told led to Ostia, the ancient sea-port. No one called after me, so I suppose I was not missed.

On, and still further, on I went, groping my way until I could no longer hear the voices of the party, nor see the light of their tapers through the dim arches of the catacombs.

"Would the monk miss me and go in search of me, thus breaking short all hopes of my exploring expedition?" I asked myself.

To avoid this, or at least to see as much as possible of the forbidden haunts before I was caught, I walked on fast, not forgetting, however, to drop my breadcrumbs all the time. There is a great sameness in all these catacombs, being long, straight, gloomy passages branching off in all directions, only varied at intervals with an occasional chapel, barely large enough to hold ten people crowded together, a simple, roughly-hewn cell in the rock, and destitute of anything that an antiquarian might be tempted to pocket; however, whenever I came across an inscription of any interest I immediately jotted it down in my notebook.

Now, the thought of being lost in these terrible catacombs with the prospect before me of gradually dying of starvation without the slightest chance of succour had often occurred to my mind, and was of all thoughts the most dreadful.

It was a daring thing I was attempting, and I own to experiencing a slight tremor, which increased the further I advanced. Yet, what had I to fear? Was I not well provided with tapers and tinder-box? Had I not marked the way with breadcrumbs besides carrying with me a good-sized roll to allay hunger in case of emergency? What danger did I incur? So I stifled my fears and boldly proceeded, passing innumerable tombs of saints and martyrs, chapels, inscriptions, rude drawings on the wall, Latin names, etc.

If I still felt any lingering tremor, it was a pleasing fear that only spurred me on the more, and I had not the slightest inclination to turn back. The situation was a new one to me, and I experienced from it a new emotion. Here was I, a solitary individual in the bowels of the earth, with the gay world above me perfectly unconscious that one of their kind was burrowing, taper in hand, beneath their very feet, treading in the footsteps of those enthusiastic workmen who had excavated these vaults, and which had been untrodden since by foot of man!

What will not an enthusiast go through in the noble pursuit of science? My stock of bread was now completely exhausted. I had not left a crumb to satisfy my hunger in case of need, such was my enthusiasm to penetrate deeply into these unknown regions.

But what matter? When I felt hungry I could return at any time. Had I not the clue? Thus I said to myself as I sprinkled my last remaining crumbs behind me. I had now penetrated a very considerable distance into this abode of the pious dead, when here an unforeseen and terrible accident befell me. Walking onward and incautiously looking behind me as I proceeded, I did not observe a flight of steep steps, slippery from the damp slime that exudes below ground, and that led— where? I never knew, for suddenly losing my footing, I fell headlong down into a dark abyss, where I lay stunned and senseless.

How long I remained thus it is impossible to tell, for when I recovered my senses sufficiently to grope around me, I could recollect nothing, but I found my head cut and bleeding profusely. I felt the warm blood trickling down my neck and matting my hair. I tried to stand upon my feet, but swooned again from loss of blood. I had just presence of mind when I awoke from my swoon to bind up my head with a handkerchief.

I remained for long on the cold ground in a sitting posture and tried to collect my ideas. Gradually I became aware of the horror of my situation. Of course my taper was extinguished by my fall. I essayed to relight it, but the material was damp with the dews of the catacomb and with my blood, besides which my strength failed me. I began to feel hungry, too, for I had eaten but a light breakfast. Could anything have been more pitiable than my plight? Wounded in the head and weakened with loss of blood, lost in the very heart of the catacombs without a light, without the barest prospect of mortal coming to my rescue, hungry, the little bread that I had taken with me wasted to make a clue which I now found it impossible to trace in the dark, and with every prospect of a lingering death before me!

With difficulty I clambered up the steps and searched in vain for the crumbs of bread on my hands and knees. I was nigh fainting again, but that strong love of life that is instinctive in us all made me screw up my nerves with a preternatural energy, and I essayed to shout for help.

Although I must have been aware of the futility of my attempts, we all know that a drowning man will cling to a straw, so bracing my strength up to its utmost possible pitch, I gave vent to a superhuman shriek, which re-echoed through the gloomy arches like the mocking laugh of demons.

The sound of my own voice in agony amidst the awful silence of this place of tombs sent a new thrill of horror through my frame, my nerves being rendered weak and sensitive by the loss of vital fluid I had sustained, and jarred upon the full consciousness of my terrible situation. I felt on the brink of madness. Every now and then I heard the rumbling of carriage wheels over my head, like distant thunder in the world above me, which enhanced still more the misery of my position, for I could not help contrasting my lot with that of the happy individual rolling over my head in his proud carriage, enjoying the bright sun and blue sky whilst I was doomed to be buried alive in those horrible catacombs, dying by inches in the greatest conceivable agony of body and mind, but few feet below that carriage road over which passed the gay and thoughtless in their fashionable equipages.

I tried to call out again, but my voice failed me. "If I die," I thought, "it must not be by inches, but at once, at a blow." I was preparing to dash my head desperately against the wall, and thus put an end to my misery, but lacking strength, I fell down once more exhausted.

When I again awoke I felt both hungry and thirsty. The wound in my head had ceased to bleed, but the handkerchief was saturated. I now felt the calmness of despair. I knew nothing short of a miracle could save me, so I tried to reconcile myself to my condition. I could just walk, but slowly. I tried to retrace my steps, though at a snail's pace and without a clue.

The hopelessness of my condition now dawned upon me more clearly than ever. It was impossible even to retrace my steps alone and in the dark, especially in my weakened state. Why should I uselessly try a thing I knew to be impossible? Why not lie quietly down and die? I sank helplessly on the ground and gave up all hope. I felt that my end was not far off, and began to review my past life. The errors, the follies, the crimes during my brief existence chased each other with painful vividness and rapidity through my memory. Not even the most trifling incident of my childhood was forgotten, but every event and thought of my life vividly, exactly and distinctly, traced with indelible finger upon the tablets of my brain, passing before my mental vision like a vast panorama.

It was then that I ventured to pray, and if I never prayed in my whole life before, I did then. Well can I remember the agony of remorse I felt for the precious time I had wasted. I was then five and twenty, a quarter of a century old, and what had I yet done to benefit my fellow creatures? and what had I not done that lay in my power to gratify my own selfish wants? Could I call to mind even one *thoroughly* good act? Were not even my best actions based upon a sort of selfishness? How I longed to live over again those five and twenty years!

What resolutions did I not make to turn over a new leaf for the future if my Creator should be pleased to spare my young life! I prayed fervently and devoutly, such praying as only the most intense mental agony can prompt the soul to, until my nervous system, overcome with excessive tension, I sank into a sort of lethargy, something between life and death. Emerging at length somewhat from this state, I began to meditate thus:

Is it possible that my young life is to be cut short in this manner? Is this what I was born for—to perish miserably from the ill-consequences of a foolish though innocent freak—or will the Almighty really hear my prayer? Have I not prayed fervently with all my heart and soul, and has He not promised to help those who trust in Him? I *will* trust in Him. I will *not* believe that the age of miracles has gone by never to return.

Miracles are wrought daily, though we do not acknowledge them as such. I felt a calmness and resignation at these thoughts, and almost indifferent if the Lord should be pleased to take my soul, or work some miracle to save me from a lingering death. Either way I would have been content, for I now felt prepared to die, and had no fear of death.

I endeavoured to keep my faith in the mercy of my Creator firm and unwavering. If for a moment a slight doubt rose in my mind as to the likelihood of the Deity working a miracle for my special benefit, it was instantly dismissed, and I prayed more earnestly. I *would* believe, I would *not* be robbed of my faith by the jeering of that mocking fiend, Doubt. I persisted in believing, and Doubt fled from me. I *felt* I should be saved. I *knew* it.

While thus meditating, methought that the extreme end of one of these long corridors had grown a trifle lighter than it was a minute ago. Was it a mistake, and merely the effect of my eyesight having grown accustomed to the darkness?

No, for the light now grew rapidly brighter. Could it be that the monks were coming in search of me?

Yes—no, for I now saw a solitary figure in the distance bearing a candle, but it was not the figure of a monk, for the garb was white, and apparently that of a female. I held my breath in wonder and expectation, whilst my heart thumped so loudly against my ribs that it might have caused an echo. My eyes were steadfastly fixed on the figure as it moved slowly towards me. It was undoubtedly the figure of a woman clad in a long white classic robe and a white head covering, such as worn by the priestesses of old. The shoulders and arms were bare, and on one arm she wore a golden armlet, on her feet sandals. She was now sufficiently near me for me to take a complete survey of her. Her face was pale and dreadfully emaciated, yet there were traces of great beauty left. She mumbled something to herself which at first I took for Italian, but on catching a word or two more, I had no difficulty in discovering it to be Latin, for she repeatedly muttered to herself the word *peccavi*, beating her breast the while. I rose to my feet as she approached. At first she appeared not to notice me and would have passed me. At length I addressed her in Italian. "*Signora*," I began, "I have lost my way in the dark and am suffering from an accident; perhaps you can show me the way out of these catacombs, for I am weak and dying of hunger."

The figure gazed blankly at me in silence, which I attributed not so much to surprise as to her not understanding the language in which I addressed her. At length she spoke in a faint sepulchral voice.

"Quis es tu qui in hoc loco versaris?"

To which I replied in the same classic tongue in which she addressed me.

"Christianus sum, tu autem quis es?" I am a Christian, but who art thou? To which she gave the following account of herself.

"Virgo Vestalis sum, aut possius eram; nunc autem nec virgo nec vestalis."

"Intelligo," I answered—I understand—not willing to extort a confession that might be painful to her, but she seemed communicative and inclined to enlighten me further.

"Audi!" she continued, *"quandam eram in mundo virum amavi. Christianus erat, et propter meum crimen quod perpetravi cum viro hoc Christiano, ad mortem damnata viva sepulta fui. Attaman cum ante meam mortem fuerim ad Christifidem conversa, nunc meus spiritus hac illuc hoc in loco versatur."*

I expressed my deepest sympathy for her sufferings in the best Latin I could muster, and indeed I was well able to sympathise with her, for did not *I* feel what it was to be buried alive and to endure the gnawing pangs of hunger?

"Alas, poor ghost!" I felt inclined to say, with Hamlet, and I could not help muttering to myself, "How hard, alas!—just for one fault, for one piece of human frailty, resulting from the over tenderness of a woman's heart, to die such a horrible death."

"An es estraneus in hoc loco?" she asked me, having overheard my soliloquy and perceiving that it was in a foreign tongue.

"Civis Brittanicus sum," I replied, and then I began to relate my history, my misfortunes, and how I had prayed to be delivered from such a dreadful death, begging her to show me the way out of these horrid catacombs as soon as possible.

"Hac conditione,"—On this condition—she said.

"Quaenam est?" What is it? I asked.

She replied thus: *"Annulus quem in digito geris quem quidem circiter quinque Sestertia valet et meus erat nom habui a viro quem delexi vende ad levandum meum spiritum."*

Here was a surprise! The ring that I had purchased previously to starting off for the catacombs belonged and had been worn by the spirit before me when in the flesh! The man of whom I bought it spoke the truth then—when he said that it had been found where the vestal virgins used to be buried alive. What a curious coincidence! Now I was called upon to sell it again to pay for masses for the poor disembodied spirit, and as a condition of being set free myself from this dungeon. I was loth to part with the ring I had paid so highly for, especially now that such an interesting history was attached to it. Yet, what will not a man do to save his life?

"*Sic erit,*" I replied. It shall be done.

"*Jamnunc sequere me,*" said she, beckoning to me with her pale emaciated finger, which together with the hand and arm was so skinny that it might have belonged to a skeleton. I followed accordingly, and was led through many a long corridor, passing many a tomb of martyred saint, though by a different route to that which I had taken. My guide walked on before me in silence. That is to say, she did not converse with me more, but ever to herself I heard the muttered words "*Peccavi! peccavi!*" beating her breast as she went.

As I followed my guide, my ears suddenly caught the tones of distant chanting.

"*Quid sibi volunt cantus isti?*" What is the meaning of that singing?

She answered merely by beckoning me on and hastening her steps. The singing grew more and more distinct, and as we approached I noticed a dim gleam of light ahead. Then, shortly turning a corner, I found myself suddenly in a little chapel, like, in appearance, to the rest I had seen, but lighted up with many candles, and with an altar on which stood a rudely-carved crucifix, a chalice, etc.

But how shall I describe my horror, consternation, and disgust on beholding the strange congregation there assembled? It was easy to see with half an eye that they were no beings of this world. They were seven, I think, in number; indeed, the chapel had hardly room for more, and to my dying day, never can I forget that horrible sight. One of them, who stood at the altar, and who seemed to be the priest, had evidently been decapitated. He stood upright, holding his head under his arm.

Another, who was naked with the exception of a cloth round his loins, was bound to a stake and pierced full of arrows, *a la* St. Sebastian. Another, who had been sawn asunder lengthways, was held together by pieces of rope. One gentleman, who had been skinned alive for the holy faith, was a most unsightly object, and reminded me of those anatomical figures you see in doctors' shops. Whenever he moved, the working of his anatomy was most painfully visible, and he wore his skin over his left arm like an overcoat.

There was another, who had evidently been burnt, for he was as black as a cinder, and presented a most woe-begone aspect. A sixth had probably been torn to pieces by some wild beast, for his flesh bore the print of talons, and here and there hung in long strips, while a seventh had been broken on the wheel, and seemed capable of bending his body into the most impossible positions.

My blood ran cold at such a spectacle, and turning to my guide, I asked the meaning of this strange sight. She informed me that they were all spirits of early Christians who had suffered martyrdom.

"Then why," I asked, "are they not in Paradise instead of celebrating mass here in these catacombs?"

The reason she gave me was that they had all been massacred in their sin, and their spirits not being yet pure enough to enter the realms of eternal bliss, they were, like herself, doomed to go through their religious duties as on earth, until masses should be said for their deliverance. This, she told me, was her object in leading me here—that I might see the misery of these wretched spirits, and pray for them. I promised I would do so, and mass being finished, she introduced me to the skinned gentleman, whom, she informed me, was her lover. He bowed, grinned horribly, and offered me his anatomical hand, after which I had a word with each of the spirits in turn, and then prepared to take my departure.

"*Ora pro nobis!*" they all cried at once.

"*Sic erit,*" I replied, and following my guide once more, she led me again through many long and dreary passages, which seemed to me interminable, she walking rapidly in front, whilst I dragged my jaded limbs considerably in the rear, led on by no other light than the luminous halo that enveloped her form, and which barely lit up the spot on which she stood, all else being in pitchy darkness. At length I thought I felt the ground ascending somewhat, and as I proceeded ever slowly upwards, I fancied that I saw a ray of sunlight struggling through a fissure in the rocky roof of the vault. I was not mistaken. The nearer I came, the larger grew the spot of light, and I now saw clearly that there was a very considerable opening, amply sufficient to admit of the body of a very large man passing through it, but quite overgrown by brambles and rank vegetation, so as effectively to veil the blue sky from my view. Even through this screen of rank herbage the light dazzled my eyes intensely, and it was some minutes before I got sufficiently accustomed to it. The ground now grew suddenly steeper, till I at length found myself within a few steps of the fissure. My guide now halted, and pointing to the opening with her hand, made way for me to pass on in front.

It would seem that the bright sunbeam as it fell upon her affected her somewhat, for I noticed that her form grew less distinct, until the vaporous essence that assumed her shape disintegrated piecemeal, beginning at the head, gradually downwards, till she completely vanished from my presence. Not, however, before I had time to thank her in her own classical language.

"Pro tuis beneficiis gratias ago."

To which she barely had time to reply *"Vale!"* when she became extinct, and I was left once more alone.

But now I had hope—I was free. Another step, and I should be launched into the outer world again. Hungry, thirsty, fatigued as I was, I should soon be able to satisfy my present wants and then—and then—with all my young life before me, what might I not achieve? My first feeling was one of intense gratitude towards my Creator, who had saved me from a terrible and lingering death. It was like being born again. I advanced towards the opening, and was just about to move aside the luxuriant growth that alone separated me from the world without, when methought I heard human voices outside proceeding from no very long distance from the aperture. Even a human shadow flitted for a moment across the opening, obscuring for a second some of the glowing sunlight.

I was loth to emerge from my hiding place into the open air in sight of men, as, besides startling them, I should myself become an object of wonderment and create a scene I particularly wished to avoid. So I resolved to pause awhile until they should presently pass on, when I could emerge alone and unobserved. In this I was disappointed; they seemed to have no intention whatever of moving on. There they sat apparently over their meal, chatting at intervals. It was impossible but that I should thus overhear some fragments of their conversation, and what I *did* hear made my blood run cold.

"Dost remember, Gaspero," said one, "on our last sally, when we captured the fat landowner from Montefiascone, and sent him back to his friends with his nose and his ears slit because they wouldn't send the ransom in time?"

"*Corpo di Bacco! don't I?*" answered another. "But I'll tell you what, if the *Cavalli leggeri* get wind of our whereabouts this time, it will be short shrift for all of us."

"Bah!" said a third, "haven't we good spies enough always on the alert to warn us of their approach?"

"True," said the former, "but don't let us talk, or we shall miss the signal."

Then silence reigned for a brief space, broken now and again by some casual remark hardly audible. Here was a pretty to do! Had I been rescued from death by starvation only to stumble upon a nest of brigands? Oh, the irony of it! I trembled for the loss of the little gold I had upon me, but more still for the precious ring upon my finger.

"I must risk nothing," I said to myself, "and bide here in patience at any cost till they depart."

I dreaded lest the beating of my own heart—so audible to myself—should betray me. Thus a full hour or more passed away, when on a sudden I heard a sound like the hooting of an owl in the distance.

"The signal—the signal!" exclaimed several voices at once, and up they jumped like one man and took to their heels with the speed of lightning.

I began to emerge from my cavern, and just managed to catch a glimpse of some peaked hats, carbines, and sandaled legs, which soon disappeared for ever from my view. I was now once more under the clear dome of Heaven. The sky was absolutely cloudless, the heat intense. I shaded my eyes with my hand to protect them from the glare of the hot sun which now shone mercilessly down upon my bare head, for my hat had been left far behind me in that subterranean burial place. I tried to realise my situation. Where was I? I was in the centre of a very arid plain with blue mountains on the horizon and lines of ruined aqueducts in the middle distance. Not a hut within sight. The sun was intolerable, and I felt ready to faint from hunger and exhaustion. I gathered some broad green leaves to protect my head, and then looked around me for something to assuage the pangs of hunger.

I recollected that the brigands had been carousing close to the opening of my cave, so I returned thither to inspect the spot. To my intense joy I discovered some broken victuals. There were sundry crusts of bread, some cheese parings, a few slices of raw ham, a whole leg of a chicken, besides other bones not quite bare, which I devoured ravenously. Also a hard-boiled egg and half a flask of good wine. All this I put away in very short time, but I wanted more. It was barely enough to whet my appetite. However, I felt better, and could now contemplate my past adventures with great complacency.

The next question was, in what part of the world was I? Which course should I steer? North, south, east, or west. I feared being benighted and losing my way altogether. I sat down on a clump of ancient ruin to collect my ideas. Presently I heard faintly in the distance the peculiar cry of a Roman bullock driver, as he goaded on his sluggish team. I raised my eyes, and saw about half-a-mile off one of those drays drawn by buffaloes and laden with large blocks of white marble from the mountains for the use of sculptors. I hastened my steps and hailed the driver.

"Accidentaccio!" cried the man in amazement and horror at the sight of my bleeding head and general woe-begone appearance.

"What a sight! *Che diavolo!*—"

Here followed a string of questions which I felt in no humour to answer, so I cut him short by asking him to let me get upon his dray, as I wanted a little sleep, and that I would remember him as soon as we arrived at the gates of Rome.

"Certainly, *signore*," said the man, brightening up, "and if you would like a covering for your head from the sun—"

Here he produced some sort of light drugget—there was no other covering, for the dray was only constructed to carry marble and not passengers.

So I mounted, and flung myself full length on a large block of marble, covering my head well up and endeavouring to sleep. So complete was my state of utter exhaustion that even my uncomfortable position and the rough jolting of the cumbersome dray when its massive wheels encountered some big stone combined with the constant cry of the driver in my ears as he goaded on his sluggish brutes of burden, was all insufficient to prevent nature from taking her proper course, and I actually slept—ay, slept like a top, spite of heat, dust, flies, noise, etc., until towards nightfall I reached the gates of Rome. The stars shone out with unusual splendour. I felt considerably refreshed after my long slumber, so I descended, and remunerating the driver liberally, entered the eternal city.

My first thought was to hasten off to a hatter's, where I purchased a hat, and then called upon a doctor. He was out, so I left my address, leaving word for him to call at my hotel in the Piazza di Spagna on the morrow, at ten in the morning. I then repaired to my hotel and heard that my friend Rustcoin had been inquiring for me, and marvelled much at my absence. I then had a wash and a brush down, changed the bloodstained handkerchief for a clean one, and ordered supper in my room.

On the morrow, punctually at ten, the doctor made his appearance. He examined my wound, prescribed me a lotion, and then asked how the accident had occurred. In my youthful simplicity I related my tale from beginning to end, omitting no detail.

He looked at me suspiciously, shook his head, and said that the danger was even more than he thought. He had no doubt that besides the wound in my head, I was likewise suffering from sunstroke, which would account for these hallucinations.

Could anything be more irritating? After all the trouble I had taken in relating my adventures, even to the merest details—to be looked upon either as a madman or impostor! He admitted that I might possibly have been to explore the catacombs, that I might have had a fall which caused the wound in my head, but as to the apparition of the vestal virgin and her unsightly friends, he would have none of it, admitting that he was deaf upon principle to all tales of the supernatural, because they were impossible. Adding that he was very much surprised to find a young man of education like myself—and moreover an Englishman—still believing in such antiquated superstitions. He took his leave and said he would call the next day.

He came and found me quite convalescent, so soon took his departure with a shrug, finding that I still believed in the actuality of my vision. As I was leaving my hotel for a stroll I ran up against Rustcoin, who was about to call upon me. You can imagine, my friends, his wonder on hearing me recount my adventures.

There is little more left to relate. I proceeded in company with my friend to several shops to endeavour to sell the ring, but at none of them would they give me back the sum I gave for it, or anything like it, so I resolved upon keeping the ring and paying the monks what I had paid for it, which amounted to the same thing. So if my spirit friends are not by this time in Paradise, it is no fault of mine.

★ ★ ★ ★ ★

"Here is the ring, gentlemen," said Mr. Oldstone at the conclusion of his narrative, taking the precious relic from his forefinger and passing it round for inspection. "You will observe it is a most exquisite specimen of Graeco-Roman art of the very best period, and believe me, gentlemen, when I assure you that the wealth of the universe wouldn't purchase it."

Loud were the expressions of admiration that passed round the table at the beauty of this antique gem, as well as the delight and satisfaction of our antiquary's story.

The Landlord's Story
Buried Alive

"Bravo, Oldstone! A very capital story!" cried several members at once. "It is a pity our host isn't here to have heard it."

"I heard a good part of it, though, gentlemen," said a voice from a dark corner of the room (for the lights had been extinguished, though it was still murky without).

"What, are you there, Jack?" cried Mr. Crucible. "We none of us saw you."

"Well, sir," said the landlord, "finding that I was not wanted outside as I thought, I ventured to enter the room quietly, so as not to disturb the story."

"Well done, Jack," said Hardcase, "and so you heard all, eh? Well, what do you think of it?"

"Pretty nearly all, I guess, sir," replied the landlord, "and a curious one it is, too, and no mistake. But talk of being buried alive, I could tell you a queer adventure that happened to myself, if you gentlemen would care to hear it."

"Only be too glad, Jack," said Oldstone. "Out with it; there is nothing like a good story to beguile the time in weather like this."

Our host, thus encouraged, drew his chair close to the fire, and his example was immediately followed by his guests. Then, refilling his yard of clay and lighting it in the fire, he gave one or two preliminary whiffs, and commenced his story thus:—

Well, gentlemen, when I was a youngster, that is to say, a lad of nineteen, I fell deeply in love with my Molly, who, though I say it, was the finest lass in the village and for miles round it. For all the world like my Helen, at her age, bless her dear heart! She was the daughter of a rich miller—his only child. Well, it had been a long attachment, for Molly and I were play-mates when we was little, but when I grew

to be about nineteen, and my father began to see that I was head over ears in love with Molly, he forbade me to see any more of her, because he and old Sykes—leastways, Molly's father, the miller—wasn't friends, d'ye see.

Nevertheless, Molly and I used to get a peep at each other on the sly like, and often took long walks together when no one was near.

Well, old Sykes also objected to me keeping company with his daughter, and sometimes suspecting what was up, used to lie in wait for us, and catch us in the lane as we was coming home from our walk. Then he'd give us both a "blowing up," for old Sykes wasn't partickler nice in his language, and Molly was locked up in her room while he went to complain of me to my father. This sort of thing occurred more than once, and Sykes, not knowing how to put a stop to it in any other way, sent his daughter on a visit to an aunt of hers some distance off.

I didn't know nothing of this for some time, and still went hovering round the house, expecting to see Molly at the window. Now, there happened to be at that time an epidemic running through the village, as proved fatal to many, carrying off both the young and the old, and when my father saw how pulled down I was in health and spirits, which was all along of my not having seen Molly for many a week, he took it into his head that I had caught the epidemic, and sent for a doctor. The doctor came, felt my pulse, and looked at my tongue, and pronounced me very bad, but said that he did not see the usual signs of the epidemic.

He ordered me, however, to be put to bed, and prescribed me some physic. Instead of doing me any good, it only made me worse, for the doctor was ignorant of the true cause of my low spirits. I was forced to keep in bed, and could do nothing night or day but think of Molly. My father, seeing me rapidly grow worse, but still ignorant of the cause—though he knew that I had been very much cut up about Molly—began to take on so—I being his only son—that the doctor was afraid that he would have to take to his bed. Once, shortly after Molly's disappearance, he told me that she had caught the epidemic and had died.

He hoped by this tale to bring me to my senses, and that I should soon forget her, and begin courting some other girl, but it had a very different effect upon me, and I rapidly sunk from worse to worse. When the doctor called again, he found me in a dangerous state, and he came to the conclusion that it must be the epidemic after all.

Whether I really had caught the epidemic in addition to my love-sickness I can't tell. All I know is that I felt so bad that I didn't expect to live, and even the doctor said it was all over with me.

My death was expected daily, and when one morning the doctor came and found me stiff and cold, he gave out to my parents that I was dead. I was no more dead than I am at the present moment. It is true that I could not budge an inch, and I have no doubt that I looked thoroughly dead, but my mind was as clear and as sharp as possible.

"Poor young man," I heard the doctor say. "So hale and strong, too. Who'd have thought it?"

"Oh, my poor son! my poor son!" wept my father. "You whom I thought to rear to be the prop of my old age, now you are torn from me for ever."

"Calm yourself, sir," said the doctor, "else you will make yourself ill."

"How can I calm myself?" cried my father, in agony. "Was he not my *only* son? and I—I—fool, wretch, that I was—*I* killed him!"

"*You* killed him!" cried the doctor. "How? Surely you rave, sir."

"Yes," persisted my father; "the poor boy was in love with a maid whose father is my enemy. I objected to his marrying her, as did also the girl's father, who wishing to save his daughter from my son sent her away to live at the house of an aunt in the village of H— in —shire. As my son knew nothing of this, I told him, thinking to make him forget her, that the maid was dead, but the poor boy took on so dreadful about it, that it has been his death, and I—yes I am his murderer!" and I thought his sobs would choke him.

"It was very wrong and foolish of you," said the doctor, "to tell him so, when you saw him so weak and ailing, yet you did it with a good intent, and I do not see that you can justly accuse yourself of being his murderer."

"Yes, yes," sobbed my father, bitterly, "I have killed him—my son, my *only* son!"

Now I had discovered a secret. Molly was not dead, but living at her aunt's. I knew her address; if I could but be restored to life, I might see her once again. I longed to be able to call out: "Father, I am not dead—comfort yourself," but my tongue refused utterance. I tried to move my limbs, and did all that was in my power to show signs of life, but I still lay powerless—paralysed, for I was in a trance. Oh! the agony I suffered! How long would it last? Should I be really nailed up in a coffin and buried alive? Oh, horror!

Some of my friends the neighbours were called in to see me and mourned over my corpse.

"Poor Jack!" one of them said; "if lads of his kidney are not proof against the epidemic, who may hope to escape?"

The next day an undertaker was sent for to measure me for my coffin.

"Where will all this end?" thought I. "Shall I awake before the coffin is made?"

This was my only hope; but if not, all was lost. Once nailed down, nailed down for ever. The thought was agony.

Here I was, struck down in the flower of my youth, to all appearances dead, yet with my mind keenly alive to all that was going on around me. Oh, that I could become insensible! I knew not how long this dreadful trance would last; all I knew was that if it lasted more than a day or two longer it would be all up with me. I was laid out in state, and all that day and the next friends poured in to gaze upon my corpse.

As the time grew nearer for my funeral the more despairing I got. At length the coffin arrived. I shuddered. Had my last moment actually come? What could I do? Nothing.

"Oh, Heaven!" I cried within myself, "for what fell crime am I doomed to bear this agony of soul?"

Two undertakers now lifted me from my bed, one of them seizing me by the shoulders, the other by the feet, and I felt myself placed within a leaden coffin supported upon trestles. I did my utmost now to make one last desperate effort to rouse myself out of my trance, but in vain.

"Oh, if they should nail me up!" I thought.

Then I was left alone all day, and remember a great bustle and whispering going on in the house. All were talking of my funeral. At length the fatal hour arrived! The undertakers entered my room again. Good Heavens! they were actually going to solder me down. The next instant the leaden lid was down upon me, and I was soon tightly secured. Then commenced the knocking in of the nails of the outer coffin. How painfully distinct was the sound of the hammer! I remember counting each nail as it was driven in. At length the task was completed, and I only awaited the hearse to carry me to my last home.

Then there was more bustle, the meeting of friends, etc., when after waiting a little longer, I heard the footsteps of the bearers. I felt myself lifted upon the shoulders of the men and carried downstairs. A crowd had evidently collected round the door, for I heard the muffled sound of voices gossipping, but could not distinguish what they said. Only the tolling of the church bell jarred upon my ears. Then the procession began. How slowly it moved along!

"Oh! if I could even now awake!" thought I, "it might not be too late. If I could make sufficient movement with my limbs to overturn the coffin, or even had strength to call out, I should even now be saved."

But all in vain—rigid, motionless as ever, in spite of my earnest prayers to be restored to life. I felt myself borne leisurely on—whither? Oh, horror! to the cold and narrow grave—to the abode of the dead. My last hope died within me when I felt the procession stop, and I knew that it was already arrived at the cemetery. I remember hearing faintly the tones of the parson's voice as he read the ceremony for the burial of the dead. The coffin was now lowered into the grave, and I heard with awful distinctness the words "earth to earth, ashes to ashes, dust to dust," followed by the rattling of the three handfuls of earth upon my coffin lid. My last hope was now gone. In another moment I should be covered up with mould and left alone to die miserably.

"Oh!" groaned I, in spirit, "it is all over with me!" as I heard the mould tumbling heavily upon me.

I knew that the grave was now covered up, for the voices of my friends were quite inaudible, and all was silent.

What a terrible feeling of isolation was mine! Cut off completely from the rest of the world by some feet of earth, alive, yet supposed to be dead, deserted by friends and doomed at length to awaken only to suffer a death of all deaths most horrible! Had I still believed Molly to be dead, it would have been some consolation to me to die; nay, how gladly would I have welcomed death that I might meet her in a better land. But, alas, I knew that Molly still lived, and after death I should be further away from her than ever. This thought was agony to me. One thing, however, somewhat consoled me, though it was but poor consolation.

"We must all die," I thought.

Molly must die, too. It might be years before she left this earth, still I should see her again sooner or later. But then came another, thought which, do all I could, I was unable to banish from my mind. In the meantime Molly might marry someone else, and rear up a large family of children, and what could I be to her then if I ever chanced to meet her in the other world? If ever human soul knew agony, mine knew it then. I longed for no eternity without Molly, and I remember praying that my spirit might be utterly annihilated and become as insensible as the clay that I was about to leave behind me. It was a dreadful and an impious prayer, but when during life, one dear idol has monopolised the heart and there reigns supreme, even the fear of eternal damnation is insufficient to drive it from its throne.

"Oh, that I could die quickly and be at rest for ever!"

Then I prayed fervently a long, heartfelt, earnest prayer, after which I felt more calm, more resigned to my fate. I had no hopes of being rescued and being brought back to life—that hope had quite left me. I now only wished for a speedy and peaceful death. Many weary hours I lay on my back within my narrow prison—rigid—immovable—a living soul amongst the dead. The silence that reigned around was intense, almost inconceivable to those accustomed to the busy world without.

I missed the rustling of the leaves, the chirping of the birds, the distant lowing of cattle, the hum of human voices, every sound of life; all was still, for it was *the silence of the grave*. The only sound at all audible, and that was so indistinct and muffled from the pile of earth that covered me that, had my sense of hearing not been excited to an abnormal pitch, I should not have heard it, and that was the sound of the church clock as it struck the hour. I had been buried in the morning at about ten o'clock, and I remember counting the hours until ten o'clock at night. Every hour appeared to me a century, until, exhausted with the agony of mind I had endured, I fell asleep and dreamed of Molly. I thought that I was by her side walking under the trees in a part of the country that I had never seen before.

There was a house at some distance, which she said belonged to her aunt. I was telling her all about how I came to be buried alive, and she was listening to me and looking up in my face with tearful eyes, for she had heard that I was dead. I also dreamed that I saw a serpent moving in the grass at her feet. I sprang up and beat it severely with my cane. At first it attempted to defend itself, but at length it escaped from me severely bruised.

The dream then changed from one subject to another, but Molly was by my side throughout. It was exceedingly vivid, and I doubted not at the time but that I was by her side in reality.

I know not how long I had been asleep when I heard a confused noise while still in a dreaming state, and I awoke to find myself once more in my coffin.

"Oh, why was not this dream allowed to last?" I groaned to myself, and tried to fall asleep again, hoping to take up the thread of my dream at the point that I had lost it, but in vain, for now I heard the same noise in reality over my head. It was the sound of men's voices. Who could they be? Was I still dreaming? No!

They were the resurrectionists, or the "body-snatchers," as we generally call them. They had come to rob my body in order to sell it to some doctor. How my heart beat for joy!

"I shall be saved! I shall be saved!" said I to myself.

"O merciful God!" I prayed in spirit, "who scornest not to make the meanest of thy creatures thine instruments, I thank Thee for having heard my prayers and delivered me from this fearful death. I am unworthy of all thy mercies, O God! Perform thy miracles on men more worthy."

The body-snatchers had now shovelled all the earth away that covered me, and they began to lift the coffin out of the grave. Had it been my friend's coffin instead of my own, I should have stigmatised the men who attempted to disinter his body as thieves, robbers, a set of midnight marauders; but in the present instance I blessed them as my deliverers, as my brothers. My heart yearned towards them, for my hopes began to revive.

It would be discovered that I was not dead, at least, I hoped so, and when my trance should pass off I should be able to find some way of seeing Molly again. The next moment the outer coffin was wrenched open; then they proceeded to force the leaden one. This was soon done, and I now felt the chill night air. To lift me out, thrust me headfirst into a sack, and shovel the earth into the grave again, was the work of a moment, and I now felt myself laid across the shoulder of one of the men, and carried off.

"Where was I bound for?" I asked myself.

The men began talking together, so I resolved to listen—to learn, if possible, what they were going to do with me.

"A fine corpse, Bill," said one body-snatcher to the other.

"Aye, my word," replied Bill, "but what a weight he be!"

"Ah! I dare say; these youngsters are so full of blood and muscle," said the other.

261

"Tell you what it is, Tom," said my bearer, "you must lend me a hand or I shall never bring him safely to the doctor's tonight. Here, just take him on your shoulders a bit!"

I then felt myself transferred from the shoulders of Bill to those of Tom.

"Begad! you're right," said the latter. "He be a load, sure*ly*."

"Well," said Bill, "the doctor has got the full worth of his money, and no mistake. For less than ten guineas I wouldn't have undertaken the task on such a night as this. Hark! how the wind howls. My teeth chatter in spite of myself. Poor Jack! Many's the good draught of malt he has drawn for me in his father's tap-room!"

"Peace, you fool!" cried Tom; "don't talk so loud, or the thing will get wind in the village, and we shall get torn to pieces. Hush! there is someone behind the hedge."

Then they walked on in silence for some time, and on the way I was once more hoisted on to the shoulders of Bill.

"Oh, you beggar, what a weight you be!" said Bill, addressing me. "Well, we're paid for it, so I suppose I must carry you," and off we trudged again.

"This is the way to Dr. Slasher's house," said Tom. "I see a light in the windows; he is awaiting us."

"Well," said Bill, "we've been pretty punctual. It is not much past twelve o'clock. Here we are at last."

The two men stopped, and one threw some earth against the doctor's window. The next moment I heard footsteps within, and the door was opened noiselessly.

"Hush!" said the doctor's voice.

The two men entered the house, when I was taken out of my sack and deposited upon a table in the doctor's study. It was the same doctor who had attended me during my illness.

"Fine specimen, sir," said Bill, "and tough work enough we've had to get him, neither; the ground's as hard as a brick-bat."

"Ah!" said the doctor, abstractedly, feeling me all over.

"Yes, sir," said the other; "and how heavy he be too!"

"Humph!" said the doctor.

"It is a bitter cold night," said Bill. "The wind howled among the trees while we was at work enough to make one's blood curdle."

"Ha!" said the doctor; "I know what that means. A glass of grog wouldn't be unacceptable, unless I mistake."

"Well, sir, you've just guessed about right," said Bill. "A glass of grog now and then, just to keep out the cold is a very fine thing, as you, being a doctor, sir, I've no doubt are well aware."

"Ha! ha!" laughed the doctor. "I perceive you understand the theory of the circulation of the blood. Well, as you have done your work well, I'll just put the kettle on the hob, and you shall have a good stiff glass apiece."

"That's the sort of thing, eh, Tom? The doctor is a real gentleman, and no mistake."

Tom acquiesced, and soon the doctor produced a tall bottle of brandy, and more than half filling two tumblers, and popping a couple of lumps of sugar into each glass, he lifted the kettle from the hob and filled them up to the brim. Then, stirring up the sugar at the bottom with the handle of his dissecting knife, he handed a glass to each of his creatures across my body.

"Here's luck, sir," said one of them, nodding.

"I looks towards you, sir," said the other, sipping his grog.

"Thanks, my man, thanks," said the doctor.

"A—h!" gasped Bill, after a deep draught, and smacking his lips, "this is something like a glass of grog. I feel myself again. I'd as *lief* set out again after another subject tonight as not."

"Well, mate," said Tom, draining his glass, "I guess we'd better toddle."

The doctor then counted out twenty guineas, and gave the men ten apiece.

"Thank ye kindly, sir," said they, "and when again you be in want of our services, your honour knows where to find us. Goodnight, sir."

"Goodnight," responded the doctor, as he showed them out and closed the door.

I was left alone for a moment, but when he returned he might begin dissecting me at once, and that would be horrible, for I was still in my trance. I hoped he would defer operations until the morrow. In the meantime I hoped to come to. Then I heard the doctor's footsteps in the passage, and here he was again. Would he really cut me up before I could call out or defend myself? Good Heavens! What was he about now? He had tucked up his shirt sleeves and seized his dissecting-knife!

All was lost. My hopes had been raised only to be dashed to the ground. My last hour had come. Already I felt the point of the murderous instrument against my chest. Rip!—an incision had been made!

"Hullo!" cried the doctor, dropping his dissecting-knife. "What is this? Why the man's not dead!"

The fact was, I was gradually recovering, and my blood had already begun to flow. The intense mental agony I had endured had caused a cold sweat to break out on my forehead. The incision luckily was not very deep, but I bear the mark of the wound to this day.

The doctor staunched the blood with his handkerchief, muttering to himself, "And have I been obliged to pay twenty guineas for a living subject? Humph! I've a good mind to cut him up all the same, no one would be any the wiser for it."

I began to fear lest he might do so in real earnest; however, he bound up my wound and carried me into his own bedroom, where he placed me on a mattress on the ground. He wiped the perspiration from my forehead and felt my pulse.

"He'll come round," he muttered to himself; "already he shows signs of life. I would not for the world, though, that this got known in the village. I should lose all my practice, and yet I don't know how to keep the matter quiet, it *must* ooze out."

Life was rapidly returning. I began to open and shut my eyes and to breathe, though with some difficulty. By degrees, however, I managed to breathe more freely.

"Ah, ha!" said the doctor, noticing the rapid change, "getting all right, now—eh?"

I remained in the same state for about an hour more, when the doctor began undressing and preparing to turn in for the night. In another moment he was between the sheets and snoring loudly. Soon after I fell asleep myself.

The following morning on awaking, I felt almost myself again. I could move my limbs and sit up in bed, though I still felt very weak.

"Well, how are we now?" asked the doctor, seeing that I moved with comparative ease. "A nice trick you've played me. Do you know that you have done me out of twenty guineas—by coming to life again—eh? I hoped to have cut you all up by this time—and I might have done so, too, easily enough at the time, but I suppose if I were to try it on now you'd halloa."

Then he began to ask me all sorts of questions, to which I answered feebly. In reply to a question of his as to whether I felt hungry, I nodded my head, and the doctor went to prepare me a cup of broth. When he returned and I had partaken of it, new strength came back to me, and I was able to relate to him all my sufferings while he listened attentively. Well, day after day I improved in health under the doctor's care, till I at length completely recovered. One morning after I was up and dressed, and breakfasting with the doctor (N.B.—Nobody, not even the doctor's servant, knew anything about either the removal of my body from the grave or of my coming to life again, for the doctor took good care to keep me locked up for a time in his bedchamber.) Well, breakfasting one morning with the doctor, I noticed that he looked rather thoughtful and confused.

"Now, I'll tell you what your thoughts are, doctor," said I, "and you see if I haven't guessed right."

"Well," said he, somewhat surlily.

"You are afraid that the affair about digging up my body may get known, and will damage your reputation, and you do not know how to keep it secret. Is it not so?" I asked.

"Well, sir," said he, "you've just guessed about right, but what is to be done?"

"Listen to me," said I. "I have a plan."

"Indeed!" said he, opening his eyes.

"Yes, a plan to kill two birds with one stone," I said. "It is to your interest that this affair should not be known—eh? Well, it is to my interest, too. All will go well if you do as I propose."

"What is that?" asked he, with eagerness.

"First you must lend me a complete disguise, consisting of one of your old wigs, a pair of tortoiseshell spectacles, and one of your suits of clothes. Secondly, you must lend me a certain sum of money to keep me for, say, a fortnight. I'll pay you back in due time, when my plan has succeeded. You needn't be afraid. You can trust Jack Hearty—eh?"

"Yes, certainly," said he, with some hesitation. "But how? I don't understand."

"Never mind that," said I; "you will know all in good time."

"Well, Jack," said he, "I know you for a sharp fellow and an honest—so I will trust you. I don't know what your scheme is; but if it fail, and the worst comes to the worst, why I can but be exposed, and there is an end of it."

"Well said, doctor," said I; "now let us commence to put the scheme into practice."

He then took from his wardrobe rather a threadbare suit of black clothes, which I immediately donned. Then I tried on an old powdered wig with a pigtail and a pair of lace ruffles, next a pair of tortoiseshell spectacles with glasses as big as a crown piece. I next corked my eyebrows, slightly stained the tip of my nose with red and made a few false wrinkles in my forehead. The doctor placed a gold-headed cane in my hand and a large signet ring on my forefinger. I then took a book under my arm, and at parting the doctor gave me a purse of gold to put in my pocket, and off I started. The doctor laughed immoderately at my successful disguise, and I heard him say as I was leaving the house, "I don't know what he means to be up to, but some devilry, *I'll* lay a farthing."

Well, gentlemen, the next thing I did was to walk straight off to catch the stage, which would pass by the village of H—, where Molly was staying with her aunt. I remember I had to run for it, and pretty hard, too, but I caught it up. Tearing along as fast as my legs could carry me, I passed by a group of villagers, some of my friends amongst them, and I heard the following remarks:

"Here comes the doctor, running for his life!"—"Go it doctor, you'll catch it up!"—"My eyes, don't he run!—who'd have thought the old boy had so much life in him?"

"It ain't the doctor, though; it's another man. I don't know him, Jim, do you? I wonder how long he has been in the village. I never see him before."

As I was stepping into the coach I heard a voice behind me say, "I thought it was Dr. Slasher, Bill, didn't you?"

"Yes, at first," said another; "he's like him—leastways the clothes is."

"By the way," said the first, "I wonder when the doctor will be ready for another subject. I suppose poor Jack's cut up long since."

"Hush! you fool," said the other.

By this time I had taken my seat in the coach, and looking in the direction of the voices, I recognised my friends of the other night, Tom and Bill. Off we then started. The coach was full of men I knew as well as my own father, most of them my customers. I appeared absorbed in my book, so as not to get entangled in conversation with anyone, for fear that my voice might betray me.

Two men, who appeared to be strangers to each other, began entering into conversation.

"Dreadful business this epidemic, sir," said the younger of the two to the elder.

"Yes, it is indeed," replied the elder; "the young fare the same as the old, they say, but I am a stranger in the place."

"Oh, indeed, sir," said the first speaker; and then added, "Yes, sir—that's true enough—the young die as soon as the old. Hardly a week ago died young Jack Hearty, son of old Hearty, as keeps the Headless Lady—a lad of nineteen, and as hale a young fellow as ever you'd find in a day's march. He was taken suddenly ill, and died in a very few days.

"Poor young fellow! who'd have thought that he would have gone along with the rest? He was an only son, too, and they say his father is devilish down in the mouth about it."

"Dear me! dreadful, to be sure," replied the elder.

The conversation then changed to various topics, and became general, the only one not joining in it being myself. I still pored over my book, appearing not to take an interest in anything that was being said, although my ears were open to catch every word.

"Who's that cove?" I heard one say to his neighbour.

"Oi doan't knaw, Oi'm sure," replied the one addressed, being a lusty farmer. "Oi never see'd un in these parts afore—looks loike a doctor."

"Why don't he speak?" said the other. "He won't talk to no one."

"Maybe un's too proud," said the former.

"I'd like to kick the surly devil," said his companion.

"What'll you bet Oi doan't make un speak?" said the countryman.

"Bet you a halfpenny you don't get a word out of him," said the first speaker.

"Done," said the farmer, and turning suddenly upon me, accosted me thus:—"Oi zay, governor, you bes a doctor, b'aint ye?"

I drew myself up with an air of dignity, and said with a frown, and in a feigned voice: "Did you address *me*, sir?"

"Ees," said the bumpkin, unawed by my assumption of dignity; "and Oi axes ye if ye b'aint a doctor."

"Well, sir," I said; "and if I am!"

"Ha! ha! ha!" he laughed coarsely. "Oi knowed ye was. Oi thought Oi knowed the breed. Vell, you doctors has made a pretty harvest of late, Oi reckon," said the farmer, bluntly.

"How so, sir," I asked. "I do not understand you."

"Vhy, vith the patients as has died in this here hepidemic," said he. "They must have brought grist to your mill, if Oi'm not mistook."

"What epidemic?" I asked, feigning surprise. "I am a stranger in these parts, and know nothing of the epidemic."

"Vhy, ye doan't mane to zay that ye never heard of th' epidemic as all th' vorld is a talking of," said he.

267

"All the world!" I cried, in astonishment. "All your little village, I suppose you mean—no, I am entirely ignorant of this malady."

"Vell then, doctor," said the boor, "if ye'd only set up in our village, there's a snug little business going on for the loikes of you."

"Humph!" I grunted, not deigning to make other reply.

"Yes, indeed, sir," said a man in the opposite corner of the coach, joining in the conversation, but more respectfully than my friend the farmer. "I assure you that a doctor's services are very much needed in these parts. They say the malady is spreading."

The last speaker was a man I knew as well as I know my own face in a looking-glass, and whom I had served to innumerable pints of our home-brewed ale—a crony of mine, in fact, yet he failed to see through my disguise.

"Dear me!" said I. "I hope it will be nothing very serious. I regret not being able to make myself useful, as I have several important cases to attend to a long distance off."

"Oh, it has been very bad indeed, sir, hereabouts," said the same man. "Most cases have been fatal. The death that has been most talked of in the village is that of poor Jack Hearty, a lad of nineteen, as strong and as good looking a young fellow as any in the village. He was took bad, as it might be, yesterday, and struck down today in the very flower of his youth."

"You don't say so?" said I.

"Yes, sir," he resumed; "and I'll be bound to say you wouldn't find a finer young fellow in all England."

"Really!" said I, inwardly feeling flattered.

"Ah!" said another, with a sly wink. "I think I could tell you what hastened Jack's death as much as anything."

"What was that?" I asked.

"There was a young woman in the case, they say," said the man, whom I also knew intimately.

"Well, sir," said I, with a well-feigned innocence; "and this young woman—?"

"Well, I believe he died pining for her, and folks say as how it was the hepidemic."

"Ah!" I said with a sigh. "That is an epidemic we all catch some time or other, but most folks get over it, I fancy."

"Well, yes," said the man; "most folks, as you say, do, but poor Jack was very hard hit indeed, sir. I happen to know the young woman, too—as fine a wench as you'll meet with in the whole kingdom."

"Ah! indeed," I said. "They would have been well matched then, had they married?"

"They would indeed, sir," was the reply. "They'd have made a pair as you wouldn't meet every day. Well, well," he sighed; "he's gone now, poor fellow, so the wench must look out for someone else."

"Did the girl take it much to heart, think you?" said I.

"Aye, I'll warrant she did, sir," said he, "though I can't say for certain, seeing as how her father sent her away from home to get her out of Jack's way. But she'll have heard all about it by this time. Poor girl! I am sorry for her. She'll have to wait a long time before she finds another like Jack."

"Perhaps she may never marry," I suggested; "that is if she really loved him."

"Can't say I'm sure, sir. You see the maid is quite young yet, and has got lots of admirers; what with one and what with another, she may in time forget Jack and take to someone else," said my friend.

"You have heard no rumours as yet, I suppose, of her showing any partiality towards anyone," I demanded, timidly.

"No, sir, I can't say that exactly, but then it is so shortly after Jack's death, that it isn't likely she would just yet. Still there's a young fellow, the son of a squire, as is very sweet upon her, and is always following of her about. If she could manage to catch him, she'd do well, but the young gent's father don't approve of it, and is like to cut him off to a shilling if he marries her. Folks say that the young squire is a bit of a scamp, and don't mean marriage. It'll be a pity if the maid goes wrong, for she is a good girl, and no mistake."

Now this was gall and wormwood to me. I knew that that rascal young Rashly had been hovering about Molly's house for some time. He had often crossed me in my walks with Molly, and we hated each other like poison, but I also knew that Molly couldn't bear the sight of him, for she was really and truly in love with me, yet the very mention of his name coupled with hers made my blood boil. Mastering my emotion, however, I asked with as much apparent indifference as possible, "And this young gentleman, where is he now?"

"Oh, up to his larks, I'll warrant," said the man, with a laugh. "The girl's father has sent her away to live with her aunt, to get her out of Jack's way, as he is not friends with Jack's father, and I guess out of the way of the young squire, too; but young Rashly has been absent now some time from the village, and I'll be bound he has found her out by this time. Now that poor Jack's dead he'll have the way all clear before him."

"The devil take him," I muttered to myself. I was bursting with rage, and to conceal my emotion, I affected to stare out of the window at some object, while my heart beat underneath my borrowed waistcoat, and must have been audible but for the coach wheels. I appeared again absorbed in my book while the rest of the passengers discoursed upon general topics.

"Give us the halfpenny," I heard my bluff fellow-traveller say to his friend; "it's been fairly von." His friend's hand was buried for an instant, and the coin was transferred from his to the farmer's breeches pocket.

"That's zum business, onyrate," said the countryman, receiving the payment of the bet with a chuckle.

The stage then rolled on for some distance further, till some passenger called out:

"There is H—, any passenger for H—?"

"Yes, sir," said I; "I am for H—."

The stage stopped, and with trembling hands and beating heart I squeezed past the other passengers.

"Good morning, gentlemen," said I, as I walked off.

The stage was set in motion again. There was no other passenger but myself for the village of H—, so I strolled off with light step to the nearest inn.

Having refreshed myself with a light luncheon, I strolled about the country a bit until I came across—you may be surprised, gentlemen—but I actually came across the very same house with the very identical country round about it, including the wood, that appeared in my dream. I certainly *was* startled.

"Yonder, then, is the house of Molly's aunt," I thought, and I walked towards it, thinking all the while how I should introduce myself.

Before I reached the house, however, two figures in the distance under the trees of the wood attracted my gaze. I looked again. One of the figures, I was sure, could be no other than Molly herself, and the other I was equally certain was young Rashly.

I hastened my steps, but by a route so as not to come directly in front of them, for I wished to overhear their conversation. Having made a roundabout cut, I concealed myself behind some brushwood, where I could both see them distinctly, and hear all they said without being seen by them.

"Come, Molly," I heard young Rashly say, "enough of this. What is the good of making yourself miserable about young Hearty? He's dead now, poor fellow—he was a great friend of mine, but now that he is gone and can never come back to you, try to forget him. I wish to console you and to raise your spirits. Now, my dear girl, do try and forget him."

"Oh, never, never!" sobbed Molly, "I never *can* forget him. I shall never be able to love anyone else. Poor fellow! He died out of love for me, I know he did. Oh, Jack, Jack, I never can forget you—never, never!" and she sobbed as if her heart would break.

"Now, Molly, this is nothing but obstinacy; you can't call him back, however you may mourn for him. Just look at the position *I* offer you. *I* shall be able to make you more comfortable than Jack would have been able to make you. Is it nothing to be made a lady of? Don't be a fool, girl, and throw such a chance away. Hundreds in your place would jump at it."

"How can I accept such terms from a man I do not love?" cried Molly. "Would I not be one of the basest of women to persuade you that I loved you just to become your wife, when my heart is another's?"

"How can your heart be another's when Jack is no more?" asked he.

"Yes, yes; in death my heart shall still be his," Molly cried.

"Come, now, you're talking like a mad girl. Just listen to reason a bit. I will settle a good round sum a year upon you to keep you as a lady in a nice little cottage with a garden, where I shall always be able to come to pay you a visit in secret, when my father is out of the way."

"Then you never from the first intended to *marry* me," interrupted Molly, "you only—only—wanted to—"

"Why, actually *marry* you, no; I never intended that. *That* would be impossible, but—"

"Exactly; I understand you," answered Molly, proudly, "but I scorn your base proposals. If you were to lay the wealth of the universe at my feet, I would never barter my good name. So *this* is what you have been trying at all this time, to make me your minion.

"When first you visited me, you gave me to understand that your intentions were honourable, and though I loved you not, and never could, yet I respected you and felt compassion for you and tried to think of you as a friend. Now I neither pity nor respect you, but *despise* you. Go, sir, and never dare to speak to me again!"

"What a trump of a girl!" I muttered to myself.

"Molly! Molly!" cried Rashly, starting backward in amazement, "are you mad?"

"I should be mad to accept your proposals," replied Molly, calmly, but firmly. "Go, sir—all friendship between us is at an end."

"My dear Molly," began Rashly, "I beg of you, I entreat you to calm yourself—to take a more reasonable view of the matter. Come, let me persuade you, dear," said he, advancing and attempting to put his arm round her waist, but he was instantly repulsed.

He essayed again.

"Dare to touch me once more, sir, and I'll scream—I'll rouse the neighbourhood and expose you."

"Hush, hush!" said Rashly, nothing daunted, "be reasonable, there's a good girl, I'll do you no harm," and he ventured to touch her again.

"Back, sir, I say!" and she lifted up her voice to scream, but instantly his hand was on her mouth.

I could endure it no longer, but bursting from my hiding-place, and grasping firmly my gold-headed cane, I sprang to the spot.

"Who are you, sir?" I cried, boiling with rage, "that dare offer to insult my niece? Begone! or it will be the worse for you."

Both started, and Rashly turned livid and trembled.

"I thank you, sir," said Molly, "for interfering."

Then thrusting Rashly aside, I cried; "Molly! I am your uncle, do you not know me?" trying to disguise my voice all the while, which was rather a difficult matter, boiling with passion as I was then.

"I do not know you, sir, though I believe your intentions to be good," said Molly.

Then seizing Molly by the hand, I whispered in her ear; "Silence!—not a word—I am Jack risen from the grave."

A piercing shriek, and Molly fell fainting against a tree.

"Who are you, you vagabond?" cried Rashly, now for the first time recovering from his surprise. "She does not know you. What have you been saying to the poor girl to frighten her so? You are an impostor, sir. Be off and mind your own business!"

"Impostor! eh?—vagabond, eh? I'll show you who is a vagabond, you scoundrel!" said I, and lifting my cane, I laid it about him with all my might and main like a cavalryman cutting down his foe.

Rashly at first attempted to defend himself, and flew at me like a tiger; he tried to snatch the cane from my hand, but I hit him so

272

severely across the knuckles that I made him howl out in spite of himself. I cut him right and left over head, shoulders, arms and legs, hacking and slashing with the force of an infuriated madman, accompanying each blow with such epithets as "scoundrel," "blackguard," till he burst out in a piteous cry and took refuge in flight. He never troubled Molly again.

The doctor's gold-headed cane had been broken with the force of the blows I had dealt my rival, for which afterwards I had to pay, but to return to Molly. She gradually recovered her senses, and gazed at me wonderingly and full of fear.

"Be calm, Molly," I said in my natural voice, "it is I—Jack, risen from the grave, but still in the flesh and no spirit." Then taking off my spectacles and wig, I said, "Molly, do you not recognise these eyes and these locks, in spite of the rest of my disguise?"

She still looked fearful and distrustingly at me, but at length convinced that it was myself—and no one else—by my voice, she flew to my arms crying, "Oh, Jack, Jack!—is it really you?"

Of course, she wanted an instant explanation of my resurrection, which I by degrees gave; and having given it, I began to unfold to her my plan, thus.

"Molly," I said, "what I have told you and am about to tell you now must remain a secret between ourselves, otherwise my plan will fail. Well then, in the first place you must get me acquainted with your aunt, and give out that I am an elderly gentleman you have known some time, and that you have met me quite unexpectedly here. You must invite me to call at the house. I shall adopt the name of Dr. Crow. You must feign illness and send for me. Thus we shall be able to see a good deal of each other. I will also persuade your aunt that she is ill, so that we shall see still more of each other. I'll worm myself into her good graces and after about a fortnight or so, I shall ask your aunt's consent to our marriage. I shall tell her that I am a doctor in good practice, and shall be able to keep you well, and when I once get the right side of her, I doubt not that I shall obtain her consent. She will then write to your father, who will hardly say anything against a match so advantageous, although our ages may be apparently unequal.

"It is not likely that he will trouble himself to come down here to have a look at me, as he is at present laid up with the gout. He will in all probability write his consent. That once obtained, I shall make all necessary preparations for the marriage, and as for obtaining my father's consent—leave that to me."

"Oh, but, Jack! if your plan should fail—if your disguise should be seen through," began Molly.

"Leave all to me," said I. "So far I have been successful, for I have not been recognised yet. Fortune seems on my side. You must aid me in every possible way to carry out my plan."

"I will, Jack!" said she.

"Well, then," said I, "you must go home now to your aunt, and say you have met an old friend of yours quite by chance here—a certain Dr. Crow. Say also that I should like to call and make her acquaintance. Meet me again tomorrow in the wood, and invite me to the house. In time, I've no doubt, all will go well."

Molly promised to follow my instructions, and we parted.

It was then late in the afternoon, so I returned to my inn. There I found a snug little parlour, with a bookcase, so I beguiled the time as well as I could by reading until the clock struck the dinner hour. After a comfortable meal, I smoked a pipe of tobacco, strolled about the streets a little in the twilight, and turned into bed.

Next morning, after breakfast, I strolled out again into the wood. I walked about for an hour, perhaps, without meeting anyone, casting anxious glances all the while towards the house where Molly lived.

At length she made her appearance; not alone this time, but with another female. This must be the aunt, I thought—so much the better. Feeling the necessity of an excuse for hovering about so near the house, I feigned to be gathering wild flowers.

"Oh, aunt!" I heard Molly say as she came up, "here is Dr. Crow, the gentleman that I spoke to you about yesterday."

"Ah, Miss Sykes!" said I, lifting my hat in the most polite manner, "I hope I see you well this morning."

Molly gave me her hand, and introduced me to her aunt, who curtseyed and smiled.

I said that I had come down here for a change of air, and that I was amusing myself with botanising.

"Oh, indeed!" said the aunt. "So that is your hobby, is it, Dr. Crow—well, and a very delightful one, too. I am very fond of flowers myself, and only wish I knew more about them. I do envy you scientific men. You always seem so happy and contented."

"Well, madam," said I, "there is nothing like having a hobby in life.

It fills up many a weary hour and makes us forget the din and the bustle of the busy world around us. For my part, when I have no patients to attend to, I am always occupied in some way or other."

"Dear me," said the aunt. "How very delightful!"

We walked on together, conversing agreeably as we went, and afterwards I was invited into the house. Need I say that I praised to the utmost the good taste of everything I saw there, her paperhangings, her worsted work, her crochet, etc. I was then shown some specimens of ferns and wild flowers that she had dried in a book, and she begged of me to write their classical names under them.

This was indeed a trial, as I had never learnt a single word of Latin, but it would not do to back out, so I exerted all my ingenuity to invent some crackjaw names. Among the rest I remember inscribing the words *Rodus sidus*, *Stenchius obnoxious* and *Herbus unnonus*. These names delighted Molly's aunt immensely, who believed she was already a Latin scholar. I found my way so well into the aunt's good graces that I was invited to call whenever I liked, and frequently asked to dinner.

As I did not like to call every day, for fear it should look bad, either Molly or Molly's aunt managed to feel unwell on the days that I did not call, and they found it necessary to send for me, so it came to much the same thing, as I saw Molly every day. Molly's aunt was one of that class of females who are always imagining that something or other is the matter with them. I soon saw, therefore, that to get thoroughly into her good graces, I must humour her in her whims.

Accordingly, I made out that she had this, that, or the other—indeed, I forget what it was exactly that I said ailed her—and promised to bring her some physic. This quite won her heart, so I at once set about making some liquorice water, endeavouring to disguise the taste of the liquorice as much as possible by adding salt, pepper, a little soap, some tobacco, and other nauseous ingredients. I wonder the mess didn't poison her, but so far from causing ill-effects, she informed me that it had really done her good.

Whether the good it had done her only lay in her imagination or whether the strange compound really did possess a medicinal property I cannot tell (I can hardly think the latter), but certain it was, she *did* seem better. I believe the real fact of the matter to be this. Molly's aunt was the daughter of a well-to-do retired butcher, and like many of her class, had over-indulged in high feeding, and consequently was always suffering from overloaded stomach. The mess that I gave her made her sick, and that, in reality, and not merely in imagination, effected a cure.

I then put her on a lower diet, recommended her plenty of walking exercise, and in a very short time there was a complete change in her constitution. She no longer felt dyspeptic and desponding, suffered no longer from nervous headaches, in fact, in her own words, she "felt quite a girl again." All the effect of my wonderful medicine. This, of course, was a feather in my cap, and she looked up to me more than ever.

A week and then a fortnight passed away, and I now thought it high time to break to the aunt my love affair with her niece, and ask her consent to our union. So I called upon her one morning and requested to speak with her alone. She received me in the back parlour, and begged me to take a seat. I did so, and began thus:—

"Ahem! Madam, I wished to talk to you upon a matter of some delicacy."

"Good gracious, doctor! What can have happened?" she exclaimed, observing a look of unwonted gravity in my face.

"Oh, nothing, nothing," I said; "at least, nothing of any great importance. Hear me. I am a physician of a certain age and in very good practice." I paused.

"Well, Dr. Crow," said the aunt.

"And I am still a bachelor," I continued.

"Well, sir," said she, wriggling about in her seat and looking coy, as if she guessed I meditated a proposal, and took the compliment to herself.

"Well, madam," said I, impatient to get through this painful duty, "to cut a long story short, I am in love with your charming niece."

"*Oh!* doctor," she exclaimed.

The "*Oh!*" was jerked out with a spasm truly painful, and her countenance fell visibly.

"I dare say you were not prepared for such a surprise, but I have known Miss Sykes now a long time, and I never saw anyone who could suit me better as a wife. Miss Sykes and I have talked the matter over together, and she only awaits her aunt's consent. Thank you, thank you, madam," said I seizing her hand, "I knew you would give it," before giving her an opportunity either to consent or refuse.

"Molly!" I cried, "come and thank your kind aunt for having given her consent to our happy union."

Molly entered, blushing and giggling.

"Come, Molly," said I, "come and thank aunt, for now we shall be as happy as two birds in a nest. I'll go and see about the licence, and we'll get married as soon as ever we can."

I laughed and appeared very merry, repeatedly seizing the aunt by the hand and patting her on the shoulder before she had time to get a word out. "Stay, sir," said she, at length, "I can do nothing without the consent of my niece's father."

"Oh, that will be easily obtained, I am quite sure," said I, hopefully. "We will at once write a note, and all will be settled."

I brought her her desk, opened it, took out pen, ink, and paper, and placing a chair for her, induced her to write.

"Yes," I said, looking over her shoulder as she wrote, "that will do—not *too* cold. Say I am in a position to make his daughter comfortable, and that you think it is a very desirable match—yes, that's the sort of thing. Give it to me, I'll take it to the post." So saying, I snatched up the epistle, bounded from the house, and returned shortly, as happy as if everything were already settled.

In due time came a reply from old Sykes, to the purport that, though he would have chosen a younger man for his daughter, yet on the whole, considering that I had a pretty good business as a doctor, and could keep her well, he saw no reason why he should withhold his consent. Furthermore, he begged the aunt that if his daughter were to be married to hasten the marriage as much as possible, as young Rashly had been missing for some time, and folks said that he was down at H— after her.

"Bravo! old Sykes," said I to myself, "Fortune seems to favour me indeed."

The next step that I intended to take was to obtain the consent of my father. Accordingly, I took leave of Molly for a time, stating that I had to absent myself on business, and promising a speedy return. I entered the stage and arrived at our village, where I put up at my father's inn. It was towards evening when I arrived.

"Landlord!" I cried, disguising my voice, "I wish to dine in half-an-hour."

"Yes, sir," said my father, coming towards me, bowing, and rubbing his hands.

"Have you got a good bed?" asked I, "for I wish to sleep here tonight."

"Yes, sir, capital beds, sir," said my father, "both clean and well aired."

"Very well, then, make me up one," said I, pompously.

"It shall be done, sir," said my father, obsequiously.

I occupied myself with reading until dinner-time. At length the dinner came up.

"A pint of your best port, landlord," I cried, magnificently.

My father returned with the port, crusted and cob-webbed, from the cellar, and I began my dinner. Having finished, I filled my pipe, and whilst my father cleared the table, I deigned to enter into conversation with him.

I began by asking him the number of inhabitants in the village, and then brought him out upon the subject of the epidemic.

"Ah! sir," said my father, deeply moved, "it carried off my only son some three weeks ago, and a finer lad you wouldn't see in all England. I hoped that he would have been the prop of my old age, but he was carried off, sir, along with the rest—struck down in the very spring of his youth, as you may say. Only nineteen was my poor boy when he was taken from me," and my father's eyes moistened as he spoke.

"Only nineteen!" I exclaimed. "Was he not strong?"

"Strong, sir! I believe you—strong as a lion," said my father.

"Dear me!" I said, "it is very strange that his youth and strength did not resist the malady."

"So everyone said, sir," replied my father, "but—but he had been ailing for some time before."

"What was his complaint before he caught this disease?" I asked.

"Ah! sir, that's just the point," answered my father. "I sadly fear that it was an epidemic of a more dangerous sort."

"How so?" asked I. "What do you mean?"

"Well, sir, my real opinion is now that the young man was too strongly attached to a maid whom he couldn't marry, and that undermined his health. Then came the epidemic, which he had not sufficient strength to shake off."

"Ah!" said I, "and why could he not marry her? Was the maid unrelenting?"

"Not that, exactly, sir. Indeed, I believe she was as much in love with him, but—"

"But what?"

"Well, the fact of the matter is, sir, the girl's father and I ain't friends, and neither of us was willing to give our consent. The girl was sent off by her father to live at her aunt's, just to get her out of my son's way. I knew all about this, but I wasn't going to tell the young man, lest he should take it into his head to run after her, so, thinking to blunt his passion, I invented the story of her death, saying that she had been carried off by the epidemic, hoping that after a time, finding she was no more, that he would cease to think of her. But instead of that, he grew worse and worse, and I attribute his death to the lie I told about his sweetheart's decease."

"You did very wrong," said I, "not to give your consent."

"Well, but, sir, if I *had* given *mine*, the girl's father would not have given *his*," replied my father.

"If you had been the first to make up the quarrel, I have no doubt that he would have given his consent," said I.

My father seemed stung with this reproach, and took out his hand-kerchief to wipe his eyes.

"Ah, my poor son! my poor son!" sobbed my father. "What wouldn't I give to have him back again?"

"Would you give your consent to his marriage with the girl he loved if he could come to life again?" I asked.

"Ay, sir, that would I, only too gladly," replied my father, "but what's the use of talking now that he has gone from me for ever?"

"You speak like a man without faith," said I. "Have you no belief in an after life? Have you no hope of meeting him in Heaven?"

"That is the only hope I have left, sir," said my father, "but in the meantime—"

"Ah!" said I, "you cannot make up your mind to be consoled for his loss for the few short years that you have to remain upon earth."

"Well, sir, it's very hard to bear," said my father.

"Have you ever prayed?" I asked.

"Yes, sir," said he, "I say my prayers regularly."

"But do you say them earnestly?" said I. "Do you believe that if you ask a thing that you will receive what you ask for? For instance, if you were to pray for your son to be restored to life, do you believe that he really *would* be restored to life?"

My father stared in surprise.

"Well, to tell you the truth, sir, no," he said; "for we all know that when a man has been buried three weeks that he rarely returns. Even Lazarus was but four days under the earth. In fact, the thought of praying for his return after his spirit had once been yielded up never occurred to me. When David was bereaved of his child by Uriah's wife, he humbled himself whilst the child was yet alive with sackcloth and ashes, but when he heard that the child was dead, he rose and ate bread. What instance is there on record of one returning to life after being buried three weeks?"

"Pray, nevertheless," said I; "the mercy of God is boundless. Who knows but that—"

"Oh, sir, sir," said my father, shaking his head, "you but mock me; it cannot be."

"It is impious of you to say it cannot be. Nothing is impossible with God," said I.

My father smiled faintly. I saw that he regarded me as a kind of well meaning madman, and after lighting my candle, he showed me the way to my room and shut me in for the night.

My room was some few doors off from my father's. I undressed and went to bed. I had not been in bed more than an hour when I heard my father's footsteps on the stairs. He, too, was going to bed. There was no other guest in the inn then, and all was quiet.

I allowed my father a quarter of an hour to get into bed. Then I opened my chamber door, and listened to hear if he was praying, for he always prayed aloud. I was satisfied that he was praying; what the precise words were I could not quite distinguish, but I fancied I heard my name mentioned once or twice. I returned to my chamber and closed the door. I allowed my father another hour to go to sleep. When the time had expired, I stepped on tip-toe across the passage and turned the handle of his bedroom door noiselessly. I peeped in. All was silent, or rather he was snoring loudly. Leaving the door ajar, I went back cautiously to my chamber to fetch the candle, and then softly and noiselessly I entered the room where my father lay asleep. I had provided myself with a pinch of salt, which I sprinkled in the flame, so as to give a look of ghostly pallor to my face. Then, tapping my father lightly on the shoulder, he started up in bed.

"Good heavens!" he cried, with every hair erect on his head—

"Jack! is it you?"

He spoke huskily, and his teeth chattered.

"Hush!" said I, in a sepulchral voice; "listen to me. Because you have prayed fervently, I have risen from my grave to comfort you. Grieve not for me, father, for I am happy. I have returned to thank you for having given your consent to my marriage. Molly is now mine in spirit, and I shall henceforth rest peacefully in my tomb. Farewell."

I strode towards the door, with long, silent, majestic strides, and closed it carefully after me, leaving my father staring after me into space and speechless with terror.

I was a very young man then, and a reckless devil-may-care sort of fellow, otherwise I should not have attempted such a dangerous practical joke. The consequences might have been fatal; as it was, my father's nerves were terribly shaken, and I spoilt all his night's rest. When he brought up my breakfast the next morning in the parlour he looked pale and haggard.

"What is the matter, good man?" said I, patronisingly, in my usual feigned voice.

"Oh, sir!" said my father, excitedly, "I saw him last night!"

"Saw him!" I exclaimed. "Saw whom?"

"My son, Jack, sir. Oh, who would have believed it?"

"What! and has he returned to life, or was it his spirit?"

"Yes, sir, his ghost," said my father, with a look of awe, and then he began relating to me the whole particulars of his son's spiritual apparition.

"Then you followed my advice, and have been praying?"

"That I did, sir, with all my heart and soul," said my father.

"You told me last evening," said I, "that if your son should come to life again you would give your consent to his marriage. If you really repent having withheld your consent during his lifetime let me see that your repentance is true by writing me the following words and affixing your signature."

"What words, sir, must I write?" he asked.

"Write," said I, "'If my son is restored to me I will give my consent to his marriage, with the girl of his choice,' that is what you have to write."

"But—but—" began my father.

"Write what I tell you, and affix your signature," said I, gruffly.

"As you like, sir," said he, complying with my request. I blotted the sheet of paper, and placed it in my pocket.

"Now, sir," said I to my father, "I have a secret to tell you. Do not faint, but be prepared for a shock."

My father looked at me in astonishment.

"Your son lives," said I.

281

"What do I hear?—my son—my son lives?" he exclaimed, staggering backwards. Then recovering somewhat his composure, he asked, "But how? I myself saw him laid in the ground; besides, I tell you I saw his ghost last night."

"That was nothing but a distempered dream brought on by our conversation before you retired to rest," said I. "I tell you your son lives—he is in my care. Listen; but what I am about to tell you, you must keep to yourself, otherwise it will damage my reputation. Hearing that your son had been buried, I, being a doctor and in want of a subject for dissection, employed resurrectioners or body-snatchers to procure me your son's body. They stole it from his grave and brought it to my house. When I began to dissect I found that he was not yet dead. He has been at my house ever since, still very weak from his recent illness. He has related to me his love affair, and knows of the deception that you practised upon him. He begged me to procure for him his father's consent to his marriage, otherwise, he said he might die in real earnest."

"Oh, doctor, doctor!" cried my father, "can it be true? Oh, say that you are not jesting with me. Do not trifle with the feelings of a poor man!"

"I never trifle," I replied, with dignity.

"Then it is true, doctor, really true! O God be praised," and he clasped his hands convulsively, whilst the tears ran down his cheeks.

Suddenly his ecstasy abated, and he grew serious.

"What is the matter?" I asked.

"Oh, but, doctor, if—if after all what I saw last night were not a dream—if whilst during your absence from home, my son really has died, and appeared to me last night to let me know. What proof have you that the vision of my son last night *was* a dream?" he asked.

"What proof?" I exclaimed. "*This* proof," I cried, throwing off my disguise and speaking in my own natural voice again. "Behold me, father, risen from the dead!"

My father's surprise, consternation and joy was beyond all description.

"What!" he cried, "and are you really Jack risen from the grave? Come, let me touch you to be sure you are no ghost.

"Ha! ha! Ha! ha! ha!" he laughed, hysterically. "What! Jack, my boy, I see it all. Ha! ha! ha! ha!" and he wept upon my shoulder till I thought he'd go off in a fit.

"Hush! father," I cried, "and calm yourself. My resurrection must be a secret between us two, for motives of policy. Do you understand?"

"Why a secret?" he asked.

"Never mind now; that is part of my plan. If you tell a single soul you'll spoil all, and I am a ruined man," I said.

"I understand nothing of all this, Jack," said my father, "but you may count upon my secrecy; but I say, Jack, how long must I keep the secret, for I am burning to tell everyone in the village?"

"For Heaven's sake, hold your tongue," said I, "until I give you permission to let it out, or I am ruined for life."

"Well, well, Jack, mum's the word," said my father.

I then resumed my disguise and prepared to leave the inn.

"Why, what the devil are you going to be up to now?"

"Mum's the word," said I. "You shall know all when I return. Goodbye, father," and off I started.

I busied myself a good deal about getting everything in order for the wedding, and returned to H—, where without further bother I was married at the village church.

Fearful that if I threw off my disguise before the wedding that something or other, I could not tell what or from what quarter, would mar all and prevent the marriage just at the last moment, after having been so successful up to this time, this feeling, or presentiment of harm, vague as it was, induced me to keep on my disguise all through the ceremony, but when it came to signing my name in the register, I signed my real name—*John Hearty.* This created some sensation.

The aunt wanted me to explain myself. However, we hurried back to the aunt's house, where we at once threw off my disguise, explained all, and craved pardon for the deception I had practised upon her.

At first the aunt seemed a little cold. She was hurt at the deception being carried on so long.

There was no necessity for such tricks, she said, if she had been told all at the beginning; nothing would have been known to anyone else.

"Do you think I would trust a woman's tongue?" I said. "Come, now, aunt," I said, "though I am not a doctor, I did you quite as much good as a court physician could have done you. Yes, although the medicine was only liquorice water mixed up with other harmless filth."

"In that, too, I've been imposed upon, then," murmured the aunt.

"Nevertheless, I cured you," retorted I; "you yourself admitted it, and what is more, I took no fee."

Soon, however, Molly's aunt recovered her good humour, and all passed off with a hearty laugh.

The only difficulty now was to reconcile ourselves with Molly's father. The comedy was nearly at an end. I donned my disguise once more, and we started off together after the wedding breakfast to our native village, and driving up to old Sykes' house, we knocked at the door.

We entered, and I introduced myself as his son-in-law. He received us well, and wished us both health and prosperity. I did not know exactly how to break the ice, so I reflected a moment.

"Mr. Sykes," said I, still in my feigned voice, "I shall expect you this evening to dine with me at six o'clock at the 'Headless Lady.' Come, I will take no refusal. If we are to be friends together, I shall expect you, if not—"

He began to make an excuse about his gouty leg, saying that he never left the house.

"Oh, nonsense," said I, "that is just the reason you never get well. Going out now and then will do you good. I am a doctor, you know, and I advise you for your good. If you do not like to walk, make use of our coach."

He still hesitated, and at length said, "Well, the fact is, I never go to that house. The landlord and I are not friends. We have had some differences together of long standing, and—"

"Nonsense," said I, "that is no excuse at all. All men have differences now and then, but we must learn to forget and forgive."

"No," said Sykes; "he was very much in the wrong."

"Well, I've no doubt that he thinks you are in the wrong," said I. "Dine with me this evening there, and I'll undertake to make matters straight for you both. Hearty is a good and honest man, and is one of my best friends. I have known him these nineteen years. If you refuse to come, it will be an offence to me, mind that."

After a time I succeeded in softening him down a little, till I at length drew from him a reluctant consent, and, according to his word, he appeared that evening at our inn.

A grand dinner was prepared, before partaking of which I succeeded in joining the hands of the two bitter enemies.

Seeing that the hour had arrived for the divulging of the secret I explained all in a few words, threw off my disguise and craved his blessing.

Old Sykes was a crusty sort of a cove, and I expected that there would have been a scare, but we had got him into a good humour previously, and he was so much amused, in spite of himself, at the whole scheme that he wrung my hand heartily and laughed much over my odd adventures.

Dinner passed off gaily, and I secretly put the doctor in possession of his old clothes again. I paid him the money I owed him, and for ever kept secret the name of the doctor who had brought me to life again so cleverly.

★ ★ ★ ★ ★

"Why, Jack," said Mr. Oldstone, at the conclusion of our host's recital, "you can tell a story like the best of us."

"Ay, that he can indeed," chimed in Mr. Crucible and Mr. Hardcase.

"There is a great deal of poetry in Jack's story," remarked Mr. Parnassus.

Mr. Blackdeed said that it ought to be adapted to the stage.

"And was it ever discovered who unearthed you, Jack?" inquired Dr. Bleedem, who had a fellow feeling for the Dr. Slasher of Jack's narrative, as he could imagine what his own feelings would have been had he fallen a victim to the infuriated villagers.

"No, sir," replied our host, "I never let out the truth, although I was pestered with questions all day long by every one in the village. At length, however, an old doctor in these parts died from the epidemic, and after his death, I gave out to the villagers that he was the man who had dug me up."

"Ah!" said Dr. Bleedem, "there was no harm in that."

"And the two body-snatchers, did you ever see *them* again?" asked Professor Cyanite.

"Ha! ha!" laughed our host, "and that *was* a joke, surely. One evening, shortly after my resurrection, leastways before everyone knew that I had come to life again, I was strolling through the cemetery alone where I had been buried, and sitting down upon my own grave, I began meditating upon my miraculous escape from death, when who should pass by but my two friends, Tom and Bill. I looked up as they passed. You should have seen how they took to their heels. My eyes! I shall never forget it."

"That was a rare joke, indeed," said our artist, "and that other young fellow, young Rashly, did you see any more of him?"

"Ay, sir," replied our host, "and that was another good joke. The

Sunday after our marriage I appeared in the village church with Molly. How the people did stare, to be sure! I recognised young Rashly in the Squire's pew with his father. He could not see me, as I was behind a pillar, and he had not yet heard of my coming to life again. Seeing that he was without a hymn book, I stepped out suddenly from my pew, and crossing the aisle, offered him mine. I never shall forget his face. He turned as pale as a ghost, and was obliged to support himself against the back of the pew. He was nigh fainting, and his father was obliged to lead him out of church."

"Your resurrection must have made quite a sensation in the village then," said McGuilp.

"My word, it did, sir, and no mistake," answered the landlord. "Everybody in the village and for miles round it wanted to shake me by the hand and welcome me back to life. People used to come from long distances to hear me recount my adventures, till I grew quite sick of it, and shut myself up and wouldn't see nobody."

"Ay, ay, tedious work I've no doubt, telling the same story over and over again to every new comer," said Mr. Oldstone. "But tell us, Jack, did young Rashly ever discover who it was that gave him the thrashing?"

"Yes, sir, that, too, came out in time," said our host, "and devilish sheepish he looked, so they said, when he heard it was his old rival in disguise. He would have liked to have had me up about it before the assizes, but he didn't like the idea of exposing himself, and so the matter dropped. After a time, however, finding that all the boys in the village laughed at him whenever he walked abroad, he went to London, and I have never heard anything more of him."

At this moment someone knocked at the door.

"Come in!" called out several voices at once.

The door opened ajar, and the head of our hostess timidly appeared at the aperture.

"Beg pardon, gentlemen," said that worthy dame, "but could Helen be spared a little just to help me a bit?"

"Oh! how very annoying!" cried our artist, "just as the weather is clearing up and I was making up my mind for a long sitting."

"I am afraid I can't do without her, sir, just now," said our hostess, "but if you wouldn't mind waiting an hour or so, she will be at liberty."

"An hour without Helen!" exclaimed several members at once. "Oh, impossible! and then to be snatched from us again so soon!"

"I'll tell you what it is, Mr. McGuilp, and you, too, Dame Hearty," said Mr. Oldstone, "you are to blame, both of you. Such conduct can't be suffered to go unpunished; therefore, in the name of the club I condemn you both to contribute to the common entertainment by telling a story, each of you, when next called upon."

"Hear, hear!" cried several voices.

"Yes, a story from Dame Hearty, and a still longer one from Mr. McGuilp for having robbed us of Helen—a most just sentence!"

"Oh, gentlemen!" said our hostess modestly. "You wouldn't care to hear any of my stories; besides, I've forgotten them all long ago."

"Come now, Dame Hearty, there is no backing out," said Mr. Oldstone. "A sentence is a sentence."

"Well, sir, if it must be so, I'll try and think of one whenever the gentlemen of this respectable club choose to command my services. Come, Helen!" And our hostess led away her fair daughter by the hand amidst the groans of her ardent admirers.

"Now, Mr. McGuilp," said Mr. Oldstone as the door closed after Helen and her mother, "we have a full hour before us. I call upon you to fill up that period to the satisfaction of the club."

"Yes, yes!" shouted a chorus of voices; "out with it; no mercy on him. Let justice be done."

"Well, gentlemen, if you will allow me a moment to compose myself, I'll endeavour to satisfy you," said our artist. Then resting his head on his hand as if to call up from the depths of his memory some long-forgotten tale or legend, he said, "Gentlemen, I recollect a story in our family, handed down to me from some remote ancestor. I used to be frightened with it in my childhood. It is long ago now since I heard it related, but I will endeavour to give it you as perfectly as possible after the lapse of so many years."

"Well, we're all attention," said one of the members.

Then our artist, after stretching himself, folded his arms and commenced the following tale—

The Artist's Second Story
Der Scharfrichter[1]

A respectable ancestor of mine, far back in the middle ages, went to study at a German university. I cannot call to mind the name of it, but that is of no consequence. I think he studied medicine, but I will not be sure even of that. I know that he belonged to a "chor," or company of students who pride themselves on their liberty, who have their own laws and customs, who fight duels with rival *chors*, and who settle disputes among themselves by out-vying each other in the drinking of beer, who revel in street brawls and other such respectable amusements, playing practical jokes upon the peaceful citizens; in fact, making night hideous.

I know not whether my ancestor was any better or any worse than his fellow students, but he seems to have entered with pleasure into all their amusements, and never to have held himself aloof when any mischief was going on. He was consequently looked up to rather than otherwise by his companions.

It was the custom then, and still is among Germans, especially among German students, to travel long distances on foot, going together often in large numbers and putting up at night, if they could, at some inn; if not, in some cottage, stables, or loft, with nothing but straw to sleep upon.

But German students are not pampered mortals, and can put up with very homely accommodation. If after a fatiguing day's march a student can find at his quarters sufficient beer, black bread, sausage, raw ham, or a little strong cheese, he is perfectly satisfied. Should he be so fortunate as to light upon a dish of *sauer kraut*, he would fancy himself in the seventh heaven.

The German is hardy, yet studious, highly sensitive, and keenly

1. *Scharfrichter* or executioner; literally, "the sharp judge."

susceptible to the beauties of nature. Though somewhat penurious, he is fond of good fellowship, and is a staunch friend.

The foot tour in Germany is a thing common to all classes, from the nobility down to the *handwerksbursch*, or journeying mechanic, which latter class is often unmercifully persecuted by the university student. From time immemorial there seems to have been a feeling of animosity between the two classes, as nearer home we find existing between the "town and gown."

The German student of the middle ages, as in our times, was fond of swagger, delighted in wearing high boots, enormous spurs, an exaggerated sword, a preposterous hat, was provoked to a duel on the slightest occasion, boasted of the number of *schoppen* or *seidel* of beer that he could stow away beneath his doublet, and ran up long bills without a thought of how they were to be paid.

In those days every student had his guitar or other musical instrument wherewith to serenade his *liebchen* or lady-love, for that latter article was indispensable to the life of a student, and though much grossness and barbarity has been attributed to him, he is, nevertheless, at times capable of being elevated by a pure and refined passion, for he has much poetry in his nature, and is both sentimental and romantic in the extreme.

In all ages students have meddled much in politics, and princes have been known to tremble before their audacity and resolution.

But enough of this digression, gentlemen. My present tale demands only that you should call up in your minds the German student on his foot tour in the long vacation, with his keen relish of the beautiful, his lusty and well-trained frame that laughs at fatigue, his love of good-fellowship, his tender thoughts of home with the image of his lady-love.

Which pined although it spoke not, and grew keen,
Entering with every step it took through many a scene.
                                        —Byron.[2]

I must now return to my ancestor, who at the time this story commences was on one of these pedestrian rambles, accompanied by some twenty of his fellow students, all stout, hearty youths who could eat, drink, and fight with any in the university, and flirt, too, I've no doubt, when occasion tempted them.

---

2. The reader is begged to excuse the anachronism. Byron did not write these lines until several years later.

These attributes, you will say, are not strictly necessary to the student preparing for honours, yet, nevertheless, somehow German students manage to find time for other amusements besides dry study. They *can* play, but when they *do* study, they study hard.

My ancestor at the time I speak of was a young man of about twenty, and had already been two years at the university. We may presume, therefore, that he spoke German tolerably well, if not well.

I believe it was in the Harz mountains, the Thüringer Wald, and about those parts that he was travelling on foot with his friends.

They rose at daybreak and walked hard, with their knapsacks on their backs, singing or conversing as they went, reposing at noon in some shady spot to avoid the heat of the day. When the sun began to abate a little they would resume their journey till night overshadowed them, when they would encamp, as hungry as hunters, in some rude quarters, where they would make merry together over a simple but plentiful supper, and talk over the fatigues of the day.

They had been following this sort of life for some time, when one evening as they were hastening towards their quarters in groups of twos, threes, and fours, my ancestor asked of his friend, "What is the name of the township where we are to sleep tonight, Hans?"

"—dorf," answered his friend; "but we shall have to hasten in order to reach it before nightfall. Look, how the mist is rising!"

"Ah! so it is," replied my relative, whose name was Frederick, but who was never called otherwise than "Fritz" by his companions.

Our Fritz had remained behind to enjoy the last dying glow of a gorgeous sunset, and was wrapt in meditation, while his friend Hans hurried on.

"Now then, Fritz!" cried one, Max, "don't lag behind so; or are your English legs not strong enough for our German mountains?"

Our Englishman was stung at this taunt, implying, as it did a disparagement of himself and countrymen, however undeserved it was, for the Germans knew that he could outwalk the best of them when he chose. Yet it had the effect of making him hasten his steps a little.

The dusky hue of night fast overshadowed our students, and the mist now rose at their feet in thick clouds, so that it was with the utmost difficulty that they could find their way.

My ancestor was still a long distance behind the rest, but he was gaining fast on them, when in the darkness, he stumbled over a clump of rock and sprained his ankle. All hope of catching up his companions was now gone. The most he could do was to hobble on slowly with the help of his staff, now losing his way, now finding it, whenever the moon peeped out to light up his path, then losing it again when the moon hid itself behind a cloud, till he began to despair of ever finding anything in the shape of a roof to shelter him from the night air during sleep, and he more than half made up his mind to encamp on the spot, but just then he felt a large drop of rain on his face, then another, and another.

It had been a broiling hot day, and the air was still sultry. Presently a flash of vivid forked lightning danced before his eyes, followed by a clap of thunder so terrific that it bid fair to burst the drum of his ear.

The storm was now overhead; the flashes grew more frequent and more vivid, and the thunder growled more fiercely than ever. In a few minutes the rain poured down in torrents, and the English student was drenched to the skin.

"Here is a nice situation for a man on a pleasure trip!" muttered my ancestor to himself. "Lost, in the dead of night, in the midst of a thunderstorm, in an open plain without shelter, drenched like a drowned rat, as hungry as a wolf, and hardly able to crawl, from a sprained ankle!"

His reflections were anything but of a pleasing sort, as you may imagine, yet he hobbled on as best he could, endeavouring to comfort himself with the vague hope of finding some sort of shelter for the night as soon as the storm should pass off.

After dragging on his limbs with exemplary patience for another half-mile, it being then about midnight, he perceived a light from a cottage window not very far distant. His courage began to revive, and with halting gait he made for the door of the cottage.

He knocked loudly, but no one answered. Thinking that he had not been heard for the rumbling of the thunder, he knocked again and again. Still no one came to the door.

"I mean to lodge here for the night," said the Englishman to himself, "if I have to break the door open to effect an entrance." And he kept up a furious knocking for about three-quarters-of-an-hour. At length he heard a harsh, grating voice within break out in a string of choice Teutonic oaths, and the word *schweinhund* (pig-dog) pronounced once or twice.

Footsteps were then heard descending the stairs, and the next moment a quaint-looking personage appeared at the door in dressing-gown and slippers, with night-cap on head and candle in hand, and demanded in a surly tone what the *teufel* he wanted at that hour of night.

My ancestor apologised with much courtesy for having roused up so worthy an individual at such an unearthly hour, but pleaded that he was a poor benighted traveller, hungry and soaked to the skin.

"Then you should have moved further on," was the curt reply.

"But whither?" asked my relative.

"To the township. This house is not a *wirtshaus*."

"How far distant is it?"

"A mile."

By this he meant a German mile—equal to four English miles.

"A mile!" exclaimed the Englishman. "I could not walk a mile to save my life. I've sprained my ankle and can't move a step further. I'm sorry to put you to such inconvenience, my good fellow, but I really must put up here."

"But there is no accommodation," growled the inmate.

"No matter. I dare say you have a little straw; if not, the bare ground will do."

The inmate sulkily suffered the traveller to enter, and showing him into a parlour on the ground-floor, was about to leave him to himself.

"Stop a bit, my good host," said the student. "I must beg to remind you that I am as hungry as a wolf, and as cold as an icicle. If you could find me something in your larder to keep soul and body together, and light me a nice little fire to dry my clothes, you will make me your friend for life."

"Food! Fire! at this time of night!" exclaimed the host, with a look that seemed to say, "Is the man mad?"

"My dear friend," said the Englishman, putting his hand in his pocket and passing a *reichsgulden* into the hand of his host, "I do not want you to do anything for me *gratis*. Make me as comfortable as you can for that—on my departure I'll give you more."

"Oh, *mein Herr*!" said our host, softening at the touch of the bright metal, "that alters the case entirely. You shall have everything you want. I am sorry I haven't another bed, but you can have some straw, and a fire to dry your clothes. I'll go and see directly what there is in the house by way of refreshment, for you must be hungry indeed!"

Our host left the apartment, and returned shortly with some fire-wood and a heap of straw.

To light a fire and arrange the straw for the traveller in a corner of the room was the work of a moment. He then hurried off to get supper ready, and returned soon afterwards with a dish of sausage, some black bread, some strong cheese and a bottle of *schnapps*.

"Our fare is homely, you see, sir," said the host, apologetically; "but it is all we have in the house. We are poor people, and not accustomed to entertain travellers."

"Never mind that, mine host," said the student, "as long as there is plenty of it, we'll excuse the quality."

So saying, he began to strip himself and to hang his clothes before the fire. Then taking from his knapsack a clean shirt and another pair of hose, he donned his slippers and drew his chair close to the table.

The host, after trimming a lamp and lighting it, placed it in the centre of the table, and was just about to return to his bed, when the student called out with his mouth full of sausage, "What! mine host, will you not honour me with your company whilst I discuss my supper? Company helps digestion, you know, and I'm sure you wouldn't like to have my undigested supper on your conscience."

The host returned with a grunt, saying that he couldn't stop long, as he had to rise early on the morrow.

"Oh, so have I, good mine host," said my ancestor, "so we are equal. Come, sit down here, and let me see you toss off a glass or two of this most excellent *schnapps*. It will keep out the cold and give you pleasant dreams, besides adding a still richer tint to that glorious nose of yours."

"Humph!" replied the host, little pleased at this personal allusion; but he drew a chair to the table and made an effort at being sociable.

My ancestor until now had hardly had time to give more than a cursory glance at the features of his host, but finding himself now at table opposite him, he took a minute survey of his countenance in all its details.

The exterior of our host was striking, to say the least. He was a man of about five-and-forty, of middle height, broad rather than tall. His neck and chest might have served as a model for the Farnese Hercules. His hair and beard, which were matted and unkempt, were of a flaming red, and he was just beginning to turn bald. His brow was low, knotted, and streaked with red. His eyebrows, which were of the same tint as his hair, were enormous, and overhung a pair of small, deep-set brown eyes that moved furtively from right to left with the rapidity of lightning, giving to his countenance a remarkably sinister expression.

His complexion was florid, and the nose, which was large and bottle-shaped, was of so bright a red that it made the eyes water to look upon it, and spoke little for its owner's temperance. His ears, large and red, stood out at the sides of his head like those of an animal, and their orifices were carefully protected by fierce tufts of red hair. The back part of his head was excessively developed, and the jaw was large and massive. His arms were very muscular, and hairy as an ape's, with strongly-defined purple veins, and his hands, the fingers of which were short and stunted, were the colour of raw meat. The legs were somewhat short for the body, and slightly bowed.

My ancestor, as he scanned the grim features of his host, could not help imagining himself a prince in a fairy-tale who had been lured by the evil genius of the storm into the castle of some ogre, who would sooner or later devour him unless rescued by the good fairies. The ogre was not a communicative person. He had not opened his mouth once since he had taken his seat at the table, save to toss down a glass of *schnapps*.

At length the Englishman, curious to know something of the life and habits of this mysterious individual, was the first to break silence.

"You live in a very isolated spot, mine host," said he.

"*Ja*," was the laconic reply.

"Have you no nearer neighbours than those of the township?" demanded his guest.

"Nein," grunted the ogre.

"And do you enjoy this solitary existence?" pursued the traveller.

"*Ja!*" was the inevitable monosyllabic response.

"I shall not get much out of him," said my ancestor to himself, and again there was silence for the space of five minutes.

As if searching for some topic wherewith to renew the conversation, the student cast his eyes round the apartment, taking in at a glance the minutest article of furniture or other commodity that the room contained.

It was a homely, undecorated apartment, built after the fashion of the period, and differed little from most other apartments of the sort. If it was remarkable for anything, it was for its extreme simplicity, not to say nakedness, but there was one object hanging on the wall that at once attracted the traveller's eye. It was a two-handed sword of peculiar shape, and appeared bright and sharp as if ready for use.

"Aha!" exclaimed the Englishman, fixing his eye on the object, "you have been a soldier, I see."

"Not I," said the host.

"No? Ah! I see that your sword is not of the same form as those used in battle. It is probably antique—an heirloom, perhaps."

The man answered with a nod of the head.

"I thought so," said the stranger; "and yet it seems bright and well cared for. It has evidently been sharpened lately. Do you always keep it well sharpened?"

"On great occasions, yes," was the reply, and our host gave a peculiar wink, accompanying it with a significant gesture with both hands, in imitation of wielding the two-handed instrument over his head, then slapping his own neck he uttered a low whistle and a sort of chuckle thus: "Wh—ew!—click!" being his mode of expressing the action of cutting off a head.

"Ho! ho!" exclaimed the Englishman, "is that in your line?"

The ogre answered by a savage laugh.

At this moment the crying of a child was heard overhead, together with the harsher tones of its mother scolding it.

"Then you do not live perfectly solitary, as I thought," said the student; "you have also wife and children?"

"One boy only," replied the man.

"Ah! An only son—a great pet, I'll warrant," said his guest, finishing his last morsel of supper. "What age may he be?"

"Ten years old—fine boy—just like me—bringing him up like his father," said the strange individual.

"If he turns out like his father, he'll be a beauty," thought my ancestor. Then he asked aloud of his host:

"And what profession may that be that you wish to apprentice him to?"

"Like his father," was the curt reply; but it was followed by the same sort of expressive gesture that I have just described.

"What!" exclaimed the student, "to cut off people's heads?"

"Yes," replied the ruffian; "I am a *scharfrichter.*"

"A what?" inquired my ancestor, who though he could make himself generally understood in German, had never yet come across the word "*scharfrichter*" in his vocabulary.

"A *scharfrichter*," repeated the man, raising his voice. "Don't you know what that means? Why, one who cuts off heads."

"An executioner!" muttered the foreigner, half-aloud. "Have I been constrained to crave the hospitality of an executioner?"

These words were inaudible to his host, but the ruffian evidently observed a change in his guest's countenance when he informed him of the nature of his profession, for he hastened to reply.

"One sees at once that you are a foreigner, and unused to the customs of this country. You shudder at meeting an executioner, and sicken at the thought of cutting off a head. No matter, it is always so at first. In fact, the pleasure derived from seeing executions is an acquired taste; but I'll show you some sport tomorrow. There is to be some rare fun down at the township at daybreak," and the wretch gave another wink and a chuckle. "I'll show you how to cut off a head. One blow—click!—cuts like cheese."

"Horrible being!" muttered my ancestor to himself in his native tongue. "Is it possible that anything human can actually revel in such brutality?" and he shuddered in spite of himself. Then he said aloud to his host—

"What was it that first gave you a taste for so horrible a profession?"

"Hm! I hardly know. I had a natural genius for it, I suppose. My father was a butcher, and I was brought up from infancy to see cattle slaughtered. At a very early age I took to slaughtering the animals myself. I seemed to take a liking to it from the very beginning. I happened to have an uncle at that time who was a *scharfrichter*, and my greatest delight was to see him cut off the heads of the criminals. I began to long to do the same.

"I was a very young man when this uncle died, and as he had no male issue to take his place, and no one else seemed to come forward, I thought I would offer my services, and they were accepted. I have been headsman of the town these thirty years, and when I die my son will step into my shoes."

"But if he doesn't take to it?"

"He *must* take to it—he'll *have* to take to it."

"Why, are there not many other noble professions just as inviting as that of chopping off the heads of one's fellow-mortals?"

"Not for the son of a headsman. I see you are ignorant of the laws of this country. Here in Germany the son of a headsman is bound by law to adopt the profession of his father, and should the executioner have a daughter instead of a son, in that case, the man who marries his daughter is bound to be headsman. Then the *scharfrichter* is obliged to build his house a mile away from other men, for he is a being hated and shunned by everyone."

"This then is the reason of your solitude?"

"It is; and so far is this superstitious fear of contamination carried in this country, that your citizen considers himself defiled if by chance he has eaten out of the same plate that a headsman has once used. Accordingly all vendors of crockery have orders to knock a chip out of every earthen vessel that they sell to the headsman."

"Dear me!" exclaimed my ancestor, "what a peculiar custom! I never heard that before. I certainly did remark that your crockery was in a most dilapidated state, but I didn't consider the remark worth making, although more than once in the course of the evening I felt inclined to ask you how on earth you contrived to knock out chips of such a peculiar shape by mere accident."

"Ah!" sighed the headsman, "what between the crockery-seller and—"

Here he put his finger to his lip and looked round the room suspiciously.

"What is the matter?" asked the student.

"Hush!" said the headsman, "it isn't always safe to talk of mischievous people—they are apt to appear. You know the saying, 'Talk of the devil.'"

"Well," said my ancestor, "but what has that to do with your broken crockery?"

"Hush!" answered his host, looking round him half-timidly; then whispered, "I have a certain mischievous lodger that does my crockery more harm than either the crockery-seller or my boy upstairs when he's fractious."

"Ah!" exclaimed the traveller in surprise, "you have a lodger in your house?"

"Ay!—a lodger who never pays his rent, and who drives me to my wit's end by shying my crockery at my head. Look here, what a cut he gave my wrist once in one of his pranks. I shall bear this mark to my grave." So saying, he bared his wrist and displayed a deep, livid wound, long since healed, but which left behind a scar which nothing could efface.

"An ugly cut, to be sure," remarked the Englishman. "But why on earth do you not get rid of so playful a lodger?"

"Get rid of him! I only wish the devil I could. He comes here uninvited and— But let us not talk of him, or he may pay us another of his pleasant visits, when you will be able to make his acquaintance.

He never stands upon ceremony, but comes just whenever he likes. He may be in the room now, for what I know. I shall be off to bed."

My ancestor gazed round the room, vainly endeavouring to discover in some hidden nook the object of his host's terror, when, marvellous to relate! a dish on the top shelf was pitched, as if by some invisible hand, from its post, and shattered into pieces against the opposite wall, nearly hitting him on the head as it passed.

The traveller stared first at the shelf, then at his host, and turned pale.

"Good Heavens!" he cried. "What was that?"

"What was it? Ay! You may well ask what it is," answered his host, peevishly. "What in the devil's name should it be but that pest of a 'Poltergeist' again. I told you you would make his acquaintance ere long."

"A what?—a *Poltergeist?*"

"Ay, Poltergeist—a malignant spirit, whose chief delight seems to be to strike terror into the house of a poor honest headsman, and smash all his crockery that he has to pay for out of his hard-earned wages."

"Holy Virgin!" ejaculated my ancestor, crossing himself (for he was a good Catholic). "A malignant spirit! Saints protect us!"

But the words were hardly out of his mouth when crash! went another plate upon the floor, just grazing his host's auburn head as it passed.

"Oh! come now, my fine fellow," said our host, in a tone of mild remonstrance; "a little of that goes a long way."

Then turning to his guest, he remarked:

"I wonder why he honours me especially with his visits, and not other people. I shouldn't wonder if he is someone that I have had the honour of decapitating, and he comes to pay me an occasional visit in order to impress upon me that he hasn't forgotten the little service I did him."

A large pointed knife that lay peacefully on the table was then suddenly and powerfully thrown from the traveller's side, and remained with the point sticking in the panel of the door opposite.

"Ho! ho!" cried the headsman; "this is getting warm work. Now, my good friend, do let me entreat you to be more moderate in your manifestations, and if you are quiet, tomorrow I will send you a companion."

This promise, so far from quieting our spiritual guest, seemed to infuriate him more than ever, for the bottle of *schnapps*, more than half full, was now raised in the air and dashed to pieces on the table, the candle being overturned at the same time, and falling flame downwards on to the spirit spilt on the table, it ignited, and in a moment everything was in a blaze.

"Fire! Fire!" cried the headsman, in a voice that roused up his wife and child, who came tumbling downstairs in no time, to learn what was the matter.

There is no knowing what mischief might not have taken place had not my ancestor, with great presence of mind, snatched up his damp clothes from before the fire, and succeeded in extinguishing the flame.

"What *is* the matter, Franz?" exclaimed our host's better half, appearing at the door just as matters were being set to rights again.

"Oh, nothing," said her fond spouse, "only that d—d Poltergeist again, who seems bent upon burning us all in our beds before he has done with us."

"Hush!" said his wife, "don't swear, or he may do as you say in real earnest. Come to bed now, or tomorrow you won't be able to get up in time. Remember—"

"Ah, true; I must have my night's rest, as it would not do for my hand to tremble tomorrow when I mount the scaffold. *Gute nacht, mein Herr.*"

And our worthy host followed his partner out of the room, leaving my ancestor to his reflections.

"Well," soliloquised my relative, "of all the strange adventures that ever occurred to me, this beats all. Oh! there is not the slightest doubt that what I have just witnessed is the work of the infernal powers— some diabolical agency.

"When I see a knife jump up from the table by itself without anyone near and deliberately fix itself in the panel of the door before my very eyes; when I see a bottle of spirit overturned and broken in pieces, and then a candle after that knocked over as if on purpose to ignite the spirit, and withal no way of accounting for such a phenomenon; moreover, when I see plates and dishes hurled from one end of the room to the other, and apparently aimed at people's heads, and yet the perpetrator of such pranks has the power of making himself invisible to the naked eye, then, I say, this is not through human agency, but something superhuman, and as it is not exactly an angelic mode of proceeding, it must be the reverse."

My ancestor shuddered, and crossed himself. The manifestations, however, had ceased for the night, and in five minutes our weary traveller was fast asleep.

His dreams that night were not of the pleasantest. He imagined that he mounted the scaffold with a crowd of eager eyes gazing at him, amongst whom were his friends and travelling companions. His host, the *scharfrichter*, stood brandishing his terrible two-handed sword, and in another moment his head would have been off, but at the critical time the dream changed, and he was being pelted with crockery in the midst of a cemetery at night by innumerable sheeted "poltergeister."

These and such-like visions were flitting before his brain, when a loud thump at the door brought him back to earth again. There was the *scharfrichter* before him, not in dressing gown and slippers, as on the previous evening, but attired in doublet and hose of a blood red, a black *barello* with scarlet cock's feather.

"Now then, *mein Herr*," said the headsman, taking down his fearful instrument from the wall, "time's up."

My ancestor, only just awake, rubbed his eyes and imagined that he was really and truly called away to execution, and that his last hour had come.

The executioner, seeing that he hesitated, added: "If you want to witness the cunning of my hand, now's your time."

My relation gave a sigh of relief when he began to recollect that his own head was quite safe, and that he was only called to witness the execution of another man.

"But I can't go; I have sprained my ankle," pleaded the Englishman.

"Oh, I don't intend to walk myself," replied the executioner. "I have my horse and cart ready, and can give you a lift."

"Oh, if that's the case," said the student, "I shall be glad to go, as I wish to meet my friends in the township."

"Come on, then," and the headsman assisted the Englishman into the cart.

As they were about starting, a little red-haired ruffian of about ten, stout and well-built, and bearing a striking likeness to our host, appeared on the threshold.

"Papa, you'll bring me home a football, won't you?" said the youth.

"Ay, my boy, that will I, a good sized one," answered his father.

"That's your son?" asked the student of his host. "Ah, a fine little fellow. Here, my little man," said he to the child, and slipping a small coin into his little fat fist, he patted him on the cheek and stepped into the cart.

301

"Ah, he's a fine boy," said our host with a paternal pride, as he whipped on his horse. "There is nothing of the milksop about him. *He's* not afraid of the devil himself."

"You do well to be proud of him. I'll warrant you buy him many a pretty toy," observed the Englishman.

"Buy him toys!" exclaimed the headsman, laughing. "As long as I bring him home a football now and then, he is quite content." And he laughed again.

"Well, that is a toy, isn't it?" said the student, not as yet comprehending the headsman's meaning.

"Yes, a toy that costs me nothing, and gives him no end of amusement. You should see how he kicks the heads about that I bring him home. It's quite a pleasure to see the youngster enjoy himself in his innocent way."

"You do not mean to say," said the Englishman, in horror, "that the football you promised him is to be *a human head!*"

"Aye, to be sure," replied the *scharfrichter*. "What else should it be? What kicks he'll give it to be sure! Ha! ha! ha! that's the way to bring up boys; makes them hardy. *He's* not afraid of a little blood. Talk of his not taking a liking to my business! Why he's always saying to me, 'Papa, when I am big enough to wield your sword, you'll let me cut off heads, won't you?'

"'Yes, my boy, that you shall,' say I, for I like to give him encouragement. That's what I call bringing up boys well. I wouldn't give a fig for one of your milksops that scream or faint at the sight of blood, not I."

"Humph," muttered my ancestor, and he remained silent for some minutes, absorbed in meditation.

The headsman whipped on his horse in silence; at length he said to his guest: "Here we are at last. Look at yon crowd waiting to receive us."

My relative lifted his head, and sure enough there was the mound of earth erected for the criminal already surrounded by soldiers, close to which thronged the crowd. All the inhabitants of —dorf were astir, and in the crowd our Englishman now recognised his fellow students. A cry of *"Der henker! der henker!"*[3] arose on all sides. Room was at once made for the headsman and his companion, and Fritz's fellow students, seeing their friend arrive in a *henker's* cart, pushed their way through the crowd to ask him all sorts of questions.

---

3. Another name for headsman or hangman.

Fritz descended with difficulty after paying his host for his board and lodging, and joined his companions. In a few minutes more the criminal's cart arrived with the *armer Sünder*, or poor sinner, accompanied by two priests. Loud execrations broke from the mob, amidst which the wretched being descended from the cart and mounted the scaffold. A dead silence reigned around. One of the priests whispered something earnestly in the ear of the condemned, who was as pale as death, and he took his seat on the chair prepared for him, while an expression of savage delight appeared on the countenance of the headsman.

He felt all eyes were upon him. The terrible two-handed weapon was raised aloft, and brandished over the *henker's* head. One blow and the head of the unhappy wretch was severed from his body. Loud cheering rent the air as the *scharfrichter*, holding the head of the criminal by the hair, presented it to the public gaze. But at this moment a most unexpected and revolting scene ensued.

Several persons from among the crowd rushed forward toward the scaffold with mugs, which they filled at the fresh fountain of blood spurting up from the severed neck of the criminal and drank off at a draught.

My ancestor sickened at so disgusting a spectacle, and demanded the reason of some bystander. He was informed that those persons believed human blood fresh from the neck of a beheaded criminal to be an infallible remedy for epileptic fits. The superstition exists to this day. Violent exercise after the draught, he was informed, was considered necessary, in order to effect a cure.

The crowd began to disperse, and my ancestor, leaning on the arm of a friend, also retired from the scene, disgusted with himself at having been present at such a spectacle. Before leaving the spot he had time to notice his host of the previous night start off in his cart towards home with the promised football.

Our English student was laid up for some little time with his sprained ankle, and some of his companions remained behind to keep him company, while others moved onward.

The ankle being cured, my relative continued his foot tour with his friends, and afterwards returned to the university, where he studied hard till the time came round for an examination, which he passed, and shortly afterwards returned to England.

We hear nothing more of my ancestor until ten or twelve years afterwards, when we again find him in Germany, whither he had been suddenly called to visit some relative, then in a dying state.

He arrived just in time to close his relative's eyes, after which he saw him quietly interred in his last home.

This sad office over, he was thinking of returning to England, when, in turning over the articles of his travelling trunk, he suddenly came across a German book belonging to a college friend of his, one Ludwig Engstein, that had been lent him when at the university, and which he had forgotten to return before leaving college. His friend used to live, he remembered, in Weimar, and not being far distant, he resolved to visit that town and to find out his friend's house.

Many changes take place in twelve years, and my ancestor only half expected to meet his fellow-student again. He might have changed his residence—he might be dead. Who could tell what might not have happened to him after so long a lapse of time?

Nevertheless, the Englishman, finding himself on German soil once more, resolved to enquire after the friend of his youth, and should he succeed in discovering him, to put him in possession of his book again, and chat with him over their student days.

Accordingly, he set off for the town of Weimar, and having arrived there, proceeded with the said book under his arm to the house of his friend. He had been once on a visit of a fortnight at his friend's house when a student, and had known his mother and sisters intimately, therefore he had no difficulty in finding the house again.

The town of Weimar had changed but little during these ten or twelve years, and once more he found himself on the old familiar doorstep.

"*Ist der Herr Advocat Engstein zu Hause?*" he demanded of an old woman who answered the door.

"*Ja, mein Herr,*" replied the crone. "What name shall I give?"

"Oh, never mind announcing me," said the Englishman; "I'll announce myself."

So saying, he pushed past the old woman, and knocked at his friend's study.

"*Herein!*" called out a voice from within, which my ancestor had no difficulty in recognising as his friend's, and the Englishman entered.

Ludwig Engstein was seated at a table strewed with papers and documents, and was busily writing. He was still young looking, but his friend Fritz noticed that his face had assumed a more thoughtful expression than when at the university. He was now a lawyer in good practice, and the moment his friend entered he was so busy that he did not even raise his head.

"I am sorry to disturb you, *Herr Advocat*," said Fritz, suddenly, "but I've come to return a book you lent me some time back."

And placing the book on the table, he marched straight out of the room, shutting the door after him. He then peeped through the key-hole and listened awhile to note the effect of his abrupt departure on his friend.

The young lawyer's ear caught his friend's English accent, and at once lifted his head, though not in time to catch a glimpse of his re-treating figure.

I have said that Engstein recognised Fritz's accent as English, but little did he suspect that it was his old college friend who had called upon him and left so suddenly.

He looked surprised, took up the book upon the table to look at the title, and muttered to himself, "Who can it have been? I do not recollect now who it was I lent it to, but it must have been a long while ago."

He was about to ring the bell, and rose for that purpose when he noticed a face peeping at him through the opening of the door, which was now ajar.

"Who's that? Come in!" cried the lawyer.

"You are busy, *Herr Advocat*—another time. *Ich empfähle mich Ihnen*," said my relative, closing the door slowly after him.

But this time Ludwig had a better view of the Englishman's face.

"*Potztausend!*" exclaimed the lawyer; "I shall know that face. *Ach! lieber freund Fritz*. Can it be really you? *Nein was für ein angenehme Ueberaschung!*" he cried, rushing forward and throwing the door wide open while he kissed his friend forcibly on both cheeks.

"Sit down here and tell me to what for a fortuitous and never-to-be-expected train of circumstances I am indebted for this friendly and to me most agreeable and blissful-past-days-recalling visit."

Fritz then went on to relate the circumstances of his relative's death, and how he had been called from home to attend him in his last moments.

"I am sorry for the death of your relation," said Ludwig, "but I cannot sufficiently express my extreme joy at seeing my old friend Fritz again after so many years! Ha! ha! ha!" he laughed, partly from delight at meeting his friend, and partly at his friend's mode of introducing himself.

"What for an eccentric and of you and your strange countryman-characteristic way of saluting your old friend after so long!"

And the German again laughed again heartily.

"And what for a busy and for-ever-with-documents-and-papers-occupied German business man, not even to notice his swiftly entering, and though long departed from German soil, speedily-vanishing and almost-forgotten English friend!" retorted Fritz, mimicking the high-flown, wordy phraseology of the German.

"No, on my honour, Fritz," replied his friend; "not forgotten, I assure you. Do you know that I had a dream of you only last night. It never struck me till now. It is strange that I should have dreamed of you just the night before your unexpected and to me most grateful arrival. How strange it is that our dreams often prognosticate coming events! It is as if the mind, partly freed from its material covering during sleep, received the power of peering with greater accuracy into that to-us-in-our-waking-state-obscure and unfathomable future which—"

"Precisely; I understand you," answered my relative, cutting short his friend's philosophic remark; "but let us talk a little over old times; that is if you are at leisure."

"Yes, to be sure," answered the lawyer; "what I am doing now has no need of hurry. Oh, by the way, Fritz, talking of old times, do you remember the night you spent at the house of old Franz Wenzel the *scharfrichter?*"

"If I remember? Shall I ever forget it? ask, rather," answered my ancestor. "It seems to me only yesterday that I witnessed that execution; and then that Poltergeist—it seems as if I had witnessed his pranks only last night. I can remember the minutest incident that happened on that unhallowed evening."

"Well," resumed the lawyer, "poor old Franz is no more."

"What—dead, eh?"

"Ay, murdered. Horrible to relate, his body was discovered minus the head, which has been carried off or hidden somewhere, for it hasn't been found yet, but his son recognised the body by the clothes, besides Franz has never returned home since, so it must be he. There appears to be a mystery about it, however. The murderer has not as yet been discovered, neither can people guess at what prompted the murderer to take the life of a man who was never over-burdened with money. Then the head being cut off without care being taken to bury the body, and all, too, within a few steps of the *henker's* own house. What could have been the murderer's object in carrying off the head?"

"A mere act of spite, I suppose," replied the Englishman.

"Well, it may be so," replied his friend, "for it seems that his life had been often threatened by the friends or relations of those he had beheaded. It may be as you say, out of spite. The murderer may, by way of wreaking his vengeance have cut off the head of the man who had put some friend or relation to death as a trophy, but why just at this moment? Why not before, as there has been no execution in the town lately? I believe there has been none since that execution we two witnessed together. If the avenger had made up his mind to avenge his friend, why did he not do so at once, instead of waiting these twelve years?"

"It may be some other private quarrel," replied Fritz. "Are you mixed up in it?"

"Yes, I shall be at the trial."

"It happened recently it would seem."

"Only two days ago."

"Then the body is still fresh—of course it has been exposed and examined?"

"Yes, but it was recognised at once by the family. I dare say it is buried by this time. I am going there tomorrow. If you have time, my friend, I should be most glad of your company."

"Well, I don't mind giving you a day or so, as I am taking a holiday."

"Agreed, then; we start tomorrow."

The two friends then discoursed until dinner-time, when Ludwig invited Fritz to share his meal.

The Englishman accepted the offer, and they chatted and laughed the time away till the evening.

Ludwig lived quite alone. His sisters had married, his mother was dead. Ludwig was still a bachelor, and so was my ancestor at this time.

"You have not yet put your neck under the yoke it appears," said my relative to his friend, in allusion to the conjugal tie.

"Not I," replied his friend. "At least, not yet."

"I understand," said Fritz; "not married, but *verlobt.*"

"No, nor that either."

"No? *Verliebt*, then, perhaps."

"No, neither *verlobt* nor *verliebt*."

"What!" exclaimed the Englishman, "not even that! Nevertheless, if I remember rightly, the student Ludwig Engstein was not once averse to the fair sex."

"Oh, recall not the follies of the past, my friend, or I may retaliate," answered the German.

"True, true," said the Englishman. "We all have our weaknesses, and youth is the season in which they mostly flourish, but now we have both grown into sober-minded *Philister*,[4] and are more wary."

"Yes, yes," rejoined his friend; "we are not to be caught now by a pair of blue eyes, flaxen tresses, and a jimp waist, however well these charms may be set off with the allurements of dress. When men get to our advanced age, they want *geist*, and look out for a good housewife who can cook them a dish of *sauer kraut* or a *pfankuchen* when *das moos*[5] is wanting, which is another very useful accessory we desire to have thrown in."

Here he made a significant gesture with his finger and thumb, intended to express the counting of money.

"I hope, my friend, you have not become so worldly as to look upon marriage in the light of bettering yourself," said my relative.

"*Ach! lieber freund*," replied Ludwig. "It is all very well for you rich milords who have *löwen*[6] to talk in that style, but we *armer teufeln* are bound to take even that into consideration."

"This is what the world makes of noble fellows when it has once got them in its grasp!" sighed my ancestor to himself, and he hastened to change the conversation.

They then discoursed on various other topics, sitting up to a late hour of night, until wearied with incessant talking, each retired to rest.

Early the next morning both were dressed and ready to start on their journey. They reached —dorf towards evening, and having fixed their quarters at the very same inn they had put up at on their memorable tour, they beguiled the time until the morrow by discoursing with the townspeople about the mysterious murder.

The body, it seems, was not yet underground, but was to be buried the next day. They accordingly both resolved to examine it.

---

4. *Philister* or Philistine.

5. The moss. Slang word among German students for money.

6. *Löwen*—also money.

"The head has not been found yet?" asked Ludwig after supper of the landlord of the inn, who had come in for a gossip.

"No, sir, not yet," replied their host. "Ah, there are some strange rumours in the town about that same murder."

"Indeed!" cried Fritz; "what do the people say?"

"Some say one thing, and some another, but all seem to agree that there is something supernatural about the murder of the *henker*."

"Something supernatural! Why—what reason have they to jump at that conclusion?"

"Well, sir, I don't know if you have ever heard of the *henker's* Poltergeist, but it is a fact well known to all in the township."

"Yes, yes—even we know it. In fact—but never mind, proceed."

"Well, gentlemen, this Poltergeist—this evil spirit—that no doubt was permitted to haunt the headsman for his sins—for a headsman must of necessity be a cruel, hard-hearted, unnatural villain to choose such a profession."

"Well, well—this evil spirit."

"Well then the *scharfrichter*, at least, so people say, had sold his soul to this demon, and when the time came round for him to give up his soul according to the bargain, he refused, and the demon wrested it from him by force by cutting off his head and carrying it away with him."

"Oh, but why this strange supposition? Why put down a thing to supernatural agency before sufficient time has elapsed to investigate the matter properly? A person is murdered, and the body discovered without the head, and because the head cannot be found at once, you say that the devil has run off with it. My dear sir, the thing's absurd."

"Well, we must wait and see what evidence will turn up," said the host.

"Yes, but if everybody merely *waits* for evidence to turn up instead of actively searching for it, the matter will come to a standstill," said the Englishman. "I myself am interested in the murder, as I knew the *scharfrichter* twelve years ago, when I was a student."

"Ah, in that case, sir—of course you would. By-the-by, there is another murder now talked about besides the *henker's*. They seem to be getting in fashion."

"What! another body?"

"Well, sir, the body isn't exactly found yet, but there is a certain count, well-known to be rich, who was taking a foot tour through

309

the country alone. His family expected him home on a certain day, and as he hasn't turned up yet, they suspect that he has been robbed and murdered."

"That may be merely a suspicion. How long has he been missing?"

"Three days, they say."

"Three days! Why, a man doesn't bind himself to a day or two when out on a foot tour. He may remain another three days, or a week longer, and then return unhurt."

"Well, sir, it may be as you say, but as the count was known by his relations to be a very punctual man, and never to fail in his appointments, you see, it is natural they should feel uneasy."

"True, especially as three days ago was about the time of the other murder, and they may get it into their heads that the two murders occurred in the same night. Was he a married man?"

"No, sir; quite young, they say."

"Humph! When did you say the body of the *henker* would be buried—tomorrow?"

"About ten, I think, sir."

"Ah! then I must be there early, as I want to examine the corpse myself."

"Oh, decidedly, sir. I will bring you to the place tomorrow in good time."

Our friends now felt inclined for their night's rest, so their host showed them into a room with two beds, and wishing them a good night, left them to undress, and before many minutes had passed both were sound asleep.

The following morning early our two friends, in the company of their host, started from the inn to visit the corpse of the murdered executioner. As they entered the hall where the body lay exposed, Fritz instantly recognised the clothes; if not the identical vestments worn by the defunct twelve years ago, at least, of the same colour and material, being, as I have said before, a doublet and hose of crimson, a colour that he seems to have been partial to.

"Yes," said Fritz; "these are the *henker's* clothes, I've no doubt."

Then, after examining the form laid out before him, he was observed to start slightly, and he added in a whisper to his friend: "Ludwig, this is not the body of Franz Wenzel—I'll take my oath of that."

"How! Not Franz Wenzel! Who else should it be, then?"

"That I am not prepared to say, but it is not the body of the *henker*, that is certain. Remember that I passed a night at Wenzel's house; during that time I took note of the features and figure of the *scharfrichter*, and though twelve years have passed since I saw him, I can swear—"

"But how! His own family have recognised him. What further proof would you have?"

Then addressing the landlord, Ludwig said: "Is it true, landlord, that his own family have recognised the body?"

"Yes, sir; at least, the son did. I don't know whether his wife did or not, as she has been laid up for ever so long with paralysis, poor soul. It may be she has never been informed of the murder. One does not like to frighten invalids, you know."

"Well, well—enough if the corpse has been recognised by the son."

"Yes, sir, he recognised it. It is true, he was a little the worse for liquor when they brought him before the corpse of his father; but when is he otherwise, for the matter of that? As sad a young dog as ever lived that same—inherits all the vices of his father. Nevertheless, who is there in the township that does not recognise the *henker's* red legs?"

"You see, therefore, my friend," said Ludwig, turning to his companion, "that you are mistaken. Everybody recognises him."

"I see nothing of the sort," replied the Englishman, doggedly; "and I am still prepared to swear that the corpse before us is not that of Franz Wenzel."

"My dear Fritz," said Engstein, "you are obstinate. What reason can you possibly have for saying so?"

"Observe the hands of the corpse," said Fritz, in a low tone. "Do they look like the hands of an executioner? They are long and delicate. Those of Franz Wenzel were hard, rough, and hairy, with square stunted fingers; besides, the headsman wore no ring. This hand, though no ring is visible, has a depression on the forefinger, as if the owner were in the constant habit of wearing one."

"Ha! say you so?" exclaimed his friend, and a strange expression came over his face.

"Then," pursued Fritz, "observe the clothes. Do they look as if they were made for the body? Franz Wenzel had enormously developed calves, and his hose fitted tightly. Do these hose fit tightly? Look at these limbs, that, compared with the *henker's*, are but those of a boy."

"Humph! I believe you are right, Fritz, after all," said Engstein; "but it never would have struck me if you had not pointed it out, as it is so long ago since I set eyes upon him, and then only for a moment. You took a more complete survey of him, and your evidence may prove useful. We will look into the matter together. It is strange, however, that no one should have been struck in the same manner as yourself."

"Well, I don't know," responded Fritz. "The people in these small villages are not always of the brightest. Then the headsman's house being so far away from the town, few people have the opportunity of taking a minute survey of him. The people here content themselves with recognising the clothes. Franz's wife is laid up with paralysis, and has not seen the body, while his son only recognised it when in a drunken state. Do you call that sufficient evidence to prove that the corpse before us is that of the executioner? Would you like another proof that this is no more Franz Wenzel than I am?"

"Well," said Ludwig.

"I remember a scar upon the right wrist that he showed me the night I put up at his house," said the Englishman; "and which he told me had been inflicted on him by a piece of broken plate hurled at him by his Poltergeist. I remember that he said he should carry that mark with him to the grave. If this is the corpse of Franz Wenzel we shall not fail to discover the mark."

So saying, he bared the right arm of the corpse and examined it carefully. No such mark was to be found. The arm was free from scar or brand, and was delicate in form, almost like that of a maiden's. Moreover, there was a scanty covering of dark hair upon it, while the hair on the arms of the executioner, if you remember rightly, was red and profuse. Even Engstein remarked this, and was now convinced beyond a doubt that the murdered man was not Franz Wenzel. "Is any search being made now for the head of the corpse?" demanded Engstein of his host, who had withdrawn some paces from the two friends, and consequently had not heard the doubt that had been suddenly cast upon the public opinion.

"No active search, I believe, sir," was the reply.

"We will make the search ourselves, my friend," whispered Engstein to Fritz; then added to his host, "My friend and I will take a stroll together. It is uncertain when we shall return to the inn, but get something savoury for us against we come back," and he waved his hand towards his host, who doffed his cap and walked towards his inn, while our two friends set off together in the direction of the *henker's* house, which they reached in about an hour.

"Yes," said Fritz, "this is the place. I remember it well. What did our host tell us? That the murder took place only a few paces from the headsman's door. Let us look well round the spot. How solitary it is! Just the place where a murder would be committed. What do you say to yon hollow flanked with brushwood, Ludwig? Is it not a likely place for a murderer to await his victim?"

"You are right, Fritz, let us make a strict search, but if the head has been carried far distant—"

"Let us, nevertheless, search well here first," said my ancestor, and the two friends set to work at once, lifting up every bush and bramble, following every track, until finally they came upon some blood stains.

An old dried well they discovered not far from this spot. Common sense would have suggested this as a likely place for the concealment of the missing head, and there is no doubt that the same idea struck the inhabitants of —dorf, for there was evident traces of a great number of feet in the sand round about it; besides which there was a chip recently made in the brickwork, which appeared caused by the letting down of a rope or chain.

This seemed evidence enough for our two friends that the well had already been searched, and without effect. Further search in that direction appeared to them to be useless, especially as no bloodstains were to be found near.

They then proceeded to examine more closely than ever the bushes around, stamping on the ground to ascertain if a hole had recently been made, but the ground was firm, and there was nothing to attract suspicion save a few bloodstains, which, instead of leading up to the well as one would have imagined, led up to the foot of an old chestnut-tree, and there seemed to end.

On examining the bark of the tree attentively they observed blood also on the trunk, but this might have been occasioned by the splashing of the blood from the neck after the decapitation of the head. There was no hollow visible in the tree where suspicion would lead one to suppose that the head could be concealed; nevertheless, when men make up their minds to make a rigid search, they often pry into the most unlikely and impossible places, so our friends determined to ascend the tree to ascertain if by any chance the head could have lodged between its leafy branches.

Previous to mounting, Ludwig, who, together with his friend, had provided himself with a long branch wherewith to beat down the bushes, struck the chestnut-tree a blow on the trunk with the branch he carried, when a hollow sound proceeded from the tree, and instantly a large owl fluttered out from the foliage before their faces with its beak and plumage stained with blood. Blinded with the sunlight, it hovered distractedly hither and thither for a time, and then vanished with a screech.

"Did you notice the beak and feathers of the bird?" asked Fritz.

"I did," said Ludwig, "and what is more, I am convinced that the whole of this seemingly robust chestnut-tree is hollow, and I have not a doubt that the murderer, aware of the fact, has hidden the head of his victim at the bottom, and that this fell bird has been gorging itself and its young upon it ever since."

"That is just my opinion," said Fritz. "Let us climb the tree and look within."

My ancestor was the first to mount, and having arrived at the point where the trunk divides itself into branches, he discovered a large hole thickly covered over with leaves. Sitting upon the edge, with his legs dangling within the hollow trunk, he proceeded to strike a light, and having ignited a taper, he commenced carefully to descend into the hollow of the tree. In his descent, however, his foot slipped, his taper extinguished itself, and he came down rather suddenly upon his feet. He soon became aware from a feeble smothered shriek that he was treading upon a nest of young owlets.

He began to dread lest he might encounter some venomous reptile in this unexplored region, but taking courage he struck another light and searched about. He had not looked long when he discovered what appeared to be a human scalp. He grasped it firmly by the hair, and by the light of his taper soon knew it to be in reality the head of a man, one half of which had been already eaten away to the bone.

"Eureka!" exclaimed Fritz, "I have it."

His friend uttered an exclamation of delight, while my relative clambered up again, and the two friends examined the disgusting treasure under the fair light of day.

"You see the hair is black," said Fritz. "I hope you are satisfied now that this is not the head of the *scharfrichter*."

"There is no doubt about that now, I think," said Ludwig. "And do you know, Fritz, now that I scan these features, they seem familiar to me as my own in the looking-glass. *Himmel!* Can it be possible!"

"What?" demanded my ancestor, anxiously.

"Why, I'll swear that this is no other than my old friend and fellow-student, the Count of Waffenburg!" exclaimed Engstein.

"What! Graf von Waffenburg! Is it really so? I knew him well. Let me examine the features," said Fritz.

"Yes, it is he beyond a doubt," said Ludwig. "We had a quarrel once, and I wounded him in the cheek. Here is the wound I myself inflicted; but afterwards we became staunch friends."

"True," said Fritz. "I remember the duel well, being present myself on the occasion. What a curious coincidence! It is certainly he, and no other. The more I look at the features the more satisfied I am. Let us hasten with this proof of the identity of the murdered man to the township and spread abroad the news of the murder of the count. His relations will then come to claim his body."

The two friends then made a covering of chestnut leaves for the head, and tying it up in a handkerchief, retraced their steps towards the township, discoursing on the cunning of the murderer, who appeared to them to be no other than the *scharfrichter* himself.

"For when a body is found minus the head," argued Ludwig, "and dressed in the clothes of another man, and that other man is nowhere to be found, it follows as a matter of course that the man missing must be the murderer."

"Yes," said the Englishman, "unless the murdered man had previously stolen the clothes of another, and then afterwards been murdered by some unknown assassin."

"But when the deceased has been proved beyond a doubt to be the Graf von Waffenburg, a man whose name is above so ridiculous a suspicion," said Engstein.

"Oh, of course the blackest suspicion attaches itself to Wenzel," said Fritz; "yet, in the case of a mysterious murder, evidence, occasionally of so startling and unexpected a nature, turns up as to completely alter the state of the case.

"The headsman is missing, and a corpse has been found dressed in his clothes. We presume, therefore, that *he* is the murderer, but if after a time the *henker's* corpse should also be found—"

"Oh, in that case," said Ludwig, "the aspect of the whole affair would be changed. Well, we must wait for further evidence. Tomorrow the case will begin in court, and my services will be required. I doubt not before long that sufficient light will be thrown on the subject to enable us to discover the true murderer."

Thus our two friends chatted by the way, till in due time they arrived at the township, and having deposited the head of the murdered man at the town hall, where the body had been exposed, they spread abroad the result of their expedition, and clearly proved to the somewhat obtuse inhabitants their error. On the following morning, then, the trial began. The court was crowded to suffocation. Evidence of a very extraordinary nature had turned up, so it was said, and Ludwig Engstein, attired in his professional robes, was preparing to conduct the case.

My ancestor was amongst the crowd, and had placed himself as near as he possibly could to his friend.

"Call in Gottlieb Kräger," cried the examiner.

A hoary peasant entered the witness-box, and the examination proceeded in this wise:

"You are a farmer from the village of —, are you not?"

"I am."

"Just inform us, if you please, what you were doing on the night of the murder."

"I was returning home after selling some cattle at the —dorf market, and it was about midnight when I passed close to the *henker's* cottage. I heard cries and groans as of someone being murdered not far off. I stopped and listened for a moment, then set off on tip-toe to the spot whence the sounds proceeded. It was very dark, and the groans at length ceased.

"I placed myself behind some brushwood to watch who should issue from the copse, when a friar passed me."

"Stay, are you quite sure the friar came from the very spot from whence you heard the groans?"

"Well, as to swearing to it, I don't know, but I heard the sound as of brushwood being trampled under foot, and the next instant the friar passed close to me. He did not appear to observe me, but moved onward in the direction of the village of Ahlden."

"Did you follow him or take any further notice of him?"

"To say the truth, I was too frightened to move, but I kept my eye on him as far as I could see him."

"But you tell me it was very dark."

"Just at that moment the moon had burst from behind the clouds, and enabled me to see distinctly."

"Well, did you observe anything peculiar in the manner or gait of the friar?"

"Yes; after he had passed me some ten paces he halted, as if he were counting money, after which he threw away something that glittered in the moonlight and then walked on. I followed stealthily behind to discover what it was that he had thrown away, when I picked up this."

The witness held up a long silk purse knitted with silver beads.

"Give it to me—so—can you recollect anything else about this friar? Could you manage to catch a glimpse of his face?"

"No, I could not exactly distinguish the features, but—"

"But what?"

"I observed a peculiar patch in his amice over the left shoulder."

"Should you be able to swear to the amice?"

"Aye, that I should, among a thousand."

"Is this the amice of the friar you saw issue from the copse?" asked Ludwig, holding up a patched amice such as is worn by the Capuchin friars.

"The very same, I'll swear to it."

"Take care, you are on your oath."

"Well, if it is not the same, it is one made after the same fashion, patch and all complete. I'll swear to the shape of the patch, for I observed the garment well."

"Enough; you may retire. Call in Hans Schultz."

A dapper little man with oiled hair and closely-shaven face entered the court, and having taken his post at the witness-box, gave his evidence as follows:

"I am by profession a barber. The morning after the murder I was shaving an elderly gentleman in my shop. I suggested that a little hair dye would improve his personal appearance, and offered him a bottle. He refused to buy it, so I placed it on a table behind me, and continued to shave him. Whilst I was recommending the hair dye to my customer I noticed a Capuchin friar pass several times in front of my shop. He appeared to be listening to our conversation.

"Shortly afterwards he entered the shop and begged for alms for the convent. I gave him a *kreuzer*, and after he had chatted a little he left the shop. I could not see his face well, as he kept it covered with his hood, but I remember that he had a red beard. He had hardly left my shop when on looking on the table behind me I found the bottle of hair dye gone. No one else but the friar and my customer had entered the shop since I laid the bottle down upon the table, yet I could not suspect my customer of having stolen the bottle, and I was much at a loss to conceive what a Capuchin friar should want with hair dye.

"I concluded, therefore, that I must have been mistaken, and must have laid the bottle down somewhere else without thinking, so I thought no more of it.

"On the same day I was called to cut the hair of a gentleman at the other end of the village, when I passed a friar who appeared to be the same as he who not long ago had entered my shop. I looked at him in the face, but he had a black beard. I could have sworn it was the same, for his amice was patched in a peculiar manner on the shoulder, as was that of the first friar."

"Is this the amice that the friar wore?" asked Engstein, holding up the patched garment.

"It is like it. I could all but swear to it."

"Did you address him when you met him, as you thought, a second time?"

"I was about to do so, but he pulled out his beads, and began counting them. Not liking to disturb him in his devotions, I passed on, thinking that after all I might have been deceived."

"That is sufficient, you may go."

The little barber left the court, and another witness was called for.

"Your name?"

"Max Offenbrunnen."

"Profession?"

"I am host of the Bear Inn in the village of M—."

"Can you tell us anything that happened at your inn within this last week?"

"Yes; three days after the murder a Capuchin friar stopped at my inn and called for a tankard of beer. He kept his hood down all the time, so that I could not see his face, but I remember that he had a black beard, and I also noticed that he had a patch in his amice over one shoulder of rather an unusual form."

The patched garment was held up again in court, and recognised also by the third witness, after which he proceeded as follows:

"He called for more beer, and I began to enter into conversation with him and asked him where he came from. He told me from a Capuchin convent at W—, about a mile off. Just at that moment another friar, an old friend of mine, passed my inn, who belonged to the aforementioned convent.

318

"'Then you know each other,' said I to my friend the second friar, and I sought to bring them together, but my friend, after eyeing the former from head to foot, denied all knowledge of him. The first friar then somewhat confusedly stammered an excuse, saying that he had spoken without thinking, but that he had intended to say St. Mary's, another Capuchin convent, six miles further off. Then my friend the second friar said that he knew all the friars at St. Mary's, but still denied that he knew this one.

"The former began to mumble that he had only lately arrived, and began to turn the conversation. My friend whispered to me that he didn't believe he was a friar at all, but someone in disguise. After my friend had left, the former friar called for more beer (I never saw a friar drink so much beer as this one), and being curious to discover who the man was I tried to draw him out. At first he answered cautiously, but after drinking deeper he became less cautious and more confidential, but his utterance was now thick and unintelligible. He drew his chair closer to mine, and seemed about to let me into some secret, when some other customers of mine at the next table began to talk about the murder.

"I noticed that the would-be friar started, and instead of continuing his conversation with me, got up suddenly and muttered some excuse for taking his departure. He paid me hurriedly by lying down a *reichsgulden*, saying that whatever change there might be I might keep for myself. He had hardly left my house when certain of the guard who had been on the track of the murderer stopped to question him, and finding he could give no satisfactory account of himself, took him into custody."

Other witnesses were then examined in their turn, among which were certain members of the family of the murdered count, and a certain Fraulein von Berlichingen, his affianced bride, all of whom recognised the body to be that of the missing Graf von Waffenburg. The silken purse with silver beads picked up by the first witness was also recognised by Fraulein von Berlichingen as having been knitted by herself and presented by her to her lover.

The remains of the murdered count were decently interred. The melancholy event caused no small commotion in the neighbourhood. The funeral was followed by a large crowd of relatives and intimate friends, among which were our two heroes Fritz and Ludwig. The grief of Fraulein von Berlichingen was too great to allow her to appear at the funeral. She was inconsolable, and shortly afterwards entered a convent.

But to return to the trial.

The prisoner was now conducted into court. He was a man somewhat passed middle-age, though his frame was square built and powerful, and his hair, beard, and eyebrows were of a deep black, yet an observer might have noticed that whenever a ray of sunlight entered the court and shone full in the face of the prisoner that his hair and beard turned to a glowing purple, demonstrating beyond a doubt the presence of dye. Those who chanced to be stationed near the prisoner declared afterwards that the hairs of his head towards the roots were of a bright red, and many were they who recognised, in spite of this disguise, the person of Franz Wenzel, the executioner.

The prisoner, however, when examined, gave his name as Adolf Schmidt, and denied stoutly that he was Franz Wenzel, or to having ever had dealings with such a person.

He denied having stolen a bottle of hair dye for the purpose of disguising himself, and maintained that he was an honest citizen who had donned a holy garb for penitence, which had been imposed upon him by his father confessor.

The prisoner was then asked if such were the case, why he had tried to deceive the host of the Bear Inn and the Capuchin friar when they asked him whence he came. To this the prisoner replied that he loved not to gratify the idle curiosity of others respecting his private affairs. Ludwig Engstein then asked the prisoner how he came in possession of the friar's amice, for which he responded that it had been lent him some time ago by his father confessor, who had obtained it from some Capuchin friar of his acquaintance.

When asked for particulars concerning his father confessor, he replied vaguely and confusedly, and when begged to be more explicit, he refused, saying he had private reasons for not divulging the affairs of his friends.

Other witnesses were then called for, who stated that they had been robbed of money and various sorts of ware more than once within the last three years, about half a (German) mile from the house of the *scharfrichter* by a man who wore a mask, and who corresponded in height and width of person to the prisoner. Among these latter was a Jew peddler, who three years ago had been robbed of a large sum and various articles of clothing, among which he declared was the identical friar's amice held up in court, and which he perfectly remembered to have patched himself.

This and such like evidence naturally went very much against the prisoner; neither will it be wondered at that his disguise was easily seen through, and his person recognised as that of Franz Wenzel, the executioner. He was consequently found guilty of wilful murder and finally condemned to be beheaded. The day of the execution was fixed, and the prisoner conducted to the condemned cell.

We have mentioned before in an early part of this story that the profession of the headsman was hereditary, that the law forced the son of an executioner to follow in the steps of his father.

The unhappy wretch then, according to this law, was doomed to lose his life at the hands of his own son. Much speculation, however, among the inhabitants of —dorf had arisen as to whether the law would actually enforce so rigorous a decree, and whether the son of the *scharfrichter* would rebel against it if it did, or bow submissively to so harsh and unfeeling an order.

Some there were who thought that an exception ought to be made in this case, and a new *henker* selected, as it was hard for the son to suffer for the crimes of the father; but even if the law were disposed to be lenient, who was the new aspirant to be? Who would like to come forward to offer his services?

The office of the *scharfrichter* was in such bad odour that it would be difficult to find a man in the whole village who could be persuaded to undertake the task, even by the offer of a large reward.

However, after much speculation and gossip, the inhabitants came to the conclusion that everything might be done with money, and that someone would be certainly found to accept the bribe.

Others began to spread throughout the village that the man had already been found, and ventured to point out such or such a citizen as the new practitioner. Meanwhile the law had remained passive and had not troubled itself to make an exception in the case, and the *burgomaster* who had the superintendence of such affairs was far too phlegmatic and indifferent even to give the matter a thought.

He knew that an execution had to take place, that someone would be paid for amputating the head of the criminal, but whether it was to be one man's duty or another's was all the same to him.

The headsman's trade was hereditary, and he (the *burgomaster*) had never heard of any such innovation as that of selecting a new headsman during the lifetime of the rightful heir; therefore, as a matter of course, the young *scharfrichter* was to decapitate his own father, and there was an end of the matter.

What to him were the feelings of the son at being forced to obey so unnatural a dictate? He was paid for it like anyone else, and very good pay he got, too.

What to him was the additional anguish of the criminal at being executed by his own son? He knew well enough that his son would step into his shoes when he himself should be deprived of office, and if he didn't like to lose his head at the hands of his own son, he ought to have reflected before he committed the murder.

Now, the *burgomaster* had a confidential servant, one Heinrich Göbel, a man of heartless and revengeful nature, who cherished an ill-will against the prisoner's son for having dared to supplant him in the affections of a certain blue-eyed damsel, the daughter of a tavern-keeper in the village.

The father of the lady in question was not over pleased with the attentions of either of these individuals towards his Lieschen, one of the aspirants for his daughter's hand being a drunkard, the son of an executioner, who besides the stigma inevitably attached to his character for life, would be obliged to maintain his daughter by the scanty proceeds of his loathsome profession.

The other, a man of notoriously bad character, and dependent upon the wages he received from his master for a living. Of the two, the maid herself decidedly favoured Leo Wenzel, the young headsman, and seeing this, Heinrich Göbel inwardly resolved to take vengeance on his rival upon the first opportunity.

Whilst plotting vengeance thus in his heart, Göbel sought his master and shaped his conversation in this wise:

"*Herr Bürgermeister*, this will be a somewhat difficult business, this execution."

"How so?" inquired his master.

"Why, according to law," answered his servant, "young Leo will have to take the life of his own father."

"Well, what of that?" said the *burgomaster*.

"They say he is a young man of spirit, and he might refuse to take his father's life."

"Refuse! would he? The law will force him."

"But if he is obstinate and persists? He is a young man of spirit."

"Ugh! I hate these young men of spirit, they are always making trouble and subverting order. Well, if he makes a disturbance, he will be imprisoned, that's all."

"Yes, yes, of course; but for all that, if he positively refuses to lift his arm against his father, the law cannot force him to do it."

"Well, not exactly, but—but what has put it into your head that he *will* refuse? He will be rewarded for his services."

"But if he could not be tempted by a reward, if by chance he should refuse at the last moment to act the part of executioner towards his own father, and no one should be found to accept the post—why, in that case, if *my* services should be accepted, I should be most glad to officiate."

"What, *you*, Heinrich! *you* turn *scharfrichter*! Ha! ha!—this is something quite new. I was not aware that that was anything in your line."

"Well, sir, knowing your dislike to a disturbance among the populace (a thing very likely to occur if the headsman should not be found at his post)—rather than such an old vagabond as Franz Wenzel should get off in the confusion, why, I'll undertake the job myself."

"You would? Ha! ha!—but stay, if there *should* be a disturbance (which Heaven forfend, as any excitement sadly upsets my digestion), I am not so sure that I should like my servant to take upon himself the office of *scharfrichter*, for the odium of the populace that he would naturally incur would reflect likewise upon his master, and—"

"Well, sir, if you fear that, I should then advise another line of conduct."

"Indeed! What may that be?"

"To keep young Leo in ignorance that it is his father that he is called upon to execute. Listen to me! The *scharfrichter*'s house is a mile distant; our villagers have a superstitious dread of the spot, and are not likely yet to have communicated with the young man, and I know that he hasn't been in the township since he was last called to swear to the identity of the murdered man, then commonly believed to be his father. You will recollect that he identified the corpse as that of his father. In his lonely dwelling, he can have heard nothing of the trial, and is consequently still under the impression that it is his father that has been murdered.

"Now, if you will leave the matter to me I will contrive that he shall not be undeceived until too late."

"Yes; but how?"

"First of all I will go there myself with the news that the murderer of his father has been arrested, that the day has been fixed for his execution, and that he will have the pleasure of trying his hand for the first time in his life on his father's murderer. Everything will go straight, provided he has as yet heard nothing from other tongues."

"But if he has?"

"Then our plan is frustrated; but I go to ascertain that, and if he has not, the greatest care must be taken that no one communicates with him from this town, to which end you should give orders for the gates of the town to be closed for some days, under the excuse that you have been robbed of certain valuables, and have taken this precaution to catch the thief. It would be as well, perhaps, to hurry on the execution as quickly as possible."

"Well, but there is one point I don't understand. Supposing all to go on smoothly, as you seem so confident that it will, won't the young man recognise his father when led up to the scaffold in the 'poor sinner's' cart, and afterwards takes his seat on the chair placed for him?"

"There is our great difficulty, but let us hope for the best. The prisoner, as you know, took the precaution to dye his red head black in order to escape recognition. This will aid our project. The 'poor sinner's' garb that he will don the morning of the execution will also help the disguise. Young Leo is but a superficial observer, and before he has well taken note of the criminal his head will be off."

"You are very hopeful as to the success of your scheme, but if the father, in his last moments, makes himself known to his son—should rush into his arms to embrace him and say: 'My son, do you not know me? I am your father—you will not have the heart to execute your own father, the author of your existence.'"

"We must prevent this. Let a handkerchief be tied round his jaw that he cannot open his mouth to speak. This, after all, will be nothing more than is usually done to catch hold of the head in order to exhibit it to the public after decapitation, the only difference being that it is generally tied on after the criminal has taken his seat on the scaffold, while in this case it will be done before. Another bandage should be bound round his eyes at the same time, which is also customary; thus a great portion of the prisoner's face will be hidden. His arms will be pinioned firmly to his sides, so as to render all attempt at the removal of the bandage impossible, and everything will pass off quietly."

"Well, well, you're a queer dog. See that it *does* pass off quietly, that's all, and don't bother me any more about it. Mind, I leave the matter entirely in your hands."

"Never fear, sir, I am off at once to the house of the *scharfrichter*, trust everything to me. Stay, you had better issue an order for the gates of the town to be closed at once. You can give me a pass before I start, or they will shut me out with the rest."

"True; just wait one moment. Here—the pen and ink—so now be off as fast as you can."

Off started the servant of the *burgomaster* with the order to the gatekeeper to close the gates, and the pass which was to admit none but himself, and after the gatekeeper had received the necessary instructions, Heinrich passed rapidly through the gates and directed his steps towards the house of the *scharfrichter*. He chuckled to himself as he contemplated the success of his scheme.

"What would the death of his father at my hands be to him to the discovery of having taken his father's life himself! That will be revenge indeed! Now to the fulfilment of my scheme there is no obstacle."

He had proceeded about an English mile on his way when, suddenly lifting his eyes, he descried in the distance the figure of an aged man, who appeared to be going the same road as himself. He hastened his steps, and soon overtook the veteran, whom he now recognised as one of his fellow citizens, a certain Gustav Meyer, and known to be one of the greatest gossips in the neighbourhood.

"Good-day, Gustav," said Göbel, with forced good humour. "Where are you off to on those venerable pins of yours?"

"*Ach! lieber, freund Göbel!*" exclaimed the loquacious old man; "how are you? I have not seen you for an age. You have grown proud since you have been in the *burgomaster*'s service, and forget that it was I who got you the situation, for you never come to see me now, though we used to be such cronies, you know. But you young folks never think it worth while to give us old fogies a call to see how we are. Why, I might be dead and buried for all you would know about it, and even if you did hear of it, I suppose it would be all the same to you, eh?

"Well, well, 'ingratitude is the reward of the world,' as the proverb says, and we old fogies with one foot in the grave and the other about to follow must make up our minds to be put on the shelf. We all have our turn; I have had mine, you are having yours, but old age comes at last, and then there is an end of us all, even to the best of us. Even I have been young, friend Göbel. Ha! ha! You'd hardly think so to look at me now with these silvery locks and tottering limbs. I say you'd hardly think so now, would you, eh? Now, how many years should you think I could count, friend Göbel, tell me?"

"I haven't the slightest idea," said Göbel, impatiently.

"I am hard upon ninety years old, and all tell me that I carry my years well. I may say I haven't had a day's illness in all my life. I have nearly all my teeth yet, and—"

"I have no doubt all you say is very true, my friend," interrupted Göbel; "but you have hardly answered my question satisfactorily yet. I asked you where you were going?"

"Friend Göbel," said the old man, "now I'll just tell you what I propose doing this morning, just by way of stretching my old limbs, seeing that I have not had a walk for an age. It does old folks good to go out for a stroll every now and then in the country. Too much staying at home over the fire isn't good, even for the likes of me."

"Well, well," broke in Göbel, beginning to lose all patience. "I asked you where you were going."

"Did you? Ah yes, I had nearly forgot. We old folks are apt to lose our memories at times, you know, my friend, so you young folks ought to have compassion on us, and recollect that we were once like you, and that you will one day become like us, therefore—"

"This is insufferable," burst out Göbel, whose forbearance was quite at an end. "I ask you a plain question, and I expect a plain answer. I repeat the question—Where are you going?"

"Hoity, toity! friend Göbel," cried the old man, in great surprise. "What! so impatient with your old friend Gustav! Don't you remember how often I have taken you upon my knee and danced you? We used to be great friends then. Don't you recollect? But I suppose you have forgotten all that now, eh?—since you have become a man. Let me see, how long ago must that be? Full thirty years ago, if it's a day, I'll warrant."

"Will you, or will you not, give me a plain answer to a plain question. Tell me where you are going?" cried Göbel, now quite furious, and shaking the old man violently by both shoulders.

"Softly, softly! friend Göbel," cried the veteran, much alarmed. "Save my life. Prithee, save my life, and I will tell you where I am going, if you will have patience."

"Well, tell me at once, and let us have no more chattering," said Göbel, leaving go his hold.

"Well, in the first place, then," began old Gustav, recovering himself—"in the first place—but stay, upon second thoughts, I'll just leave you to guess where I am going. Now, where do you think?"

"Dotard, have a care!" cried Göbel, threateningly, "and trifle with me no longer. Tell me where you are going, or—"

"Well, well, friend Göbel, I'll tell you; don't be afraid, don't let two such old friends as we are quarrel for a trifle—I'll tell you where I am going, although I must say that I think you seem to take an uncommon interest in the doings of an old man like me, who, though he be an old friend—"

"Take care now!"

"Well, well, my friend, wait one moment; I'll tell you. I told you before that I would tell you, and I will be as good as my word, if you will have one moment's patience—for patience, friend Göbel, patience, I say, is a virtue that we ought all to cultivate, and which we all of us more or less are sadly wanting in. But to proceed; though, after all, my friend, what hurry can you possibly have to learn so simple a fact? It appears to me that the world has grown wondrously impatient since my time; that is, if everybody is like you, but as I said before—"

"Tell me! tell me!" screamed Göbel, seizing his venerable friend a second time by the shoulders.

"Well, then, my friend," said Gustav, drawing out his words at a most provoking length, "if I *must* tell you, and you are quite sure that you have sufficient patience to listen to me, learn that I am going to pay a visit at the house of the *scharfrichter*, to have a quiet little gossip. You know I am fond of a nice little gossip. Well, I am just going to have a little chat with that poor young man Leo Wenzel. What do you think? He doesn't know yet that his father is the real murderer, for he lives so far off and no one ever goes near the house to tell him the news, and he is still under the delusion that his father has been murdered and that the assassin has not yet been caught. Poor young man, I shall have to break the news very gently to him, for he will feel it deeply. He must know the truth sooner or later, so I have taken upon myself to be the first to communicate the unwelcome news.

"According to the law he will be obliged to take the life of his own father. It will be a dreadful blow to him, poor boy, and I am sure I don't know how he will be induced to act executioner in the present instance. I know not if the law in this case will make an exception and choose someone else in his place; it will be very hard upon him if the law really should insist on being carried out to the very letter. Let us hope that mercy will be shown to the son, but in any case it is a very dreadful affair, so I thought I would just go to comfort him a little, to see how he takes the matter, and give him courage, in case—"

"I thought as much!" muttered Göbel to himself; then aloud to his friend, "So that is where you are going is it? Ah, then I will save you the trouble. Being a matter of no importance, you need not be in a hurry. Listen to me; my master has lost certain valuables, and has given orders for the gates of the town to be closed until he has discovered the thief, and has strictly commanded me to arrest any person I might find leaving the town, until his valuables shall have been recovered. I should be sorry to suspect you, but as the law respects the person of no man, it is my painful duty to take you back to the town. Let us have no more cackling or resistance, but come at once."

"But, my dear friend Göbel!" pleaded the veteran, "you surely can't suspect—you will not for one moment imagine—nay, if you have any doubt of my honesty search me. I can assure it will be useless, I am innocent."

"If you are innocent, you will be proved so in due time, meanwhile I have orders—"

"But, friend Göbel, I assure you again and again upon my oath that I have taken nothing. There—look—search me all over, if you will, and let me go in peace. Is not my character enough? Am I not well known in —dorf? Have I ever been known to touch my neighbour's goods? Pray satisfy yourself that I have taken nothing, and let me go. Why trouble yourself to bring back a man to the town to be searched whom you know to be innocent. Besides, it will upset my plan. I wouldn't miss my little gossip with young Leo for all the world just at this moment. Just consider, my friend—"

"Cease your cackling and come along with me!" shouted Göbel, seizing him by the collar and dragging him forcibly back towards the town.

"But—but—" stammered the astonished and terrified old man.

"But me no buts, but do my bidding instantly, Sir Driveller, or it will be the worse for you."

So saying, he dragged his old friend home again at a hurried pace, regardless of his tottering limbs and of his prayers and entreaties.

It was just mid day, and the sun shone hot, when Göbel returned to the township, perspiring at every pore, and deposited his charge, more dead than alive, within the walls of —dorf. He then retraced his steps under the broiling sun, cursing and swearing as he went at his plan having been so nearly frustrated by the cackling gossip of an old dotard.

"*Potz—Himmel, Donnerwetter, Schock, Schwerer, Noth, noch mal!*" he muttered to himself. "A pretty obstacle in my path! *Tausend Teufel!* I had a mind to dash his brains out on the spot, the old idiot, for his drivelling."

With these and such like elaborately strung together oaths the servant of the *burgomaster* beguiled the time, until at length he arrived at the door of the *scharfrichter's* house, where he discovered young Leo at work in his garden. The young executioner looked up at the sound of stranger footsteps, and though he would rather the visitor had been anyone else than his rival, yet upon the whole he was not displeased to see a human face after so long. His manner even warmed towards his visitor when he saw him advance with a smile on his face and an extended hand.

"Leo," began Heinrich Göbel with feigned friendship, "we have long been enemies, but everything has an end. I have now come to offer you my hand in friendship, for henceforth we are no longer rivals, but friends. Lieschen, think of her no more. Her father positively refuses to give her to either of us, so she has at length plighted her troth to another man."

"What! Lieschen? Impossible!" cried Leo, mopping his forehead.

"Ay, my friend, it is too true; nay, pray calm yourself. I, too, loved her as you did, but since the matter has turned out thus, I have made up my mind to console myself by paying my addresses to another as soon as possible."

"You never *could* have loved her as I loved her," gasped out Leo, as he staggered for support against the garden wall.

"Well, well, my friend, I knew you would feel the blow, but calm yourself and dismiss these gloomy thoughts. I have better news than that in store for you."

"What care I for news now that *she* has deserted me?" groaned Leo distractedly.

"Come, come now, let me comfort you a little," said Göbel. "What do you think? *The murderer of your father has been discovered!*"

"What do I hear? Caught? Safe?"

"Ay, the murder has been proved, and the murderer condemned to die by the sword. The execution has been fixed for the day after tomorrow. It will take place at daybreak as usual, and you will have the satisfaction of taking vengeance on your father's murderer with your own hands. You will wield your father's sword for the first time in your life before an admiring crowd. Think of that."

"Vengeance at last!" cried the young headsman, with flushed face and distorted features. "Vengeance at last! Thank God! thank God!"

"Bravo, old friend!" cried Göbel, slapping his heartily detested rival on the shoulder in the friendliest manner possible. "I knew you would take heart at this piece of news. Come, let us sit down together and console ourselves."

Leo, then entering the house, took from a cupboard a large bottle of *schnapps* and two glasses. The two companions, seating themselves, began to drink deeply and to chat incessantly, the subject of the discourse being the particulars of the murder according to the version of Göbel. We need hardly say that the whole was a fabrication of Heinrich's own brain. At length the servant of the *burgomaster* rose to take his departure, and having enjoined his rival to be of good cheer, bent his steps again towards the township, chuckling by the way at his own devices. Arrived at the gates of the town, he showed his pass, and was permitted to enter without let or hindrance. Hurrying through the streets until he reached the *burgomaster's* house, he presented himself before that worthy, whom he found seated at a table before a plate of sausage, and in the act of draining to the dregs an enormous tankard of beer.

"Well, what news?" asked his master.

"Oh! the very best; he took the bait greedily. It was quite a pleasure to see how he enjoyed the news. No one had been before me, so I had him all to myself. The matter will now go off as smoothly as could be desired; but, by the saints! I had a narrow escape of failure."

"Indeed! How was that?"

"When I was nearly half way to the *scharfrichter's* house, who should I see just ahead of me but that cursed old gossip, Gustav Meyer. I stopped him and asked him where he was going. *Potztausend!* what a chatterbox! I thought I should not get an answer out of him before nightfall, and when I did, where do you think he *was* going? Why, straight to the house of the *henker* to have a quiet chat with young Leo upon the subject of the murder, and reveal to him all that

I had taken such pains to keep secret. He seemed delighted at the idea of being the first to deliver the news."

The *burgomaster* laughed heartily.

"Well, what did you do?" said he, at length.

"What did I do! I told him his presence was particularly wanted at the township, and seizing him by the collar, dragged him all the way back again, regardless of his cackling. I informed him that you had lost some valuables, and had given me orders to arrest anyone leaving the town on suspicion. He was indignant at the charge. Protested, declared his innocence, and spoke of the high character he had always borne in the town, etc., etc. He seemed in despair at being deprived of his little gossip with the *henker*'s son, and begged and entreated me to let him have it out quietly; but, deaf to all his chattering, I dragged him home again in spite of himself, and lodged him safely within the gates of the town. *Donner und Blitzen!* but it was enough to raise the bile of a saint to listen to the wanderings of that antique driveller, to say nothing of having one's plan so nearly frustrated; by such a worm as that too!"

Here and again the *burgomaster* burst into a loud laugh, in which Göbel, in spite of himself, joined.

"Ah," said he, at length recovering himself, "there is one thing yet to be done. I must go to the jailor of the prison with private orders from you to prevent the prisoner having an interview with his son, should he ask for one. This accomplished, there will be no more difficulty."

"Ah, yes," said the *burgomaster*, "it would be as well. But what an interest you seem to take in this case, Heinrich! One would imagine that you had a private grudge against the prisoner."

"I like to see things well done," was the reply, and the servant shortly after left the presence of his master.

A great sensation was caused in —dorf when it was given out that the execution had been hurried on a week, and much speculation arose as to what could have been the *burgomaster*'s motive. Half the town already knew by the tongue of old Gustav of his having been arrested by the servant of the *burgomaster* on suspicion of having robbed his master of certain valuables just at the very time when he (Gustav) was contemplating the pleasure he would have in being the first to communicate the melancholy tidings of the murder to the young headsman. They therefore concluded that Leo must still be in ignorance of the real state of the case. The other half of —dorf, however, never gave a thought as to whether he knew it or not; enough for them that someone was going to be beheaded and that they should have a spectacle to vary the monotony of their humdrum lives.

At length the fatal day arrived. The gates of the town were thrown open (for the servant of the *burgomaster* gave out that the thief had been discovered and the valuables regained), and now all —dorf was in an uproar, while crowds of peasants from all the surrounding villages flocked to witness the bloody spectacle.

The scaffold, or the mound of earth which was to serve as such, had been erected half way between the township and the house of the executioner, and was already surrounded by a file of soldiers, around which thronged the mob so closely that they were every now and then repulsed by the military. From the sea of human heads that inundated the place of execution resounded a hum of voices, in which salutations, sallies, bad language, coarse jokes, and coarser laughter, together with murmurs and imprecations, and an occasional scream from the women when the crowd pressed too closely, were confusedly mingled, and resembled at a little distance the bleating of an immense flock of sheep. Classes of all sorts were jostled together, from the lowest grade of *handwerksbursch* to the university student. There were pretty peasant girls in their holiday costumes, and sturdy peasants from all parts of the country. There were Jew hawkers, sharpers, pickpockets, ruffianly bullies, cripples, and mendicants. There were mothers with young children in their arms, which latter contributed their feeble cries to the general buzz.

All had turned out to feast their eyes upon the death of a fellow mortal. Nor was this an ordinary execution like that described in an earlier part of this story. No; this was an exceptional case—something out of the common way, a sublimer spectacle.

In this case the condemned was no obscure *handwerksbursch*, of whose career the multitude knew nothing, and cared as little about. The criminal was no less a man than Franz Wenzel, the far-famed *scharfrichter*, who had amputated the heads of "poor sinners" for the last thirty or forty years, and was now doomed to lose his own.

The interest in the case was considerably heightened when it was known that the veteran executioner was to be operated upon by the hands of his own son. Then the facts of the murder were so strange, so unnatural. Fancy the cunning of that hardened old sinner, the ex-headsman, who, according to his own confession, made in prison the day

332

before the execution, had waylaid, robbed, and murdered the innocent Count of Waffenburg, a scion of one of the most wealthy and respected noble families for miles round, disguised as a Capuchin friar, and in order to conceal the identity of the murdered man, had dissevered the head of the corpse, which he had endeavoured to hide for ever from the eye of man by throwing it into the trunk of a hollow chestnut tree. Then having stripped the corpse of its clothes, and afterwards having stripped himself of his outer garments, he dressed up the corpse of his victim in his own well known crimson-coloured doublet and hose, thereby conveying the idea to the public mind that the corpse found was his own, after which, returning to his house close by, having again donned the friar's habit, he deposited the sword usually set apart for the beheading of criminals, and in this case used for amputating the head of the murdered count, and wiping it well, he lighted a fire on his hearth where he burned one by one the habiliments of his victim. He then left his house a second time, still disguised as a friar and laden with his ill-gotten treasure, passed once more the scene of the murder and wandered all night in the direction of —. How strange the evidence, too, that convicted him, the theft of the bottle of hair dye, the remarkable patch on his amice. Every particular of the murder had an indescribable interest in the minds of the populace of —dorf and its surrounding villages. No wonder the adjacent townships vomited forth their scum of the curious, idle, and depraved! This was a sight not to be missed on any account, and would furnish them with gossip for the next six months at least. At length, when the long streaky rose-tipped clouds announced the approach of the fatal hour, the crowd burst out simultaneously into a cry of "He comes! he comes! the *henker* comes!"

The crowd made room for a young man in a cart, who, having thrown the reins on the horse's neck, passed through the file of soldiers and mounted the hillock of earth, armed with the two-handed weapon that he was about to use for the first time in his life.

"Look!" said one of the crowd; "it *is* young Leo, after all. I thought they had found a substitute."

"What a hard-hearted young ruffian to consent to take the life of his father with his own hands!" said another.

"And he doesn't seem to feel it a bit," said a third; "why, he is actually smiling."

"Some folks say that he does not know who it is that he is going to behead," said a fourth.

"Not know that the criminal is his father?" exclaimed the former speaker. "Nonsense, I don't believe it."

The young headsman was attired in a buff leather jerkin slashed with red and hose of a dark green. He appeared about two-and-twenty, and was as yet beardless. He was considerably taller than his father, but his frame, though powerfully built, was devoid of that excessive and almost preternatural muscular development that characterised that of the old executioner. His hair was of a reddish brown, his complexion florid, his eyes light blue, and his features, though somewhat coarse, had something in them not altogether disagreeable. He leaned firmly on his sword and gazed around calmly on the crowd, when suddenly the human sea became violently agitated and began to groan and hiss in its fury.

The cause of this tumult became speedily known. It was the arrival of the "poor sinner," who was drawn in a cart between two priests and habited according to the custom of the condemned on such occasions. Loud hooting and execrations burst forth on all sides from the crowd as it made way for the condemned cart.

"But that is not Franz Wenzel," said one to his neighbour. "The old *henker* had red hair; this man's hair is black."

"Fool, don't you know how that is?" said his neighbour. "Haven't you heard yet how he dyed his hair black in order not to be recognised?"

"No, did he though?" said the former. "But look! why is his head tied up so with two handkerchiefs? I can't see anything of his face."

"H'm, I don't know; some innovation I suppose. The handkerchief always used to be tied on when on the scaffold in my time," answered his friend. The criminal had now alighted from the cart, and, followed by the two priests, ascended the place of execution, where he took his seat on the chair placed for him. The assistant executioner, whose face was most successfully disguised with a black mask, pushed his way through the crowd and mounted the platform.

"Who is *he*?" was a question asked by everyone of everybody; "and why is he masked while Leo, who bears the sword, is unmasked?"

"Who knows? Perhaps he is the new headsman that they all talked about, and young Leo will not really behead his own father; but we shall see."

The crowd had grown more curious than ever. Every one stood on the tip-toe of expectation with his eyes and mouth wide open. An intense silence reigned around, during which the man in the mask bound the criminal firmly to his seat with a strong cord, then seizing the handkerchief that was tied round the head of the condemned, he gave the signal for the blow. The two priests who had hitherto been whispering consolation in the ear of the criminal now retreated a few paces to the rear, while young Leo advanced, flushed and triumphant, his whole countenance distorted with an expression of malice and revenge. Before brandishing his sword to give the final blow he lowered his head close to the ear of the victim and hissed out in accents sufficiently audible to be overheard by that part of the crowd that had assembled nearest to the scaffold: "Wretch! thine hour has come at last. Learn now the vengeance of a wronged son. Thou shalt see if I am the son of my father or no, and whether it is for nothing that I have been bred a *scharfrichter*. Prepare now, for thou art soon to learn how I have profited by my lessons—whether I am an apt pupil. My sword is sharpened well on purpose for thee, and when thou feelest the cold steel close to thy neck, then, then, to h—l with thee, and bear throughout eternity the curses of a ruined son!"

During this speech of the young headsman the criminal was observed to tremble convulsively, as if struggling to speak, but the assistant executioner grasped the handkerchief still tighter round his head and repeated the signals impatiently.

"Did you hear?" said one of the foremost in the crowd. "Did you hear how he cursed his father? He actually reproached him in his last moments for having brought him up a *scharfrichter*! Oh! the unfeeling young villain! What a heart he must have."

"Ah! neighbour," answered another, "these executioners are not like other mortals; they do not know what it is to feel. They are brought up to kill their fellow creatures as butchers are to kill cattle, and they think nothing of it. Bless you, there is nothing these men would not do for money."

"'Tis strange, too," said another close by. "I always thought young Leo loved his father. I never thought so bad of him as to think that he would curse him in his dying moments, wretch though he may have been."

"Take my word for it, neighbour," said a sturdy inhabitant of —dorf, "that young Leo does not know yet that it is his father."

At this moment everyone suddenly broke short his discourse, and the crowd again was silent for a moment. The two-handed weapon was raised high in the air, glittered for a moment in the rays of the rising sun, then descended with the rapidity of lightning, while the head of the murderer having slipped out of the handkerchief with the force of the blow, fell with a crash on the platform.

A loud cheer is raised by the crowd, and young Leo having thrown away his sword and pushed aside the assistant executioner, has seized the head of the criminal and torn off the bandage from his eyes. He holds it high in the air by its purple locks and gloats with fiendish satisfaction on its writhing features. The muscles of the face are fearfully convulsed, as if the spirit had not as yet quite departed, but still lingered about the corpse, being loth to leave its tenement. The eyes roll hideously and appear to gaze reproachfully upon the face of the young executioner. Suddenly a change comes over the features of the young man. His countenance, the moment before so flushed with triumph and revenge, now assumes a ghastly pallor; a cold sweat breaks out on his forehead, his matted locks stand on end. His eyes start from his head, his jaw drops low. Then, with a preternatural shriek, he drops the head, which rolls down the hillock of earth among the crowd, staggers and falls heavily upon the platform, gasping out *"Oh, Gott! mein Vater!"*

No words can describe the sensation created among the crowd at this horrible scene. Questions and explanations ensued, and a rush was made towards the scaffold. Assistance was at length procured, and the son of the late executioner was lifted from the ground and driven toward his own house in the cart that he had set out in that morning to execute his fearful mission. A doctor was sent for, who declared that he was in an apoplectic fit. In time, however, he recovered, and the doctor left someone with him to attend to him and keep him quiet. Nevertheless, when he came to reflect upon what had happened that morning, in spite of all restraint, he rushed wildly into the chamber where his poor paralytic mother lay on her death-bed, and losing all caution and reflection in his emotion, he related in a wild and excited manner the dreadful events of the day. The result may be anticipated. The poor woman, long given up by the doctors, sank under the startling news, and expired almost instantaneously.

Young Leo, who, with the exception of his drunkenness had really nothing very bad in him, now gave way to the most excessive grief, for he loved his mother tenderly. He felt himself now guilty of the murder of both his parents, and refused all consolation. What had he now to live for, thought he. His father he had murdered with his own hands and sent with curses to the tomb; his mother, so dear to him he had hurried to the grave through his insane want of self-restraint. His lady-love, false (as he thought), for secretly they had plighted their troth together. What was life to him now but a burden? He loathed it. These gloomy thoughts clouded his mind with a profound melancholy, a deep incurable despair. On the following morning Leo Wenzel, the young executioner, fell upon his own sword, yet moist with the blood of his father, by him so unconsciously shed on the day before.

With the death of Leo Wenzel the family became extinct, and the profession of the *scharfrichter* went begging. But who was the assistant executioner? Nobody could find out. He had disappeared as mysteriously as he had made his appearance. Some said it was one, and some another, while the most settled belief was that it could be none other than the arch-fiend himself who had come to carry off the *henker's* soul. In the confusion that followed the swoon of young Leo he had vanished, and no one had seen whither. No human being could have passed through a crowd without being seen by someone, therefore it must have been the arch-enemy of mankind. Thus reasoned the people of —dorf.

And Lieschen, what became of her? Poor girl! the news of her lover's suicide, for she had truly loved the youthful headsman, had completely overwhelmed her. She fell into a decline and outlived her lover but one year.

The servant of the *burgomaster* was mistaken in believing that after Leo's death the course would be now clear for him. His heartless scheme had come to light (for it was difficult to keep anything long a secret in —dorf), and he found the door of Lieschen's house closed upon him for ever.

He soon knew himself hated by all the town, and tradition goes on to relate that some years afterwards, when he was in the service of another master, his employer having missed certain articles of plate and called in the police to search his coffers, they found not only the missing articles, but also a black mask and a suit of sad coloured clothes, recognised as having been worn by the assistant on the day of Wenzel's execution.

Finding his reputation lost in —dorf, he deemed it advisable to retire to another village, where he afterwards married. The last we hear of him is that he ultimately accepted the office of *scharfrichter*, and took up his abode in the house of Franz Wenzel, where he reared up a long line of executioners, which was only broken many years later by the profession of the *henker* ceasing to be obligatory.

But what of our two friends Fritz and Ludwig? We had nigh forgotten them. That they were both of them present at the execution is undoubted from certain passages in their correspondence after my ancestor had left Germany for ever. The day after Wenzel's execution was the last time they met on earth. They each of them passed the remainder of their days in their own respective countries though they corresponded frequently. The most recently dated letter from Ludwig Engstein bears with it the news of his marriage, and in a postscript he mentions having been just informed that since the execution of Franz Wenzel the tricks of the Poltergeist had ceased for ever.

★ ★ ★ ★ ★

Murmurs of applause were upon every lip as our artist finished his narrative, when Mr. Oldstone, rising, thus addressed the club. "Gentlemen; I think you will all agree with me that my friend Mr. McGuilp has fully earned his sitting from the fair Helen?"

"Yes, yes," cried several voices; "he has paid us beforehand. Let him have his rights."

At this moment the door opened ajar and the head of Dame Hearty appeared at the aperture to inform the club that her daughter was now at their disposal.

"Let her be brought in!" shouted a chorus of voices. "It is but fair that we should have one more look at Helen before Mr. McGuilp walks off with her."

Helen then appeared in the doorway and was greeted enthusiastically by the whole club, in the midst of which the painter, after looking at his watch and ascertaining that it was yet early enough for a good sitting, left the room and made for his studio, where, having set his palette, he was joined shortly afterwards by his fair model. Having arranged his colours and placed his canvas on the easel, he sat contemplating the portrait he had commenced so recently. Alas! how flat and insipid his poor work looked after having gazed on the bright original! It was but the first painting, it is true, and we know that nothing really good can be done at once; but, then, what drawing he found to correct now that he looked at his work with a fresh eye! The awfulness of the difficulties in art now rose up in his mind to appal him, and he uttered a sigh.

"Can all the glazing and scumbling in the world," muttered he to himself, "ever advance this portrait one step towards the divine original?"

Thus musing, the painter seized the canvas in both hands and breathed over its surface. Immediately afterwards, mixing up some colour sparingly, he scumbled over the entire surface of the portrait. Helen, whose eye dwelt upon the artist's every movement, whether from curiosity, or from some mysterious sympathy she felt for the young painter, demanded of him why he breathed on the face of her picture.

"To breathe into it the breath of life, Helen," replied McGuilp, smilingly.

Helen opened her large blue eyes with an expression of half wonderment, half doubt, not knowing whether the painter spoke in jest, or whether an artist really had some occult power in his very breath that could vivify the canvas. How was she to know, poor innocent child! Village bred and born in an age, as our readers will recollect, before photography had rendered too familiar the representation of the human face even for the veriest peasant any longer to wonder at the art by which it is produced?

In the days we speak of the painter's art was the only mode of transfixing the lineaments of a dear friend or parent and rendering them immortal. Painters, too, were much less common then than now-a-days, for art was still in its infancy in plain matter-of-fact old England. The painter, or limner as he was then called, was a being of far greater interest than at the present day. He was patronised by royalty and nobility, and though the prices that he received for his works were considerably less than in our times, and he was nearly always a poor and needy individual, yet he met with a certain amount of respect from his patrons, as they knew that by his hand alone could they hope to become immortal. Everyone liked to see his own features represented upon canvas, or those of his wife and family. Oft times his favourite horse or dog. In order to secure the services of the limner therefore, it was necessary to court him, nor was this respect or appearance of such ever denied him, save perhaps by the pampered menial of some nobleman or wealthy squire, who looked superciliously down upon the itinerant painter as a being far inferior to himself. We will hope, however, for the honour of humanity that the number was comparatively small that measured the painter's respectability by the length of his purse.

Indeed, the titled and the wealthy seem to have prided themselves in doing everything in their power to set the example of respect towards a disciple of the fine arts. Among this class the painter had seldom anything to complain of; in fact, provided he were affable in manner, decent in appearance, could paint the ladies' hands and ears small enough to please them, their eyes sufficiently large and languishing, and, lastly—but which was of no small importance—could represent faithfully the texture of their silks and satins, their lace, velvet, fur, or swansdown, oh, then he was caressed, petted, and acknowledged by all as a most agreeable member of society and sure of making his fortune. But woe to him if he were above his business and attempted high art—we mean subject pictures that were not portraits. However much he might be gifted in that line, his friends would instantly desert him, and he might starve in a garret. His patrons knew nothing of high art and cared as little. All they wanted was to see their own effigies adorning the walls of their mansions, and as long as the limner was content to be of service to them they were willing to support him, but no longer. It was set down as an axiom that the human *face* divine—by which they meant their own faces—was the highest aim that a painter could aspire to. This was the sort of high art they wanted, and no other.

A painter must be content with the work his patrons set him to do and not indulge his own caprices. Well, well, admitting the range of the painter's art to have been cramped and limited, has any age or country the power to cramp the genius of an artist? Is high art only to be found in imaginative pictures? Does not a portrait become high art under a master hand? Can that be called a mechanical art that gives intellect or sentiment to the eye, firmness or softness to the lip, the natural bloom to the cheek, truth and beauty to the whole? Few, let us hope, even in this matter of fact age, but would rank the real artist before the photographic artisan who usurps his name. If, in the present age, now that we are accustomed to a much more rapid process of reproducing the human face, there are to be found those who honour the true artist, imagine how his art must have been held in honour when it was the only way of immortalising men! It need not be wondered at that among those classes where the appearance of a painter was less common, that the respect he inspired almost amounted to awe in certain instances. This was the case with our Helen, who never having set eyes before on a real artist, looked with awe and wonder on our painter as a species of magician who possessed an art not merely unknown in her humble sphere, but which she was sure that the worthy members of the club were alike ignorant of, however learned they might be in other respects. The painter's youth and good looks, together with his possessing this mysterious art at such an early age, elevated him at once into a hero in her eyes. Then there was the strange fact of his having seen and spoken to a ghost in the same house where she herself had been born and bred, the very ghost she had been frightened so often with in her childhood, but which was, nevertheless, so chary of its appearance that it had found no one for upwards of half a century worthy of revealing itself to until now, and had chosen for that purpose the young artist before her, and that, too, the very first night that he arrived at the Inn. What was there peculiar in the organisation of our painter, that he should have been selected before all others to gaze on the august presence of one risen from the dead? The haunted chamber had been repeatedly slept in by all the members of the club in turn, and by many strangers beside, for years back, and yet never before within the experience of our host had the headless lady vouchsafed a parley with any one of them. The preference, therefore, shewn towards our friend McGuilp by the tenant of the haunted chamber had raised him at once in the esteem of the whole club, and the marked respect with which he was treated by the other guests, all of them older men than himself, did not fail to escape the quick eye of Helen, who felt inwardly flattered that the man for whom she had conceived so warm a sympathy, should be so honoured among his better fellows.

Our artist and his model had been left together for upwards of three-quarters of an hour, during which time McGuilp had not opened his mouth to exchange a single word with his sitter, a habit of his when unusually engrossed in his work. He had glazed and scumbled, chopped and changed about his drawing, laid on impasto, worked upon the background, and so absorbed was he with his picture, the time had passed as if it had been five minutes. A considerable change, however, had taken place in the portrait. There was more life and vigour, the tints were more natural and the head now stood more out in relief. Helen never once attempted to break the silence, but remained modest and immovable in her position as a statue. Had she been a vain and foolish girl or a coquette, she might have been irritated by the painter's silence, misconstruing it into a sign of insensibility to her charms, but no such thought for a moment entered the head of our Helen. On the contrary, she looked with the deepest awe and reverence on the painter whose art required so much silence and concentration, and instead of calling away his attention from his work by some frivolous remark, she mentally resolved to aid him to the utmost by posing as patiently as it lay in her power.

Nevertheless, after a long sitting, a change is apt to come over the face of the sitter. The muscles become flaccid, the colour vanishes, the eye grows vacant, and an expression of languor and weariness takes the place of the bright healthy look that the sitter bore at the commencement. This is especially the case with young people, and so it was with Helen, who, spite of her laudable endeavours to do justice to her portrait painter, had unconsciously grown several shades paler, and had so altered in expression that our artist, finding it impossible to continue his work, deemed it advisable to give his model a little repose.

"That will do, Helen, for the present," said he; "take a little rest, until you can call back the roses to your cheek and the life to your eye. There, then, you may look if you like, but there is much to be done yet, I can tell you."

"Oh, I think you have done wonders this sitting," said Helen, as she stood contemplating her own portrait from behind the artist's chair, with her head resting on her hand.

"It appears to me as like as it can possibly be already. I do not see what more there is to do to it."

"Do you not, Helen?" said McGuilp. "Then you are very easily satisfied, but it is not so with us. We artists are the most discontented people under the sun. We know that however well a portrait may be painted, it can never come up to the original, and yet we are never contented, even with our utmost endeavours to approach it."

"Then, we who know nothing about your art are happier in our ignorance than the artists themselves who have studied art all their lives," remarked Helen.

"Very often," replied McGuilp with a sigh; "nevertheless, there is a pleasure in the mere pursuit of art, however far removed the work of the artist may be from his ideal, that he would not exchange for the calm satisfaction of the uninitiated who perceive no fault."

At this moment a sound of cheering and clapping of hands proceeding from the club-room interrupted the dialogue between the painter and his model.

"What can all that noise mean?" ejaculated Helen. "Ah, I can guess. Mother has just finished telling her story to the gentlemen of the club, and they are applauding her."

"Is it so, Helen?" said McGuilp.

"Well, as they have been enjoying a story from which we have been excluded, I see no reason why we should not have a story all to ourselves. What do you say?"

"Oh, by all means," said Helen; "but I am a poor storyteller. Pray do not ask *me* for one, but if you know of a story, why of course I am all attention."

"Let me see, then," said McGuilp. "What sort of story would you like to hear?"

"Oh, tell me something about Italy. *I should* like to hear so," answered Helen.

"Would you? Then I think I can remember a little circumstance that occurred in Italy within my experience, which I will relate to you if you will resume your seat, for I have but little time to lose. We can work and talk at the same time. Your colour has now returned, and my story may possibly help to preserve it until the end of the sitting."

Helen then resumed her seat, and McGuilp having seized once more his palette and brushes and placed himself in front of his easel, continued his portrait whilst he related the following story.

LEONAUR

ALSO FROM LEONAUR
AVAILABLE IN SOFTCOVER OR HARDCOVER WITH DUST JACKET

THE EMPIRE OF THE AIR: 1 *by George Griffiths*—*The Angel of the Revolution*—a rich brew that calls to mind Verne's tales of futuristic wars while being original, visionary, exciting and technologically prescient.

THE EMPIRE OF THE AIR: 2 *by George Griffiths*—*Olga Romanoff or, The Syren of the Skies*—the sequel to *The Angel of the Revolution*—a future Earth in which nation states are given full self determination when the Aerians, the descendants of 'The Brotherhood of Freedom,' who have policed world peace for more than a century, decide they are mature enough to have outgrown war.

THE INTERPLANETARY ADVENTURES OF DR KINNEY *by Homer Eon Flint*—*The Lord of Death, The Queen of Life, The Devolutionist & The Emancipatrix.*

ARCOT, MOREY & WADE *by John W. Campbell, Jr.*—The Complete, Classic Space Opera Series—*The Black Star Passes, Islands of Space, Invaders from the Infinite.*

CHALLENGER & COMPANY *by Arthur Conan Doyle*—The Complete Adventures of Professor Challenger and His Intrepid Team-*The Lost World, The Poison Belt, The Land of Mists, The Disintegration Machine* and *When the World Screamed.*

GARRETT P. SERVISS' SCIENCE FICTION *by Garrett P. Serviss*—Three Interplanetary Adventures including the unauthorised sequel to H. G. Wells' *War of the Worlds-Edison's Conquest of Mars, A Columbus of Space, The Moon Metal.*

JUNK DAY *by Arthur Sellings*—". . . . his finest novel was his last, Junk Day, a post-holocaust tale set in the ruins of his native London and peopled with engrossing character types . . . . perhaps grimmer than his previous work but pointedly more energetic." *The Encyclopedia of Science Fiction*

KIPLING'S SCIENCE FICTION *by Rudyard Kipling*—Science Fiction & Fantasy stories by a Master Storyteller including 'As East As A,B,C' 'With The Night Mail'.

DARKNESS AND DAWN 1—THE VACANT WORLD *by George Allen England*—A Novel of a future New York.

DARKNESS AND DAWN 2—BEYOND THE GREAT OBLIVION *by George Allen England*—The last vestiges of humanity set out across America's devastated landscape in search of their dream.

DARKNESS AND DAWN 3—THE AFTER GLOW *by George Allen England*—Somewhere near the Great Lakes, 1000 years from now. Beneath our planet's surface tribes of near human albino warriors eke out an existence in a hostile environment.

LEONAUR

ALSO FROM LEONAUR

AVAILABLE IN SOFTCOVER OR HARDCOVER WITH DUST JACKET

THE COLLECTED SCIENCE FICTION AND FANTASY OF STANLEY G. WEINBAUM 1—INTERPLANETARY ODYSSEYS *by Stanley G. Weinbaum*—Classic Tales of Interplanetary Adventure Including: A Martian Odyssey, its Sequel Valley of Dreams, the Complete 'Ham' Hammond Stories and Others.

THE COLLECTED SCIENCE FICTION AND FANTASY OF STANLEY G. WEINBAUM 2—OTHER EARTHS *by Stanley G. Weinbaum*—Classic Futuristic Tales Including: *Dawn of Flame* & its Sequel The Black Flame, plus The Revolution of 1960 & Others.

THE COLLECTED SCIENCE FICTION AND FANTASY OF STANLEY G. WEINBAUM 3—STRANGE GENIUS *by Stanley G. Weinbaum*—Classic Tales of the Human Mind at Work Including the Complete Novel The New Adam, the 'van Manderpootz' Stories and Others.

THE COLLECTED SCIENCE FICTION AND FANTASY OF STANLEY G. WEINBAUM 4—THE BLACK HEART *by Stanley G. Weinbaum*—Classic Strange Tales Including: the Complete Novel The Dark Other, Plus Proteus Island and Others.

THE COLLECTED SCIENCE FICTION & FANTASY OF JACK LONDON 1—BEFORE ADAM & OTHER STORIES *by Jack London*—included in this Volume Before Adam The Scarlet Plague A Relic of the Pliocene When the World Was Young The Red One Planchette A Thousand Deaths Goliah A Curious Fragment The Rejuvenation of Major Rathbone.

THE COLLECTED SCIENCE FICTION & FANTASY OF JACK LONDON 2—THE IRON HEEL & OTHER STORIES *by Jack London*—included in this Volume The Iron Heel The Enemy of All the World The Shadow and the Flash The Strength of the Strong The Unparalleled Invasion The Dream of Debs.

THE COLLECTED SCIENCE FICTION & FANTASY OF JACK LONDON 3—THE STAR ROVER & OTHER STORIES *by Jack London*—included in this Volume The Star Rover The Minions of Midas The Eternity of Forms The Man With the Gash.

THE CRETAN TEAT *by Brian Aldiss*—The Cretan Teat is a wry and comic novel that interweaves its own fiction with an inner fiction about the discovery of a Byzantine painting of the Mother of the Blessed Virgin Mary suckling the infant Jesus and a fake ikon that becomes an instrument of Nemesis.

LEONAUR

ALSO FROM LEONAUR
AVAILABLE IN SOFTCOVER OR HARDCOVER WITH DUST JACKET

THE FIRST BOOK OF AYESHA *by H. Rider Haggard*—Contains *She & Ayesha: the Return of She.*

THE SECOND BOOK OF AYESHA *by H. Rider Haggard*—Contains *She and Allan & Wisdom's Daughter.*

QUATERMAIN: THE COMPLETE ADVENTURES—1 *by H. Rider Haggard*—Contains *King Solomon's Mines & Allan Quatermain.*

QUATERMAIN: THE COMPLETE ADVENTURES—2 *by H. Rider Haggard*—Contains *Allan's Wife, Maiwa's Revenge & Marie.*

QUATERMAIN: THE COMPLETE ADVENTURES—3 *by H. Rider Haggard*—Contains *Child of Storm & Allan and the Holy Flower.*

QUATERMAIN: THE COMPLETE ADVENTURES—4 *by H. Rider Haggard*—Contains *Finished & The Ivory Child.*

QUATERMAIN: THE COMPLETE ADVENTURES—5 *by H. Rider Haggard*—Contains *The Ancient Allan & She and Allan.*

QUATERMAIN: THE COMPLETE ADVENTURES—6 *by H. Rider Haggard*—Contains *Heu-Heu or, the Monster & The Treasure of the Lake.*

QUATERMAIN: THE COMPLETE ADVENTURES—7 *by H. Rider Haggard*—Contains *Allan and the Ice Gods, Four Short Adventures & Nada the Lily.*

TROS OF SAMOTHRACE 1: WOLVES OF THE TIBER *by Talbot Mundy*—55 B.C.--an adventurer set during the Roman invasion of Britain.

TROS OF SAMOTHRACE 2: DRAGONS OF THE NORTH *by Talbot Mundy*—55 B.C. —Caesar plots, Britons war among themselves and the Vikings are coming.

TROS OF SAMOTHRACE 3: SERPENT OF THE WAVES *by Talbot Mundy*—55 B.C.--Caesar is poised to invade Britain—only a grand strategy can foil him!.

TROS OF SAMOTHRACE 4: CITY OF THE EAGLES *by Talbot Mundy*—54 B.C.—Rome—Tros treads in the streets of his sworn enemies!.

TROS OF SAMOTHRACE 5: CLEOPATRA *by Talbot Mundy*—Tros and the Roman Empire turn to the Egypt of the Pharaohs.

TROS OF SAMOTHRACE 6: THE PURPLE PIRATE *by Talbot Mundy*—The epic saga of the ancient world—Tros of Samothrace—draws to a conclusion in this sixth—and final—volume.

LEONAUR

ALSO FROM LEONAUR
AVAILABLE IN SOFTCOVER OR HARDCOVER WITH DUST JACKET

THE PRISONER OF ZENDA & ITS SEQUEL RUPERT OF HENTZAU *by Anthony Hope*—Two famous novels of high adventure in one volume.

THE GLADIATORS *by G. J. Whyte Melville*—A Classic Novel of Ancient Rome—Three Volumes in One Special Edition.

THE COMPLETE CAPTAIN DANGEROUS *by George Augustus Sala*—The Adventures of a Soldier, Sailor, Merchant, Spy, Slave and Bashaw of the Grand Turk.

ORTHERIS, LEAROYD & MULVANEY *by Rudyard Kipling*—The Complete Soldiers Three stories.

SIR NIGEL & THE WHITE COMPANY *by Arthur Conan Doyle*—Two Classic Novels of the 100 Years' War.

THE ILLUSTRATED & COMPLETE BRIGADIER GERARD *by Arthur Conan Doyle*—All 18 Stories with the Original Strand Magazine Illustrations by Wollen and Paget.

THE OHIO RIVER TRILOGY 1: BETTY ZANE *by Zane Grey*—The land along the Ohio River is newly settled. Indomitable men and women—Col. Zane and his family, the McCollochs, Wetzel, the "Death Wind" Indian killer, among them—have hewn a life out of the frontier wilderness.

THE OHIO RIVER TRILOGY 2: THE SPIRIT OF THE BORDER *by Zane Grey*—Fort Henry still stands as a bastion for the settlers on the frontier along the Ohio River. More pioneers are now moving west to carve new lives out of the wilderness.

THE OHIO RIVER TRILOGY 3: THE LAST TRAIL *by Zane Grey*—This final volume of Zane Grey's Ohio River Trilogy is a gripping finale to a great series—another thrilling story of life and death on the early American frontier and a classic in the tradition of Drums Along the Mohawk.

THE NAPOLEONIC NOVELS: VOLUME 1 *by Erckmann-Chatrian*—This book comprises two linked novels—*The Conscript & Waterloo*—about the adventures a young conscript in the French Army. during the Napoleonic wars.

THE NAPOLEONIC NOVELS: VOLUME 2 *by Erckmann-Chatrian*—*The Blockade of Phalsburg & The Invasion of France in 1814*—the events portrayed in these two novels of the Napoleonic period properly fit in time between those of the first volume. They appear together here since each—unlike the other two in this series—is a stand alone work.

LEONAUR

ALSO FROM LEONAUR
AVAILABLE IN SOFTCOVER OR HARDCOVER WITH DUST JACKET

THE LONG PATROL *by George Berrie*—A Novel of Light Horsemen from Gallipoli to the Palestine campaign of the First World War.

NAPOLEONIC WAR STORIES *by Arthur Quiller-Couch*—Tales of soldiers, spies, battles & sieges from the Peninsular & Waterloo campaingns.

THE FIRST DETECTIVE *by Edgar Allan Poe*—The Complete Auguste Dupin Stories—The Murders in the Rue Morgue, The Mystery of Marie Rogêt & The Purloined Letter.

THE COMPLETE DR NIKOLA—MAN OF MYSTERY: 1 *by Guy Boothby*—*A Bid for Fortune & Dr Nikola Returns*—Guy Boothby's Dr.Nikola adventures continue to fascinate readers and enthusiasts of crime and mystery fiction because—in the manner of Raffles, the gentleman cracksman—here is character far removed from the uncompromising goodness of Holmes and Watson or the uncompromising evil of Professor Moriarty.

THE COMPLETE DR NIKOLA—MAN OF MYSTERY: 2 *by Guy Boothby*—*The Lust of Hate, Dr Nikola's Experiment & Farewell, Nikola*—Guy Boothby's Dr.Nikola adventures continue to fascinate readers and enthusiasts of crime and mystery fiction because—in the manner of Raffles, the gentleman cracksman—here is character far removed from the uncompromising goodness of Holmes and Watson or the uncompromising evil of Professor Moriarty.

THE CASEBOOKS OF MR J. G. REEDER: BOOK 1 *by Edgar Wallace*—*Room 13, The Mind of Mr J. G. Reeder* and *Terror Keep*—Edgar Wallace's sleuth—whose territory is the London of the 1920s—is an unlikely figure, more bank clerk than detective in appearance, ever wearing his square topped bowler, frock coat, cravat and muffler, Mr Reeder is usually inseparable from his umbrella.

THE CASEBOOKS OF MR J. G. REEDER: BOOK 2 *by Edgar Wallace*—*Red Aces, Mr J. G. Reeder Returns, The Guv'nor* and *The Man Who Passed*—Edgar Wallace's sleuth—whose territory is the London of the 1920s—is an unlikely figure, more bank clerk than detective in appearance, ever wearing his square topped bowler, frock coat, cravat and muffler, Mr Reeder is usually inseparable from his umbrella.

THE COMPLETE FOUR JUST MEN: VOLUME 1 *by Edgar Wallace*—*The Four Just Men, The Council of Justice & The Just Men of Cordova*—disillusioned with a world where the wicked and the abusers of power perpetually go unpunished, the Just Men set about to rectify matters according to their own standards, and retribution is dispensed on swift and deadly wings.

LEONAUR

ALSO FROM LEONAUR
AVAILABLE IN SOFTCOVER OR HARDCOVER WITH DUST JACKET

THE COMPLETE FOUR JUST MEN: VOLUME 2 *by Edgar Wallace*—*The Law of the Four Just Men & The Three Just Men*—disillusioned with a world where the wicked and the abusers of power perpetually go unpunished, the Just Men set about to rectify matters according to their own standards, and retribution is dispensed on swift and deadly wings.

THE COMPLETE RAFFLES: 1 *by E. W. Hornung*—*The Amateur Cracksman & The Black Mask*—By turns urbane gentleman about town and accomplished cricketer, life is just too ordinary for Raffles and that sets him on a series of adventures that have long been treasured as a real antidote to the 'white knights' who are the usual heroes of the crime fiction of this period.

THE COMPLETE RAFFLES: 2 *by E. W. Hornung*—*A Thief in the Night & Mr Justice Raffles*—By turns urbane gentleman about town and accomplished cricketer, life is just too ordinary for Raffles and that sets him on a series of adventures that have long been treasured as a real antidote to the 'white knights' who are the usual heroes of the crime fiction of this period.

THE COLLECTED SUPERNATURAL AND WEIRD FICTION OF WILKIE COLLINS: VOLUME 1 *by Wilkie Collins*—Contains one novel 'The Haunted Hotel', one novella 'Mad Monkton', three novelettes 'Mr Percy and the Prophet', 'The Biter Bit' and 'The Dead Alive' and eight short stories to chill the blood.

THE COLLECTED SUPERNATURAL AND WEIRD FICTION OF WILKIE COLLINS: VOLUME 2 *by Wilkie Collins*—Contains one novel 'The Two Destinies', three novellas 'The Frozen deep', 'Sister Rose' and 'The Yellow Mask' and two short stories to chill the blood.

THE COLLECTED SUPERNATURAL AND WEIRD FICTION OF WILKIE COLLINS: VOLUME 3 *by Wilkie Collins*—Contains one novel 'Dead Secret,' two novelettes 'Mrs Zant and the Ghost' and 'The Nun's Story of Gabriel's Marriage' and five short stories to chill the blood.

FUNNY BONES *selected by Dorothy Scarborough*—An Anthology of Humorous Ghost Stories.

MONTEZUMA'S CASTLE AND OTHER WEIRD TALES *by Charles B. Cory*—Cory has written a superb collection of eighteen ghostly and weird stories to chill and thrill the avid enthusiast of supernatural fiction.

SUPERNATURAL BUCHAN *by John Buchan*—Stories of Ancient Spirits, Uncanny Places & Strange Creatures.

www.ingramcontent.com/pod-product-compliance
Lightning Source LLC
Chambersburg PA
CBHW022205010726
47493CB00002B/419